MW01027877

AN ARTIFICIAL LIGHT

ALSO BY PETRA DURST-BENNING

The Photographer's Saga

The Photographer

The Seed Traders' Saga

The Seed Woman

The Flower Shop

The Century Trilogy

While the World Is Still Asleep

The Champagne Queen

The Queen of Beauty

The Glassblower Trilogy

The Glassblower

The American Lady

The Paradise of Glass

AN ARTIFICIAL LIGHT

THE PHOTOGRAPHER'S SAGA, BOOK TWO

PETRA DURST-BENNING

TRANSLATED BY EDWIN MILES

AMAZON CROSSING

This is a work of fiction. Names, characters, organizations, places, events, and incidents are either products of the author's imagination or are used fictitiously. Any resemblance to actual persons, living or dead, or actual events is purely coincidental.

Previously published as *Die Fotografin—Die Zeit der Entscheidung* by Blanvalet Verlag in Germany in 2019. Translated from German by Edwin Miles. First published in English by Amazon Crossing in 2020.

Published by Amazon Crossing, Seattle

www.apub.com

ISBN-13: 9781542008624
ISBN-10: 154200862X

Cover design by Shasti O'Leary Soudant

Printed in the United States of America

In photography, the smallest thing can be a great subject.

—Henri Cartier-Bresson (1908–2004)

CHAPTER 1

Laichingen, Swabian Jura, Pentecost Monday, June 5, 1911

Mimi all but floated into her uncle Josef's house, her feet barely touching the floor. It wasn't the success of the Pentecost market that had her on cloud nine—rather, it was Hannes, the man she hadn't been able to get out of her mind since they'd first met nearly two months before in Ulm, the man who'd found his way into her dreams.

Mimi still could not believe that he'd come for her. When he appeared at the market as if from nowhere—just minutes before!—her joy at seeing him again had nearly made her faint. Given everything stacked against them, she'd almost lost hope of ever seeing him again.

Yet here he was in Laichingen because of her, even though in Ulm he'd made it very clear to her that he was finished with his hometown, that he'd never set foot there again. She hadn't known then that Hannes was originally from Laichingen. For her sake he'd evidently put his resolution aside, she thought happily.

She cheerfully tended to her uncle—fatigued by the busy market, he only wanted to rest—and helped him to bed, then she got ready to go to sleep. Hannes had said that he would come to her "as soon as possible," but when would that be? Mimi wondered as she lay in bed.

Now that she knew he was close by, she could hardly bear her sense of longing. She sighed and snuggled deeper under her blanket.

Their first meeting in Ulm had felt predestined. The evening they had spent in each other's company had been marked by an intensity that Mimi had never known. To be with someone else, or to be free? For Mimi, freedom had always come first.

But now, with Hannes, she could imagine almost anything.

It was eight in the morning, and her uncle was still asleep when she heard a soft knock at the front door, which faced the back garden. Mimi, unable to sleep and out of bed since six, knew at once that it was him.

"Hannes . . ." Her voice was a mere whisper. "You've come." She looked at him cautiously, as if she still could not believe that he was really here. His brown-black eyes as warm as the coals of a fire. His mouth a touch too large, but just right for a man with so much to say. The dark-brown, unruly hair crowning his tall, powerful frame. The broad shoulders to lean on.

In the bright light of that June morning, Hannes returned her gaze intently, almost as if he wanted to be certain that his decision to come back to Laichingen had been the right one. "It wasn't easy for me. I couldn't shake you from my mind. I just could not accept that something that had not even started could already be over."

What a declaration of love! Mimi had never heard more beautiful words. "I couldn't stop thinking about you, either," she admitted in a whisper. She wanted to nestle against him, but Hannes took her by the hand and led her to a corner of the garden between Josef's little woodshed and the back of the studio, where no one could see them from the surrounding houses. In the shadows behind the studio, he finally took her in his arms. They held each other for a long, silent moment, enjoying each other's warmth and closeness.

"How did you even find me?" she murmured.

"I went to the guesthouse in Ulm where you'd spent the night and asked the landlord if he knew where you were going next. At first, he hesitated, but when I made it clear how important it was, he told me where you'd gone. You can imagine how I felt when I heard you'd left for Laichingen—of all the places you could have traveled, you were in my old village."

"And you still came after me. Oh, Hannes . . ."

He released himself from their embrace and looked into her eyes again. "May I ask you for one thing?"

Mimi nodded. He could ask her for anything.

"From now on, would you call me Johann? I called myself Hannes when I was traveling. Whenever someone in America said my real name, it sounded like a girl's name: Joanne. Hannes was easier for them, but it will only confuse the villagers here to hear you use that name."

"Of course," said Mimi with a smile. Names meant nothing. "As long as you don't call me Minna. That's what my mother used to shout, whenever I'd been up to something."

He laughed. "And? Have you been up to something these last few weeks? Have you already managed to catch the eye of one of the weavers?"

"Oh, wouldn't you like to know!" As if one of the pale, worn-out weavers slaving away from morning to night in the factories could be even half as attractive as Johann, she thought.

He took a lock of dark-brown hair that had come loose from her elegantly pinned coiffure and twirled it around the index finger of his right hand. "With all the people around your stand at the market, you seem to have made quite an impression here."

Mimi grinned. "Thank God I have, or I'd be packing my bags again already. I have to earn money for two now, you see—for myself and for my uncle, who is quite ill and needs care." She pointed to the house behind her.

He looked at her with admiration. "You're so strong, so beautiful," he whispered. "I can hardly wait to get to know you better. You and me . . ." He pulled her close to him again.

Mimi closed her eyes in sweet anticipation of his kiss. For the moment of a heartbeat, the world seemed to stand still, then his lips finally touched hers. Mimi's knees grew weak, a warm trembling filled her, and with a commitment unfamiliar to her, she opened her lips to his.

The morning after the Pentecost market, Anton was a changed man. Feeling on top of the world, he stood at the kitchen sink at his parents' inn, The Oxen, and washed the countless dirty beer glasses as if he were counting gold coins instead.

It had been good to talk with Alexander the previous evening, he thought while he polished the glasses with a clean cloth.

He was still amazed at the intensity with which his friend had sworn that he would do *anything* to take the entrance exam for Stuttgart Art School that the photographer Mimi Reventlow had organized for him. Anton hadn't suspected that such a fire burned inside the weaver's son. As Alexander spoke, one thing had become clear to Anton: It wasn't enough to complain all the time about the work at the inn—about the kitchen smells he hated so much, or about the monotony or the same old faces he constantly saw. Whining about those things was no different from making yourself comfortable in a rocking chair: yes, you moved, but you didn't go anywhere. If he, like Alexander, wanted to turn his back on Laichingen, then he had to do something about it. And that was exactly what he was planning. Even better, he already had a pretty good idea of how he could manage it. But he had to talk it through with Christel first. Christel, his secret sweetheart, still struggled with the idea of abandoning her hometown, but in her parents' house she was worse off than he was at his parents' inn. At least he got paid for his work, but Christel was no more than an unpaid maid for her parents, Paul and Sonja Merkle. Christel deserved more.

"I'm going out for a little while," he yelled to his mother, who was sitting at one of the tables in the barroom, sorting coins into small piles.

What a beautiful morning, Anton thought as he stepped out into the square in front of The Oxen. The sky looked as if it had been wiped clean, the cobblestones gleamed in the sunlight like polished jet, and birds twittered in the trees in front of the church. How good would it feel to shoulder his pack on a day like this and hit the road! *Soon,* he promised himself. *Soon.*

He wondered if the photographer was already up. She must be, he thought as he strode across the square to the house on the opposite side. Mimi Reventlow was smart and hardworking, a capable businesswoman. And time was money, right? Anton laughed.

Mimi Reventlow didn't know it yet, but when she left Laichingen, he would be at her side. He would have to be patient a while longer since he knew that she wouldn't leave town while her uncle needed care. But that didn't stop him from dreaming, did it? He got along well with Mimi, as he'd discovered on their outing to Ulm. Together they could conquer the world. It certainly wouldn't be much longer, he thought as the closed shutters on the upper floor caught his eye: Josef Stöckle was likely still asleep. The old photographer was gravely ill, and God would certainly call for him soon.

Anton would use the time that Mimi stayed in Laichingen to his advantage. He would offer a helping hand here, a favor there, and make himself increasingly indispensable. When the day of her departure finally came, Mimi would have no choice but to let him go with her. *That* was his plan.

Anton went around back, swung the garden gate open, and was already at the door of the house when he saw a shadow move back by the studio. A burglar? The photographer had done good business at the market, and many had seen it. Was someone trying to get his hands on her money? Fists raised and heart pounding, Anton crept closer, ready to leap into action. But when he peeked around the corner of the woodshed, he saw only Mimi herself—in the arms of Johann Merkle!

Anton froze in astonishment.

"There's another thing," he heard Johann say as the two broke from their embrace. "For the time being, it's better if we . . . well, if we're not seen together. And no one needs to find out that we already know each other from Ulm."

They knew each other? Anton found it hard to trust his ears.

"But why all the secrecy?" Mimi asked, not understanding.

Anton risked another peek. Johann seemed a little impatient as he said, "In the weeks you've been here, haven't you noticed that things in Laichingen are a little different than in other places? Everyone hears everything about everyone else. I don't want people gossiping about you. As a businesswoman, you have a reputation to protect. It's no good if they mark you with an affair with someone like me."

"With someone like you!" Mimi ran her fingers through Johann's curly hair and smiled. "What's that supposed to mean?"

An affair? The two of them had had an affair? What was going on? Anton's head was swirling, and he couldn't think clearly.

"An emigrant. A vagabond. Someone who can't be trusted an inch," Johann said.

"A unionist?" said Mimi, teasing him.

"For now, no one needs to find out I work for the unions, either, or I won't get a foot in any doors here at all."

Johann Merkle was a unionist? Anton had recently read a report in the newspaper about a workers' uprising in Berlin. Apparently, unionists had riled the men so much that not even the police had been able to make the mob see reason. This was getting more and more interesting. Anton hardly dared to breathe—he didn't want to miss a word . . . or be discovered.

"But there's nothing dishonorable about that," said Mimi, still pressed close to Johann. "The weavers would be grateful for a little support, I'd imagine. The unwritten rule that says the son of a weaver also has to become a weaver . . . I find it incredible. And the hours they work—for a pittance! It's time someone told the mill owners that they can't exploit people the way they do forever."

"Mimi, Mimi," said Johann cheerfully. "That's exactly what I admire about you. The fire in your eyes when you talk about what you believe in. I've only ever seen that in men, never in a woman."

"And what's wrong with it?" Mimi shot back. "You also speak your mind about the things you believe, don't you?"

Johann nodded. "But to just come out and say what I really believe would be the worst thing I could do here in Laichingen. I've been gone many years. Why should the villagers trust me?"

Damn well right! thought Anton vehemently. All these years, Johann Merkle hadn't cared a bit about what went on in the village.

Mimi nodded her understanding.

"I have to settle in and show the people I'm one of them again. My first impression is that conditions for the weavers haven't improved in the years I've been away."

It's unbelievable! Johann Merkle strolls into town after years away and imagines he knows about everything and everyone, thought Anton angrily. *The self-important blowhard!*

"You've had my trust from the start. And when the people hear you speak like I heard you on the plaza in Ulm, they'll follow you like lambs," said Mimi, her voice so full of admiration that Anton had to bite his lip to quell a groan of dismay. The photographer was in love. Head over heels.

"Let's hope so." Johann grinned. "But here in Laichingen I can't simply set up in the square and talk about worker protection laws and better pay. No, I'll start as a weaver, probably with Herrmann Gehringer since I used to work for him. I'll only find out where things truly stand when I'm in the lion's den."

"You actually want to work for that monster?" Mimi sounded surprised.

"What have you had to do with Gehringer? You haven't been picking fights with him, have you?"

"Depends on how you look at it . . ." In as few words as possible, Mimi told Johann what she'd been through with the weaver baron.

As far as Anton was concerned, Mimi had acquitted herself very well indeed. Far better than any of the men, he thought; all they did was bow and scrape to Gehringer. Anton noticed that Johann also seemed impressed by Mimi's behavior. His laughter, at least, sounded encouraging.

"You and me—at least there are two of us willing to stand up to the man. But if I start at Gehringer's, there's something else to think about." He paused for a moment before he went on. "My brother will be mad as hell. He was overjoyed to see me leave back then. He thought the way I stood my ground with Gehringer was damaging his own career."

There was an intimacy to the way they laughed then, as if they had known each other a long time.

"I have to go. I have a lot to sort out today. I'm staying at my mother's place. Edelgard . . . you might know her. She's a seamstress."

"Yes, I do know her. When will I see you again?" Mimi asked, a little sadly.

"As soon as I can manage it, I promise. But I don't know how the next few days will go." He raised her chin and looked into her eyes. "From now on, we have all the time in the world, don't we?"

Confused and angry, Anton crept away. It was infuriating—and terrible timing—that Johann Merkle had decided to come back now. It seemed as if the prodigal son already had the photographer wrapped around his finger. Anton kicked a stone, which went skittering across the market square. Mimi had sounded as if she already had visions of standing at the altar with Johann. Damn it! The last thing she needed was to put down roots here in Laichingen. She was supposed to leave the village when her uncle passed away—and with Anton himself at her side.

For a moment, he thought about trying to find Alexander, whom he wanted to tell about Johann and Mimi. But he decided against it.

His friend was ignorant when it came to women. And perhaps it was an advantage if he was the only one who knew about this liaison.

Anton stopped and took a deep breath. He had to keep a cool head. He had to think about the changed situation and not do anything stupid. Only time would tell how he should play his hand. One thing was certain, however: he would not give up on his plan.

Eveline stood at the well, drawing water into a large bucket as she held her face to the sun, enjoying the warmth. The sun had shone just the same the day before, when she had stood face to face with Johann at the Pentecost market. And how he'd looked at her, so intense, so sensitive.

She was impatient to see Johann again, but Edelgard would surely keep a tight grip on her son. And she wasn't the only one staking a claim, thought Eve angrily. At the market the day before, half the village had swarmed Johann—including the photographer. Mimi didn't even know him! Couldn't people give him a moment's peace? Eve had wanted nothing more than to protect him and shoo everyone else away, but they'd been granted no more than a few hastily whispered words. That had been enough, though, to give her the courage she needed to go on.

Eveline smiled. She could still only dream about Johann, but they certainly would see each other again in a little more than a month at the *Heumondfest*, and very likely before that. At the July harvest festival, Johann would ask her to dance, she knew, just as they had once before . . . And in his arms, she would forget the world around her, if only for a moment. He would whisper how beautiful she was and how much she enthralled him, just like he had back then, before he left seven years ago, when they had met secretly several times.

For a while, she really had believed that Johann would help her escape her despair. What would it mean if she ran off with a man a second time, but instead of Klaus, this time with Johann?

When Johann suddenly disappeared to try his luck in the wide world, she had been utterly surprised. It had taken almost all her strength to remind herself over and over that she was married, that she should be thankful fate had not tempted her into adultery, or worse.

Now he was back, and it seemed the good Lord had plans for the two of them after all. She knew one thing for certain: Johann would be horrified to discover how terrible things had been for her in the years that had passed, and he would do everything he could to help her.

The soft sound of crying snatched Eveline from her thoughts. She turned to Marianne and Erika, who sat on the ground, looking miserable. A fat tear rolled down Erika's cheek. "My tummy hurts so much, Mama," she sobbed.

"Oh, children," said Eveline gently. Her own stomach was growling with hunger, but Eveline tried to ignore it. "It's only a few hours till dinnertime, then we'll have a good bread soup." She still had half a loaf of decent bread. The other half had mysteriously gone moldy overnight. Her pantry was bare, nothing edible would come from the field for a long time yet, and her purse was all but empty after Klaus had spent his wages at The Oxen. She needed the few coins she had to pay the photographer.

She heaved the heavy bucket onto the handcart. The young plants in the field needed water urgently to thrive and give them a rich harvest in the autumn.

"When we come home from the field, we'll collect some delicious dandelions along the way. I'll make them into a salad, all right?" she said as brightly as she could.

Marianne held her stomach and said, "Can't I eat my piece of bread now? Maybe I won't want anything for dinner tonight."

Eveline fought back the tears that suddenly threatened to overwhelm her. Johann would want her to be strong, she knew—simply because Klaus was not.

"You know what we can do? We can go to the chicken pen right now and find an egg for each of us."

Her daughters' pale faces instantly brightened a little.

The chickens were old. A short while later, with two pitiful eggs, Eve returned to the house, the children at her heels.

There were still some hot coals in the stove, enough to fry the eggs. Eveline put the heavy cast-iron pan on the stovetop, then took the moldy half loaf of bread. Wisely, or in desperation, she hadn't yet thrown it out, and she cut off the moldy sections of crust as best she could.

"Mold for beauty, as the old people here promise," she said, and gave each daughter a piece of the bread.

"Don't you want anything?" Marianne asked when Eveline put a plate with a fried egg in front of each girl.

"I'm still full from the porridge this morning," Eveline lied. The mere sight of the crispy fried eggs made her mouth water. To distract herself, she looked at the pictures that her son, Alexander, had drawn on old cardboard and wrapping paper from Helene's store. An owl. A swallow's nest: a mother swallow feeding her babies . . . He'd drawn every blade of grass so finely, so precisely.

Wasn't it typical of Alexander to choose a motif like that? He could have drawn the rooster out in the street or something else, but no, Alexander had chosen to draw an unselfish mother bird. The thought was enough to give Eveline new strength. She would try everything she could to change Klaus's mind about giving Alexander permission to take the admissions test for the art school. If she managed that feat, she was sure Johann would have a few good words of advice for her son about leaving Laichingen.

A ray of sunlight fought its way through the narrow opening between the neighboring house and their own, dousing the dark yard in golden light.

Eveline smiled.

CHAPTER 2

Mimi would have liked nothing more than to sit on the steps in front of Uncle Josef's house and spend the day dreaming about Johann, but she needed to pull herself together. Thanks to the Pentecost market, she finally had some money in her pocket again, and she wanted to restock the groceries. Uncle Josef needed good food to have any defense at all against succumbing to his tuberculosis.

She was just stepping out of the house, shopping basket over her arm, when she saw Josef's neighbor Luise waving to her over the garden gate at the back.

Mimi had no choice but to go over to her. "Good morning. You're up early."

"Just like you," said the older woman, smiling. "Happy with the Pentecost market?"

"Very," Mimi replied proudly. "We're going to reward ourselves with a few salted herring today. Uncle Josef says that Helene always opens a barrel after the Pentecost market. I want to get to the store before they're all gone." *And maybe I'll run into Johann along the way, just by chance?* she thought hopefully.

"And what about that?" Luise pointed sternly over the garden fence to the vegetable bed that lay untended in Uncle Josef's garden. "Don't you want to plant anything? If you've got your own turnips, kohlrabi, and onions, you don't have to go shopping three times a week. The Ice Saints are a long way behind us already. With no more worry about a frost, it's about time!"

For a moment, Mimi was so dismayed that she was at a loss for words. What business was it of Luise's how often she went shopping?

"I had no idea where to get seedlings here," Mimi finally said in her defense. "I was probably supposed to buy them from a seed merchant weeks ago, but back then . . ." She shrugged. Back then, she'd believed that her visit here would be short. But her uncle's illness had changed everything. She looked thoughtfully at the vegetable beds, where dandelions and other weeds were running wild. "It would probably be fun to look after a little garden like that."

"It's not magic. I'd be happy to show you what to do," Luise said. "You've already got the housework under control, and you'll do fine with the garden. I still have a lot of seedlings in pots and no room for them out in the field. If you like, you can have them. A few turnips, cabbage, kohlrabi—when autumn comes, we want Josef's pantry to be full, don't we?"

If he lives that long, thought Mimi with concern. She knew he would not recover from his tuberculosis, but the doctor had told her that a healthy lifestyle, good food included, would help keep the bacteria at bay. Vegetables from his own garden, harvested and cooked with love—that would certainly do Josef good.

Mimi looked at her neighbor enthusiastically.

"What do I have to do?"

"No herring?" asked her uncle, disappointed, when Mimi put bread and butter on the table at midday.

"You have your neighbor to thank for that," Mimi said, cutting a slice of bread for each of them. "Luise gave me dozens of vegetable seedlings, and I've spent all morning getting the garden in order. I didn't have time to get to Helene's. But the plants are lined up like little soldiers," she said with a trace of pride in her voice. "I have no idea how they'll turn out, but let's be surprised, all right?" Mimi laughed. *My hands!* she thought at the same time, horrified. The soil had found its way into the folds of skin and under her nails, and neither soap nor scrubbing brush would get it out.

"The vegetable garden was always my beloved Traudel's pride and joy. She'd be happy to know that you've taken it over. Oh, Mimi, it's so nice to have you here." Her uncle smiled wistfully. "Still, when I think of how you've given up your career because of me, I admit I feel awful. You're a traveling photographer, and in great demand. And instead of earning good money in spa towns and tourist destinations, you're sitting here watching me die! Child, that doesn't sit right with me."

Mimi could only watch in dismay as his eyes filled with tears. "I'm happy to be here," she said gently. Back on the road, chasing one job after another? *Never again,* she thought.

The one thing that, in all her years as a traveling photographer, she had thought impossible had actually happened: she was happy as a resident photographer. How many times in the past had she regretted only fleetingly getting to know the people she photographed? A few friendly words, a click of the shutter, and then "adieu." Here in the village, she'd begun to make a few tentative friendships—with their occasionally nosy neighbor Luise; with Eveline, whose son, Alexander, showed such promise as an artist; and with clever and capable Anton from the inn. And then there was her beloved uncle Josef—she would always be there for him, until the day he died. She'd sworn that to herself, and nothing would shake her resolve. Now that Johann had come, she had no reason to want to leave again.

Spontaneously, she cut the bread that she had buttered for Josef into the shape of a fish. "There. A herring!" she said with a grin, and put the plate in front of her uncle. It made her happy to see a small smile appear on his face.

"Really, though, right now I'm enjoying being a resident photographer very much, and I like not constantly setting off to somewhere new. I can manage everything as I like, with no more compromises—that's completely new for me!"

The old photographer nodded, satisfied. "There's nothing better than having your own studio."

Mimi laughed. "But you know what bothers me a little? I feel so *watched.* People notice how often I go shopping and how clean the laundry is when I hang it out to dry. They check if I've thoroughly swept the steps in front of the shop, if I've weeded the garden, and . . . and, my God, how could I dare go and sit on the bench for half an hour and get a little sun. I get looks from the other side of the garden fence as if I'm the laziest slug in the world. No one misses anything here." And because of that general curiosity, she and Johann had to keep their relationship a secret, too, she thought.

"You're hardly the one to talk," said her uncle with a laugh. "Your photographic eye doesn't miss anything, either. Like yesterday, when that young fellow tried to pilfer a postcard without paying. Or how you spotted our returnee, Johann Merkle, among all the turmoil of the market. Your eyes nearly popped out of your head, I have to say."

Mimi looked aside, embarrassed. "That was just because everyone else was making all that fuss around him. You would almost think it was the second coming. What's so special about Johann Merkle?" As casually as she acted, she could not keep a sudden trembling out of her voice.

"Johann Merkle . . ." Her uncle leaned back in his chair. "I don't know so much about him. A year after I first met Traudel, he left for America, and no one has seen him or heard from him since. Until yesterday, that is. Just before he left, his father died. Now, I know you're not supposed to speak ill of the dead, but it seems that Robert Merkle was quite a violent man. Traudel once told me that Edelgard was often heard crying, and that Robert used to beat her."

"What? And no one stood up for her?" If her own mother heard about that! Amelie Reventlow, a priest's wife, would have told the man what was what, and in no uncertain terms, thought Mimi, incensed.

"Things that go on behind closed doors are private. And no one likes to get mixed up in marriage matters at the best of times. Traudel also said that ever since he was little, Johann tried to protect his mother by deliberately turning his father's resentment onto himself. Then he was the one who'd take a beating."

Mimi looked at her uncle in disbelief.

"Well, when Johann grew up and was his father's equal, physically speaking, I'm sure he knew how to defend himself." Josef shrugged. "And almost immediately after his father died, Johann left. Everybody was thinking that he would continue living with his mother and look after her. But it seems that when his brutal father died, Johann saw his duty as done. At some level, he was right. Even in her year of mourning, Edelgard was a changed woman. Happy, full of life, always concerned for the welfare of others. She complained about Johann's departure, of course. Many times. But mostly she seemed relieved to be free of her tormentor." Josef sat quietly for a moment, then said, "I wonder why Johann has come back now."

It's fate, Mimi thought dreamily.

"I'll bet you that Johann starts working for Gehringer," her uncle said. "He used to work at Gehringer's mill, you know."

Mimi raised her eyebrows in surprise. Her uncle had a very good sense for what was going on in the village, she realized once again. "After the pitiful amount Gehringer offered you for your shop, I imagine he also pays extremely low wages. A smart man like Johann Merkle will surely find another place to work, won't he?" Mimi said, pushing Johann's words from that morning to the back of her mind.

"You and your aversion to Gehringer! Mimi, I don't want to keep on at you about this, but if you plan to spend any length of time here in Laichingen, you'd be well advised to not make an enemy of the man. Although it might be too late—you've already stood up to him. If Gehringer takes a disliking to someone, that person will not have an easy life here."

"I'm not afraid of him," Mimi replied cockily. "We're not living in the Middle Ages anymore, are we? It's not as if the lord of the manor can do what he likes with his subjects. I'm a free woman!"

"Keep in mind that Gehringer hasn't had an easy life, either," Josef said, as if he hadn't heard Mimi's words at all. "His wife passed away fifteen years ago, and no one knows exactly what was wrong with her. Not long after that, his only son went off on a trip to Italy and has been missing ever since. People say the young man had always been a bit peculiar."

No surprise, with a father like that! Mimi thought.

"Gehringer will no doubt give Johann a warm welcome, despite their past differences. There aren't enough people here who know their way around a loom, and it's not as if you can just bring in someone from outside. Johann Merkle comes from an old weaving family, and *he* certainly has weaving in his veins."

Her uncle stopped speaking and coughed, and Mimi covertly cast a glance at the handkerchief he used to cover his mouth. *No blood,* she thought with relief.

"And I've got photography in my veins. For just that reason, I have to get into the shop. After the market yesterday, I dumped everything, so it's a bit of a mess. If people look in the window now, they'll start calling me too slovenly to tidy up," Mimi said, smiling wryly. She threw her arms around her uncle spontaneously. *How thin he is,* she thought, shocked by feeling his bones as she embraced him. Once again he hadn't eaten anything. The bread she'd cut into the shape of a herring lay untouched on his plate. He seemed to be disappearing more and more every week.

"Lie down for a bit and rest," she said gently. "I'll go off to Helene's this evening and get you a real herring, a fat one, all right?"

Her uncle looked at her with gratitude in his eyes.

CHAPTER 3

Mimi was about to unlock the door of the photography shop when she saw two young men crossing the square toward her: Anton Schaufler, the son of The Oxen's owners, and Fritz Braun, one of the confirmands she'd photographed. Anton carried a wooden stand under his arm and glanced back over his shoulder every few steps as if afraid his mother would call after him any second.

"Here's the postcard stand you wanted. I'm sorry it wasn't finished in time for the Pentecost market, but I'm sure you'll still be able to use it." He set the stand down proudly in front of Mimi.

She looked at Anton in disbelief. "You kept your promise?" Since the Laichingen carpenter had died the year before, people had been going to Mr. Meindl, the wagonmaker, for their carpentry work. Mimi had even sketched what she'd wanted him to build, but he hadn't had time. Anton, whom she had run into just after leaving the wagonmaker's shop, had promised her on the spot that he would get her the stand she wanted. Honestly, though, Mimi had not counted on him delivering. Anton had helped her out of difficulties a number of times, but Mimi had also learned that the good-looking young man was not always reliable.

Anton grinned. "Let's say it was a joint effort. Fritz built the stand, and I found the materials. What do you think? We made the rails just the right height for postcards and photographs—we've already tested it."

Mimi crouched to inspect the wooden stand more closely. The left side was shaped a little differently than the right, but with the evenly proportioned rails that joined the two, the stand was still very pleasing to the eye. At the top was a carved vignette. It looked like a large flower, and each petal had been sculpted so finely that Mimi could see every vein.

"The carving is very lovely," she said. "And the stand will certainly be a great help to me. I don't know what to say . . . You really built this?" She looked at Fritz Braun.

The weaver's son nodded proudly. "Anton got the wood for me, and I built it. I love to carve wood more than anything. I could carve all day long!"

Mimi smiled. "You can count yourself very fortunate indeed. A talent like that is a gift from God."

But instead of accepting her words of praise happily, the young man's expression turned gloomy.

What have I said wrong now? Mimi wondered.

"Shall we take the stand into the shop?" Anton asked hurriedly.

Mimi looked up at the sky. No clouds, no sign of rain, and if that changed, she could quickly get the stand inside by herself.

"Let's just leave it here for now. A little advertising can't hurt. Everyone who crosses the marketplace to go to the church has to pass by here." As she spoke, she went up the steps to the shop, unlocked the door, and brought out some of the postcards of Laichingen she'd been selling at the market the day before. A moment later, the cards were in neat rows on the rails of the stand.

Mimi beamed at the two craftsmen. "It's perfect! What do I owe you?"

Anton and Fritz exchanged a glance, and Fritz gave Anton a quick nod.

"We don't want any money," Anton said slowly.

Mimi crinkled her brow. "Then what do you want?"

"Fritz has something he . . . well, we wanted to ask if you . . . I mean, you've seen how things are here in Laichingen. Fritz is supposed to train as a weaver with Gehringer, just because his father works there. But Fritz would much rather become a carpenter. We thought, because of what you did for Alexander—because of you he has the chance to take the admissions exam at the Stuttgart Art School—well . . . could you maybe think of something to help Fritz, too?"

Mimi laughed softly. "I can *think* of a few things, I'm sure. But whether I get anywhere with them is another matter, as I'm sure you've heard in grim detail from your friend Alexander. If Klaus Schubert continues to forbid his son from going to Stuttgart, then anything I did was wasted. Also, I don't know any carpenters," she said. Still, she could not stop herself from turning the situation over in her mind. After all, Mr. Meindl was drowning in work, and surely he could use some help!

She looked at the two youthful faces in front of her. Both gazed at her so full of hope, as if they thought she could work magic. "Keep your nose out of it, child!" she heard her uncle warn in her mind. "Mr. Gehringer needs every weaver he can get."

She hesitated for a moment longer, then said, "Perhaps Mr. Meindl could use an apprentice? Why don't you go talk to him?"

"I already thought of that. If my father heard about it, he'd hit the roof," said Fritz, and his cheeks flushed red. "Besides, I don't think it would work, coming from me."

"What about you, Anton? You're not exactly the shy type—why don't you try talking to our wagonmaker?"

Anton waved dismissively. "No one cares what I have to say."

"Stop painting things so black! If you don't try, you'll never find out if it's even possible."

"Easy for you to say," said Anton. "You know your way around in the world. You're independent, you earn your own money . . . Maybe if we were like that, we'd try reaching for the stars. But people like us are told from when we're kids that it isn't right to turn your back on the place God put you. We're worse off than slaves!"

"It isn't as dramatic as that," said Mimi, amused, but her heart softened at so much youthful despair. "All right, I'll talk to Mr. Meindl."

"You'd do that for me?" Fritz exclaimed.

Anton jabbed him in the ribs. "Didn't I tell you?" he said.

Mimi laughed. "Hold your horses! I can talk to Mr. Meindl, but even if he likes the idea, it's still up to your parents to say yes." She looked sternly at the two young men.

Fritz seemed not to hear a word. "Me as the wagonmaker's apprentice . . . that would be my dream come true!" With that, he said a hasty goodbye—his parents were waiting for him.

"Anything else I can help you with?" said Anton.

"Don't you have anything to do?" said Mimi in surprise.

"Sure I do. I have to get back to The Oxen," he said. "But there's something else . . ."

"Oh yes?" Mimi rolled her eyes inwardly a little.

"It's about Alexander. If he gets to take the exam, what do you think his chances are?"

Mimi shrugged. "It's just my gut feeling, but I'd say he has a very good chance of being admitted and perhaps even receiving a scholarship."

A few weeks earlier, in a fit of frustration, Mimi had decided that if her mother was unwilling to do anything for Uncle Josef, then at least she could do something to help Alexander. So Mimi had sent her mother a letter along with a few of Alexander's drawings and had asked her—as a priest's wife with many good contacts—if she would make some inquiries on behalf of the talented boy. And Amelie Reventlow had, in fact, shown Alexander's drawings to the Stuttgart Art School. In her last letter, Mimi's mother had written that, this year, there didn't seem to be many good candidates among the up-and-coming young artists in Stuttgart, so Alexander's chances were even better. Mimi decided to keep that to herself.

"Are you really sure?" Anton pressed, frowning.

"Why do you want to know?" Mimi asked as she sorted her various postcards on the stand. Swans on the pond. Laichingen view one, Laichingen view two . . .

"Just because."

"You're not planning anything silly, I hope." She narrowed her eyes at Anton.

"What would I be planning?" he asked calmly. "Alexander's father is never going to let him go to art school. Everyone knows that."

"And if I talked to the man?"

"You can save your breath," said Anton with a sniff of disgust. "Klaus Schubert is a die-hard weaver. He'd sleep at his loom if they let him. It would never cross his mind that someone might want to spend their life with something other than warps and wefts. The only chance would—" He broke off abruptly.

"Yes?"

"Nothing. I'd better go."

Mimi was still in front of the shop—along with postcards, she was also displaying all sorts of photographs and picture frames to advertise her business—when a woman stopped to look. With a hoe and fork balanced on her shoulder, it seemed she was on her way to work in the fields.

"Those are Eveline's children!" she exclaimed, and pointed to the pictures that Mimi had just positioned on the stand.

"Yes, they are. Not only did Mrs. Schubert have a picture of Alexander done for his confirmation but also pictures of her daughters."

"I've got two boys of my own at home—"

"I have some good props for boys: sailor suits, a wooden toy sailboat, a spinning top, and even a rocking horse they might like."

"But could I afford it? I'd certainly have to save money for a while," said the woman.

Mimi told her what a photograph would cost, and before she walked off, the woman promised to think about it. Mimi rejoiced: the new stand was already opening doors with the locals.

"Is it true?" Mimi started at the sound of a woman's voice. She hadn't heard anyone approach, but when she turned around, her neighbor Luise was standing there. "There's word you'll be opening on Sundays. Is it true?"

"I am. I'll be starting next Sunday, June eleventh. It was my uncle's idea. Everybody is so busy working during the week, but they have time to have their picture taken on Sunday," said Mimi with a smile.

Mimi needed new customers. In all her years of traveling, she had never known a resident photographer to have so much trouble making a living. On the contrary, the studios in which she had worked as a guest photographer were successful, and none of the resident photographers had ever complained about a lack of customers. But here in the Swabian Jura, other things took priority over a visit to the photographer.

"Georg and I have our fortieth wedding anniversary soon. It's only right that we have a photo taken, as a memento. You said a little while ago that you'd photograph us for free, because I taught you to cook. My youngest daughter, Berta, will be marrying soon, and she will certainly want to have a wedding photo, too. Paid for, of course."

It seemed as if the new stand was her lucky charm, Mimi thought happily. "Just come by when—" She broke off when she saw Eveline Schubert hurrying across the market square in her direction.

Eveline stared at the stand in horror. "How could you think about putting these photographs on display? What if my husband had seen them here?" She snatched the pictures from the shelf. "I've already got enough trouble at home because of you."

Luise was all ears.

Mimi gritted her teeth. "But Laichingen women earn their own money. Can't you decide for yourself what you spend it on?" she added defiantly.

Luise laughed. "Young lady, you still have a lot to learn," she said, then walked away.

"Do you at least like the photographs?" Mimi asked with some remorse when she and Eveline were alone.

Eveline ran her fingers reverently over the pictures. Marianne held a porcelain doll in her arms and smiled blissfully. Erika was seated on the rocking horse and beaming from ear to ear.

Mimi, relieved to see that Eveline's anger seemed to have evaporated, said, "In many studios, children are still made to sit like austere little adults. No smiles, no expression at all—it's so old fashioned. And yet a child's smile is a gift from heaven."

"You're absolutely right," Eveline said. Before Mimi could react, Eveline grasped Mimi's hands in hers. Her voice heavy with emotion, she said, "They're beautiful. Thank you! As soon as I have some money saved again, I'll buy a picture frame for them." She briskly took out her purse. "What do I owe you?"

Mimi told her the price. The sight of Eveline counting out the amount coin by precious coin broke Mimi's heart. She seemed to have really scrimped and saved, and Mimi guessed she had made considerable sacrifices for the sake of the pictures.

"You're a wonderful woman," Mimi said, spontaneously stroking Eveline's arm.

Eveline sniffed and shook her head. "So wonderful that all my husband and I do is fight. If he heard that you called a child's smile a gift from heaven, he'd say the devil is dancing in your house, too. Laughter's forbidden, you should know," she said, her words laced with bitterness and irony. "Klaus is getting more and more joyless every day, and he expects the same of us. And he'll never admit that Alexander's talent is also a gift from heaven. It's the damned Laichingen disease."

Mimi let out a confused laugh. She'd never heard the expression before. "What do you mean?"

"Depression. Klaus is melancholic. It started a few years ago and has only gotten worse. I don't recognize the man I married anymore." She took a deep breath. "But I can't let it bring me down too far. Somehow, things go on. This evening I'm going to talk to him again. I *want* Alexander to have his chance at art school."

Mimi, deeply affected by Eveline's words, said nothing. Was his depression the reason that he was so obstinate about Alexander's chance at Stuttgart? She had no experience with melancholic people, and she admired Eveline for the way she dealt with her husband's illness.

"Doesn't your doctor have some advice for—" Mimi broke off when she saw Karolina Schaufler crossing the square. Karolina hadn't quite reached Mimi's shop when she began pointing at the wooden stand.

"But that's . . . that's . . ." The proprietress stepped closer to the stand, inspecting it closely, running her hand over the uneven sides. The lines on her forehead grew deeper and her expression more dour.

"Yes?" said Mimi slowly. "Fritz Braun built the stand, and your son got the materials for him. I'm very grateful to them for it, too."

"This *used* to be my bench. I put it out in the barn and was planning to get it fixed when the wagonmaker had time. Now my son has gone and sawed it to bits!"

Mimi didn't know whether to laugh or cry. "I had no idea. I just assumed the wood was left over. How can I make it up to you?"

Beside her, Eveline let out a suppressed squeak. Mimi didn't dare to look at her for fear of bursting out laughing.

"Anton's going to get the thumping of his life. I don't care if he's a head taller than me ten times over!" Karolina Schaufler turned and glared grimly across the square toward The Oxen as if she could hardly wait to get her hands on her son.

"I've got another idea," Mimi said quickly. "In exchange for the wood, what about a photograph of your inn? On a clear day, if I stand off to the left a little, I might even be able to get a reflection on the surface of the *Hüle*. You and your husband could be standing in front, and I'll include a frame, as well. But only if you forget about the beating. Your son meant well."

Barely mollified, Karolina walked off, and Mimi exhaled the breath she'd been holding in. "Looks like I've gotten off with just a black eye again," she said, laughing.

Eveline also smiled. "Anton is a prime example of a rogue, and I say that as praise for my Alexander. He's such a good boy."

"It's really something that the two of them are such good friends." Mimi shook her head, laughing.

"It's been like that since Alexander could walk," said Eveline. "He'd go through hell for Anton. And vice versa."

Mimi smiled, but she was not completely at ease with the idea. Anton had asked her so insistently about what she thought of Alexander's chances at the art school . . . He wasn't thinking of some new scheme to help his friend, was he?

CHAPTER 4

Herrmann Gehringer stopped in his tracks, stunned, when he came to Benno Klein's machine. "Cleaning the loom with your bare hands?" He pointed to the bits of fluff that had to be removed with every change of warp or other major adjustment. "You need a brush for that. You're leaving too much lint behind!"

The weaver scratched his head in embarrassment. "Sorry. My brush disappeared."

Gehringer couldn't believe it. Had everyone completely taken leave of their senses? Wherever he went on his morning rounds, sloppiness and outright negligence were one step ahead of him.

"You've managed to lose equipment, too? For your sake, I hope you find that brush, or it's coming out of your wages," he shouted over the noise of the looms, before shaking his head and moving on.

The next loom was Klaus Schubert's. *Nothing good to expect here,* thought Gehringer as he looked at the list of pick counts that his assistant, Paul Merkle, had handed him at the start of his rounds. The list reflected the number of times each weaver had sent his shuttle and its weft thread from one side of the loom to the other the previous day. For almost all the weavers, the pick count was below the daily quota set by Gehringer, but none had performed as badly as Klaus Schubert.

"Did you take a half day off or something?" Gehringer snarled at the weaver. "Looms as good as ours ought to manage six thousand picks an hour."

Klaus stepped behind his huge loom, as if to put it between them as a shield. "My stomach . . . I wasn't well. I had to go to the bathroom a lot." His eyes flickered restlessly.

Herrmann Gehringer sighed. Schubert was one of those men cursed with a feeble constitution. "Either you pull yourself together or start looking for a new job. This is no place for a man with a weak system."

Without another word, Gehringer walked on. "Can you tell me what's going on?" he snapped at Paul Merkle, trotting at his heel. "Broken warps, low pick counts—weaving demands the highest level of concentration. It seems as if the men have other things on their minds besides their actual work."

"If you say so," his assistant replied sourly, as if it had nothing to do with him.

Herrmann Gehringer glanced surreptitiously at his assistant. Could it be that his right-hand man was . . . pouting? He hadn't even told him yet that his brother, Johann, would soon be starting work.

Back in his office, the mill owner took his place behind his enormous desk. Merkle already had sorted the day's incoming mail into neat piles: orders, invoices, and other correspondence. Three new commissions, very nice! But Gehringer's pleasure faded when he saw the message his long-time—and very good—Berlin customer Alfred Stoll had included with his purchase order. *Please note! Important!* he had written in red ink.

> *This order, for a hundred pieces each of slips, nightshirts, and shifts, will only be considered binding if you agree to a price reduction of 10 percent. If you are unable to accommodate this request, Boutique Stoll will be obliged*

to look for an undergarment supplier who works with cotton. I await your earliest reply as to whether you are prepared to offer said reduction. Otherwise . . .

Otherwise? Had things gone so far that his customers were starting to threaten him? Gehringer let the letter fall onto his desk. The air in the room suddenly felt stale and stuffy. He stood up abruptly, crossed the room, and threw the window open. Inhaling and exhaling deeply, he swept his eyes across the expansive company grounds. Usually, the view of the buildings with their tiled roofs pleased him and the rhythmic clacking of the looms was music to his ears. But today his thoughts were gloomy, and the noise in the mill droned in his head. Worse still, he now had to put up with ill-mannered demands from his customers! This one complained about old-fashioned designs, that one requested discounts, and the third in line wanted his goods yesterday or sooner—how long could he keep his life's work afloat in a world like this?

It's the damned cotton, he thought. He would never have believed that the British colonial yarn could assert itself on the European market as strongly as it had. For centuries, tablecloths and sheets made of Laichingen linen had been a synonym for quality, like cuckoo clocks from the Black Forest or knives from Solingen. And people were prepared to pay a corresponding price for that quality. But for several years, cotton had been surpassing linen. It was cheaper, softer, and easier to manufacture than linen.

His order books were still full. Overfull, even. But the bulk of the orders consisted of simple garments for which the profit margin had never been high. If he started granting reductions now, he'd soon be making no profit at all.

Gehringer narrowed his eyes as he gazed out toward the weaving shed. As if the pressure from customers wasn't enough, his weavers were lazy. He closed the window again and returned to his desk. "Paul!"

His assistant instantly appeared in the doorway. Gehringer waved him over. "Pad and pencil! There's a lot to be done. If we want to survive until our company's thirtieth anniversary next year, we have to put our heads down and work. The competition from cotton producers is getting stiffer by the day. They're flooding the market with their cheap goods and driving prices down, and it's become something of a fashion among our customers to ask for price reductions. My colleagues here in town don't seem to be faring any better, either—at least, that's the talk when we meet at The Oxen. Some of them might be willing to buckle, but I'm taking up the fight!"

"Which fight, exactly?" Paul Merkle asked, eyebrows raised.

Gehringer looked at his assistant with a fierce expression. Was the man putting him on? "I won't let anyone interfere, neither our esteemed clientele nor my own people. New times are upon us, Paul, and the measures I'm about to introduce will not be to everyone's liking. Take this down. Item one: starting next month, working hours will be increased by two hours per day, with no adjustment to rates. That by itself will help balance some of the price reductions I'm being forced to make."

"Should I call an employee meeting?"

"Wait for now. The less notice we give, the better. It's not as if they won't get paid for their labor, but there's no need to give them too much advance notice to think about the extra work," said Gehringer dismissively. "Item two: when selecting apprentices, I'll be separating the wheat from the chaff. Physical constitution is one thing, but mental resilience is just as important. That miserable Schubert spoils my good mood every time I see him."

"A wife like his would get any man down," Merkle mocked. "There isn't another woman here with airs like Eveline Schubert. I could tell you a thing or two. Sonja's always on top of what's going on in the village."

That made Gehringer smile. Paul Merkle's wife, Sonja, was one of the biggest muckrakers of them all. Not that Gehringer minded: he'd picked up some useful tidbits from her over the years. She was quite an expert with an embroidery needle, too. Right now, however, he didn't have time to listen to gossip about Eveline Schubert's latest "airs." "Wife or not," he said sternly, "if Schubert doesn't pull himself together, he's out. On to point three . . ."

Barely pausing for breath, he rattled off the next two points. It wasn't as if he was thinking about these problems for the first time—he had had many sleepless nights—but he was more than ready to face the future now. And he'd step on anyone who stood in his way without a second thought.

"Item five: I'll be pressing ahead with the hiring of good weavers, to which end I'll be taking out an ad in the Ulm daily paper. If we want to stay afloat, we have to grow.

"Item six: I'm not entirely certain about this yet, but I'm considering tying wages to some kind of quality check. The pick count is only one criterion for how well or badly a man works. More mistakes mean less money! Still on the agenda is whether I employ an inspector for this or continue to carry out inspections myself."

"If you like, I can take over the inspections," Paul said.

Gehringer thought about that for a moment. Why not? He already suspected that his assistant spent too much time twiddling his thumbs. Besides, Merkle had accompanied him on his daily rounds for years, so he knew exactly what to watch for. Merkle was also hard nosed enough to deal with the men.

"Agreed! Now to item seven, and this one's particularly important to me. One or more of the new apprentices will have to take on some additional duties. Otherwise, this mill has no future at all. If one of them happens to be artistically gifted, like the Schubert boy, then after his regular shift, he can work up a few new embroidery designs. If another is mechanically inclined, I'll send him off to a mechanics course. Then he can do minor repairs, and I'll save the cost of bringing in expensive experts. Speaking of talent, have you compiled the list I asked for of this year's school graduates?"

Merkle stood and went to his office. A moment later, he returned with a sheet of paper in his hand. "I've noted which particular skills the boys have, at least for the ones I know something about."

Gehringer glanced over the list. "You didn't need to write that Vincent Klein has no particular skills," he said with a laugh. "Like father, like son, I'd say. But Fritz Braun . . . a skilled woodworker, that's interesting. How do you know?"

"Fritz gave my daughter, Christel, a little wooden horse some years ago. It was carved in so much detail that it might have come from the hand of one of the *Herrgottschnitzer*, the master carvers down in Oberammergau."

Gehringer was impressed. "Very good. Then we can certainly use him. Maybe Fritz could be our new technician—if a loom breaks, we'll have just the man we need right here!" He read on. "Your son Justus—strong and reliable, all right. Martin Steudle, Josef Krautwickel, nothing special there . . ." He looked up with a frown. "You don't have Alexander Schubert?"

Paul Merkle shook his head. "I wasn't sure if I should put his name on the list."

"Why not?" Alexander Schubert was a gifted artist, and Gehringer had plans for the young man. The patterns his embroiderers used for the pillow covers and nightshirts all came from the last century—it was imperative to breathe fresh air into things! The one illustration of Alexander Schubert's that Merkle had shown him had convinced Gehringer that the young man's artistic talent was just what he needed for his new designs.

"Because he's probably going to Stuttgart."

"Stuttgart? What's he doing in Stuttgart? He belongs here!" Gehringer was shocked. "This is the first I've heard about this."

Merkle looked at his boss in disbelief. "Sorry, have you really not heard? The photographer has contacts at Stuttgart Art School, and she's put in a word for Alexander. He's supposed to take an admissions exam there at the end of June, and there's even talk of a scholarship." Paul Merkle shrugged. "The word in the village is that Klaus Schubert is against it, but his wife is thrilled by the idea. If you ask me, Eveline

Schubert and Mimi Reventlow are cut from the same cloth. Both of them put ideas into people's heads, and when people get ideas in their heads, they start to think they're above their station."

"You're right about that photographer. Those lunatic photographs of the most recent confirmands were an affront, if I'm any judge. A simple picture of the boys and girls with the Bible wasn't enough? Oh, no, it had to be an atlas or a world globe! As if we need something like that here." He shook his head in disapproval. "I should have sent the pigheaded woman packing the minute she arrived."

Merkle grinned. "May I remind you that you actually tried that? Unsuccessfully, however. Mimi Reventlow won't let herself be sent packing so easily, especially now that she's looking after her sick uncle. And she seems to earn a living here, too—her stand at the Pentecost market certainly drew customers." He sounded downright smug.

"The old photographer won't live forever," said Gehringer sullenly. But Merkle, unfortunately, was right. Mimi Reventlow had stymied him more than once, and so far he'd found no way to stop her making a living. Now she was stirring up the youth of the village against him, and that was going too far.

"Put Alexander Schubert on the list. He'll work for me; I'll make damn sure of it. And I'll put a stop to that photographer's maneuvering, too. Item eight: think of ways to foil Mimi Reventlow's plans!"

A smirk played on Merkle's lips, and it occurred to Gehringer that his assistant seemed to despise the self-assured photographer almost more than he did himself. "That's all for today," he said, signaling to Merkle to leave. He had to think of some way to stop young Schubert from going off to Stuttgart. The first step was to go to Klaus Schubert and get to the bottom of this ridiculous farce, and find out why he wasn't man enough even to override his wife.

That's what you get when you marry above your station, he thought with scorn. Even after all her years in the village, and even though her life as the daughter of a rich Chemnitz industrialist had come to a sudden end seventeen years earlier, Eveline Schubert hadn't given up her high-society delusions.

Until today, he'd always found it a source of amusement that the daughter of his loom supplier, Karl-Otto Hoffmeister, had actually eloped with *his* weaver and had settled here in Laichingen. But his smile vanished at the idea of Eveline Schubert trying to stop her son from becoming his apprentice.

Gehringer was so caught up in his thoughts that it took him a moment to realize that Paul Merkle was still standing in the doorway.

"Is there something else?"

"Mother tells me you've hired my brother as a weaver."

Ah-ha! So he hadn't been mistaken: he'd sensed a certain defiance in Merkle and he'd been right. He appreciated that his assistant didn't kowtow to him the way so many others did, and Merkle had provided him with useful information on many occasions. Still, now and then, it was necessary to remind him of his place.

"Johann will be starting tomorrow. I've already started to recruit some new, good weavers, as you can see," said Gehringer with obvious relish. He knew, of course, that the two brothers couldn't stand each other, but he could not factor that in. Johann Merkle was a good weaver, just as his father had been. Gehringer hadn't forgotten how headstrong Johann had been years ago, but as long as he toed the line now, he was what Gehringer needed.

Paul Merkle puffed softly through his nose. "My brother was and is a troublemaker. I hope you haven't misstepped by taking him back on."

Gehringer let out a loud laugh. "Don't worry. The way he walked in here in his worn-out clothes, it's clear that the world beyond Laichingen wasn't especially kind to him. Believe me, your brother's happy he can hole up at your mother's house and that he has work. I think it's safe to say that he's not about to cause any trouble."

CHAPTER 5

It was the second Sunday in June. The weather was comfortably warm, the day was clear and bright, and the air was free of the noise and fumes from the factory machines. Mimi had opened all the windows in the studio, letting in the scent of the first blooms on the rosebushes climbing the walls of Josef's house.

"If you would put one arm around your wife," Mimi instructed her neighbor. He was standing behind Luise, who was sitting in an armchair and holding a fan.

Georg Neumann placed one hand on his wife's shoulder awkwardly.

"Maybe with a little more affection? You're celebrating forty years of marriage," said Mimi with a smile as she focused the Linhof camera.

Georg Neumann moved his hand one inch.

"Forty years is a long time. What's your secret?" Mimi asked chattily. Maybe Georg would relax a little if she could get him talking.

Luise answered instead. "There's no secret. We were lucky we could marry young. Georg inherited a little money from an uncle, so we were able to build our house. It was like that for Sonja, too, when she married Paul. But marrying young isn't typical."

"I see. Well, what is typical here in Laichingen?" Mimi asked from beneath her black cloth as she looked again at her composition.

"Normally, you're only allowed to marry if you can afford your own home. With everyone living so close and the houses so small, it's not easy." Luise cleared her throat. "Do I really have to hold the fan? I feel silly."

Mimi appeared from beneath the black cloth and said, "We can certainly try something else." The fan was new—she'd bought it recently in Ulm with some other props—and she thought it was exceptionally pretty.

"What if you, Mr. Neumann, sat in the armchair with your wife sitting on your lap?"

The couple looked horrified at the very idea. Both shook their heads.

"Where's the head support your uncle usually used? Aren't we going to use that?" Luise asked brusquely.

"To me, head and body supports usually make pictures look lifeless. Let's try it without, all right? Besides, supports like that can be very dangerous. Last autumn, I visited the Countess von Hohenfels, and she insisted on body supports for everyone. I was taking a group photograph of all the court ladies, and one of the supports collapsed and fell into a window, which smashed to bits. We don't want to risk that, do we?"

Luise and her husband smiled, and Mimi clicked the shutter. Now the picture would have a natural, warm radiance.

While she slid the next plate into position, Mimi decided that she would trim Luise's waistline and fill in Georg's beard—both just a bit—when she retouched the photograph. As much as she loved her work, she was finding it difficult to concentrate: Hannes—she still wasn't used to calling him by his real name, Johann—had dropped a note in her mailbox. He was going to try to stop by later.

Georg Neumann cleared his throat. "Excuse me for asking, but . . . will it be much longer? I need to be gettin' out to the field."

"I'd like to try one more pose, so you can choose between two pictures later," Mimi said as she was hanging a backdrop: climbing roses decorating a trellised arch. "Could I get you hand in hand in front of the arch? The rose is a symbol of all your married years—to enjoy the scent, one also has to live with the thorns."

Luise and Georg looked doubtfully at Mimi, then at the rose-covered arch. "Wouldn't Jesus on the cross be better? It's by God's grace, after all, that we've had so many married years," said Luise.

Mimi gave Luise a small brass cross to hold. "Maybe like this? Mr. Neumann, please stand still."

"The potatoes in my field aren't standin' still."

"It isn't always necessary to work, work, work. One also has to take the time to rest. Or have your picture taken," said Mimi patiently. "'Thus the heavens and the earth were finished, and all the host of them. And on the seventh day God ended his work which he had made; and he rested on the seventh day. And God blessed the seventh day, and sanctified it.' That's from Genesis, chapter two." Mimi surprised herself sometimes with all the Bible passages she still remembered from her father's sermons.

"But you're workin' on Sunday, too," said Georg Neumann. He was practically scraping one foot on the floor like a restless old plow horse.

Mimi laughed. "Touché! And me a good priest's daughter!"

"Your father is a priest?" Luise seemed impressed. "Your uncle never said a word about that."

Mimi went to the cupboard and brought out the body support that she'd thought she'd put away for good when she first arrived. Luise's husband was simply squirming too much.

Luise and her husband had just left when a family stepped into the studio. They were thin, their pale faces gaunt and careworn.

The man introduced himself as Kurt Kleinmann, and in a somber voice he asked if Mimi could photograph him and his family. His wife wanted one after seeing a family portrait hanging on the wall in their neighbor's house. With every word, the man seemed to grow more pallid.

Oh dear, Mimi thought, sympathizing with the man's plight. For reticent, reserved people, being photographed—and thus the center of attention—was torture.

"Would you like to take a look at my props? Then we'll think about how your picture could look. With family portraits especially, the possibilities are countless," she said in a cheerful voice.

The man nodded uncertainly, but instead of going to the shelf that held the props, he stood where he was.

His wife, however, didn't need to be asked twice. Reverently, she ran her fingers lightly over a summer hat decorated with white silk roses. "It would be nice to be a real lady, just once . . ." She looked doubtfully at Mimi while her children, with no less reverence, gaped at the rocking horse.

"I also have a handbag and a parasol with silk flowers to match the hat, see?" she said. "You can try everything on, and there's a mirror out in the entrance."

The woman continued in her melodic voice, "It's like you're living a different life . . . allowed to dream for a moment." She carefully placed the hat on her head.

Mimi smiled. Giving people the gift of beauty—that had always been her dream. As she looked at the woman now wearing the hat, she had an idea.

She quickly took down the backdrop of the rose-covered arch and put up one of Josef's: a clearing in a forest. Then she spread a blue-and-green checked wool blanket on the platform. While the woman adjusted the hat in front of the mirror, Mimi set out silk roses and porcelain cups and saucers on the blanket and added a wine bottle and glasses. When the rather romantic-looking scene was ready, she said invitingly, "What about a picnic, like the kind the high-society ladies and gentlemen enjoy?"

Mrs. Kleinmann's eyes lit up and her cheeks glowed with excitement.

"If you think so," said her husband, resigned to his fate.

The couple sat down on the blanket, and Mimi positioned their children and the rocking horse in the foreground. And just as she tripped the shutter, the sun appeared and shone a golden ray of light on the picnic scene. Quickly, not wanting to lose a single valuable moment, Mimi stretched a fine silk net in front of the lens, inserted a new glass plate, and took another picture.

How radiant the woman had been! Mimi thought as she carefully packed the glass plates in lightproof wrapping. The slightest bit of light would destroy the plates immediately, and all her work would have been for nothing. She was just packing the last plate when she saw Hannes—Johann—opening the garden gate. He'd made good on his promise! Mimi's heart was pounding in her throat in an instant. She jumped in front of the mirror and ran her fingers frantically over her hair. Every pin was in place, and her hair was smoothed back evenly from her forehead. Everything was perfect. Only the red flush on her cheeks was new.

She'd just made it back to the platform and was pretending to be busy when the door opened. But it wasn't Johann. It was his mother, Edelgard Merkle. Mimi's mouth opened and closed, but she couldn't get a word out.

"Good morning, Miss Reventlow. Seems the cat's run off with your tongue, has it? Who'd have thought an old woman like me would have reason to pay you a visit here in the studio." With a loving mother's gleam in her eyes, Edelgard turned and pulled Johann through the doorway and into the studio. "You met my son at the Pentecost market, and he had the good idea of having a picture taken to remember his homecoming by," she said, beaming at Johann.

Johann, who so far hadn't said a word, only grinned.

Mimi had trouble suppressing a giggle. What a charade! Why should they keep their relationship a secret? She was a grown woman and could do what she wanted. If her reputation in Laichingen suffered as a result, so be it.

But if Johann wanted it this way . . . She held out her hand formally and said, "Congratulations! You're certainly full of good ideas." Then she turned to his mother. "Maybe you'd like to have a look at the props and accessories? You could also pick something nice for Johann. A top hat, perhaps? Or a gentleman's suit?"

Edelgard Merkle nodded enthusiastically, then she went off to look at the props and clothes.

"A gentleman—you don't actually think I'm going to dress up for a photograph, do you?" Johann whispered to Mimi.

She smiled with exaggerated charm. "*You're* the one who wanted a picture," she said, and acted as if she were adjusting her camera. But then she couldn't hold back any longer. "I thought you were coming alone!" she said.

"Sorry. I couldn't shake Mother off. First she wanted to go to The Oxen with me, then for a walk, and next I'm supposed to go visit Paul's family with her." He snorted.

Mimi glanced at Edelgard. Johann's mother had just draped a silk scarf with a long fringe over her shoulder and was admiring herself in the mirror.

"I've missed you . . . ," Mimi said, stroking Johann's arm tenderly.

"And I've missed you," he whispered back. "But I've been working at the mill since Thursday, and when I'm finished with work, it's evening, and I've got a dozen things to take care of."

"Miss Reventlow?"

"Coming!" Mimi called.

"Will I see you this evening?" she whispered. "We could go for a walk, or sit here in the garden."

He shook his head. "A few of my workmates have agreed to meet at The Oxen. I want to try to find out from them what's been going on at Gehringer's mill."

Mimi frowned her disappointment.

"I'll think of something," he said. He kissed her quickly on the cheek, then went back to his mother. "Well, did you find yourself something nice?"

"Look at this silk scarf—doesn't it have an elegant sheen to it?" Like a young girl, Edelgard pirouetted in front of Johann, and the fringes of the scarf flew out around her as she turned.

"The 'elegant sheen' of *silk*! From the mouth of a linen-weaver's wife? Isn't that a sin?" Johann said, and laughed.

But his mother wasn't about to be put off. "I've found this top hat and walking stick for you. They'll make you look like a real nobleman."

Mimi laughed, too—Johann dressed like that seemed so absurd.

"I worked in the cotton trade, Mother, not at the New York Stock Exchange. And 'noble' really doesn't apply in that business. I think we should just let the photographer do her job—I'm sure she knows what she's doing." He winked conspiratorially at Mimi.

Mimi suddenly felt a tug of desire deep inside her. *Oh God, don't let me get distracted now.* She glanced up at the sky. A cloud covered the sun again, but it was a bright day. "The perfect light for a picture outdoors!" she said.

Johann Merkle didn't want his picture taken in front of the apple tree in Josef's garden. Nor did he want to sit on the bench in front of the house and strike a thinker pose with one arm propped on his knee. Instead, he stood in front of the weathered, gray wooden wall of the studio. His mother stood rather listlessly beside him—she would have preferred a picture taken inside the studio but gave in to her son's wishes, just as Mimi had.

When Mimi looked through the viewfinder of her camera, she realized, to her astonishment, that the plain background was ideal for Johann's expressive face. *Now if only my hands would stop shaking,* she thought.

How old is he? she wondered as she sharpened the focus. That night in Ulm, it seemed they had talked about everything under the sun—except their ages. On his forehead, a wrinkle had dug its way in, and there were a few small folds around his eyes, but the lines came from laughter, not age. He looked young and strong. *What a beautiful man,* she thought dreamily. But the way everyone in his hometown monopolized him, well, there was nothing either he or she could do about that.

"Now smile!" Mimi said.

After seeing Johann, Mimi floated through the day as if on a cloud. She was putting away the props and clothes when the door opened again. In front of her stood a man in his Sunday best. The woman beside him had braided her hair elaborately and wore a small costume-jewelry crown as an ornament.

"But you're . . . you're . . . ," Mimi stuttered.

"The wagonmaker who didn't have time to make your postcard stand. Balthasar Meindl's the name," said the man with a smile. "And this is my wife, Emilie. When we got married, we were so poor we didn't even have enough to pay for a picture of our wedding day. But now that you're open, and we can afford it, we thought we'd make up for that."

Mimi welcomed the couple warmly. "How nice of you to visit. I'm so glad you did." She'd been meaning to visit the wagonmaker for days to put in a good word for Fritz Braun, and now the man had come to her. If that wasn't a stroke of fortune . . .

Balthasar Meindl nodded toward the street, where Mimi had once again set up her wooden stand in front of her business. "Looks like someone else built your stand after all. The wood isn't ideal for the job, but with the carved rose on top, you don't notice that."

Well, this could hardly be better, Mimi thought. "A young man here in Laichingen built it for me. He loves to work with wood, and if you ask me, he's very talented."

"A young man from here did this?" The wagonmaker raised his eyebrows.

Don't stick your nose into other people's business, child . . . It wasn't the first time Mimi heard her uncle's voice in her mind, but she ignored his warning and summoned up her courage. "One of the boys finishing school this year, actually. Mr. Meindl, could you imagine taking on an apprentice?" She held her breath in anticipation.

The wagonmaker laughed bitterly. "There's a lot of things I can imagine. And when I look at the chaos in my workshop, I can see well enough that I desperately need some help. If I had a son who wanted to follow in my footsteps, things would be different, but I don't, so where am I going to find an apprentice? The boys here in the village all want to work in the mills. Like father, like son—you must have heard that before, young lady."

"Since Balthasar took over the customers from the carpenter who died, he's been working day and night. It really can't go on," said Emilie Meindl reproachfully, as if Mimi herself were responsible for their state of affairs.

Mimi nodded. "A hardworking apprentice would certainly be a great help. The boy who built my stand was Fritz Braun, by the way."

"Walter's son Fritz can carve like that? Likes to work with wood, too, does he?"

Mimi nodded. "Fritz would like nothing more than to learn woodworking. He even asked me to talk to you because he couldn't bring himself to do it."

For a long moment, nobody spoke. The Meindls exchanged a look. "It certainly wouldn't please Mr. Gehringer if you stole one of his weaver boys," Emilie finally said to her husband.

Balthasar Meindl snorted. “You know what? I don’t care.” He looked from his wife to Mimi. “If there’s anything to fix at the Gehringer mill, he always brings in someone from outside. I told him years ago that I could do most of the smaller repairs, but no—for his oh-so-sacred looms he wants ‘experts’ from the city.” Meindl laughed scornfully. “It would serve him right if Fritz came to work for me.”

“So he”—Mimi swallowed excitedly—“he can come by?”

Balthasar Meindl hesitated a heartbeat, then said, “He should come by tomorrow. If I like him, we’ll draw up a contract on the spot.”

CHAPTER 6

When Anton stepped out of The Oxen with a tray of freshly drawn glasses of beer, he was met with a sweet, summery breeze drifting in from the fields and meadows. He was about to take a deep breath when the breeze—and Anton—was overwhelmed by a wave of kitchen smells: fried potato, meat broth, and fat heated too many times. *If you could only close your nose the way you can close your eyes,* he thought.

As on every Sunday, the benches in front of The Oxen had been full since early afternoon. The first men had come for a drink right after the church service. While their wives hurried home to cook the midday meal, they drank cider at the regulars' table. Usually, these men went home around one o'clock, just about the time when others came in to eat: the clerks from the weaving mills, the blacksmith and his wife, Helene from the shop next door, and there were always one or two unfamiliar guests.

Now it was midafternoon, and at a table to one side sat Herrmann Gehringer, the parish priest, and a man from the mayor's office whom Anton recognized but whose name he didn't know. When he went to clear their plates, Anton wondered what the unlikely trio was whispering about. The men immediately stopped their conversation when Anton arrived at the table, but as he stepped away, he thought he heard Mimi Reventlow's name mentioned.

Gottfried Hirrler and Egon Morlock, businessmen like Herrmann Gehringer, sat at another table. They had catalogs spread out in front of them and seemed to be comparing numbers. Sometimes, with a flourish, they crossed out an item in a catalog. Were they planning on joining forces? Bed linen, table linen . . . it would make sense. Anton let out a sigh—he would love to be a businessman! Leading negotiations, making plans and deals. It would be the right thing for him, he was certain of it. But no, he had to be here at The Oxen, wasting away. Annoyed, he wiped down a table where someone had spilled cider.

Some distance from everyone else sat Johann Merkle, his expression vacant. Probably daydreaming about the photographer, Anton thought. Or did he already have his eye on someone else? Since the meeting he'd witnessed in Mimi's garden, Anton hadn't seen the two of them together at all. But that didn't mean their "affair" was over, did it?

Anton had an idea. He went inside, drew another beer, and took it out to Johann. "On the house," he said, then leaned in closer and said, more quietly, "So what's it like to be home again? Must be boring as hell after all your adventures. You wouldn't have a tip or two for me about getting by out there, would you?"

But Johann only shook his head peevishly. "Leave me be. I have to think."

Damn, why did I even bother asking? Anton thought, annoyed at himself. He knew he had to seize every chance to find out about the world, but he could have saved himself the trouble just now: he was perfectly aware of how arrogant Merkle was. Johann probably still saw in him the dumb eleven-year-old Anton had been when Johann turned his back on Laichingen. But those days were long gone. Now, at eighteen, Anton knew more than most people in town—he read every newspaper, every book, everything that came his way.

His mood was slowly plunging toward despair when he heard a stone skittering along the side street beside The Oxen. He brightened instantly. Christel! A stone tossed along the street was the signal they'd worked out long ago for their secret meetings. Anton quickly put down the tray he'd been carrying.

"So you finally decide to show your face?" she barked at him the moment he came around the corner. "I've been standing here for five minutes! My brother is wandering around somewhere—if he sees us together, he'll snitch to Father." Her deep-blue eyes sparked with anger. "Besides, Mother isn't doing well. She's afraid she's going to lose the baby, and I have to go home again in a minute."

"Sorry, I didn't hear you at first. I've been busy with customers," Anton said.

Before he knew it, she threw herself into his arms. "Oh, Anton, everything is so horrible! I don't think I can bear it much longer," she sobbed.

Did she miss him so much? Flattered and touched, Anton stroked Christel's silken hair. "I'll be done by eight at the latest. We could go for a walk then, if you like?" He would have loved to take Christel to a café or a dance or an afternoon concert—somewhere the scent of luxury filled the air. But there was none of that in dingy little Laichingen, and instead, the air reeked of fryer fat.

"What are you talking about?" She pulled away from him. "This isn't about you, for once."

Anton looked at her in confusion.

"It's Father," she said. "I hate him!"

"Ah. Why?" Anton dutifully asked. It was nothing new for Christel to blow off steam about her strict father, and Anton despised Paul Merkle, too. But didn't they both have better things to do just then than vent their anger about him? His mother was bound to appear any moment and demand to know where he'd been hiding so long.

Christel grasped Anton's arm. "I was in Helene's store yesterday, and Mr. Gehringer came in. He took me aside and told me he was planning to build a glass pavilion at his mill. He's going to use it as a showroom for his customers."

"Why in the world did he tell *you* about it?" Anton asked.

Christel's eyes glittered with excitement. "Because he uses models. You *might* remember that I told you my father mentioned Mr. Gehringer hires models in Stuttgart for pictures of his garments. Well, now he's asked *me* if I want to work for him as a model! Imagine that! When customers come, I'd show off the finest embroidered blouses and aprons in the glass pavilion. Paid, of course, and he also said that he would only take a pretty girl for the job." Pride filled her voice. But a moment later, her tone turned despairing. "I think I could do it really well, too," she said, wringing her hands.

Anton couldn't believe his ears. Now Gehringer wanted to tie down the most beautiful girl in town—*his* girl—to this place? The thought of the businessman using Christel's beauty to help him sell his aprons made Anton furious, but in as natural a voice as possible, he said, "So what's the problem?"

"Father!" she spat. "He forbids it. 'As long as you're under my roof, I'm the one who says what you do and don't do,'" she mimicked Paul Merkle. "I hate him. I hate everything here."

"Christel!" Before she wallowed in her misery any longer, Anton took her hands in his. "You don't need Gehringer. With your beauty, you could model dresses in the finest fashion houses in Berlin or Munich. What are we waiting for? Let's get out of here, once and for all. I already have an idea for how we can manage it soon." He couldn't do anything about the touch of desperation that had crept into his voice—they had had this talk too many times. But he now had a pretty clear idea of how he could "escape" Laichingen—he could not describe leaving the village any other way. But Christel didn't yet know anything about it.

She shook his hands off her as if she were shooing away an insect. "You're just as tied to Laichingen as I am. Just look at yourself!" She pointed contemptuously at the damp rag drooping over his left shoulder. "Dream on, Anton. But I'll tell you here and now, you'll rot in this village like the rest of us." Without another word, she turned and ran away.

Perplexed and hurt, Anton watched her go.

"Took a little nap, did we?" his father snarled at him the moment he reentered The Oxen. "Dessert for Gehringer and his guests is on the counter. Hurry it up!"

Gehringer, Gehringer, Gehringer! He couldn't hear the name anymore. When he saw that his mother had added a second piece of cake to the plates for each of the three men, it only made him angrier. She wouldn't give a weaver so much as an extra potato.

"Then we're agreed—no more work allowed on Sundays," Anton heard Gehringer say as he approached their table. "It's best for everyone. The photographer might try to seduce the people, but we'll make sure they don't get tempted into sin. Sunday is the Lord's day, after all."

The priest nodded.

Gehringer really seemed to have his sights set on Mimi, Anton thought. Should he warn her? "Apple cake for the gentlemen. Coffee and schnapps are on the way," he said, and set the plates on the table with so much energy that a few crumbs of cake found their way onto Herrmann Gehringer's trousers.

"Watch out, you oaf," Gehringer snapped at him.

Anton grinned inwardly. He was about to make a half-hearted apology when he saw Alexander creeping along at the far side of the square—and it looked like he, too, had had a bad day. Anton dropped everything and crossed the square to his friend. His father, The Oxen, and most of all, Herrmann Gehringer be damned.

"Well? How's it looking?" he said when he reached Alexander.

"Don't ask. All hell's broken loose at our place," Alexander said. "Nothing but fighting for days. Mother wrote to Stuttgart thanking them and telling them I'd be there for the admissions test. You should have seen my father! He pushed her against the wall and choked her. For a second I thought he'd kill her." He looked as if he was close to tears. "It looks like Gehringer heard I might not be his slave after all and raked Father over the coals."

Gehringer. Again. Who else? Anton felt like he might explode with fury and frustration. "So what now?" he asked.

Alexander shrugged hopelessly. "No idea. The end of my dream, I guess. I'll never know if I have what it takes to be a good painter."

Anton furrowed his brow. "Didn't you tell me just a few days ago that you'd do anything to get to that test?"

Alexander nodded. "Yes. But that was before my father nearly killed my mother. Marianne and Erika are terrified of him, and no wonder. I'd rather keep drawing on old wrapping paper with pencil stubs if it would keep the peace at home. Maybe I'll be able to come up with an embroidery design now and then." Bitterness filled every word.

"What?" Anton said. Not because he hadn't understood what Alexander had said, but because he couldn't believe—and didn't want to believe—his ears. Christel wasting away as a housekeeper and needle-woman in her own home. He trapped at The Oxen. And Alexander spending his life as Gehringer's slave? Never! At least one of them had to make it. Anton grasped his friend by his thin shoulders and shook him. "Man, Alexander, when I think about how you talked about your dream, about being a painter, how intense you were less than a week ago, I can't believe you want to bury the whole thing."

"Do you think it's easy for me? But what chance do I have?"

"You have every chance. But you have to take matters into your own hands. Imagine you weren't able to work a loom . . . Gehringer would lose all interest in you."

"What's your point?" Alexander frowned. "You know Gehringer will hire just about any boy who isn't blind or on crutches, and that's especially true if he's the son of a weaver."

"Well, there's your solution . . . ," said Anton softly.

Alexander laughed. "You think I ought to hobble around like a cripple? But I'm healthy, and my parents and Gehringer know it."

Anton fell silent.

Alexander looked at him sharply. "Are you saying I should—"

"You'll have to give up something, there's no two ways about it." Anton shrugged. "As a painter you need your sight, so if you want to escape Gehringer, that's out of the question. But a walking stick, well . . ." Even as he spoke, he realized how insane their discussion sounded. For a moment, he questioned whether he was making a grave mistake. But he leaned closer and whispered his idea in Alexander's ear. Summoning all his courage, he added, "I'll help, but we can't put it off. Your exam isn't even three weeks from now."

When Alexander looked at him, Anton saw his friend was pale as death.

CHAPTER 7

It was Tuesday evening. Hands trembling with exhaustion, Eveline combed her hair in front of the piece of mirror before braiding it for the night. The girls and Alexander were already in bed. She would go up soon herself, but she couldn't let herself sleep, not yet. No, she would wait for Klaus to come home from The Oxen. Now he went there during the week as well as on the weekends. Eveline hated it, but there was nothing she could do about it.

If Johann were the father of her children, everything would be different, and he would care for her and the children above all else. Johann . . . Earlier that day, when she'd taken Klaus his lunch—yet again, he'd forgotten to take it with him—her eyes had met Johann's across the looms, and she believed she had seen the same yearning in his eyes that she felt. Oh, to get away from the noise and the other weavers . . . They had so much to say to each other.

Eveline had begun to smile discreetly at Johann when suddenly Klaus had come running toward her and, without a word of thanks, snatched his lunch from her hand. Johann had watched, and Eveline had seen from his raised eyebrows how displeased he was at the way Klaus treated her. If he knew that Klaus drank away half his wages, well . . .

And the wasted money wasn't all of it. In his drunkenness, Klaus had raised his hand against her many times, only to stop at the last moment as if shocked by his own behavior. Indeed, just a couple of days before, he'd nearly throttled her. What would happen if the day came when he could not control himself? Eveline thought fearfully.

A sense of doom threatened to overwhelm her. *Focus on what you have to do,* she chided herself as she plumped up her straw mattress and climbed into bed. With the task ahead of her, no one could help, not even Johann.

Her heart beat hard and fast when she heard Klaus's heavy footsteps on the stairs around nine. When he reached their small room, he silently took off his shoes, shirt, and trousers, then flopped onto the bed beside her in his underwear. He stank of sweat and schnapps.

Forcing herself to smile, Eveline rolled to face him. Timidly, as if she were touching a stranger, she stroked his arm. "Klaus, dear, how was your day?" Instead of asking him where he'd been, she pressed a kiss to his cheek. "Guess what the girls got up to today?" She told him how Erika and Marianne used the stones they'd picked out of the dirt in the field to create shapes of animals on the ground. "I think they're both almost as talented as Alexander." Was that a good way into the discussion? she immediately wondered. If not, what would make him at least a little receptive?

"And you're proud of foolishness like that, aren't you," he said. "Didn't they have anything useful to do with their time?"

Beneath his reproachful eyes, Eveline looked away, hurt. She'd have done better to hold her tongue.

"If the girls are as clever as you claim, it's time they learned to embroider. Marianne's eight. At her age, my sister, God rest her soul, was already helping Mother with the embroidery."

"All right," said Eveline, while at the same time she thought, *Like hell she'll do that!* Neither of the girls would hold an embroidery needle before they were ten years old. She didn't care what other families did. But she kept that to herself.

As he did every night before going to sleep, Klaus folded his hands together in prayer. He spoke softly:

Lord, how glorious will it be
To wake with you, as by a new birth
Cleansed from sin, pure and free
Released at last from this earth.

A shudder ran through Eveline. Other men prayed for the safety and well-being of their families, but her husband prayed to one day meet the Lord.

"Klaus, dear, about Alexander . . . ," she began. "Won't you think it over one more time? I am sure God would be happy if our son were to take this opportunity."

"How dare you twist the Lord's name to your own ends." Her husband's voice was dangerously low. "I won't hear another word on the matter. Let a good man have his well-earned sleep, can't you? I work from morning to night, and all I find at home is a wife who provokes me."

Damn it! Eveline bit down on her lip. What was she supposed to say that she hadn't said so many times already? "Klaus, please . . . I'm begging you."

"Begging me? For what? To show you who's in charge in this house?" He held both hands to his head, and his eyes looked almost crazy.

"What is it? Do you have a headache?" she asked, shocked by his appearance. A terrible thought came to her: Did Klaus perhaps have a tumor? Something wrong with his head? Was that behind his depression, his aggressive behavior in recent months?

Before she could follow the thought further, he threw himself at her. "If anything is giving me pain, it's you. You with your disobedience!

Your arrogant talk! Your never-ending begging!" He heaved himself on top of her, pushing her body into the bed, as if to stop her from slipping out from under him. With one hand he tore away her underwear and with the other he pulled up her nightdress. "Is this what you're begging for?" With his right knee, he pried her legs apart violently, and she felt his stiffness. He forced himself inside her.

It took all of Eveline's will not to cry out in pain. "Shut up!" He punched her in the face and kept pushing into her. "Wives submit to their husbands. The husband is to rule his wife as Christ is to rule the church, and as the church submits to Christ, so, too, should wives submit to their husbands. It is written as such in the Bible, and I will teach it to you, until you finally understand!"

This can't be happening, Eve thought, as if in a trance. A nightmare, she told herself, and soon she would wake up. But she had the metallic taste of blood in her mouth. And the thrusts grew harder, more brutal.

In the next room, Alexander lay in his bed and listened helplessly. The blows against the wall. His mother's muted sounds. The hate-filled grunts of his father. Alexander curled his hands into fists. How he would love to go into the other room and—

Drag his father out of bed? Bash him over the head with a stick? Shout, *Enough!*? Anything Alexander did would only make his father wilder and more likely to terrorize his mother and sisters. And how would his mother feel if she knew he'd heard? Alexander knew what a proud woman his mother was. Like this, at least, she could tell herself that no one knew a thing.

Alexander swallowed hard and faced the bitter truth: here and now, he could not help his mother, but in the future, he would take things into his own hands. Anton was right. And though the price might be high—he had to pay it.

He pulled on his clothes, went as quietly as he could down the stairs, and ran to The Oxen. There was still a light burning in Anton's room. Alexander tossed a pebble at the window. A shadow appeared, and a ragged Anton looked down to Alexander on the street.

"Your plan," Alexander called up softly. "I'll do it!"

Josef Stöckle's darkroom was tucked away in a small room in the cellar. There was no window, and a black cloth draped over the door blocked even the slightest ray of light from that direction. While Mimi had always disliked cellars in general, she had never once felt any apprehension in her uncle's darkroom.

She had looked forward to today's work even more than usual. Her Sunday in the studio had been a success, and after spending Monday with Josef, now she finally had time to develop the pictures.

First, her eyes had to adapt—the only light in the darkroom came from a single red-brown safelight. As soon as she started the developing process, she would turn even the safelight off and work in total darkness, trusting herself entirely to her senses.

Whenever she was at work in the darkroom, and today was no exception, she was overcome by an exhilaration that was hard to describe. Something akin to stage fright, perhaps? Anticipation? Maybe even a little nervousness at the possibility of damaging her images? Mimi wasn't sure, and she had never talked about it with anyone, not even her uncle.

Preparation, as Mimi had learned years before, was everything. In front of her on the long, narrow table, neatly lined up in the correct sequence, were four trays, each holding a different fluid.

In the first was the developing fluid. With this chemical, the image on the colorless glass plate became visible as a negative. Of course, there were guidelines for how long a plate had to stay in the tray before it was lifted out and placed in the second, but Mimi usually made the decision based on instinct. For her, it was this first part of the process, when the image emerged, that bordered on the magical.

The moment she took the glass plate out of the first tray and put it in the acidic mixture in the second, the developing process came to an abrupt halt.

In the third tray was fixer, which made the image permanent. Only when this stage of the process was complete, and the last remaining light-sensitive silver bromide was rinsed from the glass plate, could Mimi turn on the safelight again. Then, for a final rinse, she put the developed negative into the fourth tray, which held clear water.

Four simple steps, some chemistry, and the right timing. That was it. Or was there really a little magic involved? Mimi wondered as much every time she was in the darkroom. Her male colleagues would probably have laughed at her reverence for the process, she thought, mocking herself gently.

Almost devoutly, she took a pair of tongs and dipped one of the silvered plates in the tray of developing fluid, then used the tongs to push the plate gently back and forth. When it was time, she used a second pair of tongs to move the plate to the second tray.

For each tray she had a corresponding pair of tongs. This way, she didn't risk transferring any of the fluids from one tray to the next and avoided the yellow or brown spots on the edges of a plate that resulted from contamination.

While the first glass plate from the photographs she'd taken on Sunday was still in the fixer, Mimi took the next plate and began the developing process again. Once she'd developed a dozen glass plates, she turned on the safelight. She took the plates out of the water bath, drained off the last of the water, and dabbed them dry with a soft cloth.

Luise and her husband in front of the rose arch. The family on the picnic blanket. The ray of sunlight was black, but the five figures on the blanket were almost ghostlike. What Mimi had developed on the glass plate was just the negative. The plate would only become a "real" photograph when she projected the negative onto special photographic paper. The stiff, card-like sheets of paper were a little larger than the glass plates. The surface of the paper was covered with a light-sensitive emulsion, and this was where the finished picture would later appear. As with developing the plates, producing the paper photographs also happened in several steps and took a considerable amount of time. And in between, of course, came the retouching.

She took the negatives with her upstairs to the shop, where her retouching desk was set up. The first plate that Mimi worked on was the negative of Luise and Georg. The anniversary couple looked very dignified in front of the rose arch, and seemed very close. Mimi found the picture moving: Luise's proud smile, Georg's slightly impatient expression . . . She would draw the corner of her nervous neighbor's mouth upward a little. With a freshly sharpened fine pencil and a great deal of intuition and accuracy, she began to make tiny strokes on the plate.

The next picture, the family on the picnic blanket, hardly needed any retouching. Mimi planned to make an extra print of the image and let the family have it for free—the parents could have a picture to hang in the children's room.

A disquiet came over her when she reached for the next plate. It was the portrait of Johann Merkle and his mother. Hands trembling, Mimi affixed the plate to her retouching desk, then did what she could not do in real life: she gazed at the man intently and for a long time. It was not only the defiance and clarity in his eyes that made him special but also the evenness of his features and the contrast between his strong chin and his soft, full mouth. A mouth that kissed very well indeed. Instinctively, she ran her index finger over her own lips. Johann . . . since he'd arrived in town, she thought about him constantly.

After she developed the two prints for Edelgard and Johann, she made a third print from one half of the glass plate, a picture of Johann alone. She would keep it in the drawer of her nightstand—and keep him close, always.

CHAPTER 8

It was two days later when people came by the shop during their lunch break for their pictures. The day before, Mimi had sent word they were ready, and now she was happy to be able to hand over their photographs.

"It's so beautiful! Like in a fairy-tale forest." The woman looked at the picnic scene with disbelief. "Is that really us?"

The moment in which a customer first saw their picture was always special. "To be someone else, just for a change—it's what you wanted. You look as if you go out on picnics all the time," said Mimi with a smile.

The woman's husband looked from the picture to his wife and back. "There's a lovely spot near the old oak, where there's a view of the entire valley. If you like, we could have a picnic there on the weekend. The children would like it, wouldn't they?"

A photograph wasn't only magical for herself but for her subjects, too, Mimi thought with satisfaction as the woman looked at her husband with affection.

"My wife's hands look different . . ." Frowning, Bernhard Scholz, a weaver at the Hirrler mill, held a photograph close to his eyes. He had come to the shop during his brief lunch break to collect the picture of him and his wife taken to mark her fortieth birthday. In the picture, Mrs. Scholz sat at a small desk and pretended to be writing a letter, while her husband looked on benevolently. "Somethin's not right."

"It's amazing what a little retouching can do," Mimi said. She'd spent more than half an hour on the woman's hands, callused from her daily labor, to make them look more ladylike.

"Hard work gives a woman's hands their character," said the man reproachfully. "Should my Emma be ashamed of that?"

"Good God, no!" Mimi said, horrified. "I was just trying to make her more beautiful—"

"So you're the one who decides that?" The man tossed his money on Mimi's desk and stomped away without another word.

"I meant well," Mimi assured herself.

Josef, who was keeping her company in the shop for the first time in weeks, laughed. "You meant *too* well, child. Maybe you should stop sticking your nose into other people's business."

"Excuse me? I don't do anything of the sort," Mimi replied.

"Really? What about Alexander Schubert?"

Mimi looked at her uncle guiltily. "An invitation to an admissions test at the art school—what's wrong with that? The boy should have his chance," she replied more grumpily than she intended. First an unhappy customer and now Josef was criticizing her! "Anyway, how do you know about that?"

"Half the village knows about it," Josef said.

"What?"

"Did you seriously think something like that could happen quietly? People here are betting on which of them wins out, Klaus or Eveline." A coughing fit nearly swallowed the couple's names.

Mimi frowned. "Who's in front?" she asked when Josef's coughing subsided.

"I don't know anyone who's betting on Eveline," Josef said drily. "Mimi, there is no dishonor in helping the boy, but you're not doing him any favors. One day, you'll move on, but everybody else still has to live here. Don't make things unnecessarily hard for them. A spirit, once it grows, can't be pressed back into its old form."

"And that's exactly the point," Mimi replied defiantly.

She had just gotten Josef back to the house and was tidying up in the studio when there was a knock at the door. "It's open!" she called.

A moment later, a messenger from the town hall handed her a letter. "From the public order office?" Mimi's brow creased.

> *You are hereby accused, on the basis of the Labor Protection Act of June 1, 1891, in which it is stated that engaging in work on a Sunday is fundamentally prohibited, of disturbing the Sunday rest on June 11 of this year. We hereby request that you immediately cease your photographic enterprises on Sundays. Should you not comply with this request, a penalty of one hundred marks will be imposed, to be paid to the municipal cashier.*

"I don't believe it!" Mimi said when she finished reading, and she let out an incredulous laugh. For a moment, she could only sit there, stunned. Her Sunday revenues had been better than all the other days of the week, when practically nobody came to the studio, put together. Now that the weather was warmer, everyone was busy day and night.

Besides, Josef had opened on Sundays in the past, so why shouldn't she be allowed to do the same?

Mimi chewed at her lower lip. Somebody must have something against her to do this just for the fun of it. But who? Could Johann advise her in this particular predicament? She would at least have a reason to call on him. Since he'd come to visit her the first time, they hadn't seen each other in private at all. On the other hand, what was Johann supposed to tell her? Even he couldn't do much about an official edict.

Mimi stared at the letter, her mind churning. Maybe the local office wasn't behind this at all. Maybe it was someone else entirely? The more she thought about it, the more she could imagine who she probably had to thank for this surprise.

She jumped to her feet, locked the studio, and marched toward the town hall.

The public order office was on the ground floor. Mimi went in without knocking, making the clerk, who was slicing an apple, jump.

"Can you explain this, please?" Without introducing herself or offering a word of greeting, Mimi slapped the letter down on the man's desk. "I know perfectly well from my travels that the Labor Protection Act mentioned here allows for numerous exceptions, for example for those who trade in fresh produce. Businesses in tourist regions are also exceptions."

"And does any of that apply to you?" the public order officer asked, wiping his fingers on a handkerchief.

"No, but my uncle also used to—" Mimi began, but the man interrupted her.

"You can take all the photographs you like during the week. People are supposed to have Sunday to rest so they can do their work on Monday properly."

"As if they're wearing themselves out by standing in front of my camera," Mimi mocked. She narrowed her eyes and glared at the man. "But I'm starting to see which way the wind blows . . . Would our dear Mr. Gehringer have anything to do with this? Is he trying to tell people how to spend their Sundays now, too?"

"I beg your pardon! Sunday as a day of rest is legally protected. Mr. Gehringer has nothing to do with it," said the man, whose face had turned beet red.

"Then this law is particularly suited to the mill boss," Mimi replied. She turned on her heel and left.

It was just after one o'clock when Anton knocked on the door of Josef Stöckle's house. When there was no sign of anyone inside, he knocked again. He didn't want to call out—that would draw too much attention.

"Yes?" Finally, the old photographer stood blinking in the doorway. Apparently, Anton had woken him from a midday nap.

"Good afternoon, Mr. Stöckle. My mother sends her greetings. We have some potato soup left over from lunch. I've brought some for you." Anton held out a small pot invitingly. "You liked this very much when you used to come to The Oxen." He hoped his mother wouldn't notice the missing pot before he brought it back.

Josef Stöckle looked at him in surprise. "You went to all that trouble for me?" When he reached out for the pot, his hands shook so violently that Anton feared he would drop it.

"Allow me. I'll take it to the kitchen for you. There's enough for your niece, too."

"Mimi isn't here. She went out earlier, but don't ask me why or where."

Even better, Anton thought. They would be on their own. Where was Alexander? He hadn't lost his nerve, had he? "Alexander will be here soon, too. We agreed to meet and cut some firewood for you. We'll stack it and bring a load into the house. Then your niece won't have to do it."

"I'm not one to look a gift horse in the mouth. Mimi does so much for me as it is," the old man said with a smile. "But there's not much wood left, I'm afraid."

Anton looked out the kitchen window and, to his relief, saw Alexander crossing the square. "We'll take care of what there is," he replied. "Why don't you have some soup, then lie down again for a while. Alexander and I know our way around."

"You made it," said Anton. When he saw how ashen his friend looked, he added, "You can still change your mind."

"Let's just go." Alexander's voice sounded like cracked porcelain. Without another word, he led the way back to the woodshed.

The door squeaked a little, and it was dark inside. It smelled of mice and dust.

Anton looked around. Josef Stöckle's wood supply was minimal—a couple of hundred pounds, if that, he estimated. Most of it had already been cut into oven-sized pieces, and there were only a few bigger blocks still to be cut. Well, that was what they had to work with. The main thing was to make the "accident" look genuine. Anton took the ax from the wall and inspected it. The end of the handle was ragged, as if someone had accidentally cut into it with a saw, but the shaft was smooth and balanced in his hand. He tested the blade with his thumb and index finger: blunt.

"What now?" Alexander said, his voice still shaky.

"Now we do everything just the way we planned it," said Anton as calmly as he could. He hauled the chopping block that was leaning against the wall into the middle of the woodshed. *My God, what are we doing? This is crazy!* he thought, and his feigned calm vanished. He lowered the ax to the ground.

"Are you really sure? Really, truly positive?" he asked, his eyes pinched nearly shut.

Alexander nodded almost imperceptibly. "Yes. I'd say I am."

Anton shook his head. "If we go through with this, there's no turning back. You realize that, don't you?"

He still did not know exactly what had led to Alexander's decision. When he'd probed Alexander about it, his friend had just waved it off.

Now Alexander was looking at him defiantly.

"Fine." Anton took a deep breath, then produced a hip flask of schnapps from his trouser pocket. "Here. Take a good mouthful. It might make it easier." He held out the flask to Alexander. "Remember what we said: hit the lower leg. Don't hit your knee! And not too hard—you want to keep your leg."

Alexander drank greedily from the flask.

"That's enough," said Anton, taking the schnapps away from him.

Was it his imagination, or did his friend stagger slightly? But no, not from just a couple of swigs of schnapps . . . He held out the ax.

"I'm here. As soon as the 'accident' happens, I'll get you to the doctor." He made a motion as if heaving a sack of flour onto his shoulder.

Alexander took the ax and swung it back and forth, getting used to its weight. There was despair in his eyes as he said, "What if I cut my leg off completely?"

"You're not that strong," said Anton. "Accidents happen all the time when people cut wood, and they're usually not so bad. Think about Schorsch last year. He sliced a tendon. And Karl Müller whacked himself in the knee, but after a few weeks he was getting around well enough. He just can't work on a loom anymore."

Alexander nodded, but he didn't look particularly convinced.

Anton leaned against the wall and wished he had a cigarette on him.

They'd worked through the idea so many times. An accident while cutting wood. Nothing deadly, and a wound that would heal passably well, in time. An injured leg, lameness, stiffness—that would be in the doctor's report. And that would put an end to ten hours a day at a loom. It all *sounded* simple.

He'll never be able to do it, Anton suddenly thought. After a long, silent moment, he said, "Should *I* do it?"

Alexander looked at him, his eyes lighting up with hopefulness. "You'd do that for me?"

Anton shrugged. "If I have to."

"What if I can never walk again?"

"I'll be careful," said Anton, and he felt like bawling his eyes out.

That certainly didn't get me far, Mimi thought as she stormed out of the town hall, angry and frustrated. She stopped when she reached the market square. She was on the verge of going to confront Gehringer with her suspicion that he was scheming against her when she saw Eveline sitting on the bench beneath the chestnut tree. Her two daughters were waiting patiently close by. Alexander was nowhere in sight. Beside Eveline stood a handcart piled high with buckets of water. *When was the last time I watered my vegetable patch?* Mimi wondered, but then she turned her attention to Eveline again. She was swaying a little from side to side where she sat, as if she might faint at any moment.

Concerned, Mimi went toward her. "Eveline, is everything all right?"

Eveline quickly wiped away a tear. "I was just feeling a little dizzy. It's the sudden change in the weather, that's all. This heat . . . I've been on my feet since four."

"Couldn't you sleep?" Mimi was shocked by how drained she looked.

"My working day always starts early in summer," said Eve, and with a groan she stood. "Just getting out to our field takes an hour."

"Are you hurt? Can I help?" Mimi asked. When she saw that the woman's arms were covered in blue blotches, a terrible thought came to her. "Has your husband hit you?" Mimi's hand flew to her mouth in shock. Blast it, hadn't her uncle just warned her not to get mixed up in other people's affairs? "Excuse me, I didn't mean to say that. It's none of my business." Had they fought over Alexander, and Mimi's action on his behalf? she wondered, feeling dazed.

"Everything is all right," Eveline said.

Mimi nodded, unconvinced. "If you ever need any help, or someone to talk to . . . I've got real coffee at home. Sometimes a good cup of coffee is the best medicine." She tried to offer a smile.

"I might take you up on that one day," said Eve softly. Spontaneously, she reached out and squeezed Mimi's arm. "Thank you for worrying about me. Life isn't always easy, but I'll manage."

The two women exchanged a brief smile, then Mimi saw Luise and Edelgard running across the square in their direction, skirts billowing.

"Eve, come quickly! There's been an accident!" Luise cried.

"Klaus?" Eveline asked, eyes wide with fear.

"No, it's your boy. It's Alexander."

CHAPTER 9

"Why didn't I send them away when they offered to help? I could have cut a few pieces of wood myself, but no! Instead I was asleep while Alexander was bleeding half to death out in the woodshed, and I didn't even know!" Josef Stöckle's shoulders slumped even more than usual. "What a useless old man I am."

"What are you talking about? It was a horrible accident, but that doesn't mean you're to blame. They wanted to help," said Mimi, as she had already assured him several times.

They'd been sitting at the dinner table for more than an hour. Josef ran his hands through his hair, coughed, and continued to berate himself. He didn't want any of the *Hefezopf* sweet bread and wouldn't drink any tea. She should have just kept her mouth shut when she returned a little earlier, Mimi thought, angry at herself. She could have waited until the following day to break the news to Josef about the accident. Then he would at least have had a quiet evening and maybe even eaten a little.

They had all run to the doctor's office together—Luise, Eveline and her children, Edelgard, and Mimi—only to have Sister Elke tell them that they couldn't go in to see Alexander yet, that the doctor was still attending to him. There was no danger to his life, but the wound he'd suffered was bad, and she said that without Anton's quick action, what might have happened didn't bear thinking about at all.

All the color instantly drained from Eveline's face, and Mimi was again afraid that Alexander's mother would pass out. Poor Eveline. As if the woman didn't have enough on her plate. Mimi grasped her hand and held on tightly, and together they sat down on the hard chairs in the waiting room. After a while, Luise offered to take Erika and Marianne, both of whom were distraught, home with her. Eveline, her eyes fixed on the door to the doctor's treatment room, nodded her head, but she said nothing when she kissed the girls goodbye. Mimi eventually had to leave, but she did so with a heavy heart. It had been hours since she had rushed off to the town hall, and Josef had no idea where she was. When she arrived at the house, she was so upset that she blurted out the bleak news.

"But Alexander has helped me so many times! Nothing's ever happened before!" Josef cried, utterly distraught.

"Uncle Josef, don't worry too much. Accidents happen sometimes," Mimi said. "Here. Drink. Your cough sounds worse today." She set a fresh cup of tea in front of him.

"Tea? I need schnapps for a shock like this, but there's none left. You treat me like a little child, or, worse, as if I were already dead." Without another word, he stood up and left the kitchen. Mimi heard his shuffling footsteps in the hallway, and a moment later, the front door closed.

Upset and hurt, Mimi stayed behind. She hadn't realized that the schnapps bottle was empty, and her uncle hadn't said anything about it until now. He wouldn't go off to The Oxen alone, would he? What if he suddenly felt weak crossing the square? She was relieved when she looked through the kitchen window and saw him heading for the studio. He probably just needed a little peace and quiet.

Mimi had just begun sweeping the path in front of the door when she heard a clatter from the garden. What in the world was Josef doing back there?

Filled with sudden foreboding, Mimi threw the broom aside and started to run.

It was six in the evening, and Anton was still feeling queasy. He would never forget the moment the ax blade had penetrated his friend's leg. It had made a strange dull sound, very much like a punch. Alexander had looked at him with huge eyes. Then his eyelids fluttered like a dragonfly's wings and he collapsed. He lay as if dead, while the floor turned red with his blood.

Oh God. Anton let out an agonized moan. The next moment, he felt a hand on his shoulder.

"Can you even work, my boy?" his mother asked, full of concern. "There's not much going on today. I can manage things by myself."

Anton thought for a moment. Alone in his room, the pictures in his mind would only torment him more. "Maybe I can just sit for a few minutes?" He nodded toward the tables and chairs, only a few of which were occupied.

"As long as you want," Karolina Schaufler said warmly. "I'll bring you a cider."

Anton, as dazed by his mother's kindness as by what he'd been through earlier, sat down at a table and stared into space. So this is what it felt like to be a "hero."

In the end, Alexander had swung the ax himself. "I'll be in Stuttgart, but you'll still be here in Laichingen. I don't want people blaming you for my accident," he'd said, and Anton could only marvel at Alexander's clearheadedness and courage. His words had struck Anton as a kind of ax blow of their own.

Like hell I'll stay in the village! Anton thought dully. He was ready to make his sacrifices, too—anything to get away from here. Away from the dishwater. Away from his tiny room, so cold in winter that the frost formed a layer half an inch thick on the inside of the window. Away from the never-changing faces. But should he simply pack his things and hit the road? It would be far better to have some sort of springboard, like Alexander had with his opportunity at the art school.

From the corner of his eye, Anton saw Johann Merkle come in and head straight for his table.

"So you're your own guest today?" Grinning, Johann sat down opposite him. "I heard what happened. A damn good thing you were there and could get your friend to the doctor fast. You did a fine job!"

Anton's brow creased. Just recently, Johann had hardly been willing to give him the time of day, and suddenly this praise . . . He'd have preferred to just ignore the man completely, but he decided to use the opportunity to try to find out where things stood between Johann and Mimi.

Anton went to the bar, where the pitcher of cider stood, and lifted it invitingly. "Thirsty?" he asked, trying to sound friendly.

Johann nodded. "God, yes! I'd forgotten how exhausting it is to stand at a loom all day. Plus the dust flying around dries my throat. It feels like my tongue is twice its usual size."

Anton poured a generous glass. "I don't know why you came back. If I'd left here, ten horses couldn't drag me back."

"That's what I thought, too," said Johann lightheartedly. "But sometimes a man has to do what he has to do."

Anton wondered if it would be more clever to sound out Mimi than Johann. Women were a bit more talkative about things, weren't they? He raised his glass to Johann. "So tell me, what's it like out there in the world?" Here he was, drinking cider with Johann while Alexander lay seriously injured at the doctor's office, he thought guiltily. He had to sweep the thought aside and focus on Johann now.

Johann thought it over for a moment. "If you've got money and power, it's a good life, but tough luck for you if you're poor."

Anton frowned. He'd been hoping for exciting stories about beautiful women, adventure, freedom.

"But America is the land of opportunity," Anton said. "I read about it recently."

"You have enough opportunities here. You don't have to leave Laichingen for that," Johann said. "What's needed now is men to make use of those opportunities, but men like that don't seem to exist. I still can't believe how bad things have gotten here in the years I've been away. The men work more hours than ever, the women sew until their fingers bleed, and on top of that comes the hard work on barren fields. No wonder life here robs people of their strength."

Anton nodded grimly. He hadn't seen Christel for days. Now that her mother's pregnancy was worrisome and she couldn't do any of the heavy work, Christel was being worked like a dog. If Johann wanted to change something, he could start with his own family and improve his niece's life, Anton thought bitterly.

"Conditions here are as hard as in the worst working-class districts anywhere. *Here* is where we have to tackle things, Anton, not America! I don't know for sure how things are in the other mills, but as far as Gehringer's is concerned, I know already that things can't go on the way they are. The way he treats his employees, it's utter exploitation."

"You sound like one of those unionists they write about in the papers," Anton said mockingly. Was he mistaken, or did Johann's face turn a shade paler?

After a moment of silence, Johann said, "Let's just imagine what it would be like if someone took things into his own hands. Don't you think it's about time things changed for the better?"

"Definitely," Anton said, feeling more and more uncomfortable under Johann's penetrating gaze. "But I don't think anything's going to change. The people here *like* to dance to Gehringer's tune." *Even Christel,* he added silently.

"Because they don't know any other tune. And because, so far, nobody has even tried. That's why someone who can lead the way and give them courage is so urgently needed. Think about it; without weavers, every mill owner here would be in dire straits. I'm certain a good negotiator could make a difference: better working conditions, longer breaks, and better pay. It works in other places, and times are changing!"

Despite himself, Anton was impressed by Johann's inflammatory words. Gehringer caught up in a labor dispute with his weavers? The idea had something going for it.

Johann leaned across the table and grabbed Anton by the wrist. "To know I had a smart fellow like you at my side would be a real advantage. I'm fairly sure we could get the photographer on our side, too. She's seen a lot of the world, and she's got guts. People trust her. Together, we could come up with a battle plan and figure out how we can get Gehringer and the other mill owners to do things differently. The time for change has never been riper." His gaze drifted off into the distance, as if he could already see swarms of weavers marching to battle for their rights.

"Better leave the photographer out of it. She's got enough to do looking after her uncle and running her business. And to be honest, I don't have the time, either," Anton said. He at Johann's side? Forget it! And he didn't like the thought of Johann harnessing Mimi Reventlow to his wagon at all. What was the man thinking? The photographer was Anton's springboard to the wide world! He was still betting that, when her uncle died, she would leave Laichingen, and he would go with her. If she got caught up in something here, that would put a serious kink in his plans.

But Johann ignored Anton's words and kept talking. "Your inn here would be a good place for us to meet, too."

That was going too far! Anton pulled free of Johann's grip. "You can forget The Oxen for your intrigues and uprisings. My mother would throw you out on your ear. She thinks the world of Gehringer and the other mill owners," he said sharply. "And forget about me. I'm not going to jump into the breach for anyone." He stood up angrily and took his empty glass to the sink behind the bar. Talking to Johann hadn't made him any the wiser at all!

CHAPTER 10

Eveline looked up at the paintings on the wall of the doctor's waiting room. The pictures were expressive and full of life, painted in heavy oils. A bullfighting scene, a sunset over the sea, men and women harvesting grapes—surely the doctor had brought them back from his long sojourn in Spain. The pictures were as out of place here as . . . Eve struggled to find a comparison, but her heart was so heavy and her head so full of worry that she couldn't think straight. She had no interest in bringing the pictures to Klaus's attention, either. Since his violent assault on her just a few days earlier, they had only spoken about what was absolutely necessary.

Alexander would certainly like the pictures, Eve thought sadly, then the door to the treatment room opened and Sister Elke appeared. "The doctor will see you now."

Eveline leaped from her chair. Finally! Dr. Ludwig had sent her home in the late afternoon. He needed more time to examine Alexander more closely and to treat the wound. There was no point in Eveline's sitting in the waiting room.

At Eveline's request, a boy from the neighborhood had gone to Gehringer's mill to tell Klaus about the accident. Instead of coming home early, as Eveline had expected, he'd worked his shift dutifully to the end. If Alexander's condition worsened, she should let him know, he told her through the boy who'd brought the message. In the meantime, she had relieved Luise of the girls and given them something to eat before taking them to Edelgard, who had offered to help. Deep inside, Eveline had hoped to meet Johann at his mother's house—in vain.

Only now, in the evening and on her second trip to the doctor's office, was Klaus finally at her side. His expression revealed nothing, as if Alexander's accident meant nothing. Eveline, in her anger and disappointment, felt like punching him. How could anyone be so unfeeling?

"How is my son?" Eve asked the moment they stepped into the doctor's office.

The doctor directed them to the two chairs on the other side of his desk.

"Alexander suffered a deep laceration with severe contusion where the ax went into his leg. Thank God the knee is not injured. The blade struck his lower leg about a hand's width below the knee."

Eveline gulped. That's where the skin was thinnest and the bone closest to the surface.

"What does that mean?" Klaus asked.

"Alexander has lost a great deal of blood, which is to say that, apart from the shinbone, some major blood vessels have been damaged. I've been able to stop the bleeding and have cleaned the wound. His leg is in a splint and elevated. No operation will be necessary." The doctor sighed. "For the moment, that's all I can do. Wounds like this take time to heal."

"How long will the boy be lying around?" Klaus said.

Eve shot him a hostile look.

"Eight to ten weeks before he can really walk. At least six weeks confined to bed."

"Oh God." Eveline inhaled sharply. Eight to ten weeks! There was the graduation ceremony at school. The hay harvest. The potato harvest. Alexander would miss all of it, and he'd also miss—

She swallowed back a sob. "But after that, he'll be well again?" she said, her voice sounding tinny in her own ears.

"The most important thing now is to keep the wound clean and prevent any infection from finding its way in. A bone infection could mean he'd lose—" The doctor paused. "I don't want to burden you with any horror scenarios. Let's hope for the best." He smiled encouragingly at them.

Eve stared at him aghast. "You mean you don't know if Alexander will ever be able to walk properly again?"

"We'll know more in a few weeks," said the doctor. "If it's all right with you, I'd like to keep Alexander here for a few days to keep an eye on him, mostly because of the danger of infection—" Before he could say any more, the door flew open. "Doctor, come quickly! Mr. Stöckle's fallen off a ladder!" Sister Elke cried.

Eveline blinked in confusion. The old photographer had also had an accident? She heard Mimi Reventlow's voice from the next room.

The doctor rose quickly. "Try not to be too worried," he said as he rushed out. "I've given your son a strong painkiller to get him through the night. He's sleeping now and I'm very happy about that. Sister Elke and I will take good care of him, I promise."

"What an idiot!" said Klaus when they were out on the street.

Eve sighed. "Dr. Ludwig will know what's best. I wanted to see—"

"I wasn't talking about the doctor. Alexander should have been helping at home instead of messing around for someone else."

Eve flinched as if she'd been pricked with a needle. "You act like it's the boy's own fault!"

"So? Isn't it?" Klaus spat back. "That's that for an apprenticeship at the mill. Gehringer will never take the boy if he's a cripple."

"How dare you speak like that about our son? He had an accident, but that doesn't make him a cripple!" Eveline snapped.

"Didn't you see how the doctor wouldn't say it straight? A wound like that always leaves something behind. Karl hardly gets around since he whacked his leg with an ax, and that was last year. Who knows? Alexander might end up losing the damned leg completely."

Eveline suddenly felt so ill she thought she might throw up. Her son, an invalid?

"Alexander will be healthy again," she said vehemently. "And besides, Gehringer is always bragging about how well he looks after everyone. Alexander can work in an office."

"Our son in an office, in a fine suit? And I guess Paul Merkle takes over at the loom? Eveline, you're a dreamer, and you'll always be a dreamer." Klaus looked at her with contempt. "You ask me, we'll be feeding Alexander for the rest of our lives. All he deserves is a good beating, and that good-for-nothing Anton, too."

"How can you say that? Alexander is our son. And I'll look after him as long as I have to, even if it means a lifetime!" As she spoke, another thought came to her: If Alexander was really no use to Gehringer, what was there to stop Klaus from giving him permission to go to Stuttgart? But then her fleeting hope disappeared. The admissions exam at the art school was at the end of the month, and there was no way in the world Alexander would be on his feet again by then.

"How are you feeling?" Anton asked when he arrived at the infirmary the next morning. He clumsily handed his friend a ham sandwich and hoped Alexander would eat it before the old photographer in the next bed woke up, or he'd probably feel obliged to share it.

Anton still couldn't get used to the idea that Josef Stöckle had had an accident of his own just hours after Alexander's. Sometimes life was crazier than you could imagine.

"My leg's throbbing like mad. And it's hot," Alexander said.

"So . . . what's the doctor say?" Anton whispered, although there was no one except for himself and the sleeping Josef in the small infirmary beside the doctor's practice. Dr. Ludwig was seeing patients at his office, and Sister Elke was nowhere in sight.

Alexander stared at the ceiling. "The ax went almost half an inch into the shinbone, and I damaged some big blood vessels, too. The doctor says it'll be eight to ten weeks before it heals. And that I might never be able to walk right again."

"But you didn't hit yourself so hard! We were careful about that," Anton blurted.

"Could you say that any louder?" Alexander hissed. For a long moment, silence fell between them. Neither dared say what was in his head.

When Anton had his idea for the "accident," he'd felt like Michelangelo, who had the bright idea of painting ceilings instead of plain old walls. Now, however, it looked as if his flash of inspiration had turned into a disaster. He was ashamed of himself. Admittedly, Alexander probably wouldn't have to go to work on a loom. But that his friend might not be in any condition to make it to the admissions test in Stuttgart? Neither of them had thought about that.

Sleep the night before had been impossible for Mimi. Her worry about her uncle, her concern for Alexander, and the question of whether she somehow could have prevented their accidents—the thoughts had swirled in Mimi's head, with no sign of coming to a stop. *Johann, where are you?* she had wondered through the night, while loneliness wrapped around her like a too-heavy coat. He must have heard what had happened, so why hadn't he come to visit her, at least for a little while? A little consolation, a strong shoulder to lean on—she could have used both.

Dr. Ludwig had asked Mimi to come in after his morning appointments to discuss Josef. She found herself sitting in front of his desk shortly before noon. After her sleepless night, she felt like an old woman. The doctor, by contrast, looked the picture of vitality, even though he had handled two emergencies the day before.

"All things considered, your uncle is doing reasonably well. He suffered a clean fracture to his femur when he fell. By some miracle, no bones were actually pushed out of place, so an operation isn't necessary," the doctor said. "I've put his right leg in a splint, and with the painkiller, he had a quiet night. He even ate a little this morning. He's not alone since Alexander is in the bed next to his. He's also holding up well, by the way."

Mimi pressed both hands to her eyes as if to staunch her tears of relief. "Thank God," she said. What if he'd broken a hip or shoulder, too? She didn't like to think about it.

"My uncle was inconsolable after Alexander's accident. He blames himself, which is nonsense, of course. I tried to make that clear, but he just got up and left. When I saw him heading toward the studio, I thought he just wanted to have some time to himself. I never thought he'd suddenly get it in his head to touch up one of the backdrops, and certainly not up on the high ladder." Mimi shook her head.

"Old men can be unpredictable. You should keep a better eye on him in the future."

"What's going to happen now?" Mimi asked meekly. "Can I see him?"

"Best if you come back this evening. I'll keep him here for a week, at least. If he has injured any blood vessels or if there's new bleeding beneath his bruises in the next day or two, I'll be able to get it under control. I can also see how he responds to the opiates. As soon as he doesn't need any more painkillers, we'll put him on a stretcher and carry him home. But it will be a long time before he's climbing any stairs, so you'd better start thinking now about where he'll sleep."

Mimi's relief at the news of Josef's clean fracture faded with every word the doctor spoke. "Does that mean he won't be able to use the toilet by himself?"

The doctor nodded. "Sister Elke can tell you the things you'll need to look after Josef, besides a bedpan. Sooner or later, given his illness, you'd need to get them anyway."

When she left the doctor's office, Mimi knew that she had to write to her mother urgently. Mimi didn't expect any help from her—Amelie Reventlow was no doubt called to higher things than standing by her brother. But her mother needed to know what had happened.

Now things get serious, she thought as she crossed the square. From the corner of her eye, she saw Anton, cleaning the window of The Oxen. They waved to each other, but a moment later Mimi was lost in her thoughts again.

Although she had known that she would need to take care of Josef as he approached the end of his life, she had never thought that the time would come so soon. She would have to assist him with every facet of his life. A glass of water? The newspaper? The window open or closed? Even tearing the next page of his page-a-day calendar on the wall. In his helpless state, he'd depend on her day and night, and he wouldn't even be able to make it up the stairs to his bedroom. She would have to set up a bed for him in the parlor. Would she be able to do it all?

Back at the house, she had just taken out paper and pen when there was a knock at the door. Something about Uncle Josef? Her heart instantly beat faster. She jerked the door open and was overcome with relief to see Johann.

"You're here. Thank God!" Mimi pulled him into the house and threw herself into his arms. The tears she'd so far managed to keep in check now poured from her eyes.

"I heard about your uncle's accident. What is it they say? Misfortune seldom comes alone," Johann murmured while she pressed against him.

"First Alexander, then Josef . . . It's terrible," she sobbed.

"Alexander is young. He'll be fine, I'm sure. And your uncle broke his leg, not his neck. Our doctor will get him sorted out, too."

"I know, of course. But an accident like that, at his age," she said. Would being even less mobile make his tuberculosis worse? She would have to ask the doctor about that.

With a sigh, she stepped back from Johann and said, "I've just brewed a pot of tea."

He followed her into the kitchen, and they sat at the table.

"I don't have much time. It's the lunch break, and I just ran off to see you. I wanted to console you a little."

Mimi smiled gratefully. "Honestly, I'm worried about how I'll stay on top of everything," she said as they sat holding hands. "Josef's care and the studio, and I still have to earn money, even if certain people are tripping me up wherever they can." She was about to tell him about the ban that had been imposed on her Sunday work, but Johann spoke first.

"Here in the village, when it really matters, we're here for each other. I'm sure you'll find someone to help you. But I have to tell you what happened in the weaving shed this morning: on his morning rounds, Gehringer ranted at Klaus Schubert so hard about his pick count I thought the man would burst into tears! Gehringer gave him a dressing down yesterday morning, too, for a trivial loom breakdown that could have happened to any of us. I don't know what he's got against the man."

"Herrmann Gehringer ought to hang his head in shame," Mimi said. Given everything that had happened since the day before, she decided not to mention the Sunday ban. It would have sounded petty and trivial.

Johann nodded, his expression stony. "It's high time someone taught him a lesson," he said. "When the men go on strike, Gehringer will find out where his slave-driving has gotten him." Johann's eyes blazed.

Mimi's brow furrowed. "Strike? Have things gone that far?"

"I wish! I'll need at least another six months before I get the men to that stage. They have to trust me first," Johann said with a snort. "I have to go for now. I don't want Gehringer to have any reason to fire me. Being a dutiful weaver at his mill is my best shot at gaining the men's confidence." With a promise to return as soon as he could, he gave her a hurried kiss and said goodbye.

Pensive, she watched him go. *"I'm sure you'll find someone to help you."* Couldn't he have offered that himself?

Mimi was thinking about how to best word the news of Josef's accident in the letter to her mother when there was another knock at the door. Mimi's face lit up. Had Johann perhaps changed his mind? Had he realized after all how much she needed him?

It was Anton, his face as grim as a grave. "I was at the infirmary this morning, to visit Alexander. The doctor said . . ." Anton's voice failed him.

Mimi's hand rose instinctively to her heart. "Yes?"

"The doctor said he might never walk right again."

"Oh, how terrible!" Mimi swallowed. How pale Anton looked, altogether wrung out. No wonder, considering he'd been there when the accident happened.

"The most terrible thing would be for Alexander to miss the admissions test because of how long it'll take him to heal," Anton said. "It's at the end of the month." He grasped Mimi's hands and squeezed them tightly. "I'm begging you, could you do something so that Alexander can take the test later?"

"I thought his father wasn't going to allow him to go," said Mimi, frowning.

Anton sniffed. "Now that Alexander's chances of being a weaver are fading, Mr. Schubert will have to let his son go, won't he?"

Mimi flinched. "To put it rather bluntly."

"Sorry if that's how it sounded," Anton replied coolly. "But you agree, don't you? That it's more important than ever that Alexander gets accepted at the art school?"

Mimi thought it over for a long moment. As brutal as he'd sounded, Anton was right. If need be, one could still study art from a chair.

"I'm writing a letter to my mother right now. If she talks to her contact at the school, maybe he'll be able to take the test later."

Anton looked relieved. "Then I say let's get started," he said, rolling up his sleeves.

Mimi frowned. "I can write the letter by myself, don't worry."

"And what about your uncle? When the doctor sends him home, Mr. Stöckle won't be in any shape to climb the steps to his bedroom. If you like, I'll take his bed apart upstairs and rebuild it down in the parlor. And if there's anything else you need, just let me know."

For a moment, Mimi was silent. "Thank you," she finally said, her voice hoarse. "My knight in shining armor once again."

"One hand washes the other, right? Don't mention it."

Anton's grin was infectious, and Mimi smiled, too. It was curious, somehow, how often she found herself relying on him.

CHAPTER 11

A few days later, Josef was still in Dr. Ludwig's infirmary, and Mimi didn't have any work at the studio. Boredom threatened to drive her crazy, and she wanted to visit Eve and offer her some help. With Alexander out of action, perhaps Mimi could do something around the house or even out in the field.

She had visited her uncle earlier and brought him a hard-boiled egg, which he ate with gusto—a good sign, she felt. She'd also talked with Alexander. It seemed to pep him up to know that she was trying to get the admissions test in Stuttgart delayed. Mimi hoped daily for a positive reply from her mother or, better still, from the school itself.

Eveline was just closing the front door when Mimi arrived. Her daughters were nowhere in sight. When she saw Mimi, Eve immediately began to cry.

Mimi took her awkwardly in her arms and rocked her back and forth. "I'm so sorry," she murmured.

Eveline freed herself from the embrace. "Forgive me. I don't know what came over me."

Mimi waved it off. "It's only natural for you to worry about Alexander."

"It's not just Alexander," Eve said despairingly. "It's my husband, too. Since Alexander's accident, he's been unbearable. Deep inside, I'd hoped that Alexander's accident might bring us together again, but we're further apart than ever. He doesn't say a word to me, and when he thinks no one's looking, he stares at me and the girls strangely, as if we're all just a burden to him. If I ask him what the matter is, he just mumbles to himself about the devil dancing in our house—what a load of rot!"

Mimi raised her eyebrows. That really did sound terrible.

"Sometimes I don't know what's worse: when he talks or when he doesn't. The girls are scared to death of their father. Thank goodness Edelgard is looking after them for now. They feel more at home with her than in their actual home." She sighed deeply. "I'm sorry to bother you with my troubles. But sometimes . . ." She shrugged helplessly.

Mimi nodded. "Sometimes it's just good to talk. I know how that is, really."

"Maybe I should just stop thinking about things so much," said Eveline with admirable resolve as she dried her weepy eyes. "I have to go to the mill to take Klaus his lunch." She held up bread wrapped in paper. "He forgot it again this morning. Sometimes it's like his mind is somewhere else completely."

"May I walk with you? A little stroll would do me good," Mimi said spontaneously. It was just before twelve, and with a little luck, the lunch break would have begun when they arrived. Maybe she and Johann would catch a glimpse of each other. Wouldn't he be surprised she'd shown up like that!

Eveline shrugged. "Why not? I could use the company."

To Mimi's disappointment, however, there was no way to see inside Gehringer's mill from the street. A large wrought-iron gate blocked the entrance. She wouldn't see Johann after all, Mimi thought glumly while Eveline told the gatekeeper the reason for her visit. The man, who seemed to know Eveline, let her enter.

Eveline turned to Mimi to say goodbye. On an impulse, Mimi said, “I’ve never been to a weaving factory like this, let alone seen one of the famous looms inside. Do you think I’d be allowed to come in with you?” At the same time, she hoped she wouldn’t bump into Gehringer—that would be awkward.

Eveline looked inquiringly at the gatekeeper.

“You don’t look like you’ll do anything,” he grumbled, waving them through.

“It looks more like a park around a villa than a factory!” Mimi was impressed despite herself. In front of them was a straight path lined with large, carefully manicured bushes. Beyond the bushes stretched broad expanses of lawn dotted with huge old trees. Small tables and chairs stood on the well-tended grass. A sign with an arrow read “Library.”

“A library? For the workers?” Mimi asked with a frown.

“A relic of the old days. Back then, Klaus actually used to bring home books all the time—edifying biblical texts, mostly. As if anyone has time to read these days,” said Eveline harshly. “There’s a canteen, too, and now, in the warm months, the men bring lunch with them and eat at the tables there,” she continued. “In winter, most just eat a snack at the loom. That building there is the weaving shed.” She pointed to an elongated building beyond the lawn on the right. “And the big building on the left is where the seamstresses work. Gehringer’s office is there, too.”

Mimi frowned. She’d pictured a weaving mill a little differently, less stylish, less manicured, and more stuffy, terribly loud, and dusty.

“Strange that everything is so quiet. The looms don’t seem to be running at all,” Eveline said just then, pushing open the large wooden door of the weaving shed.

Mimi’s heart began to pound, and she didn’t know whether it was from the fear of crossing paths with Gehringer or the anticipation of catching sight of Johann any minute. *No kiss, no effusive greeting!* she warned herself. More than a glance would be impossible.

The looms were, in fact, at a standstill. The smell of machine oil filled the air along with a strange tension. Some kind of assembly was taking place. Up ahead, at a lectern, stood Herrmann Gehringer, delivering an address to the men. Johann's brother, Paul, was beside his boss.

Eve and Mimi exchanged a look. What now?

Gehringer! Just the man she'd most wanted to avoid. Gone was any thought of Johann. She quickly turned toward the door, ready to leave, but Eveline whispered, "Could you stay with me?"

Mimi nodded uncertainly.

The men stood close together, all in faded trousers and aprons. With their narrow shoulders and stooped posture, they all looked very similar, Mimi thought, looking as unobtrusively as she could for the one who was most important. There he was, on the left, close to the front. Johann.

"As you know, we've come through some difficult times together, and we'll get through this one, too," Gehringer said from his lectern. "Gehringer Weaving is a company with traditions and a good name to uphold, and that will continue. But times are changing! Costs are going up, and pressure from the competition is increasing like never before. For me, simply surviving as a businessman is getting harder and harder. If I'm to ensure that your sons don't have to worry about finding a good job, a job like their father's, then I have to make changes here and now."

Mimi felt Eveline stiffen beside her.

"What I ask of you now does not come easily. And you can believe me when I say that I would not do it if it were not absolutely necessary."

Mimi's expression darkened. Something bad was coming, and the workers were on the receiving end. She stole a glance at Johann and saw how grim he looked.

"Men, we have no choice. From today onward, the looms have to run an extra two hours a day. We have major orders that need to be filled, come what may! I cannot say yet when we'll return to the old hours, but I hope by the end of September, at the latest. I know you won't let me down now, as I have never let you down. Next year, the Gehringer mill will be celebrating a major milestone, our thirtieth anniversary, and that's something we want to see together, am I right?"

Mimi raised her eyebrows. Gehringer's threat couldn't be more clear.

A murmur of unrest and indignation rippled through the crowd of men. Gehringer nodded as if he could fully understand their anger. "I like this no more than you! But it is necessary if we are to remain competitive. And don't think that things will be any better elsewhere. Just a few days ago, I spoke to Egon Morlock and Gottfried Hirrler, and they are in the same situation."

The men fell silent. Mimi wondered what Johann was thinking.

"I know I can rely on you!" Gehringer said, winding up his speech with satisfaction. "No point in fooling ourselves. This summer will be no picnic for any of us. But remember what they say: what doesn't kill us makes us stronger." With a final wave, he and Paul Merkle made their exit. An uproar broke out the moment they were gone.

"It's the last straw," Eveline whispered. As if in a trance, she dropped Klaus's lunch and, without a word, turned and ran out of the building.

Mimi picked up Klaus's lunch. Should she go after Eve? Or try to find Klaus in the crowd? She looked around helplessly, then saw Johann coming toward her, his face dour.

"What are you doing here?" he snapped, as if she'd been whispering Gehringer's speech straight into his ear. "Didn't I tell you no one was supposed to find out about us?"

"I came with Eveline. She brought Klaus's lunch," Mimi said quietly. She handed him the bread Eve had wrapped for her husband. "Would you give it to him?"

He took the package from Mimi, and his expression softened. "Sorry. But what Gehringer just announced is too much! Twelve hours a day at the loom—over time, that's going to knock down the strongest of us." His eyes glinted, and his body trembled with anger. "It's time someone put a stop to his games."

Mimi nodded grimly. "Not a single man dared to speak back to him. How is that possible? Have you been able to win a few of them to your cause?"

Johann shook his head. "Many of them still hold a grudge because of the way I left years ago. But who knows? Maybe Gehringer is playing into my hands with his outrageous demands. I need to talk to one or two of the men at The Oxen over a glass of cider, and tonight's the night for it."

"I thought we could finally spend some time together today," Mimi said. "As long as my uncle is at the infirmary, I have time. Could we go for a walk together?"

"That sounds very tempting." Johann grinned charmingly. "But you've seen for yourself how urgent it is to push things ahead." He nodded toward the group of weavers.

"Yes, of course. But we haven't had an hour to ourselves since you got here." Mimi could do nothing to keep the yearning out of her voice.

"We'll take that evening stroll together as soon as we can. And I'll show you all my favorite places around the village—promise!"

CHAPTER 12

Eveline had to read the letter from Stuttgart three times before she could believe it. Given Alexander's serious accident, the art school was willing to delay his test. If his health allowed, he could attend an admissions test at the end of July. The school year started in September, so if he were to be accepted, there would still be enough time to make the necessary arrangements.

What a whirlwind of emotion, Eveline thought. After Alexander's accident, everything had looked blacker than black. Now she saw a shimmer of hope on the horizon. Once again, it was Mimi Reventlow who had spoken up for Alexander—she had truly brought something positive to the family.

Eveline ran as quickly as she could to Dr. Ludwig's infirmary to tell Alexander the good news. His disbelief turned into a wide grin as he listened.

"I know I won't be as healed as I'll ever be by then, but I won't be laid up in this bed anymore. I'm sure Father will let me go now," he said.

She nodded. "Oh, he must. Everything will work out."

The work in the house, in the field . . . everything Eveline did that day was easier than usual. She'd even managed to pass on her happy mood to Erika and Marianne. When Eve went to Edelgard's house to tell them that they would be allowed to stay overnight, they bubbled over with excitement. They loved the seamstress, who always had candy or cookies for them. Thank God Johann's mother was there whenever she needed help, Eveline thought gratefully as she waved a cheerful goodbye to the girls.

Back home again, her energy and high spirits continued. She peeled and cut potatoes for a soup, added a little ham she'd reluctantly accepted from Edelgard, and spiced it all with fresh herbs she'd gathered herself. *How delicious it smells,* Eveline thought as she stirred the soup. Maybe she could rouse Klaus's appetite with it? It seemed that since Gehringer's announcement that the men had to work even more, he ate even less.

Around eight, just before the end of Klaus's shift, Eveline had finished preparing the soup and had a little time to devote to herself. She pulled all her hairpins out, then combed her hair in front of the shard of mirror beside the sink. She looked at her reflection, satisfied.

Since the night more than a week ago that he had taken her so brutally, she had rejected any attempt by him to touch her. But things could not go on like that—they were still husband and wife. This evening should be just for the two of them, she'd decided, and with Edelgard watching the girls, they would have that chance. He'd been in better spirits that morning than she'd seen him in for . . . well, for about as long as she could remember. He'd stroked the girls' hair and called them lovely. Then he'd placed his hand on her arm and told her she was a good wife. Eveline thought she'd misheard him. Hardly a word out of him for weeks, and suddenly saying nice things like that?

She turned and looked at the wall, where a pale square showed the place that, for years, a picture had hung: *The Broad and Narrow Way*. "I know you hate this picture," Klaus had said to her, and he had taken it off the wall and added that, from now on, the picture would no longer be needed. Alexander ought to paint something beautiful for the wall instead. Eveline had been struck almost dumb, managing no more than "thank you."

She'd spent the day thinking about what his gesture might have meant. And his remark about Alexander painting a new picture—was he somehow miraculously agreeing to the admissions test? She didn't dare to believe it, but perhaps the signs of a new beginning were real. The good news from Stuttgart couldn't have come at a better time. And if Klaus was ready for a new beginning, then she had to be ready for it, too.

The clock caught Eveline's eye. A quarter past eight already. If only he'd come home.

At a quarter to nine, when he still hadn't arrived, Eveline's stomach began to protest uncomfortably. Klaus hadn't said a word about going out to the field after work. Was he perhaps visiting Alexander? He'd never gone on his own, and besides, Dr. Ludwig was strict: at seven o'clock, visiting hours were over for the night. *Where* is *he?* Eveline wondered, a little irritated, while she stared at the pot of soup, untouched. At The Oxen? Was he getting drunk again? She'd probably misinterpreted his cheerfulness that morning. She set off to find her husband.

He wasn't at The Oxen. Nor had anyone seen him. Eveline stood helplessly in the market square. What now? Where to? Was there an explanation for his disappearance that she was simply overlooking?

She turned her eyes to the sky, where a raven turned in a slow arc. It almost seemed to her as if the bird were escorting her, or wanted to show her the way. She shuddered and hoped it wasn't a sign of misfortune. Then, she saw Johann Merkle walking in her direction.

The sight of him thrilled and panicked her. She tried to banish the distress from her face.

"Eveline! Our paths finally cross . . ."

The intensity in his eyes when he looked at her! As if they were the only two people in the world. Eveline felt the old yearning well up inside. She bit down on her bottom lip so hard it hurt.

His smile was as warm as the evening sun. "You would not believe how often I've thought of you over the years." *And a lot of good that did me,* she thought, startled at herself. "How have you been?" he asked. He reached out to stroke her cheek, but she shrank back. How was she supposed to sum up seven years in one or two sentences? And as much as she longed for Johann, she needed to find her husband.

"I'm looking for Klaus. He . . . he's disappeared," she said. The raven high overhead caught her eye again, and her sense of foreboding increased. It took all her strength not to throw herself into Johann's arms and weep. "I feel as if our lives are breaking apart, and I can't do anything to stop it. All I can do is watch as we more and more become shadows of ourselves."

Johann's expression darkened as she spoke. "It's the same tragedy everywhere. The burden each one of us has to bear is simply too much. If I could only ease some of yours . . ." The way he looked at her, scrutinizing her, as if he wanted to find out for himself where things stood between them.

Eveline shifted her weight uneasily and suddenly felt the same uncertainty he seemed to. Could she forgive him for simply taking off all those years ago? Did she want to rekindle their little dalliance from those days? A bit of flattery, a stolen kiss—would that be enough for her today? She was no longer the woman she was seven years ago, full of naïve illusions. Hard times had robbed her of some of her hope.

"Why do you look at me like that?" she asked, unsettled, as his eyes rested on hers with both tenderness and admiration.

He hesitated for a moment, then said, "Perhaps because I can't believe you're still here. I was certain that, like me, you would have left Laichingen long ago. I couldn't have blamed you if you'd gone back to your parents in Chemnitz."

"Not everyone is able to turn their back on the village as easily as you did," she said archly. "As for my parents, I was dead to them the day I eloped with Klaus." She let out a short, bitter laugh, but caught herself and, more mildly, said, "And how have you been?"

He laughed. "Can you ask me something easier? Since my return, I've been seesawing from joy to misery and back again. There have been moments I've regretted coming home. And then there have been moments, like now, when I ask myself how I could ever have left . . ." He stroked her cheek tenderly, then looked around. When he saw that no one was close by, he took her in his arms, embracing her for just a moment. "In all these years, I've never been able to forget you, Eve. You're the reason I left. Did you know that? You were another man's wife . . . I saw no chance for us."

"So you decided to pack your things and go?" A suppressed sob rose from deep inside her. "Why didn't you ask me to go with you? I would have, in a second." She could not help the tone of complaint in her voice.

He shrugged, and she read the hurt in his eyes. "Maybe I was scared. To destroy a marriage—who wants that on their conscience?"

"You can't destroy something that is already beyond repair," she said, feeling empty. "I have to go. Klaus . . ."

Johann nodded hesitantly. "I'd like to help you look, but I have to meet someone. The future of Laichingen is at stake, and maybe our future, too. One thing is certain: this time I won't stand by and do nothing as everything here goes to the dogs. Everything will work out, I promise." And then, suddenly, he was in a hurry, striding away.

She watched him leave, her mind turning over. *"Everything will work out"*—she wished she could believe him. But she had long ago given up relying on other people. If life had taught her one thing, it was that she had to take matters into her own hands. And that meant talking to Klaus about Alexander, urgently, whether she wanted to or not. And if he'd holed up somewhere with a bottle of schnapps, then she'd have to teach him a thing or two!

The note that Johann had slipped into her mailbox said they could meet at the train station at nine in the evening for a walk. Mimi had been standing in front of the station for almost half an hour, and now she was starting to feel like forgotten luggage.

Had she perhaps gotten the day wrong? she wondered as the clock in the church bell tower rang for half past the hour.

Finally, Johann came running. "Sorry I'm late. I got held up. You know what it's like," he said, then took her by the hand.

Instead of being angry at him, Mimi smiled.

The path that Johann suggested led them up and out of the village and away from the fields, where, taking advantage of the long summer days, people worked late into the evening. After a few minutes, they were the only people far and wide.

It was a wonderful, warm evening. The sun settled toward the horizon in a blaze of orange, and the hills and forests of the Swabian Jura seemed soaked in honey.

Several times, Johann stopped and looked around as if he were seeing everything for the first time. "My hometown," he said, his voice heavy with emotion. "It's crazy, but since I've been home, I've felt my roots more strongly than ever before. The people, the unspoiled countryside . . ."

Mimi smiled. "That must be a wonderful feeling. But here's me on the other side, with no roots at all. I'm free as a bird, and that's just as wonderful." She spun around, her skirts flying up, and she enjoyed the kiss of the breeze that touched her legs. Secretly, she waited for Johann to say something like *Just wait—with me at your side, you'll start to put down roots of your own here in Laichingen.* But instead, he crouched and plucked an inconspicuous green herb. "Smell that? So sweet. That's woodruff. Here at the edge of the forest, it's still growing in June. After a long, hot day, you can smell it everywhere. I've missed this smell so much." He crushed the fine leaves between his fingers and breathed in the aromas released.

The sultry air was making Mimi quite dizzy.

Walking closely at each other's side, Mimi felt the warmth Johann's body radiated. *Like another sun beside me,* she thought happily.

"Beautiful handiwork," he suddenly said, gently stroking her right arm. "Finest linen."

Mimi smiled. She'd spent more than an hour thinking about what to wear to this rendezvous, but nothing she had was good enough. In the end, with her uncle's permission, she borrowed a blouse decorated with embroidered eyelets from Traudel's collection.

"What would you have said if I'd chosen a cotton blouse?" she teased.

"You would never have done that. You might not know it yet, but you're as much a captive of linen as the rest of us." He sounded almost solemn.

I'm afraid I doubt that, Mimi thought, while his fingers moved over the linen appreciatively.

"Linen is a fabric like no other! It's part of the people here, from christening sheet to shroud. It's soft and supple, but also strong and durable, smooth but tough. It's as special as the people of these parts."

Mimi struggled to hold a nervous giggle in check. They had finally managed to get away by themselves, and Johann found nothing better to do than declare his love for linen. Not her! Something like that could only happen in Laichingen, she was certain. Despite herself, she had to laugh.

"I'm so glad we met again," she said, her voice betraying her emotion. "The first time, in Ulm . . . there was something fateful about it."

"That may be," he replied vaguely, but he seemed far away in his thoughts.

Mimi frowned. Didn't he want to admit his feelings for her? Johann was a free spirit, after all, just as she was. Finding the love of his life had had no part in his plans.

An almost imperceptible shudder seemed to go through him. He took her hand and they walked on, while the sun transformed into a fiery red ball. Mimi felt she ought to pinch herself: she and Johann, hand in hand. This could only be a dream.

At the top of a hill, he pointed to a large flat stone. "One of my favorite places. Shall we sit?"

Mimi smiled and nodded. What a beautiful view they had up here, back over the village and, in the distance, the neighboring villages. In the rapidly approaching dusk, houses, trees, and bushes took on strange forms. What a pity it wasn't possible to take photographs in that light, she thought.

"It's incredible," she said. "In the weeks I've been here, I've seen practically nothing of the surrounding countryside. And I've seen practically nothing of you since you've returned." She gave Johann a playful push. "Luise told me there's a big festival in Laichingen every July. Might we go together? We could even dance—or would that also damage my reputation?"

"*Everyone* goes to the *Heumondfest*, so certainly we can go together, and my family will welcome you at our campfire," he said with a grin. "As far as dancing goes, I'll spin you on the dance floor till you're dizzy." Then he grew serious again. He pointed down toward the village. "When you look down on Laichingen from here, it's difficult to imagine how hard the people have it, isn't it?"

Mimi, her mind elsewhere, just nodded. Did they have to talk about Laichingen now? She edged closer to him.

"If and when I lead the workers against the mill owners, any semblance of an idyllic life will be over, at least for a while. Different factions will form, and everyone will have to decide for themselves where they stand. Even you, Mimi. Will you be on my side?"

"Of course I'll be on your side. But I'm a photographer. I have nothing to do with unions," she said. "Apart from that, I'm honestly a little skeptical about how far your ambitions will get you. I have the feeling that most people here are proud to be weavers. They don't want to change anything about their lives."

"I have nothing against the old weaving traditions. They've been weaving here in the Jura for five hundred years. The skill is in our blood. But that doesn't give the mill owners any right to take the workers' last drops!" He took her hands in his. "You're one of the few who doesn't grovel to Gehringer. I could picture you, for example, speaking a little with the people who come to you to have their picture taken. You could tell them that labor disputes and strikes are normal in other parts of the country, and that they don't mean the end of the world. Laichingen is desperately in need of encouraging words—I'm sure you'll think of more."

"I don't know . . . ," Mimi said, and laughed. "First, when I take pictures, I have to concentrate. And second, I think you're miscalculating the influence I have on people. I've had one or two run-ins with Gehringer, it's true, but the people hold that against me. My uncle is always telling me to keep my nose out of other people's business, too."

"And what about Alexander Schubert?" Johann said. "And Fritz Braun? I've heard a thing or two in The Oxen. The people have a lot of good things to say about you. Believe me, you're far more important to the inhabitants of Laichingen than you think."

Whether she wanted to be or not, Mimi was flattered.

Johann looked deep into her eyes. "You're right: you and me, here in Laichingen—fate had that in store for us. We can do a lot here, you and I." He laughed and ran his hands through his hair, as if his words were embarrassing to him. "It's rare for me to wear my heart on my sleeve like this. I hope I haven't put you off with my aspirations."

"Maybe it really is God's will," said Mimi, her voice low, her heart beating feverishly.

They sat in silence for a moment. It was an agreeable, intimate silence, while high overhead three ravens turned in broad circles against the darkening sky.

"Those birds are so lovely," said Mimi, and felt a lump forming in her throat. It was clear to her in that moment what she'd been missing more and more in the last few months: being able to share a special moment with someone else. *No good thing is pleasant to possess, without friends to share it,* Mimi thought, recalling a quotation from Seneca. She remembered reading the line somewhere, and at the time had thought, *Nonsense! A self-sufficient person is never lonely.* But she could not say with certainty exactly when, despite her self-sufficiency, she had begun to feel very lonely indeed.

When she had left Esslingen after Heinrich's proposal six years earlier, there had been several men on her travels she could have had. A couple of years earlier, a man in the Palatinate region had spoken to her of marriage. Mimi had found him nice enough, and they had laughed a lot together. And in the Palatinate, where grapes grew and wine was made and people were happy, she had felt very at ease. But she had not felt love, not even a passing infatuation. She didn't want just any man. If she ever married, it would be to the "right one."

She looked at Johann. Could it be that she had found him?

The encounter with Johann had upset Eveline more than she had already been. *Calm down,* she told herself. What mattered now was finding Klaus. Later, in bed, she would be able to think in peace about the things she and Johann had said.

A step at a time. That was the only way to get through life. And nature showed the way. Eveline's eye was drawn to a knotty apple tree on which the first signs of fruit were showing. A few weeks earlier, walking along this path, she had still been enjoying the apple blossoms. Now the apples would grow until harvest in late summer. The leaves were still a juicy green, but of course, in autumn they would wither and fall.

Arrival, departure. Living and dying. Love blossomed. Love withered away. A new love stirred. It was the same everywhere.

Now you're getting sentimental. Stop it! Eveline thought. She shaded her eyes with her right hand to be able to see better against the setting sun. Klaus wasn't at the meadow, either—Eveline reminded herself that they would have to cut the second crop of hay there in the next few days. The people in the Jura called second-cut hay *Öhmd*, Klaus had explained many years earlier. Since then, the word had become part of her, along with so much else from here.

Then he must be at the potato field after all. She groaned with annoyance. Couldn't he have let her know? She wouldn't have worried and could have saved herself the long walk. What was he trying to do? Give her a bad conscience because she'd spent more time at Alexander's sickbed than pulling weeds out here? She warned herself not to fight with him when she found him. He still hadn't given his permission for Alexander's trip to Stuttgart, though she was sure he soon would. Now, when nobody really knew what would happen with Alexander's leg, the second chance from Stuttgart seemed like a gift from God.

After walking five minutes longer, the potato field came into view. Eveline narrowed her eyes to see better. Nobody in sight, and not a hoe or any other tool lying around. But there, farther left. Eveline blinked. Beneath the old pear tree that hadn't borne fruit in years . . . was that a shadow?

"Klaus?" she called.

And then she ran.

Klaus's body hung lifeless from one of the old, strong branches. His head was snapped to one side, like a puppet's neck broken in the too-rough hands of a child.

In silence, smothering the scream in her throat, Eveline stepped up to the tree.

He had slung a rope around his neck. Eveline knew the rope. In her first years here, they tied a bucket to that same rope and drew water from the old *Hüle*, the village pond. Now the rope was old and frayed, but it had not broken.

"Oh, Klaus . . ." Eveline's sigh rose from the abyss inside her. She felt no panic. She didn't even feel grief. The thing she had feared most, deep down, had come to pass.

At his feet lay the picture *The Broad and Narrow Way*. The glass that had covered it was smashed into a thousand pieces and reflected the bloodred sunset. Beside the picture lay a letter. Eveline could not remember the last time her husband had written anything. Trembling, she picked up the letter.

My dear Eveline,
You gave me everything you had. Your youth, your beauty, your life. Instead of leading a wealthy life in keeping with your station and running a fine household, you followed me into bitter poverty. Trust me, I wanted to make you happy, but I did not succeed. The way was too narrow, too stony, and too hard. I know that I am a great disappointment to you.

So my way ends here. I am happy about this, for a man can lose his life long before death. There can be no happiness in a house where the devil dances.

Look after the children, and look after yourself. I hope your way will be broader without me.

With love, your husband.

Her face wet with tears, Eveline let the letter fall. Love? What in the world did a rope around the neck have to do with love?

"Everything all right?" As he did every evening, Otmar Ludwig did a final, late-evening check at the infirmary. The doctor could not remember the last time he'd had two patients in here at the same time. He hoped to release both of them in a few days.

Josef Stöckle was asleep with his mouth open, but Alexander Schubert was still awake.

"How's the pain? Do you need another drop of morphine?" the doctor asked his young charge.

"No, thank you. I've had much less pain today," Alexander replied.

The doctor nodded, satisfied, then pulled the door closed quietly behind him.

Alexander lay back on his pillow. He smiled.

All the uproar, the fear, the pain—in the end, it had all been worth it. The Stuttgart Art School was giving him a second chance! In his mind, he could already see the white canvas in front of him. The smell of oil paint filled his nose, and in his ears sounded the voice of the professor explaining to him and his fellow students how to decipher the human face and capture it on canvas.

Alexander closed his eyes. His leg was a small price to pay for what he would gain.

CHAPTER 13

It was a small group of mourners who congregated on the evening of June 24 to usher Klaus Schubert to his grave. From where she stood off to the side, Mimi had the sense that she was seeing the scene in sharp focus through the lens of her camera.

Eveline and her daughters stood at the front, beside the grave. Eve's face was a stone mask. She looked so slight and exhausted, as if she were ready for the grave as well. *Poor Eve,* Mimi thought. Her heart ached even more when she looked at Eveline's daughters. Marianne at eight and Erika a year younger looked even more delicate and lost than usual. At least Edelgard Merkle and Johann were there to stand by Eve and the children. A small degree of solace, but something.

Alexander wasn't there. He was still bedbound at the infirmary, and with the wound not yet fully closed, the doctor felt there was too much risk of infection to move him.

"So much misfortune in one family," whispered Luise, who stood with Georg next to Mimi.

Mimi nodded. Eve had confided to her more than once that she was afraid for Klaus and that his melancholy was getting worse.

Just a few steps from Eveline stood Herrmann Gehringer. With his black top hat and even blacker frock coat, he could have passed for one of the pallbearers. As little as she liked the man, Mimi counted it to his credit that he had come to the funeral. He had given the rest of his weavers the evening off, as well, but only a handful had turned up. Not many of the other villagers had come, either. Paying one's last respects to someone who died by suicide was done reluctantly, if at all.

They could at least have come for Eveline, Mimi thought sadly, with a nod across the grave to Anton and his parents.

It was a hot evening, and the warm wind carried with it the dust from the surrounding fields and the sounds of people still working in them. From far in the distance came a faint growl of thunder, but overhead the sky was its usual evening blue.

Heads bowed, the congregation stood around the freshly dug grave. It lay on the outer edge of the graveyard, where the foxes sometimes slipped through the hawthorn hedge in search of something edible on the compost heap.

No bells rang, no one sang as the priest delivered his final words, his face rigid.

"Out of the depths have I cried unto thee, O Lord. Lord, hear my voice: let thine ears be attentive to the voice of my supplications. If thou, Lord, shouldest mark iniquities, O Lord, who shall stand? But there is forgiveness with thee, that thou mayest be feared. I wait for the Lord, my soul doth wait . . ."

As the priest finished the psalm, the four pallbearers lowered the coffin into the grave.

Mimi hoped that Uncle Josef was all right at home. She had arranged for Sister Elke to stay with him while she was at the funeral. He'd been brought home the day before and was not happy to discover that his bed had been moved to the parlor. He did not want to accept that he could not climb the stairs to the upper floor, and they had argued almost as soon as he arrived. Why couldn't she just have been good-natured about everything? Mimi wondered now, suddenly fighting back tears. She saw how Josef's strength was waning day after day. According to Dr. Ludwig, it would not be much longer before they were once again standing at a grave. Josef's grave. The very thought was too much for Mimi to bear. From now on, she thought, she would keep her brash mouth to herself. It was her task—no, it was her duty!—to make her beloved uncle's last days as comfortable and pleasant as possible.

All at once, she felt very alone. From beneath her lowered eyelids, she looked yearningly toward Johann, but his eyes were fixed on the grave. Since their walk two days earlier, when Klaus had taken his life, they had not seen each other. *What a wonderful state of "affairs,"* she thought ironically, but instantly reproached herself: *And don't you have anything else on your mind?*

"For dust thou art, and unto dust shalt thou return." Almost aggressively, the priest tossed a shovelful of earth into the grave. Then he turned on his heel and walked away. Not a word of solace to the widow and her two daughters. No farewell to the mourners who had assembled.

Mimi frowned. Could he have been any more cantankerous? With a heavy heart, she was about to give her condolences to Eveline, but Herrmann Gehringer stepped up to the widow first. "My commiserations," he said. "A terrible mishap. Falling from a ladder at that height."

The furrows already marking Mimi's forehead dug deeper. What appearance was the businessman trying to keep up? And for whose benefit? Everyone in the village knew the truth. Klaus Schubert had not slipped off a ladder, nor had there been any "mishap." Klaus Schubert, depressed and desperate, had hung himself from an old pear tree.

With a flourish, the mill owner presented Eveline with an envelope. "A small contribution from our widows and orphans fund. Normally, the money is only paid if one of the men passes away at the mill, but that never happens, so I have taken the liberty of diverting some of the money."

Hesitantly, and with what looked to Mimi like distrust, Eveline accepted the envelope. As she did so, Gehringer grasped her hand. Loud enough so that everyone could hear, he said, "There's another matter close to my heart. Your son, Alexander, will have a position at my mill whether or not his leg heals completely. You will be needing him to be earning wages now, naturally." With his free hand, he took a second envelope from his trouser pocket. "This is a blank signed contract of employment—blank because we don't yet know in what capacity we'll be able to make use of Alexander."

At Gehringer's words, Mimi audibly inhaled. This was the height of impertinence! The man was acting as if Alexander was permanently crippled, but even Dr. Ludwig didn't yet know if the accident would leave any lasting damage. Everyone hoped that Alexander would soon be back on his feet and walking normally.

Her expression empty, as if she had no idea what it all meant, Eve accepted the second envelope, too. Gehringer tipped his hat, murmured something about important business, and left. His assistant, Paul Merkle, followed at his heel.

"What a noble gesture, don't you think?" Luise whispered. "A person can rely on Gehringer."

"What's noble about it? Alexander doesn't even want to work at the mill," Mimi answered testily, then she stalked off after Father Hildebrand. The churchman couldn't be allowed to shirk his responsibilities like that! When Mimi thought about the efforts her own parents put into cases of hardship in their parish in Esslingen . . .

The priest had almost reached the church when she caught up with him. He did not look particularly happy to see her. "Yes?"

"Excuse me, but I . . ." Mimi was suddenly unsure of her ground. She really had no right to speak to the priest, but likely no one else would, so she worked up her courage. "Eveline Schubert is all but penniless, and she will need support. I wanted to ask if the church could perhaps help the family in some charitable way."

"But of course. The Lord is close to those with broken hearts, and helps those whose souls have been hard hit." With an exaggerated nod, he turned and went into the church.

And I'm sure the widow and her children will eat themselves fat on that, Mimi thought.

When Mimi got back to the grave, only a few mourners were still there, Johann among them. His mother was also still there, holding Erika's and Marianne's hands.

"I haven't yet offered my condolences to Eveline. Do you know where the reception will be?" Mimi asked when she saw Eve disappear through the graveyard gate.

"Reception?" asked Johann bitterly. "Who's going to pay for a reception?"

The day just gets worse and worse, Mimi thought. "Isn't it comforting to at least sit together for a little while after a funeral? To raise a glass to the dead man? To shed a few tears *together* instead of alone . . . I'm sure it would do Eveline good."

"Oh, Mimi . . ." Johann looked at her. "Life here is much harder than you imagine."

"So we just go our separate ways in silence? Then at least let's go to The Oxen, you and I, and drink a schnapps to the dead," she said with a touch of defiance. "Or come to my uncle's. We'd have the studio to ourselves," she added in a whisper.

"Johann? Are you coming?" Edelgard demanded. "Marianne and Erika want you to take them to feed the rabbits."

"Well? How was it?" With effort, Alexander sat up in his bed at the infirmary.

"Your mother and your sisters were very brave," said Anton. He went to the window and jerked it open. The infirmary smelled of disinfectant and old sweat. Anton couldn't understand how Alexander put up with it—he wanted to leave the moment he got there.

How red his friend's eyes were, Anton thought as he pulled up a chair. Was he crying his eyes out about his father? He sneaked a look toward Alexander's left leg, splinted and protected by a thin gauze bandage. It had been nine days, and the healing was taking its time.

"And Father Hildebrand?"

Was it just his imagination, or was Alexander holding his breath? *Don't say the wrong thing now,* Anton thought.

"I think everyone found his words very comforting." The priest! He felt like wringing old Father Whatawaste's neck, but he kept that to himself.

"What kind of sermon was it?"

Anton imperceptibly raised his eyebrows. Damn! It wasn't easy to fool Alexander. They were like fire and water, people said, not that either of them gave a damn what people said. But they trusted one another, and recognized each other's every mood. They had never deceived each other, either. But just now, Anton did. Sometimes, for the sake of friendship, one had to lie.

"As if I'd remember every word! Nothing you wouldn't expect, in any case," he said. Alexander said nothing, and Anton exhaled. Was he supposed to tell his friend about Father Hildebrand's spiteful looks or about how reluctant he'd seemed to give the service at all?

"Were there a lot of people?"

Anton shrugged. Should he say that maybe two dozen had bothered to attend? That not a single one of Alexander's classmates had been there?

"Your father had a dignified escort to his grave. His colleagues, your neighbors, my parents . . . even Gehringer paid his last respects. Johann Merkle was there, and Mimi, too."

Alexander's expression grew almost tender. "Mimi Reventlow . . ."

How reverently he said her name! He spoke about Mimi as if she stood on a pedestal and was lit by a halo. "Guess what I heard—the photographer and Johann know each other from before. And if you ask me, there's something going on between them," said Anton grimly.

"Why do you think that?" Alexander asked.

Anton shrugged. "Just a feeling . . . and I saw them walking together a couple of days ago." The same day Alexander's father died, he thought. They'd probably gone off to share a little romance. *How nice for them,* he thought bitterly. He couldn't remember the last time he and Christel had gone for a walk. "By the way, Gehringer told your mother you could start an apprenticeship with him anytime you like. The man has a vivid imagination, I'll give him that." Then Anton's face brightened. "Now that your father can't forbid you anything, there's nothing to stop you becoming a famous painter."

"What are you talking about? When Father died, my dream died with him, and you should know it," Alexander growled.

Anton thought he must have heard wrong. "Uh . . . what?"

"What am I supposed to do? Abandon my mother and sisters to their misery? I'm the man of the house now, for whatever I can do." Alexander looked at his leg, and his anger died as quickly as it had flared. He let out a small, pained groan. "I'm a cripple, Anton. I'm no good for anything! I won't be able to walk an hour out to our field, which means my mother is left with all the work. I'll probably end up having to do her embroidery at home while she digs up the turnips. If Gehringer takes me at all, all I can do is smile and say thank you. Without that money, we'll starve to death."

"But you don't know for sure that you'll be crippled." Anton swallowed hard. He wanted to believe that, but it hadn't occurred to him that Alexander would have to provide for the family.

Alexander stared at him. "Don't you get it? It was all for nothing, Anton! The fear and the pain and all of it. Father's ruined everything for me again."

CHAPTER 14

Eveline sat at the kitchen table and wept. She didn't know how long she'd been sitting here. She had gratefully accepted Edelgard's offer to look after her daughters, but when had that been? The day before yesterday? A week ago? Maybe two weeks? Tears took no notice of the calendar. The basket of dirty laundry was overflowing and dishes filled the sink, but Eve couldn't bring herself to do anything about it. It was only when she had no choice anymore that her stiff legs somehow carried her through the house to the toilet. She ignored the gnawing hunger in her belly. Her eyes burned from lack of sleep, and crust had formed at the edges of her eyelids. She didn't care. Had Klaus felt like this? Alive but dead? Like a ghost?

Occasionally, Luise or one of the other villagers came to check on her and bring her food. Eveline accepted the food and stored it away. She didn't want to eat anything. She didn't ask anybody in, and she accepted none of her neighbors' invitations. She should have visited Alexander long before now, but she couldn't even rouse herself for that. Grief was tearing her apart, like a wolf dismantling its prey, and all she could do was cry.

She wasn't crying for her dead husband, as everyone assumed. She'd wept enough for Klaus. All the days he'd been unkind to her and their children, all the nights he'd turned away from her, she'd cried, half-frozen and horribly alone.

Eveline's tears now were for the young girl, full of hope, that she'd once been, the girl who'd dreamed of the love of her life and who was now a widow at thirty-seven. She cried for the dreams that she and Klaus had never allowed themselves. To have time for each other. To do whatever they felt like every so often and not give everything of themselves just to finish their work. Once, just once, to walk the broad way instead of the narrow. *"The way was too narrow, too stony, and too hard,"* Klaus had written in his suicide note. But what about *her* way and their children's?

She cried for Klaus's laughter, which she could no longer even remember. He had once been a cheerful soul, and aside from his earnest exterior, it had been his sense of humor in everyday situations that she had so appreciated. Their life together had never been easy, even from the start, but in their early years, they had laughed away their share of tribulations.

But laughter had fallen by the wayside years before in their small, gloomy home. She had taught herself not to laugh—laughing would only have set Klaus off again about the devil dancing in their house.

Eveline cried for her children, too. How would they remember their father? As a man who was only rarely there? Who emanated despair like the smell of sweat? Who drifted along with a vacant look and dark shadows beneath his eyes?

What a life. What a death. She actually could understand what Klaus had done. There was some consolation in the thought that in a moment, all her problems could be resolved. If it were she, she wouldn't use a rope. Instead, she would leap from an outcropping at the edge of the Jura into the valley below, and feel as free as a bird for one final moment.

The thought vanished as quickly as it came. She was not Klaus, and she never wanted to become like him.

At some point, all her tears had been wept and her pain washed away, and in its place came emptiness. She sensed that the door to her old life had been irrevocably closed. What lay behind her had not been good for her. Was it true what they said, that when one door closes, another opens?

From her seat at the kitchen table, Eveline looked around her house as if she'd never seen it before, and that was exactly how she felt: like a stranger in her own home. Who was she? Where did she belong? She'd stopped being a daughter long ago—the day her father had declared her dead to him because she'd followed the call of love. She was no longer a wife, either, and she could not accept the word "widow." It felt unyielding, confining.

She was still a mother, and she was glad of that. There was never as much time for her children as she wanted, and yes, sometimes in the day-to-day turmoil she had been harsh. But she loved Erika, Marianne, and Alexander more than her own life. Suddenly, she could hardly wait to hold her daughters in her arms again. And to visit Alexander.

Eveline looked out the window and watched the summer evening slowly transform into night. The past was the past. Wouldn't she be better off thinking about what kind of life might now be possible? Could she patch together something new and good from all the torn pieces? Strangely, she did not doubt that it was possible. She knew she had to fill the void created—that was her task, her obligation. But it was unclear what she was supposed to fill it with. More work? More worry? More hunger, more fear of tomorrow, more of the desperation that made her scream inside?

Or would it be better to fill it with a new love? One day, certainly . . . that way now lay open before her.

The "way." As it often was, her eye was drawn to the place on the wall where the only picture they had ever owned had hung. Not an original painting, not a copper etching, but a cheap print. *The Broad and Narrow Way*, a picture she knew decorated the walls of many houses in the Swabian Jura. Along the broad way, all the geese laid golden eggs, and a cornucopia of pleasure opened to those who walked it. But the broad way also led straight to hell. The narrow way, in contrast, was marked by toil and torment, but led those who followed it to heaven.

Eveline stood up, her arms and legs leaden. The motion was abrupt, and made her so dizzy that she had to hold on to the table. When she was steady, she went to the stove and lit the fire. She was low on wood, as usual.

Finally, with a cup of tea, she returned to her seat at the table.

She had no idea where things were supposed to go from here, but Klaus's death could not be allowed to have been in vain. It was a warning for them all.

Unlike Klaus, she didn't believe the broad way would lead to hell. Her childhood was filled with pleasure and beauty, and none of that was sinful—rather, it had been quite beautiful. From now on, she would make sure that the way was broad and beautiful for all of them. *One step at a time,* she thought.

Life went on. The three envelopes on the table in front of her were witness to that. They had lain there since the burial. As if playing a game of cards where it mattered which one she drew, Eveline's gaze ranged over the envelopes before she reached for one.

She didn't need to take the paperwork out completely to see that it was the contract for Alexander's apprenticeship, and she stuffed it back into the envelope. Whether or not they needed every pfennig they could get, Alexander would hate the work at Gehringer's.

The second envelope was from the art school offering the new date for Alexander to take the test. Dr. Ludwig had said that, from a purely medical standpoint, her son most likely would be able to make the journey to Stuttgart by the end of July.

Eveline reached for the third envelope, the one that contained the money from Gehringer's widows and orphans fund. There were coins inside. Valuable gold coins, maybe? Gehringer had trumpeted his generosity so loudly at the funeral that there had to be a decent sum inside. If it was enough to get the family through the next few months, then she would send Alexander to Stuttgart, she thought, her heart pounding.

She opened the gray envelope with a fingernail, and five one-mark coins clattered onto the table. For that, she could buy a hundred pounds of potatoes. Or four pounds of coffee. Or she could take the children to eat at The Oxen, once.

Eveline, distraught and amazed, sat and stared at the coins. At least now she knew how little a human life was worth.

CHAPTER 15

"Mimi! Mimi!"

Frantically, Mimi dried her hands. It was half past seven, and she had almost finished getting ready for the day ahead. All she had left to do was pin her hair in place, but she was interrupted by Josef's impatient shouts.

"I'll be right there!" she called back, then hurried downstairs, her heart thumping.

She knew what was coming, of course, and she felt like running away. Josef needed to use the toilet, and because he still couldn't walk, Mimi had to help him. Not long ago, she would never have believed how much she would come to dread the task.

"Where were you? I have to go . . . ," Josef growled the moment she appeared.

As she did every morning since he'd come home nearly two weeks ago, she fetched the bedpan. When she tried to pull Josef's covers back to push the pan under his rear, he held on to his blanket tightly. "I'll do it!"

"But—" she began.

"No buts. I'll do it myself," he interrupted. "Don't treat me like a child."

She handed him the heavy pan without a word. Josef's hand trembled so much that Mimi was afraid he would drop it. She hoped he'd be able to manage it by himself.

"Shout when you're finished, all right?" she said, already in the doorway.

The old man grumbled something she didn't catch.

Mimi had just put the last hairpin in place when she heard him call for her again. She took a deep breath, then went back downstairs.

His face was wet with tears.

"Josef! What's the matter?" Shocked, she ran to the bed. Had he spat blood again? Sometimes when he used the bedpan, he had to cough and . . .

"Why hasn't God called for me?" he cried. "Why Klaus? I'm old and useless."

"Oh, Josef, don't talk nonsense."

When Mimi pulled back the blanket, she saw that Josef hadn't positioned the bedpan properly, and half of what he'd produced had missed its mark. He had tried to deal with the mishap himself but had only made a bad mess worse. Mimi had trouble containing her anger—this was exactly what she'd foreseen. But how was she supposed to make him do something that, for him, so clearly went against his nature?

She helped him get his feet over the side of the bed and propped up his splinted leg on a chair, then said, "Just sit. We'll get this sorted out in a minute."

Half an hour later, she had washed her uncle, spread fresh bed linens, and put the soiled sheets in the washtub to soak. When she looked in on Josef again, he lay staring rigidly at the ceiling, the blanket pulled up to his chin.

"What would you like for breakfast? Bread with honey or with marmalade?"

"I have no appetite," he said so quietly that she could barely hear him.

"You should eat something. You're—" *just skin and bones,* she'd been about to say, but her uncle had pulled the blanket all the way over his head.

Like a temperamental little boy, she thought sadly. What could she do to make him feel even a little better?

There was a knock at the door, and Mimi was almost relieved to leave her uncle for a moment. When she opened the door, she brightened instantly.

"Johann!" she said in delight, and when he stepped inside, she threw herself into his arms.

Since her uncle had come home from the infirmary, she had hardly dared to leave the house. Johann had come by in the late evening a few times since the funeral, but far too seldom for Mimi. When he did, they would creep around—God forbid Luise or someone else should spot them!—until they reached the studio, where they talked and held hands. Their intimacy went no further, though, because Mimi always had her ears pricked for any sound from the house. What if Josef needed something and she wasn't there? What if he tried to get up and fell again?

"Shall we go out to the studio?" Mimi asked, even though it was morning and Johann was likely only on a break from the mill.

"I don't have time. I just came to remind you about the *Heumondfest* the Sunday after next. Have you found someone who can stay with your uncle that evening?"

Mimi shook her head. "Not yet, I'm afraid. Luise wants to go to the festival, too, and I don't know many other people I could ask for a favor." She chewed her lip, considering for a moment. "I might ask Sister Elke. Perhaps I could offer to take her photograph in exchange, and she would be willing?"

"I can't tell you how much I'm looking forward to the *Heumondfest,* just to have something different to do. The monotony of weaving is suffocating me."

She wished he would say he was looking forward to the festival because they would be going together, but she understood what he meant about doing the same thing day in, day out, from morning to late—that was not the life for her, either, Mimi thought. "Could you try to find another job?"

"Another job? There's nothing else here to do," he said with a snort. "Besides, it's about time things took a turn for the better in the weaving trade, and I'm happy to be the one to make that happen." He stepped close to Mimi. "Maybe we'll have a few minutes just for us at the festival? I'd like to know how you see things in Laichingen. As an outsider, so to speak—you already know quite a few people here, after all."

"I hope very much that we can find a little private time for ourselves," Mimi whispered, but just then, a shadow appeared behind Johann. She hadn't closed the door! They stepped apart like thieves caught in the act.

"Anton! How nice of you to drop by," Mimi said with exaggerated warmth.

"I don't have to work this morning, so I wanted to see if you needed any help with Josef. But if it's a bad time . . ." He looked meaningfully from one to the other.

"No, it's fine," Mimi squeaked.

Johann nodded at both of them and walked away.

"Josef isn't having a good day. He hasn't had a bite to eat yet, either, but maybe he'll try to eat something if you're here," Mimi said.

How she smiled even while talking about her sick uncle . . . no doubt thinking about Johann, Anton thought, irritated. "What did Johann Merkle want?" he asked as ingenuously as he could.

"He . . . he invited me to the *Heumondfest*," she said dreamily.

And how her cheeks flushed, like a teenage girl in love! Anton abruptly blocked Mimi's path in the hallway, and she almost collided with him.

"That's very nice for you. But what about Alexander?"

She looked at him in surprise. "Excuse me?"

"The test at the art school is at the end of the month, but everyone seems to assume he'll have to start working at Gehringer's, and it looks like you do, too!" he snapped. "It can't be that Alexander has to suffer for what his father did. There's no way a family can live on the few marks that cutthroat pays his apprentices, anyway, so why not try for art school?"

"Why take it out on me?" Mimi said sharply. "If that's Eveline Schubert's decision, then that's what it is. It's rotten that Alexander might have to give up his dream, but everyone has to find a way to get by, me included. If I don't get more customers, Josef and I will soon be in the poorhouse ourselves."

Let Johann help you out! Anton thought. "You won't starve just yet. The week before the *Heumondfest*, the graduating students will come for a class picture. If every family with a graduate buys a print to keep, I'm sure it'll add up nicely," he said.

"I wouldn't have imagined the families could afford photographs again so soon after confirmation."

"The school principal thinks that finishing school is at least as important as confirmation, so it has become tradition to have a photographer for the occasion."

"I didn't know. Josef never said a word," Mimi said, abashed. "I'm very relieved to hear it, of course . . . though I'll have to get ready quickly. That's next week." She took a deep breath, and added, "Maybe if the earnings are good enough to take care of Josef and myself for a bit, I'll have more time to help the Schubert family after all, or at least Alexander. I imagine Johann might have some ideas, too." Again, her eyes took on their faraway look.

Anton already had his hand on the door handle to the parlor when he paused again. "You ought to watch yourself around Johann Merkle. He's not exactly an open book."

"What's that supposed to mean? You can keep that kind of talk to yourself," said Mimi, irritated. "Did you come to visit my uncle or not?"

"OK, OK." Anton raised his hands to pacify her. So the prodigal son had truly turned Mimi Reventlow's head. He was probably all she dreamed about these days, Anton thought bitterly.

It looked as if there was only one person who could help Alexander, and that was Anton. And while he was at it, he could plan his own escape as well.

CHAPTER 16

Not long after Anton left, there was another knock at the door, but this time it was the mailman. He handed Mimi a large and oddly shaped parcel. It had been mailed a week ago from Esslingen and was wrapped in thick paper. When Mimi unpacked it in the kitchen, she didn't know whether to laugh or cry.

With a resigned sigh, she read the enclosed letter from her mother.

Esslingen, June 28, 1911

Dearest Mimi,
Please excuse my slow reply. This summer is starting to feel truly hexed! So much to do in the parish, and I feel myself called upon to help from all sides, so I am all the happier to know that you are caring for Josef and that I don't have to attend to him as well.

Mimi frowned. As far as she was concerned, her mother could certainly do a little "attending" to her own brother and to Mimi herself. She "attended" to every other waif and stray, so why not to them, too?

How is Josef getting on? I am so proud of you, my child, for how well you have taken to looking after him.

What could her mother know about that? Nothing! But it was naturally far more pleasant to assume that Mimi was getting along swimmingly than to actually "attend" to anything herself. Churning inside, Mimi read on.

No doubt you are aware that exercise is extremely important for elderly people, especially after such an accident, to stop the old bones seizing up. Not too much and not too little. Perhaps you can get Josef to do a few gymnastic exercises? Water exercises of the hydrotherapeutic kind espoused by Father Kneipp would also do him good.

I'll leave you with the hope that the enclosed crutches might help with his walking, and with my best wishes from Esslingen.

Your mother

Crutches. Gymnastics. Hydrotherapy? Mimi sighed loudly—she was happy if she could get Josef to sit up in bed and eat a little, or even to sip a cup of tea. Shaking her head, she put the crutches out of the way. Some motion outside the kitchen window caught her eye, and she saw Luise, a pot in her hands, heading for the house.

"I brought some *Schwarzer Brei*. It's hot and well dosed with butter, the way your uncle likes it," she said when Mimi opened the door, and handed her the pot of dark spelt porridge.

"That's very nice of you. Thank you," said Mimi, with no real enthusiasm.

"Oh, child, you seem so down—is everything all right?" Luise reached out and stroked Mimi's arm.

Suddenly, Mimi had a lump in her throat. Luise Neumann cared more about her than her own mother did.

"Everything's fine," she said bravely.

Luise beamed at her. "You know what? You need to get out of the house! Go for a long walk. The weather's so lovely. And take your time. I'll stay with Josef while you're gone, all right?"

A few minutes later, Mimi found herself standing in front of the house and feeling a little lost. A few hours, just for herself? She wasn't used to having much freedom anymore. How lovely it would be to spend the day with Johann, she thought longingly. But the incessant clopping of the looms could be heard through the village, and the sound reminded her that Johann, like all the other men, was shackled to his loom well into the evening.

So what now? She looked across the market square to The Oxen. Anton had been more than a little agitated that morning, and the way he'd snapped at her was practically rude. But now that she had some time to think about it, he was not entirely wrong. She really should look in on Eveline and see if there was something she could do to help.

Filled with good intentions, she marched off.

She found Eve and her daughters in front of their house with two large baskets beside them. "We're going out to the field," Eveline said. "The wagon has a broken axle, so we have to carry everything, but we must go. It's our first time out since . . . well, you know . . . It's hard to believe it's been nearly two weeks since Klaus died."

Eve picked up one of the baskets, and although Marianne tried to imitate her mother, the basket was too heavy for her, so Mimi took it. "I'll come with you."

Eveline seemed calm and composed, Mimi noted with relief, and it was only a moment before Eve nodded in agreement.

"I owe you an apology. I'm sorry I haven't come by sooner, but my uncle . . . ," Mimi said. "Never mind. How are you?"

"Life goes on. I miss Klaus, of course. Every day. I even miss his tossing and turning at night. And his snoring!" She laughed sadly. "But if I'm to be honest, he had separated himself from me and the children long before he died. I was alone with everything for so many years, and that hasn't changed." She looked toward her daughters, who had run ahead to pick flowers.

Mimi nodded. In all likelihood, she thought, some people felt more alone in their marriages than she had in all her years of traveling by herself.

It wasn't long before the village was behind them, and the knocking of the looms faded. Gone, too, were the smells of the mills and village life. Here, the air was filled with a clear freshness that Mimi could hardly get enough of. She filled her lungs with the clean air, reveling in the feeling. With every breath, she grew more aware of the expanse of the landscape around them—there were no high mountains to stop one from gazing into the distance, and no dark forests to cast gloomy shadows. Instead, sunshine all around.

How lovely it is here, Mimi thought. No wonder Johann felt so connected to the region.

"Do you have any plans for the future?" Mimi asked.

"If you mean, do I spend all day and night thinking about it, then yes, I have plans for the future," said Eveline cautiously. "Right now, we're getting by on what I make with my embroidery, but it's not enough. Since Klaus's death, Paul Merkle has given me extra embroidery. He always acts as if he's doing me a favor. Of course we need the money, but I can only sleep five hours a night if I want to get all the work done. I'd like to try something else, but no one is hiring for house cleaning or such, so I really don't know what else I can do."

Her shoulders suddenly drooped, and Eveline put her basket down and looked at Mimi. "The worst part is that the whole miserable situation is going to rob Alexander of his dream. I worry all the time about that. He says he'll make the best out of his apprenticeship with Gehringer, but he's hiding a lot of tears behind a brave face. I'd do anything I could for him to go."

That isn't good at all, Mimi thought. If only the photo studio were busier, she could hire Eveline as a housekeeper and caregiver for Josef, and everyone would be better off.

"Having your own field must count for something, though. I can't wait to see what I'm going to get out of my little garden bed at home." She gave a friendly grin, and Eve actually laughed, then picked up her basket again.

They walked on. "Don't be too disappointed if your harvest turns out to be less than you imagine. When I followed Klaus to Württemberg, I also thought I was coming to a rich region. All around the empire, people talk about the 'Württemberg oasis,' where you can live a good life without working your fingers to the bone. That may be true in some parts, but it's a different story here in the Jura. The soil is poor and full of stones." Eveline crouched, scooped up a handful of earth, and held it out to Mimi—in just that small sample were three white, misshapen lumps of rock. "When we take the wheat to the mill to be ground, there's almost as much stone in it as grain. They say we've got rocks in our bread around here, and there's truth in that." She flung the handful of dirt away.

"I didn't know about any of this," Mimi said.

Eveline nodded. "There's more. The individual fields these days are too small for a family to live on what one produces. The local 'free-division customs,' as they're called, are to blame."

"What do you mean?"

"Anyone who owns a piece of land can divide it among their descendants any way they see fit. Sooner or later, every child here gets a piece, and none is left empty handed—unless they commit murder, which would exclude them from an inheritance," Eve explained. "The custom is well intentioned, but it means that with each passing generation, the individual plots get smaller and smaller. Look at this patchwork!"

Mimi's gaze followed Eveline's. The many small fields really did look a little like the patchwork blanket Uncle Josef used for his noonday nap.

"Often enough, it also means you own individual pieces of land that are far apart, and you have to walk forever to get from one to the next. It's horrible!"

"But if that old custom just makes everything worse for everybody, why don't they change it?"

"You can't ask me that. I'm still an 'outsider' here," said Eve. "As if all that wasn't enough, you've got the cold climate. Up here in the Jura, only the toughest plants grow, and only sparsely at that. Now you know why we live hand to mouth."

"But there's more to Württemberg than just the Swabian Jura. I just have to think about the Neckar Valley, for example—fruit trees, grapevines, cereals, vegetables, everything grows there in abundance. It's like paradise. Why don't people just go and try their luck somewhere else?"

Eveline laughed out loud. "Leave here? Don't even think about it! With all the stones in the soil, they talk about farming here as 'plowing the devil's skull,' but the Laichingers would rather dig up the devil for a lifetime than go anywhere else."

After a good hour, they finally reached Eveline's field. Mimi couldn't believe it. "You do this trek every single day?"

"Some days more than once. Sometimes I'm on my way at three thirty in the morning, and other days we don't get home until after ten," Eveline said. She pointed to the surrounding fields. "Look around. That field belongs to Edelgard Merkle, and the one beside it belongs to the

Kleins—you photographed their son, Vincent. They're no better off than we are. Our second field is even farther out. I don't like to think about all the useful work I could be doing in the time it takes me just to get here. Of course, there are some fortunate enough to have their fields closer to the village. Sonja Merkle has one, and her mother, Luise, too. Enough talk now. We have work to do." She turned to her daughters. "OK, stone picking, both of you. While you're doing that, I'll loosen up the soil to let the rain soak in better when it finally decides to come."

The two girls immediately crouched and began gathering one stone after another with their bare hands. Once they had collected quite a few, they carried them in the baskets to the edge of the field and piled them up. Eveline moved behind the children and broke up the soil between the plants with a small hoe.

Without a word, Mimi also crouched and did as the girls did. The work was more difficult than she'd imagined: the stones were often locked in the soil as if they'd been baked into it. Her fingers already scraped, she looked around for a stick or something else she could use as a tool to help her get the stones out, but apart from Eveline's hoe, there were no other tools to be had.

My God, she thought, *this kind of work is far too hard for women and children.*

"Mama, I'm thirsty," Erika said.

Without putting down her hoe, Eveline picked up a small stone and popped it into her mouth. When she'd licked it clean, she gave it to her daughter. "Here. Put that in your mouth. It'll stop the thirst."

Amazed, Mimi said, "Don't you have any water with you?" How could a mother forget to bring something for her children to drink?

"I had the baskets to carry. I can't carry a jug of water, too. Besides, they'll survive a few hours without a drink." She pressed her lips in a thin line and carried on in silence.

Mimi also stopped talking.

After two hours, they had picked a sizable pile of stones out of the now loosened earth and set off wearily for home. For Mimi, the work had been a kind of torture. Her legs were on fire. She had not been able to work in a crouch for long, so she had spent more of her time crawling along on her knees. Her back hurt and her hands were so feeble that she was afraid she might not be able to hold her camera the next day. Her uncle and Luise were no doubt wondering where she'd gone, and she suddenly longed for her uncle's house. But instead of making a good pace on the return trip, Eve and the children stopped every other step to collect sticks and brushwood, which they carried in the baskets.

Mimi reluctantly held out her basket for the brushwood. Despite her bad conscience, she could no longer pull herself together to help them—her back simply hurt too much. "What do you need all this for, anyway?" she said irritably as the two baskets slowly filled.

"We need it for the oven, to bake our bread. And for the fire, we need the kindling." Eveline wiped the sweat from her forehead. She nodded toward a patch of forest. "Around the end of winter, some people go over there to collect wood, but before you do that you have to lease somewhere to store it. We don't have the money for that, so I spend the whole year looking for things to burn."

"I don't know how you put up with it . . . ," Mimi blurted before she could stop herself.

"Who says I put up with it?" Eve replied. "All that keeps me going is the hope of better days," she said with a grimace.

When Mimi finally lay in her bed that night, she felt as if her spine was as fragile as glass. One wrong move and she would shatter! But instead of falling into a rejuvenating sleep, her mind was tormented by thoughts that would not rest.

The housework. Raising children. The field. And on top of it all, the delicate embroidery for Gehringer. How did Eveline manage it, day after day? How did the other women manage it?

One image flashed through her mind: all the citizens of Laichingen she'd had in front of her camera, their faces marked by hardship, their callused hands and hunched backs. With shame, she thought of how much energy she had put into retouching the photographs to do away with all those "flaws." She should have painted a laurel wreath into every picture instead, as a symbol of the strength and will to survive that the people of Laichingen possessed.

Worn out and depressed, Mimi finally fell asleep. The last question on her mind before she drifted off was whether there was any way to help Eveline and her family. It wasn't a new question, but with what she now understood, finding an answer was much more urgent.

CHAPTER 17

"The crutches could be worse," said Anton when he visited Mimi on Thursday.

Mimi, who had learned that "could be worse" was the Swabian way of saying "very good indeed," looked at him in astonishment.

Anton grinned. "Alexander can use them when I go to Stuttgart with him. And I'll come up with something your uncle can *really* use to get around, if it's all right with you."

"What do you mean? You're going to Stuttgart with Alexander?" Mimi was astonished.

"Someone has to." Anton shrugged. "If I scrape together my savings, I'll have enough for the train ticket. Alexander doesn't know anything about it yet. I'm going to help him get home from the infirmary so his mother doesn't have to leave her work. I'll tell him then, or else he'll just lie there brooding about it." He grinned. "And I'll send Fritz to come see you about something for Josef."

On Saturday, Fritz Braun came by with a walker crafted from two wooden crates with four small wheels screwed to the bottom. The wheels had been donated by his boss, Mr. Meindl, Fritz announced, smiling broadly. Then he demonstrated how Josef could push the walker ahead of him and lean on it for support.

"I can't believe it," said Mimi. "As soon as Josef is a little stronger, we'll practice with it every day. You're a wonder!" With the new walker, Josef would soon be able to make it to the toilet unaided, she thought with relief.

She threw her arms around Fritz and, despite his protests, wouldn't let him leave without accepting two marks as payment.

Mimi was dusting the props she thought she might need for the graduating class pictures she'd take on Tuesday when Sonja Merkle, propped on the arm of another woman, stepped into the studio. "I'd like to introduce my sister, Berta. She's getting married soon and—" In the middle of her sentence, Sonja suddenly lurched forward; her face was twisted in pain as she clutched her hugely pregnant belly.

Mimi, startled, quickly pulled up a chair. "Sit, please! Would you like some water?"

"Yes, thank you. It's been like this for days," Sonja groaned. "It feels like the child is going to come any minute, but it's really taking its time. The births of my boys were just as drawn out, and each time, when the baby finally came, it was always when I was out with Berta. So I thought I'd come here with her today." She grinned mischievously.

"Have you lost your mind?" asked Berta with a laugh. "You want me to play midwife for you yet again?"

"Let's not tempt fate," said Mimi. "You'll end up having the baby here in the studio." As if on command, Sonja was seized by another contraction.

Mimi frowned. "I don't want to send you away, but wouldn't it be better if you were at home, resting?"

"It would certainly be better, but Berta has to work during the week, and besides"—Sonja Merkle paused—"at home it's like the walls are closing in. I can't stand the atmosphere there just now."

"The atmosphere?" Mimi asked while she surreptitiously scrutinized Berta from the corner of her eye. Like Sonja and Christel, Berta was also an uncommonly attractive woman, though by the faint lines that were starting to show around her eyes and the many silver strands in her brown hair, Mimi guessed she was in her midthirties.

"Mr. Gehringer would like Christel to model his best blouses and skirts for the buyers from the big department stores. It's a great honor, as I told my husband, but he's against it, and Christel's been moping around ever since he forbade her from doing it."

"I'm sure Christel would enjoy something like that very much. No wonder she's disappointed," said Mimi sympathetically. "Gehringer's customers would probably buy twice as much if a girl as pretty as Christel modeled his wares for them."

When she refilled Sonja's water glass, Mimi noticed Sonja raising her eyebrows. "Good heavens, what happened to your hands?" Sonja exclaimed.

Mimi quickly pulled her hands away, embarrassed. "I went out to the fields with Eveline Schubert and helped her a little. It would seem my delicate hands aren't used to hard labor," she said with a wry smile.

With one hand on her belly and the other on her back, Sonja groaned and leaned forward. "What I'm about to say can never be allowed to reach our mother's ears, but I absolutely *hate* working in our field. Thank God Paul earns enough for us not to have to rely on the harvest. If I had to break my back with that, too . . . oh, God forbid!"

"There are some fortunate enough to have their fields closer to the village. Sonja Merkle has one, and her mother, Luise, too," Mimi suddenly heard Eveline's voice in her mind.

"Then what are you doing with your field?" Mimi asked, furrowing her brow.

Sonja shrugged. "Last year we had potatoes, but this year it's lying fallow. Which my mother isn't happy about, by the way, but she doesn't have a horde of children to deal with."

Mimi cleared her throat. "We walked over an hour yesterday to get to Eveline's field. I was horrified by how long it takes just to get there," she said. "And your field is really so much closer to the village?"

Sonja nodded proudly. "Just a few minutes away."

Mimi bit down on her lip. Damn it, she was going to do it again . . .

"I know it's none of my business," Mimi said slowly, "but something has just occurred to me. Could you perhaps imagine exchanging your field for Eveline's? Or maybe just letting her use the field for a year or two? You'd be helping her get back on her feet."

"You want me to give up my little field? Out of the question!" Sonja said vehemently. Then, less fervently, she said, "I'm always happy to help, but I might get the urge to grow something there myself next year."

So much for that, Mimi thought. "It was a silly idea, I admit. It's easy to see I'm not from here, isn't it?" Mimi conceded with a smile. "Let's get to things I understand," she said, turning to Berta, who so far had hardly said a word. "So you're getting married. How wonderful."

"The wedding is set for the middle of August. My fiancé is Richard Hausmann," Berta replied happily, her cheeks turning red. "Of course, we need a photographer. Sonja mentioned you right away."

"I'm glad to hear it. I'll do the loveliest wedding pictures you can imagine, unforgettable mementos of the day," said Mimi warmly. "Were you thinking of coming to the studio before the ceremony or after?"

Berta already had her mouth open to reply when Sonja let out a loud scream. She doubled over, and Mimi was horrified to see a flood of liquid pour from beneath her skirt and onto the floor.

"Oh my Lord . . . What *is* that?" Her heart was suddenly beating so hard that she could hardly speak.

"Her water has broken," Berta said. Then, with a touch of hysteria in her voice, she said to her sister, "The baby is coming! Sonja, how can you do this to me?"

Mimi slapped her hand over her mouth in fright. "We need the doctor!"

The two sisters exchanged a look. "The baby's going to beat him," Sonja muttered through gritted teeth.

Mimi frantically glanced out the studio windows toward the gate at the back of the garden. "Then should I get your mother?"

Sonja, who in the meantime had slid off the chair and was lying on the floor in front of the photography platform, let out a groan so loud it set Mimi's teeth on edge. "Not Mother," she murmured when she could breathe again. "She makes me so nervous."

Berta looked at Mimi. "Could you stoke a fire in your stove?"

Mimi, confused, nodded.

"Then we'll manage this by ourselves," Berta said, with a level of resolve Mimi had not suspected. "Go into the house and get the fire in the stove burning as hot as you can. We need a kettle of hot water, a pair of scissors, a candle, and matches. And bring a towel to wrap the baby in and a few blankets and clean pillows for Sonja. Fast!" She drew the curtains closed as she spoke. "Spectators are the last thing we need." She turned to Mimi. "Go!"

Mimi, still half-paralyzed with fright, went.

An hour later, a baby girl with rosy skin, pale-blond downy hair, and pink pouty lips saw the light of the world. When Mimi saw her tiny, perfectly formed fingernails and toenails, she burst into tears.

Sonja and Berta joined her. Relief, joy, and friendship filled every tear.

Mimi felt as weary and euphoric as if she'd given birth to the girl herself. Never, not even once, had she experienced anything as moving as this.

While Berta washed the newborn in the basin Mimi had brought and wrapped her in a linen hand towel, Sonja lay exhausted on the blanket that Mimi had also brought from the house. She grasped Mimi by the hand. "I don't like to think about what that would have been like at Helene's store or somewhere else. Thank you forever for your help," she said. "You *must* come to the christening."

"Thank your sister," Mimi managed to say, while she squeezed Sonja's hand. She was touched by Sonja's gratitude and the invitation. She had never been invited to a christening other than in a professional capacity.

"You have to come to my wedding, too!" Berta added as she laid the infant in Sonja's arms.

"And you'll be this one's godmother, too. That goes without saying," Sonja said.

The sisters laughed together.

"The *Heumondfest*, a christening, and a wedding—I'm never going to stop celebrating," said Mimi, joining in their laughter and feeling more a part of things than she had for a very long time.

CHAPTER 18

"The wound itself has healed nicely, and faster than I expected. There's no danger of infection anymore, which was my greatest worry. Now all we can do is wait and see how strong and mobile your leg gets." Dr. Ludwig looked at Alexander seriously. "Because the bone also took some damage from the ax, I strongly advise you to use the crutches for the next few weeks and not to put all your weight on the leg until you're stronger. Be sure to do the exercises I've shown you several times a day—they will help your mobility."

Alexander nodded.

Anton, who had been standing next to Alexander without saying a word, handed Josef Stöckle's crutches to his friend. Then he shouldered Alexander's bag, and they left.

"So how does it feel to be free again after all that time in a sickbed?" Anton asked when, slowly but surely, they had put the doctor's office behind them.

Alexander inhaled, drawing a deep breath of air heady with the scent of freshly cut hay. "Good. Also strange," he said. "I feel like I've come home from a long journey, but I haven't been anywhere at all."

Anton watched him from the corner of his eye. Alexander was doing quite well with the crutches. Still, to give his friend a break, he stopped walking. "The days are flying by. We just had the Pentecost market, and it's *Heumondfest* next weekend. I can already picture all the little campfires and smell the homemade schnapps. After everything that's happened lately, I can hardly wait to have a good time." Anton puffed out a breath of air.

The *Heumondfest* was one of the few days of the year that The Oxen closed. Everybody gathered at a big meadow outside the village that belonged to the parish. Each family brought their own food and drink, there was music, and the Laichingers danced in celebration of the end of the hay harvest. Some of the small fires would keep burning until daybreak.

Maybe sometime in the night he'd manage to sneak away with Christel? If the night and the ground were warm, maybe she would finally let him kiss her and hold her close.

"I haven't seen Christel for so long. I'm going to dance the night away with her at the *Heumondfest*," he said, but instantly regretted it. Damn! He should have kept that to himself. Who knew whether Alexander would ever be able to dance again?

But Alexander didn't seem to take offense. He said, "My family and I won't be there this year, you know. It's our year of mourning."

"But that doesn't mean you won't go somewhere else. Here!" Anton stuck his hand in his trouser pocket and proudly held out a handful of coins to his friend. "The fare for the train to Stuttgart. Every free hour I had, I helped my father build a new blind in the forest, and I made sure he paid me for it."

"You gave up your free time for me?" A blotchy red flush rose into Alexander's face. "That's . . . I don't know what to say. I can't take your money. I can't accept it."

"Oh, yes you can. You're going to that admissions test in Stuttgart if I have to carry you on my back. And then you're going to paint and draw like Michelangelo himself."

"Why are you doing all this for me?" Alexander whispered.

Anton swallowed. He'd asked himself the same question. He could have saved the money just as easily and finally gone off somewhere with Christel. Was it friendship? Sympathy? Maybe a bad conscience?

"I think it's because I don't want to stop believing it's possible to make your dreams come true," he said. Then, in a lighter tone, he added, "Besides, I'm going with you. While you're at the school taking the test, I'll be hitting the town. I'm going to buy myself a tie, then go and drink a beer like a real gentleman—it's going to be a grand day!"

Alexander laughed and started to hobble ahead. "What do you need the tie for?"

"I'll need it soon, so I might as well buy it! You don't want me to come to your first exhibition like some poor relative from the Jura, do you?"

"I'd love to have your optimism for just *one* day," Alexander said, shaking his head, but Anton could see how happy he really was. "I'll think about it, all right?"

Anton grinned. That meant yes. One step at a time, he thought. Once his friend had the admissions exam successfully behind him, they would have to find a way for him to actually go to the school. Gehringer and his pitiful apprentice income could go to hell.

With Alexander on crutches, the route through the village had never felt longer to Anton, who normally strode along briskly. He was relieved when they finally reached the Schubert house.

Instead of knocking or simply walking into the house, Alexander paused just outside the front door. "It's going to be strange to go into the house knowing that Father is never coming home."

"And to make up for that, your mother and sisters will be so much happier to see you," said Anton. "By the way, tomorrow Mimi Reventlow will be taking pictures of the graduating class. She said you absolutely have to come and that it won't cost you anything . . . She said your picture is a gift for a friend."

"I can't accept it," said Alexander a second time.

"Oh, yes you can!" Anton replied. His tone left Alexander no choice.

With the fifteen graduates and Christel, who had accompanied her brother Justus, the studio was so full that Mimi would have been hard pressed to squeeze in even a mouse. There was no doubt about the excitement among the young crowd. The students chatted and giggled at a loud volume; several were red faced with excitement, and two girls were so pale they looked as if they were about to faint.

Mimi, too, was excited. She had little experience with a group this big, but she was hoping she could get the perfect picture. What a pity Uncle Josef couldn't be here with her. He would have been a great help, Mimi thought as she tried to arrange the young people on the platform. She created three rows and placed the tallest students in the back, the smaller ones in front of them, and a few kneeling at the front. She offered a chair to Alexander, who was propped on his crutches off to the side, but he wanted to stand like the others.

"All right, nobody move," she said as she went behind her camera.

It was a slightly overcast day, but when she looked through her viewfinder, she found there was just the right amount of light coming through the uncovered windows. Mimi was sure the photo would make a nice memento for the ages.

"Smile!" she called out, then tripped the shutter. "Thank you!"

Immediately, the students fell out of their orderly rows and began talking and laughing again.

Mimi smiled. "Before you go, I have a suggestion . . ." She looked expectantly from one face to the next. "I'd like to take a second picture, something unique. The idea came to me last night, but don't ask me why!" Mimi laughed, a little embarrassed. "Anyway, I'd like to take the second photograph, and you can look at it when it's done. If you like it, you can ask your parents about buying a print. OK?"

The young people nodded uncertainly.

"Who here's been to a movie theater?"

Nobody raised their hand.

"You've heard of them, haven't you?" Mimi asked.

A couple of them shrugged.

"Well, I've been a few times, and I find it terribly exciting," Mimi went on. "In the movies, anything is possible. There are Indians from the Wild West and pirates with eye patches. There are films with sailors at sea and with princesses wearing a dozen pearl necklaces. The stories they tell aren't always very true to life, but that just makes them more exciting. Anything is possible, any dream can come true, every adventure . . ." Mimi could practically see the imaginations of the young people stirring as she spoke. She seized the moment. "How would you like to pretend we're making a film? One that tells lots of different stories at once! I know it sounds crazy, but I'm sure we'll end up with a very dramatic picture."

Her young subjects, some of whom had listened uncertainly and some of whom had been spellbound, seemed to recoil a little. It was Fritz Braun who finally spoke up and asked what the picture was supposed to look like.

Mimi looked him in the eye. "If a fairy appeared right now and told you that you could be anyone you wanted, just for a day, who would you be?"

"A pirate!" he blurted without a moment's hesitation. "With a big saber. I'd board a ship, find a treasure chest full of gold coins, and be a rich man for the rest of my life."

Fritz's schoolmates laughed.

"I'd be a pioneer," said Vincent Klein. "I'd travel through the Wild West in my covered wagon, looking for a new home." His red cheeks were even redder than usual. "There was a whole page about a pioneer in Saturday's newspaper, and that man also used to live here in the Jura."

"This is going to be a strange movie, because I want to be a train conductor," said another young man.

Christel, who had so far been watching in silence from her chair, sprang to her feet so suddenly that the others jumped. "And *I* want to be a famous actress, admired by all!"

"You're not even one of us," her brother Justus jeered.

"Thank God," Christel hissed back.

Mimi, who had seen the gleam in Christel's eye, said, "For a special picture like this, I think Christel could join in, don't you?" She looked at the group—no one was brave enough to contradict her.

Mimi nodded. "All right then. Fritz and Vincent, you go and look through the wardrobe and props. There's even a saber. Christel, maybe you want to choose a dress? I also have pearl necklaces—the pearls aren't real, of course, but they look as if they are. In the meantime, the rest of you can think about what you'd like to be, and I'll look for a backdrop."

They really went at it, dressing themselves up! Fritz as a pirate and Vincent as a Wild West pioneer with a cowboy hat on his head. Gisela wanted to portray a hairdresser styling the hair of high-society ladies and actresses, and Justus wanted to be a wrestler. *Figures. He's always been a bruiser,* thought Alexander.

Mimi Reventlow was in her element as she jumped around among the props, the camera, his classmates, and the platform. Just then, she was adjusting Fritz's eye patch, the last detail of his pirate look.

A few months earlier, Alexander had had the opportunity to watch her retouch photographs and had seen how she worked. He had no doubt this picture would be something very special, despite—or perhaps precisely *for*—being so outlandish.

So far, he hadn't said anything about who he wanted to pretend to be in the picture. He felt distant from everything going on around him.

To lead a new life, a different life . . . for his schoolmates, it was all just a game, an illusion. But for him, a new life was within his grasp. Even before Anton offered him the money for the journey to Stuttgart, he'd made up his mind to take the exam. Lying in Dr. Ludwig's infirmary, he'd envisioned different ways of getting to Stuttgart. On foot using crutches, hopefully traveling part of the way on a mail wagon . . . Maybe an automobile would pick him up along the road? He could try stowing away on a train and hope the conductor didn't find him. If he was discovered, he'd pretend he'd lost his ticket. And if he got fined, then he got fined.

What was most important to him was to finally find out if his artistic talent had true merit. If the professors in Stuttgart saw that he could draw a decent picture but thought he wasn't skilled enough to take it further, then he could accept that judgment. And if it turned out that they saw talent and thought he really could be an artist, well, then he would take it from there. He knew studying art was out of the question for now. He had to earn money for his family. It was his responsibility, and he would fulfill it. But one day, maybe in a year or two, perhaps his mother would marry again, and then they wouldn't have to depend on him anymore. Then he'd be able to go his own way. He wouldn't stay in Laichingen a day longer than he had to. Not in this place he hated so much, where—

"Alexander? Who do you want to be in this picture?" Mimi asked with a smile, interrupting his thoughts.

He didn't have to think about his answer. "A weaver."

A few heads turned. "We're supposed to think up something make-believe," said Vincent with a frown.

"I know," Alexander replied. "A weaver is something I'll never, ever be."

CHAPTER 19

"These are for you." Cheerfully, Johann held out a small bouquet of blue blossoms.

"Forget-me-nots?" Touched, Mimi accepted the delicate bunch of flowers. "Thank you, but I'm not planning to leave Laichingen anytime soon."

Johann grinned. "It's a tradition here for a man to give the woman he's taking to the *Heumondfest* a few forget-me-nots in the morning, so she won't forget him in all the fun and frolicking!"

He wanted her to think of him. Spontaneously, she threw her arms around his neck. "Now I'm looking forward to this evening even more."

"What about your uncle?" He nodded past her to the interior of the house.

"Josef says I shouldn't worry and that he'll get along just fine without me. And he wouldn't even think about keeping Sister Elke away from the *Heumondfest*." Mimi laughed. "I'll look in on him once or twice. Speaking of looking in . . ." She took Johann's hands in hers. "Just the other day, you told me that the people here in the village are here for each other, and that if you need it, you'll find someone to help you. I'm getting along fine, but would you look in on Eveline Schubert? Alexander was here yesterday, and he's limping badly. I can't imagine he's of much use to his mother right now. Perhaps you could chop wood for her or take care of some other heavy work that needs doing?"

Johann shook his head. "You sound like my mother! She's been pressing me to help Eveline. I'd be glad to, but tell me when I'm supposed to do it? I work for twelve hours, then my mother commandeers me. You and I hardly see each other as it is. I've been wanting to read a draft of a speech to you for days. It's one I'm planning to deliver to the weavers when they have gained a bit more trust in me."

"I know what you mean," Mimi said. "Between looking after my uncle, the studio, and the household, there's practically no time left for anything."

"I'll stop by Eveline's and see what I can do, I promise. And just to put your mind at ease: my mother has been looking after Eveline's daughters quite a lot, and sometimes she cooks for all of them, too, which helps."

Mimi nodded, relieved. "Could I show you something?" She smiled mischievously.

"Only if it's quick. I have a lot to take care of today before the festival at five, including gathering wood for our campfire."

She quickly unlocked the door to the shop, where the pictures of the graduates were displayed on the wooden stand. Proudly, she handed him the second photograph.

In the center of the composition, Mimi had positioned Christel Merkle in front of Josef's old bellows camera, as if she were standing in front of a movie camera. Johann's niece had adopted a dramatic pose and was pretending to fan her face. Meanwhile, Gisela, a comb and brush in her hands, was applying the final touches to Christel's elaborate hairstyle. To the right, behind the young women, stood Fritz Braun, looking grim and acting as if he were about to steal the pearl necklace from around Christel's neck. The others around Christel completed the spectacle in outlandish, entertaining ways. If that didn't show artistry! Mimi was practically bursting with pride.

"Well, what do you think?"

"My niece outshines everything around her," Johann murmured.

Mimi grinned. Although she'd used no special lighting techniques, Christel's blond hair really did seem a shade brighter than everything else. The girl had a genuine, powerful radiance.

Johann abruptly handed the picture back. "It's nice. But what's the point?"

"The point? What kind of question is that?" Mimi scoffed. "Can't you see how much fun they're having? People need something to dream about, if only for a moment. They see enough of the serious side of life every day."

"The serious side of life would be easier to take if the conditions in which the people work—and live—were more bearable," Johann replied. "A lot has to change here in Laichingen. *That* is what the young people here have to learn. With your photographs, you dangle a carrot in front of them. You're leading them to believe that they're free to choose whatever they want. But the truth is, they're slaves of Gehringer and the other mill owners."

"At least with Fritz Braun, that's not likely to be true. And Alexander Schubert might also have a different future ahead of him," Mimi said passionately. "Just because something is a certain way now doesn't mean it can't change. I hope, in time, that more young people will be able to forge their own destinies."

"I'm sorry, but I find that attitude completely misguided. Going away is no solution!" Johann said.

"Excuse me?" said Mimi, unable to believe that such words could come from his mouth.

Johann's eyes glinted combatively as he said, "I know what you're thinking, and yes, you're right—I left here once myself. But how am I supposed to improve working conditions for the weavers if every man who can think for himself leaves, too? If things really go as far as a workers' rebellion, then we need every man we can get on our side."

"Oh, and that's why they should all stay weavers?" If her mother knew how the young people of Laichingen were being robbed of their future, then . . . she'd be very upset indeed, Mimi suddenly thought. *I sound just like Mother.*

"Mimi, be a little realistic, will you?" He reached for the photograph. "Don't you think it's a little mean to stir up dreams like this in the minds of the youngsters, dreams you know will never come true?" She opened her mouth to reply, but he continued before she could interrupt. "I'm not talking about dressing up as pirates and pioneers. They know perfectly well it's all just a game. But the look in Christel's eyes—it's pure yearning."

"So what? Christel is a beautiful young woman. No one knows what life has in store for her," said Mimi. If Johann had seen the enthusiasm with which Christel had thrown herself into her role, he'd think differently now.

Johann laughed. "Oh, I know that perfectly well," he said with a touch of arrogance. "In the best case, my brother might let his daughter play Gehringer's model after all. But you would have to agree that there's a difference between being a famous actress and being a garment maker's live dummy, right? Maybe it's time you started photographing reality and not pretty illusions. I have to go. See you tonight!"

Confused and hurt, Mimi watched him go. What kind of strange conversation was that? Or was it a fight?

"For you! Forget-me-nots are a symbol of the deepest love. Did you know that?" Anton's voice was full of affection when he handed Christel the small bouquet of blue flowers. He'd gotten up extra early to make sure he was one of the first to pick them at the edge of the forest. He wanted only the best for Christel.

She took the bouquet and set it on the fence beside them. "Thank you, but I don't know if I'm even going to be able to go. Mother's been crying for days and refuses to get out of bed. She always gets into a mood like this after she's had a baby."

"And that means you can't leave the house? Are you her nurse or something?"

"Psst! Lower your voice!" Christel hissed.

As usual when he went looking for her at her home, he'd tossed a small pebble against her window. A moment later, Christel had come rushing out. Behind the house, hidden by the goat pen, they now stood close together.

"Let your father look after your mother. He's the one who helped her *make* the child," he whispered.

Christel giggled.

That's something, at least, Anton thought.

"Do you actually think Father would lift a finger around the house? That's what they have me for—their maid!"

Bitterness infused every word, and it hurt Anton just to listen.

Christel looked around fearfully. "You'd better leave. Father said he wants to go and see Gehringer this morning. If he sees us together, he'll blow his top. He's already as mad as a snake about the picture."

"What picture?"

She pulled a photograph out of her apron pocket. "I went to the photographer with Justus. When she was taking the class picture, she wanted to do something unusual with us. Can you see what I am?"

Anton had to stifle a laugh. "I'll bet there isn't another picture like this in the empire!" he said, grinning. "Of course I can see what you are: you're an actress. And I am sure you're more beautiful than any real one."

"Do you think so?" She touched the picture with her fingertips affectionately. Then she looked at Anton. "I'd love to go to a theater and see one of those movies that the photographer talked about. She said they were wonderful."

"Then let's do it!" Elated, Anton grasped her hand in his. "I'm going to Stuttgart next week with Alexander, for his admissions exam. Come with us! I'll find the money for the train." *But where, though, without stealing it?* He fretted. He probably would have to steal some money from The Oxen's register.

Christel looked at him suspiciously. "You're going to Stuttgart with Alexander? I thought he was going to start at Gehringer's."

"Nothing's been settled yet," he said. "So what's it to be? Shall we make a day of it?"

"Father will never let me," Christel muttered.

"What won't I let you do?" Paul Merkle suddenly barked, and her father appeared around the side of the goat pen. "And what is this about Stuttgart?"

"Anton is going with Alexander. And I'm invited to go along for the day. Please, Father, I'd love so much to see the city where the king lives!" she pleaded.

He snatched the photograph out of her hand and, his voice now perilously quiet, said, "The king! Is that all you can think about? Get in the house and do something useful."

Without another glance at Anton, and without testing her father's wrath any further by taking the bouquet of forget-me-nots, Christel bowed her head and ran to the house.

"Now for you. How many times have I told you to stay the hell away?" Paul Merkle said the moment they were alone.

"Always the same old tune—is that all you can think of? In case you hadn't noticed, your daughter is an adult. You have no right to deny her anything. Whether you like it or not, I'm going to keep courting Christel, and one day we're going to get married," Anton said, his hands pressed to fists.

"You and Christel? Married?" Paul Merkle snorted. "Do you really think I'd let my beautiful daughter marry you? If I ever see you here again . . . you don't want to know. Get going now!"

Shaking with anger and disappointment, Anton stalked away. He'd show the Merkles of this world one day, he thought, fighting back angry tears. The day would come when no one ran him off!

If anyone had asked Herrmann Gehringer what his favorite workday was, then—softly, of course, so the priest couldn't hear—he would have said Sunday, because on Sunday the looms were quiet, and that meant the entire mill was quiet, grounds and all.

He opened his office windows wide to let in the summer warmth. Then he took a deep breath, because on Sundays the air was clear: no dusty lint to tickle his nose, no exhaust fumes from the steam engines to make him cough.

While on regular workdays he liked the bustle and noise—all evidence of his successful business—Sundays were the one day each week he could catch up on everything it took to make his mill as productive as it was. Satisfied with himself and the world, he sat at his desk and began methodically to go through the mail and paperwork he'd put aside during the week.

There was a note from the architect in Ulm, who proposed that if it was all right with Gehringer, the glass pavilion could be assembled on the premises the following week. It was absolutely all right with him! In the coming weeks, several important customers would be arriving to look at the new winter collection. Now he'd be able to welcome them to his "glass palace." He still needed a model, though, and not just any model. For that he had to talk to Merkle again, urgently. It was preposterous for his assistant to be making such a fuss about his daughter's modeling. His beautiful Christel would *dress* for the customers, not undress.

Gehringer was writing his reply to the architect when he heard a key turn in the door to the outer office. A moment later, his assistant was standing in the doorway. Gehringer was at a loss: Had he called Merkle in for the day and forgotten he'd done so?

"I don't want to disturb you for long, and I'm off to the *Heumondfest* with the family soon, but you absolutely have to see this!" He slapped a large photograph onto the desk in front of Gehringer. "All she had to do was take a standard picture of the graduating class. What does she do instead? She twists the minds of an entire generation of our children! Just look at Christel. She thinks she's an actress!"

Herrmann Gehringer studied the photo, then let out a laugh. "That Mimi Reventlow is certainly one of a kind, isn't she?"

"Is that all you can say?" His pride wounded, Merkle took the photograph back. "I'm telling you, this woman is going to cause us more trouble than she's worth. I thought you were going to do something about her."

Gehringer raised his eyebrows. Since when did he have to justify himself to his assistant? Still, he said, "It would appear it's rather difficult to stop the woman. The ban on Sunday work doesn't seem to have caused her too much difficulty, because, one way or another, she still manages to get people into her studio during the week." He shrugged. "Maybe it's for the best to just ignore her. What does it matter to an oak tree if a dog pisses on it?" he said casually. But inside, he was seething—that woman waltzes in and dares to put ideas into people's heads . . .

"Easy for you to say," Merkle grumbled. "You don't have a daughter getting pigheaded because Mimi Reventlow is giving her notions."

What kind of tone was that to take? Gehringer thought. "As far as Christel is concerned, let me give you a word of advice," he said, raising his voice. "The fact that your daughter is pigheaded, as you put it, is your own fault. You simply have to ease back on the reins a little. A pretty young girl like her doesn't want to be a maid. She needs a little joy in her life, too." He pointed to the postcard from the Ulm architect. "Let Christel start working here as a model, and I'm telling you, you'll have peace in your house again before you know it. Give someone little freedoms and they won't think about the big ones."

"Maybe you're right. I'll think about it," Merkle growled. "But what if things go for me the way they have for Walter Braun and his boy, Fritz?"

"What do you mean? What's going on with them?" Gehringer furrowed his brow. Merkle was really starting to eat into his valuable time.

"You can forget about hiring Fritz—he's long gone. The boy's signed an apprentice contract with Meindl, the wagonmaker, and his parents seem to approve."

"What?" Gehringer thought he'd misheard. "We'd been planning on adding him to our team."

"Another thing: next week, Alexander Schubert is going to Stuttgart. If you ask me, you can say goodbye to your new designer, too. All because of Mimi Reventlow."

But Gehringer only laughed. "Alexander at the art school? The family could never afford it. Daydreams, all of it," he said, although he wasn't half as convinced as he tried to sound.

"I wouldn't be so sure," his assistant replied. "Mimi Reventlow isn't short on ideas."

Gehringer looked past his assistant and out the window for a moment. If not for Mimi Reventlow, he would have had a very nice storefront right on the square. Alexander Schubert would be starting with him as a designer, and Fritz Braun would probably never have even considered being anything but a weaver! If he thought about it more, then one hand would not be enough to count the number of times the photographer had interfered with his plans. It was time someone put a stop to her tricks. But as long as she was looking after her uncle, she was certainly not going to leave Laichingen. That, in turn, meant he had to find a way to somehow get her out of his way. If she no longer had an opportunity to stir up anyone against him, then as far as he was concerned, she could stay in Laichingen as long as she liked.

Gehringer smiled broadly, amused at his own train of thought. "Keep your friends close, but your enemies closer," he murmured.

"Pardon me?" Merkle looked at him in confusion. "I'm sorry, I don't understand what—"

Gehringer cut him off with a wave. "I'll take care of Mimi Reventlow myself. You do what you can about Alexander Schubert and Stuttgart. It's time someone knocked some sense into the boy. I *need* him for my mill!"

CHAPTER 20

Eveline glumly poked in her stove with an iron hook. She would have loved to make herself a cup of tea, but not a single ember still glowed: the fire had burned itself out. Like she had. And she had no interest in kindling a new fire, nor in anything else. What a terrible day, and what a terrible year. What a life . . .

Frustrated, she sat at the table again, where Alexander also sat with his sketch pad, and she picked up the nightshirt she was embroidering.

Normally, for *Heumondfest,* by now she would have washed her hair, conjured a decent coiffure, and taken out her best dress. Perhaps she would also have tied the blue silk ribbon around her slender waist—the same ribbon she had once brought with her from Chemnitz and which she now guarded like a treasure. She liked the way the ends fluttered in the breeze when she danced.

Normally, too, she would have cooked egg pancakes in the morning, spread them thinly with marmalade, rolled them up, and put them in a bowl to take to the celebration that evening. She'd have spread drippings on bread, too, in case someone wanted something more savory—at the *Heumondfest,* everyone took plenty of food along, even if it meant going without the week before.

And, normally, her heartbeat would have started quickening hours earlier, anticipating the campfires, the music . . . and, this year, rather than being in mourning, she would have liked to have been anticipating dancing with Johann.

Instead, she sat there in her blackest smock and jabbed her finger sore, while others got themselves ready for the best and brightest party of the year.

What had she done for life to punish her like this? she asked herself bitterly, and the bit of optimism she had so recently regained was gone.

At least the girls were taken care of, she thought as she heard laughter ringing from the chicken pen. Some chicks had hatched, and Erika and Marianne spent hours with the fluffy little creatures.

A loud banging on the door snapped Eveline out of her thoughts. "Are you expecting anyone?" she asked Alexander. Anton was all she needed tonight!

Alexander shook his head.

Reluctantly, Eveline went to the door.

"Working at night—how refreshing and invigorating!" said Paul Merkle, lugging a basket of cushion covers into the house. "I was in the area and thought I'd drop by and bring you some more work. Thirty decorative cushions . . . the ones with the seven-petaled rose at the top right."

"I'm not finished with the last basket yet. The embroidery on the nightshirts is too elaborate," Eve protested. Was she supposed to work magic now? What was the man thinking, turning up on a Sunday? He usually only came by on Mondays.

"I thought you'd be happy. Or don't you need the money anymore?" Paul Merkle said, feigning surprise. He turned to Alexander. "And while I'm here, I could pick up the apprenticeship contract. Mr. Gehringer needs it for the accounts." He gestured in Alexander's direction.

Eveline felt the panic rising in her son as if it were her own emotion.

"We're in mourning! We've got other things to think about than some contract," she said.

"And it's the difficulty of your situation that makes it all the more important for Alexander to sign with us. Or did Klaus leave you so well off that you can live from the inheritance?" He looked around the meager room with exaggerated slowness and then focused on Alexander. "I'll be back next week. If you want my advice, don't push Mr. Gehringer's patience too far, or you'll end up looking for work somewhere else. Which will certainly *not* be easy . . ." He looked meaningfully at Alexander's leg, propped on a chair.

Once Merkle had left, a silence descended for a long moment over mother and son.

Eveline had trouble hiding her furious tears from Alexander. Filled with hate, she stabbed her needle through the stiff linen, wishing it were Paul Merkle's hide instead.

"Where do you really come from? Who are you really?" Alexander asked.

She looked up in surprise. Her children knew that she didn't talk about her previous life. "Why are you asking? And why now?" she said, her voice brittle.

"Herrmann Gehringer, and Paul Merkle just now . . . you're a thousand times better and stronger than they are, and they both know it. They have no right to treat you like they do." Alexander's voice cracked with indignation.

For a moment, Eveline could only stare at her son. "Maybe you're right. Maybe it's really time you found out where I come from, who I am. You'll learn a little more about yourself, too." She put her embroidery aside. Gazing out the window, she began: "I grew up very differently than people here in the village. At least, I don't know anyone in Laichingen who gets their *Schwarzer Brei* fed to them with a gold spoon." She laughed. At first haltingly and then more readily, she told her son about the wealthy house of her birth and her carefree childhood, which had come to an end when she met his father.

Alexander listened, spellbound. "But if you had such a wonderful life, it makes me wonder even more how you put up with everything here." He swung one arm wide as if to take in the entire house.

Eveline, who followed his gesture with her eyes, suddenly had the sense of seeing everything through a magnifying glass. The faded, scratchy towels. The tiny piece of soap by the stone washbasin. The crumbling putty around the windows, through which spiders and other creatures found their way inside. All the poverty, all the misery.

"Why didn't you just go? You could have left this prison years ago."

"Prison? It might look like that to you, but it doesn't matter how much Merkle and Gehringer hound me—I've kept my freedom the whole time, inside, even today," Eveline said passionately. "And I've kept my wealth—that's you and your sisters—all these years," she said more gently.

Alexander chewed guiltily at his bottom lip.

But his question was not misplaced, not completely, Eveline thought. She'd felt the house to be a prison many times.

"Besides, what choice did I have? Where was I supposed to go? To my parents, I might as well be dead, and I have too much pride to ask them for help anyway," she said, more to herself than to Alexander. "Was I supposed to leave my children behind, or take you all with me? How would we have lived? I could never have put the three of you at the mercy of an uncertain future where we would probably all have ended up on the street. And there was your father, too. He wasn't always as . . . difficult as he was in the last few years. I loved him, once. Was I supposed to leave him alone?"

Alexander said nothing, and Eveline was grateful for that. She would have struggled to deal with any careless accusations. She took a deep breath and continued, "In time, I learned one thing: where you come from doesn't matter. What matters is making the best of your life here and now. And that's what I try to do, every day, for all of us."

Alexander took her hand. "Thank you for telling me. When it comes to inner freedom . . . I'll try to do the same as you. I'll try to make the best of whatever comes my way," he said with so much adult earnestness that Eveline felt as if her heart would burst with love for her wonderful, brave son.

"You can prove that next week," she said, smiling now. She took the small scissors she used for her embroidery and, beneath Alexander's dismayed gaze, began to open up the hem of her smock. Carefully, not wanting to damage the fabric any more than necessary, she pushed out the coins she'd sewn into the hem years before. The very last money she had put away.

"Here. For you. For the trip to Stuttgart."

Her son looked at her in disbelief. "You mean . . . I should . . . ?"

Eve nodded. "I've thought about it long and hard. The Gehringers and Merkles of this world can go to . . . well, they can take a running jump. You *will* take that examination, if it's the last thing I can do for you."

They were absolutely penniless now, and Eveline hoped she would not soon regret her grand gesture. Through the open window, the scent of smoke from the first campfires coming to life wafted in. She had put the girls to bed, but a little later had heard a soft whimper coming from their room. Since Klaus had died, Marianne had been plagued by nightmares. But before Eveline could even put aside her embroidery, Alexander had hobbled upstairs as quickly as he could to console his sister, leaving Eveline alone.

Another knock at the door made her jump. If that was Paul Merkle again—

She went to the door and threw it open.

"Johann?" She had to hold on to the doorjamb to steady herself. Here he was, now, when she was on the brink of despair. Fate, she thought. Just like his return to Laichingen.

"Mother baked a cake, and because you can't come to the *Heumondfest* this year, why not at least make a nice time of it at home?" Smiling broadly, he handed her a plate covered with wax paper.

"Thank you. Come in," she said, her voice quavering.

"How are you?" he asked when he was standing inside. "Are you getting by? Can I help you with anything? I wanted to stop in sooner, but . . ." He shrugged. "I didn't have the courage."

"What?" Eve was bewildered. "Now, of all—"

"Yes, even now," he interrupted her. "You're Klaus's widow, and your mourning year has just begun. I want to be mindful of that; anything else would be disrespectful."

What nonsense was this? Eveline put down the cake and threw herself into his arms. "Just hold me," she whispered, breathing in the mixture of soap and leather he emanated.

For a long moment, they stood in their embrace.

"I would so gladly do more for you," he whispered into her hair.

She could feel his arousal, and a tremble of pleasure ran through her. Oh God, she was still alive! Eveline closed her eyes, fighting back her rising tears, her relief.

"Do you want me to stay? The *Heumondfest* makes no difference to me."

Yes! cried everything inside her. The mere thought of spending the evening with Johann made her dizzy with happiness. But she pulled herself together—*As usual,* she thought bitterly. Forcing a smile, she freed herself from his embrace.

"Out of the question. There's so little to celebrate here in the village and the *Heumondfest* is sure to be wonderful. The children are here. Besides, if anyone found out you were spending the evening here, they'd cramp their tongues gossiping." She held her breath. If he said now that he didn't give a damn about the gossip, then she'd say to hell with her year of mourning, too. She'd cried enough tears, and she was more than ready for a new life.

But Johann nodded. "It's probably better this way. Mother is waiting for me to come and light our campfire," he said, and he seemed almost relieved. "I've invited the photographer to join us for the celebrations, and I almost forgot I have to pick her up." He smiled an embarrassed smile.

Eveline flinched as if she'd suffered an electric shock. "Mimi Reventlow?" she asked, her voice suddenly shrill.

He shrugged. "It was a spontaneous invitation."

Ah. So . . . what? Perhaps because Mimi was alone and very definitely not in mourning, he felt he had to take her, Eve thought angrily.

"Now don't look at me like that. Everyone knows the *Heumondfest* is just a party, that's all, and I can't change the way things are right now. We'll have our time by the campfire next year, I promise." He stroked her cheek tenderly, and then he was gone.

Night settled slowly. A full moon the color of rosewood peered through the window as Eveline checked on the children in their room. They were all sleeping now, even Alexander, but she was too worked up to think about bed. The music of violins drifted gently to her ear, no doubt from the gypsy band that came to the *Heumondfest* every year. The stringed instruments sounded at once nostalgic and alluring, like the songs of sirens.

What if she went to the fete for a few minutes, her face covered by a dark scarf so that no one recognized her? A little fresh air, a short walk . . . it would do her good. If she had to live shut away from everyone in her mourning year, then she could at least share a little in the joy of the others, if only as an onlooker. Maybe she would even catch a glimpse of Johann at his campfire?

CHAPTER 21

As the sun sank lower in the sky, numerous small campfires flared up across the meadow. The scent of freshly cut hay hung in the air and mingled with many other scents, creating a potent perfume. Sitting as close to Johann as she could without seeming improper, Mimi breathed in the motley blend. She smelled the yeasty aroma of twist bread as it baked over the fires, the salty odor of grilled trout, and the slightly musty tang of cider. But most of all, she smelled the potatoes that had been tossed into the fires to bake. Later, when they were cooked, Johann's mother explained, they would be eaten with cheese curds and herbs, or a pat of butter.

Close friends and families had gathered around every fire. They shared the various foods they had brought, and there was cider, wine, and beer. The warmth of the fires was met by that of the camaraderie.

Mimi waved to Luise, who watched over a fire a few yards away with her husband, Georg, and son-in-law, Paul, while the rowdy Merkle boys were off somewhere else. Luise told Mimi that Sonja had stayed home with the newborn.

At the edge of the meadow, Mimi saw Anton, Christel, Vincent, and several other young people at their own campfire. Their eyes gleamed in the firelight as they told stories and laughed. Even from where she sat, Mimi saw, now and then, an amorous glance exchanged across the fire.

Johann's mother seemed to find nothing unusual in Johann's inviting Mimi. "No one should be alone tonight. There's room at our fire for everyone. It's just a pity your uncle can't be here," said Edelgard, then introduced Mimi to the others around them: an elderly widow, who was one of Edelgard's neighbors; the Laichingen blacksmith; and a bachelor colleague of Johann's. Mimi shook hands with each of them.

"So what do you think of our celebration?" Johann asked as his mother held out a plate of fritters to Mimi.

Mimi selected a fritter as her gaze drifted across the meadow. "I thought there'd be one big campfire, but all the little fires are much nicer."

Edelgard laughed. "Just don't ask me where the tradition comes from. As long as I can remember, we've celebrated the end of the hay harvest this way."

"It probably comes from every man here wanting to prove that his fire is the best and burns the longest," said Johann, laughing.

Mimi laughed with him, their strangely fraught conversation from the morning forgotten. She had clipped his little forget-me-not bouquet artfully into her pinned-up hair. She felt more beautiful, carefree, and happy than she had in a long time. She tried to be inconspicuous as she wriggled closer to Johann, whose right hand, as if by accident, brushed against her thigh. An electric vibration ran through her.

"Look, the musicians are here!" Edelgard Merkle pointed to a wagon pulled by two skittish horses at the edge of the meadow. A group of men jumped out of the wagon. Each of them had deep-black hair, sparkling eyes, and glowing light-brown skin. Their red satin vests put the red embers in the campfires to shame as the men unpacked a violin, a double bass, a viola, and a clarinet.

"The musicians travel all around the empire to earn their living, and they come here every year for *Heumondfest*," said Johann. "Their leader's name is Zoltan. He once told me they played the traditional czardas folk music for the Hungarian royal family." He jumped to his feet and grabbed two bottles of cider. "I'm going to say hello to Zoltan."

"I'll go back and check on Uncle Josef," Mimi said as she stood up.

"Don't be long," Johann said, smiling at her. "We'll dance the first dance together!"

Mimi smiled, too, then she turned and started walking back toward the village.

Uncle Josef was awake when Mimi arrived home. He was sitting on the sofa with a couple of photography magazines, and the walker Fritz made beside him. He could get around the house with it now.

"Having a good time?" he asked in a frail voice.

Mimi nodded. "All that's missing is you." She went to the sideboard and took out a bottle of plum schnapps and two small glasses. "Let's at least share a drink, all right?"

A weak smile flashed on Josef's face.

The spirits ran down Mimi's throat with a delicious warmth, but sharing the drink left a sad feeling behind. Mimi knew they wouldn't have this opportunity much longer. Josef's eyes were weary, almost transparent. His once powerful radiance had been all but consumed by his persistent cough. It broke Mimi's heart to see his thin body racked by a fit of coughing and to see his handkerchief flecked with spots of blood. Every few weeks, Luise brought an herbal tincture made by a woman she knew, but nothing really helped.

As if he could read her mind, he laid a hand on her arm. "Go, child. Go back to the party. You can't do anything here."

Mimi, close to tears, wrapped her scarf around her neck. Shouldn't she stay with him? She hesitated another moment, but her longing to be near Johann won out. She would make her uncle the best breakfast she could in the morning.

When she got back to the meadow a few minutes later, she was astonished to see most of the fires abandoned, with just one person at each to keep them burning. Everyone else was on the improvised dance floor in the center of the newly mown meadow. Mimi saw Luise and her husband swirling around, as well as Anton's parents and the Meindls. Old and young, adults and children—in the moonlight, everyone was dancing to the wild czardas sounds.

Mimi felt a knot form in her throat. So much life, so much pulsing energy! If she could give Josef the smallest part of it . . .

The next moment, she felt two hands on the back of her shoulders.

"You finally made it back! Come on!"

"But I don't know your dances at all," she protested as Johann pulled her onto the dance floor.

He laughed as his right arm circled her back and his left hand held her right hand firmly. At first hesitantly, then more and more surely, Mimi let the music carry her away. The sound of the instruments, Johann's strong arms, even the smoke from the campfires stinging her eyes—all of it combined to pull Mimi out of her gloomy state of mind. Life was to live, here and now. Her feet flew over the meadow grass as if it were the finest, smoothest parquetry.

Viennese waltzes, Hungarian folk songs, Spanish dance music—the musicians' repertoire seemed to be inexhaustible, and their music stirring. Mimi could not remember ever dancing as much! Her feet burned, sweat ran down the back of her neck, but she didn't care about any of it. She also could not remember when she had ever felt so womanly—as if her entire body was warm, soft, and supple. And with Johann so close . . .

"I need a break," she said, when the band began to play a quieter piece. Smiling, she wiped the sweaty curls from Johann's forehead.

"I agree," he said. Not letting go of her hand, he led her away from the dance area. "Hold on," he said when they reached the edge of the meadow, and he ran back toward their campfire. When he returned, he carried one of the bottles of wine that Mimi had contributed to the party, and tucked under his left arm was a rolled-up blanket. "We haven't had a chance to talk just the two of us all evening. Let's walk awhile and find somewhere quieter."

Neither Johann nor Mimi noticed, here and there, the eyes curiously following them. Nor did they notice a woman, her face covered by a scarf, watching them depart with hostile eyes.

When Mimi awoke, she lay with her eyes closed trying to remember where she was. Her carefully arranged hair had long since come loose, and a hairpin was jabbing her head, which throbbed at the slightest movement. Her hair draped her shoulders and breasts like a veil, and her clothes reeked so strongly of smoke that she screwed up her nose. Everything around her was quiet—she could not even hear any birds twittering. No one calling out in neighboring houses, no milk cans being placed noisily in front of doors, no coughing from Josef. Nothing moved. Where was she?

She opened her eyes and felt a wash of love surge through her. Johann lay beside her, sleeping blissfully.

They had left hand in hand. Johann knew a cave—no more than a hollow on the edge of a rise, really—and had led her there in the pale shimmer of the full-moon night. The smell of the fires and the music had accompanied them, but at some point all that was left to smell was the wild honeysuckle, and the music was replaced by the chirping of field crickets.

The ground inside the hollow was warm, dusty, and dry. Johann had spread the blanket out for them, then opened the bottle of wine and handed it to Mimi. She had hesitated for a second—she had never drunk out of a bottle—then took a large mouthful. The red wine tasted sweet and seductive. And yes, she was ready to let herself be seduced . . . but things had not gone that far.

Propped on one elbow, Mimi looked out into the valley as the first light of dawn appeared. It was early, maybe four o'clock? Half past? What a wonderful light for taking pictures!

The throbbing in her head grew stronger, and she struggled to remember the previous evening. They had talked for a long time—not only about Laichingen but about everything under the sun. They passed the wine bottle back and forth, and before long the alcohol had led them down more and more audacious mental paths: to a workers' revolution, and to the day, one day, when there would be justice for all. They had felt so close, like allies against the rest of the world. But somewhere along the way, their thoughts started moving in circles, and when Mimi once again raised the bottle to her lips, she found it empty. Exhausted, she had leaned against Johann, had wished for him to kiss her and take her in his arms. His gentle snoring, however, had put an end to her wishes. Then, it seemed, she, too, had fallen asleep.

Her handsome weaver . . . Tenderness coursed through her veins, and she wanted nothing more than to make up for all the kisses they had not shared during the night. The boldness of her own thoughts shocked her—she had not even been aware that she longed so deeply for that kind of intimacy.

She hadn't wanted to fall in love. Being free, not having to justify herself to anyone—in the past those things had mattered more than anything else. But it was like they said: you make your plans, and God laughs. Was Johann the man for her, for life? The two of them in Laichingen was more than coincidence. And there were certainly worse places to make your home, especially now that—

Johann suddenly moving beside her snapped her back to the present.

"Mimi . . ." He blinked. "What . . . ?" His gaze wandered around the hollow and stopped when it came to the empty wine bottle. "Oh God, don't tell me I fell asleep last night."

"I won't tell you that, but it seems *I* did." She leaned across, closer to him, with a smile. Her lips were only a few inches from his, and soon, soon he would kiss her—what the night had not given them, the morning certainly could.

Instead Johann sucked air in through his teeth and sat up.

"What's the matter?" she asked, startled.

"I feel like I've been harpooned." He pulled back the blanket and patted the dusty ground where he'd been lying, then held up a pointed stone.

"Ouch. Come here. Let me massage that a little." She reached out for him, but he struggled to his feet with a grimace.

"Thank you for the offer, but I have to go. Today's a work day at the mill like any other," he said. "You should stay here awhile. I don't like to think what people will presume if they see us together in this state."

"And yet we were so well behaved," she said and laughed. *Too well behaved,* she thought to herself.

A fleeting kiss and he was gone, striding away.

He's probably right, Mimi thought. She did her best to fashion her disarrayed hair into a braid, then, about fifteen minutes later, she crept off toward home. As disheveled as she looked, she didn't like the idea of bumping into anyone, and certainly not arm in arm with Johann. No one would ever believe they had only fallen asleep.

Uncle Josef was still sleeping, Mimi was relieved to see. After washing up and fixing her hair properly, she went to the kitchen to light the fire. Then she sat at the table with the coffee mill and ground a generous dose of beans. Today she would treat them both to a pot of strong coffee. And she'd go to Helene's store and buy some herring. She'd learned from Luise that, as with the Pentecost market, Helene traditionally opened a barrel the day after the *Heumondfest.* A fat fish would help fight the hangover some inevitably took home with them, her neighbor had said with a smirk. Mimi hoped a herring would relieve the pounding in her own head. If it didn't, then at least Uncle Josef would enjoy the fish. She grabbed her purse and set off for Helene's store.

CHAPTER 22

"Did you see how the photographer was making eyes at Johann Merkle? And how they danced, so close I blushed just looking at them!" A wife of one of the weavers shook her head.

"She's got him wrapped around her finger. And did you see? She ran off with him at the end of the night, too. I don't want to know what they got up to," said another woman indignantly.

"A roll in the hay, what else?" a third woman chimed in.

Eveline, who had just joined the end of the line inside Helene's shop, froze. The evening before, she'd tried to talk herself into believing that Mimi and Johann's dancing together had been harmless, although she had all but exploded with jealousy.

"I don't know why you're all getting so worked up," said Helene, scooping sauerkraut out of a barrel behind the counter. "The *Heumondfest* is a party, and Johann and the photographer are adults. It's no one's business who someone spends the night with."

No one's business? Helene was wrong about that, and Eveline wanted to tell her so. She and Johann were destined for one another and always had been. He knew it, she knew it, but the others in the shop hadn't the slightest idea.

"You're putting two and two together and coming up with five!" said Edelgard Merkle, who'd come in behind Eveline and also heard the last part of the exchange. "Sorry to disappoint you, but Johann slept in his bed last night." She looked around defiantly. "He escorted the photographer home, which proves only that he's a right-minded man. Your unsavory thoughts, however, show just the opposite about yourselves."

Absolutely! thought Eveline. The idea that Mimi and Johann might have fallen for each other almost drove her out of her mind.

"If that's the way it was . . . ," said one of the women.

"Escorted her home? That's all? Edelgard, you don't believe that," said the second woman with a sneer.

"Did you all just come here to gossip?" Helene said sharply. "Whose order is next?"

"The photographer's probably in bed with Johann right now, and Edelgard just hasn't noticed," whispered Franka Klein to Eveline.

Aside from a strained nod, Eveline did not reply. She clenched her hands into fists. Had Mimi Reventlow really latched on to Johann? The stab Eve felt in her heart served her right for being so trusting.

Just then, she heard a cheerful "good morning" behind her. "I heard Helene was opening a barrel of herring today?" With a rosy complexion and her usual immaculate appearance, Mimi Reventlow took her place behind Edelgard and Eveline in the line.

The women who had just been gossiping about Mimi responded to her greeting with either feigned friendliness or reserve. *Isn't she just the picture of innocence,* Eveline thought.

"Eve, it's lovely to see you," Mimi said. "The exam in Stuttgart is next week. How does it look? Will Alexander be able to take part?"

As warmhearted as ever, like nothing has happened at all. "What Alexander takes part in and what he doesn't is none of your business," Eveline replied harshly, and loud enough for everyone in the shop to hear. "I'd be grateful if you'd keep out of our lives. As Alexander's mother, I'm the one who makes decisions regarding my son, and by God, I don't need any out-of-towner to help me do so." She saw with satisfaction how Mimi recoiled, as if she'd been slapped in the face. *Serves you right,* Eveline thought.

"But . . . I thought . . . ," Mimi stammered.

Eveline let out a shrill laugh. "You thought! You, you, and you again. You think you see everything oh-so-clearly through your lens, but the truth is you only see what you want to see. You don't give a damn about us," she spat at Mimi, while the other women watched the one-sided exchange of blows both mesmerized and baffled. *What's gotten into Eveline?* they seemed to be wondering.

Wouldn't you like to know! Eveline thought grimly. Mimi said nothing, and Eve decided, now that she had a good head of steam, to press her advantage. "You come here putting ideas into people's heads and stirring everything up. But just because you *believe* we lead a miserable life doesn't even begin to make it true. Yes, there are hard times, but there are good times, too. And it's the good times we live for, right?" Eve glared at the women around her, who nodded and murmured assent.

Mimi looked at Eveline as if seeing her for the first time. "Why are you attacking me like this?" she asked in disbelief. "I never once said everything here was bad. If I've given anybody that impression, I'm truly sorry. I—" The photographer was suddenly close to tears, and her voice failed her.

Eve herself had been close to tears the night before when she'd watched Mimi and Johann dance.

"And there's another thing," Eve said, starting in again. "In the past, your uncle always gave our men a top hat to wear for pictures, and women could pick out a dusty crinoline dress from his collection. Now you come along and put our children in some incomprehensible make-believe scene and think you're being so very, very modern. You want to show the 'nature' of people, the things they carry deep inside," she mocked. Her eyes were filled with contempt as she continued. "And yet you're not one bit better than your uncle. You stick us in front of your camera like dressed-up monkeys. You're not interested at all in who we really are!"

Mimi, stunned speechless, turned on her heel and walked out.

Anton chose the nearest table and set down the tray of beer glasses that he'd been carrying to the mill owners' table. If he didn't get some fresh air this instant, he'd throw up! And it had nothing to do with the cider he'd drunk with his friends at the *Heumondfest* the night before.

Traditionally, while the weavers were hard at work despite the late-night festivities, the mill owners met at The Oxen the day after the *Heumondfest* to dine on *Kutteln*. While they shoveled down the cooked tripe with gusto, business was done, agreements settled, information passed back and forth. Anton detested the smell and taste of the boiled entrails so much that all he ever ate on that day was bread and butter.

As he filled his lungs with fresh air, he saw the door to Helene's store fly open, and the next moment, Mimi Reventlow ran past as if the devil were on her trail.

Anton hesitated for only a moment, then went off after her across the square. "Hey! What's the matter?" he called after her, but Mimi stormed ahead.

She only stopped and turned to face him when she reached her uncle's house. She'd been crying. The look in her eyes was strangely wary, as if she was wondering whether she could trust him.

Anton blinked in confusion. "Is everything all right, Miss Reventlow?" he tried again. "It's me, Anton," he added, feeling rather foolish as he said it.

She shrugged, then told him about her encounter with Eveline in Helene's store. "I really don't know what got into her. I only tried to help," she said when she was done.

Anton thought he must have misheard. "If Mrs. Schubert even tries to stop Alexander from going to Stuttgart for that test . . . Well, he'll get there if I have to carry him on my back. I've already gotten together the money for the trip," he said grimly, and clenched his jaw to stop himself from saying anything truly harsh. For Mimi's sake—she looked as if she were about to start crying again—he pulled himself together.

"You know what? Why don't you come to Stuttgart?" he said as brightly as he could manage. "You have to get out of this town sometimes. You've seen for yourself what happens if you spend all your time here," he added, trying to keep the lighter tone in his voice. "Christel's going to come, too. I don't know who to thank for that miracle, but her father actually gave her permission to come with Alexander and me."

"I'm happy for you," said Mimi, her face brightening briefly. She thought for a moment. "Maybe you're right. A change of scenery would do me good. I could ask Luise if she would keep an eye on Josef for the day."

"Do that." He reached out and squeezed her arm encouragingly. He'd had a pretty good idea there, he thought—plus, if the photographer stayed at the art school to keep her fingers crossed for Alexander, he and Christel could go to the movie theater in Stuttgart with a clear conscience.

The herring were already sold out, Mimi said curtly after wiping the tears from her cheeks in the bathroom. Josef nodded in silence. He seemed to sense that something had happened, but he didn't ask any questions. She wished he would, though. In the past, she'd always been able to share whatever was weighing on her with Josef. He was her confidant and guide in so many things. And while his mind was still clear enough, his eyes told her that he was too weary to carry the burdens of others. *And what is he supposed to tell me?* she thought sadly, refilling his cup with tea. *"Keep your nose out of it, child!"*—she had his words firmly planted in her ear.

The day went on, and Mimi's dismal mood did not improve. No matter how much the thoughts tumbled in her mind, she simply could not understand why Eveline had attacked her. If only she could have gone and cried her heart out to Johann. But he was at his loom, just as he was every day.

It was already past eight in the evening, and Mimi was watering her vegetable garden when Johann came by. As usual, he looked left, right, and behind to assure himself that no neighbors were watching.

Why all the playacting? she wanted to ask, but her annoyance was smothered by her weepy frame of mind. Instead, she put her arms around him and held on.

"Mimi, I'm sorry," he said. "My mother told me what happened at Helene's this morning."

Mimi sank. Did Johann really have to find out about it at all? "It wasn't as bad as it looked. Eveline probably just got up on the wrong side of the bed," she said, trying to salvage something.

"Not as bad as it looked? My mother said the whole shop was gossiping about us. If she hadn't shown up and told them I'd slept alone at home even though she knows I got home at first light, your reputation would be in tatters now and forever!"

"Who cares? I'm starting to think people will say what they damn well like." *Always the same old song . . .*

Johann patted her arm. "Don't get so upset. It's not worth it. You and I know nothing happened."

Unfortunately, Mimi thought. If it had, then at least the gossip would have been worth it.

"But I should never have fallen asleep like I did. Mother let me have it. She says if you can't handle wine, you shouldn't drink it, and she's right."

Mimi had to laugh. "It's funny, isn't it? The whole situation, I mean. Everybody thinks the worst, when, really, we were so well behaved. Last night, at least . . ." She ran her fingers over his cheek in a gesture she hoped was seductive.

Instead of picking up on her playful tone, Johann looked at her intently. "Mimi, just so we both know where we stand: I like you very much. I've never met a woman quite like you, and I admire your self-reliance and independence. I feel damn good around you, and you know it. I believe we could achieve great things together. But I can't make any promises to you. I don't even know how much longer I'm going to stay in Laichingen. I'm a union man! Once a labor dispute has succeeded in one place, my bosses move me to wherever I'm needed next."

He really is a man of honor, thought Mimi. "None of us can see into the future," she said lightly. "I know you have to stay focused on the situation here in Laichingen, for now. But we'll be able to find some time for us, won't we?"

Sometimes, when she lay in bed and let her mind wander, she pictured Johann and herself sitting down to dinner, united in marriage. Years ago when Heinrich had proposed to her, and again when the man in the Palatinate had mentioned marriage, the thought had felt completely alien. She could not marry without love. But these days, sometimes, she pictured herself standing at the altar in a wedding dress.

"Don't try to pin me down, please. I have enough people putting pressure on me already," Johann said. Then, more gently, he said, "But maybe I'll think of some way we can meet without half the village finding out. In the meantime, let's move slowly, all right?"

"Move slowly?" What does that mean? Mimi wondered when he was gone. Were they supposed to go for walks more slowly? Kiss more slowly? Formulate their words more slowly when they talked? She should have asked him before he left, she thought cynically. But what Johann might really have meant . . . she didn't dare even think about it.

CHAPTER 23

On the last Wednesday in July, four people with eager hearts set off from Laichingen for Stuttgart.

Alexander could barely speak, he was so excited. Today was the day of days for him. Today he would find out if he really had talent or not. What form would the examination take? Would they plunk something in front of him and tell him to reproduce it exactly? A vase? He could do that. Perhaps something figurative, too? But what if they asked him to draw a person? He'd tried that, but had never been satisfied with the results. He was so preoccupied with these questions that whenever one of his traveling companions spoke to him, he responded only with a nod or a shake of his head. The others tried—in vain—to calm him down, cheer him up, and bolster his courage. After a while they gave up and accepted his sitting there, looking at them with a vacant gaze.

Anton's and Christel's eager hearts had enough to do with being smitten and with the anticipation of a lovely day away from home and in the city. They held hands, and Mimi and Alexander acted as if they didn't notice.

Mimi, likewise, could hardly wait to get out of Laichingen for a day. After Eveline's extraordinary attack on her, the village had lost its charm. Johann, too, had obviously meant what he'd said about taking things slowly. Since the *Heumondfest* a week and a half ago, they had only seen each other twice—much to Mimi's disappointment. She wondered if she was asking too much, or if this kind of behavior was completely normal.

But the trip meant more to her than just a change of scenery. She was traveling to Stuttgart with an idea she thought showed a lot of promise, and she wanted to take it to several photo studios there. Luise had promised to spend most of the day with Josef, so Mimi did not have to worry about him.

"How are your mother and your baby sister?" Mimi asked Christel. "Does the little one have a name yet?"

Christel shook her head. "Not yet. It's like this after every birth. Mother lies in bed and cries her eyes out. Guess who ends up doing all the housework," she said resentfully.

Bright and bubbly Sonja, crying her eyes out? Why? Mimi frowned. "I'll pay your mother a visit very soon," she promised. "Maybe I can cheer her up a little." Mimi decided she would buy something nice for mother and child in Stuttgart.

Christel shrugged as if it made no difference to her, and the conversation dwindled to silence.

When they arrived at the train station in Stuttgart, they agreed on what time they would meet for the trip home, then went their separate ways. Anton and Christel headed off to a movie theater on Calwer Strasse that a customer recently had told Anton about, and Mimi went with Alexander to the art school, which was housed in a classical sandstone building close to the New Palace. It was a long way for him to go on crutches, and his forehead glistened with sweat by the time they arrived. Mimi held open the large door, which was decorated with a colorful crown-glass panel, as Alexander maneuvered himself inside.

They walked into the smell of oil paint and turpentine, and Mimi saw by the way Alexander lifted his head and sniffed that he noticed it, too. A woman in a dark-blue outfit approached them and introduced herself as the director's secretary. The examination would take place on the second floor, she explained. Other than Alexander, there was another young man taking the test—he'd been visiting Monaco with his parents, the Count and Countess von Auerwald, at the time of the original test. It was summer vacation now, the woman went on, so the building was practically deserted.

The family of a count. Sojourns in Monaco. The entrance with its impressive glasswork. Mimi's eyes turned to Alexander's too-short trousers and straw shoes. If his mother had said so much as a word, or if she had thought of it herself, Mimi would have loaned Alexander a pair of Uncle Josef's shoes, she thought, both annoyed and saddened. She and Eveline still hadn't spoken, so Mimi did not know what had gotten her so upset. Her stomach suddenly tightened, as if she herself now had to take the exam.

"You're sure you'll manage by yourself from here?" she asked Alexander quietly. Though she wasn't quite sure how he would do it, Alexander had insisted earlier that he would find his own way back to the station after the test.

Alexander, whose nostrils were twitching like those of a horse about to bolt, nodded. He was so pale that Mimi thought he might faint.

Still she hovered, uncertain what to do. She had her own business to take care of, but could she really leave Alexander alone?

As if reading her mind, the secretary said, "The examination is scheduled for three hours, and the professors will confer for an hour after that, so you have plenty of time to take care of other things. Otherwise, there is a marvelous café around the corner . . ." Friendly but firm, she pointed the way out.

Mimi had already turned to leave, but in a spontaneous gesture she came back and embraced Alexander warmly. "Good luck!" she whispered in his ear. "We're all very proud of you, whatever happens."

"I fail to understand why Maximilian even has to take this examination. In his letter, Dottore Viante in Genoa wrote glowingly about our son's outstanding talent," Alexander heard a woman proclaim as he painfully made his way up the last steps to the second floor. "You seem to forget with whom you are dealing. The von Auerwalds are not used to being tested by anyone."

"That may be," came a sonorous male voice in reply. "For us, however, it is important to know our students' abilities before they start with us. Dear lady, please, if I could ask you to leave? We will be starting soon."

Alexander stopped on the last step. He could still turn around and leave . . .

"Well, here we are." The director's secretary smiled at him encouragingly, then knocked on the door to Alexander's right, which was slightly ajar. Without waiting for a response, she pushed the door open. "In you go. They're waiting for you."

The next moment, the edge of an umbrella the size of a wagon wheel caught Alexander on the chin, and he almost lost his balance. A woman in a voluminous, billowing cream-colored lace dress was standing so close in front of him that he could not only see the powder caked on her face but smell it, too. Instead of apologizing, the woman only looked him up and down with a withering gaze, then turned back to the room.

"And how long is this circus going to take? We have a dinner to attend," she said, without letting Alexander past her into the room.

"The sooner we begin, the sooner we'll be finished. And I see our second candidate has also arrived," replied one of the three men sitting behind a large table. All three—plus the young man already in the room, his hair parted stiffly on the side—assessed Alexander, their expressions a mix of interested curiosity and slight disdain.

Alexander wanted to die on the spot.

The lovely shops, the magnificent wrought-iron streetlamps from which hung baskets filled with flowers in full bloom, the advertising pillars with all their beguiling offers—Anton couldn't really absorb it all. He and Christel walked along hand in hand.

They're all looking, he thought. They turned their heads, as if they wanted to burn into their minds Christel's creamy skin, her gold-blond hair, her high forehead. Some even stopped in their tracks and gazed at her with open mouths.

Of course he knew that Christel was beautiful. She was the prettiest woman in all Laichingen! But it had never occurred to him that she would be the most beautiful woman in Stuttgart, too, or that her beauty might provoke such a reaction from the people they passed. They were reacting to Christel like . . . Anton had nothing to compare it with.

Christel also seemed to have noticed the attention she was causing. "Why are they all staring at me like that?" she asked, half-amused, half-uncertain.

"Because you're so beautiful," Anton said.

"Do you really think so?" She straightened her shoulders and let out a ringing laugh that caught the attention of two gentlemen just then stepping out of a tobacconist's. Both automatically lifted their top hats in greeting, as if they thought Christel might be one of the stars of the Stuttgart State Theater.

Anton stopped in his tracks. He blinked as if he could not believe how blind and stupid he'd been.

All this time, he'd believed that Mimi Reventlow was his and Christel's ticket to the future—thus his plan to leave with her when she departed Laichingen. Suddenly, though, on the streets of Stuttgart, he had a revelation: his future did not depend on Mimi Reventlow but rather on Christel's allure, and he was sure there was at least one way to cultivate that. The photographer might still be useful to them, but now he saw the alternative he'd had all along.

"What is it?" Christel looked at him in surprise. "Have we gone the wrong way?"

"Oh, no," he murmured as the theater came into view. He proudly swung one arm around Christel, claiming her for himself. "We're just where we need to be."

"I'm sorry, but there's not much interest in postcards of the Swabian Jura here in Stuttgart." The photographer, an elegantly dressed gentleman, handed the Laichingen postcards back to Mimi with regret. His studio was situated very close to the art school, which Mimi had taken as a good sign.

"But Laichingen is famous for its linenware. It's in the trousseau of every bride," Mimi said.

"Yes, certainly." The photographer smiled. "Maybe you could try a shop where they sell linens for trousseaus?"

Mimi frowned. Who would look for postcards there?

She found a second studio within ten minutes of leaving the first. But there, too, she was out of luck.

"Right now, the vogue is for postcards showing our beloved Grand Duchess Vera," the photographer explained. "Postcards with King Wilhelm and his Pomeranians are also popular. You don't happen to have any like that?"

Mimi did not. "The Swabian Jura is very beautiful. Your customers might be inspired by the postcards to go on a little outing there themselves," she said, trying again.

The man laughed. "An outing? To that barren place? You know what they say about the Jura: half the year it's winter and the other half it's cold! Believe me, it's a happy soul who *doesn't* have to go there." The man narrowed his eyes a little. "Didn't we meet at Linhof's in Munich? At the start of the year, the camera maker's show? You're Mimi Reventlow, aren't you?"

Mimi smiled at her fellow photographer from the other side of the counter. "Yes, that's me. And I remember you now, too. You also bought a Linhof, if I remember correctly."

The man nodded, and they chatted brightly about the merits of the Linhof cameras before coming back to Mimi's question.

"I'm afraid I can't use your postcards, Miss Reventlow. But if you'd like to work as a guest photographer in my studio for a week or two, well, we can certainly talk about that."

"It's very nice of you to offer," Mimi replied. Crestfallen, she put her "Laichingen Views" back in her bag. "But I'm afraid I can't take an engagement like that at the moment. Family reasons."

As she sat, a little later, in the sun at a café and enjoyed the spectacle of the New Palace, she hoped that Alexander had been more successful in his exam than she had been with her postcards. The picture-perfect view she had from where she sat was no doubt a popular choice among Stuttgart's citizens and visitors. Or a picture of the wrought-iron pavilion in front of the palace, or of the imposing Königsbau building on the main square . . . Stuttgart was a treasure trove of photographic motifs! And she, like an idiot, thought she'd be able to impress studios here with the picturesque *Hüle* in Laichingen, the village pond complete with the swans she'd added. She laughed at her own foolishness.

It looked as if she and Uncle Josef would be living a hand-to-mouth existence after all, she thought, sipping her coffee. It tasted thin. Apart from the wedding photos for Luise's daughter Berta and perhaps a christening picture or two for the Merkle family, Mimi had no idea what work she might be able to find. Now that the hay harvest was behind them, the Laichingers were looking ahead to planting the grain, and after that to harvesting the potatoes, turnips, and cabbages—who would find the time to come to her studio with all that going on? She did still have a little savings put away for the long term, but she wanted to leave that where it was. That meant making every pfennig count, maybe even twice over, she thought. And she'd have to do a better job of looking after her vegetable garden, too, if she wanted to fill their pantry. Just the week before, a horse pulling a cart had left a pile of its droppings directly in front of Josef's house. Just as she'd been wondering if she ought to get a shovel and put the coveted fertilizer on her vegetable patch, Josef called for her. When she was finally able to turn her thoughts back to the free fertilizer and went outside to shovel it up, someone else had beaten her to it. She'd probably never be very good at running the house and garden, she thought, annoyed at herself.

Suddenly, Mimi felt lost and alone. It would be so good to have someone with whom she could share her woes. But it wasn't Johann "Let's Move Slowly" Merkle who appeared in her mind's eye in that moment. It was her mother, Amelie. They hadn't seen each other since the previous Christmas. Why hadn't she written her mother to tell her she was going to be in Stuttgart? Esslingen to Stuttgart wasn't far. A bit of time together, a chat over coffee and cake—it would have done Mimi good to pour out her heart a little to her mother.

She watched the waiter deliver two pieces of cake to the next table.

"Anything else for you?" the man asked—he must have noticed her yearning gaze.

Mimi, who still wanted to find something for Sonja Merkle, shook her head. She didn't want to strain her purse too much, even though her stomach grumbled.

CHAPTER 24

The examination committee consisted of the school director, Wilhelm Hahnenkamm; the senior art teacher, Gottlob Steinbeiss, who led the proceedings; and another teacher introduced by Steinbeiss only as Mylo, who was one of the most famous architects in the empire and a lecturer at the art school.

Once Alexander and Maximilian von Auerwald had taken their seats at two spacious worktables, Gottlob Steinbeiss addressed them.

"Welcome to the Stuttgart Art School. Before we begin, I'd like to say a few words. While the National Academy of Art devotes itself to a broad range of the visual arts—sculpture, architecture, copper engraving, and many other fields—we at the Stuttgart Art School have chosen to specialize in painting and drawing. Our students learn all the classical techniques, of course: in art, as in any field of endeavor, a solid grasp of fundamentals is the basis of all worthwhile creation. But beyond that, we see ourselves as an artistic 'forge of the modern'—our primary concern is with artistic expression that allows a variety of interpretations."

Steinbeiss's expression had turned almost rapturous, and Alexander could see that the man would gladly have talked longer about that point. But the senior art teacher pulled himself together and continued in a more sober tone. "The examination in which you gentlemen are taking part is therefore divided into the following three sections . . ."

Alexander gulped. Never in his life had he been called a "gentleman." But instead of feeling more grown up, he felt more insecure than ever.

"In your first task, you will demonstrate your abilities to work with perspective, light and shadow, a sense of spatial orientation—these are some of the aspects we will be looking at."

Alexander, who hardly dared to breathe for fear of missing a word, nodded imperceptibly. Those were things that Josef Stöckle had often talked about before he fell ill.

"In your second task, we would like to get a better sense of your feeling for color. I assume you have both already worked with watercolors and oils?"

Maximilian von Auerwald gave a bored nod.

"And you?" the senior teacher asked Alexander directly when he did not respond.

"No," Alexander whispered. "Never."

"Then it might be best to use watercolors," said Steinbeiss, and made a note on a sheet of paper in front of him.

Alexander had heard of oil paints and watercolors, of course, but other than the nubs of pencils lying around at home and the pens and inks that Josef Stöckle had sometimes given him to draw with, he'd never had anything else to work with. So it was with all the more reverence that he surreptitiously eyed the materials set up in neat rows on the worktable in front of him. A clay pot that held several brushes of different sizes and thicknesses. A few rags. A jar of water. A small bottle of some clear liquid, sealed with a screw-on lid: "Spirit of Turpentine" read the label. An open wooden box with a dozen tubes inside. "Finest Oil Paints" it said on the inside of the lid, and below that the names of the individual tubes: "Carmine Red," "Cobalt Blue," "Indian Yellow," "Sienna," Alexander read, and felt a slight tremor run through him. Beside the oil paints stood a smaller box, this one made of metal and containing tiny pots of watercolors. A box of inks and various ink pens were also at the ready. Alexander had to resist the urge to pinch himself.

Was he dreaming, or were there really so many different paints in one place? What a treasure! And they all looked so beautiful . . . Would he dare to touch even one of the tubes or pots, let alone paint with them?

Steinbeiss's voice jolted Alexander out of his thoughts.

"Your final task, like your first, involves spatial thinking. At the same time, we will also be looking at how well you are able to adapt to new and unexpected situations, as an artist often encounters in his day-to-day work." The three men exchanged a knowing smile.

"New and unexpected situations"? Alexander raised his eyebrows slightly. Sometimes he felt as if his life consisted of nothing else. What was in the bowl covered by a wet cloth that stood beside the paints? he wondered.

"Alexander, you have applied for a scholarship," Steinbeiss went on.

Alexander felt more than saw Maximilian von Auerwald's snide sideways glance.

"The money for the scholarship comes from a fund established by the royal family, and only one such scholarship is awarded each year. This means that very few young people are the beneficiaries of such an honor—so do your best!" Steinbeiss said with a final nod.

Alexander felt his blood run hot and cold at the same time. Only one scholarship? Somehow, he'd thought that there must be several. And the royal family would pay for it. Why should he of all people have the honor of winning something like that? What was he even thinking, coming here?

"I'd like to hand this over to Mylo now. He will guide you through the examination."

Strange. Why didn't the senior teacher say "Mr. Mylo" or "Professor Mylo"? Alexander wondered. While he didn't actually know what a real artist looked like, he had a vague picture in his head, and Mylo wasn't far from that. He wore black trousers and polished black leather shoes. His white shirt hung loosely on his thin body, and instead of a tie he wore a lightweight red scarf tied around his neck. Unlike the other two gentlemen, who both sported handlebar mustaches, Mylo was clean shaven. His gray eyes sparkled, alert, as if registering every detail of what he saw, no matter how small.

Gracefully, Mylo stood and picked up two canvases and two watercolor pads from a side table and gave one of each to both boys.

"For your first task, I would like you to look out the window, either literally"—Mylo, with a supple motion of his hand, pointed toward the large windows—"or figuratively. You may use oil or watercolor, canvas or the paper in the sketch pad. That is entirely up to you, but think about what kind of paint might better reproduce the view through a pane of glass. Remember that your focus here is perspective and spatial relationships, light and shadow. You have one hour, and at the end of that time your view from the window should have evolved to a point where we can share your vision with you."

What lovely words Mylo used to describe the task they faced, Alexander thought.

This first part of the exam certainly seemed like something Alexander could complete. At home, he looked out the window so often that he could call up every visible detail before his inner eye. The narrow alley with its straw-roofed houses. The tiny gardens with the old pear and plum trees, of which their owners were still proud despite them hardly bearing fruit anymore. Most of the neighbors, like his family, kept a few chickens, but only Else, whose house was on the other side of the alley, had a goat—which sometimes broke out of its pen and went grazing in the neighborhood, much to the annoyance of Else's neighbors, who needed every spare bit of vegetation for their chickens.

Alexander instinctively reached for pen and ink, then with a light hand began to sketch in the outlines of the buildings. A view from the window in summer . . . that was what he wanted. When the sun around midday was high enough to cast its rays into the alley and—

"What are you doing there?" he heard Mylo's voice beside him.

"I . . ." Alexander looked up uncertainly.

Mylo pointed to the pen in Alexander's hand. "The ink is really only intended for the signature. Wouldn't you like to work with the oils or watercolors?"

"Sorry." He put the pen aside as if he'd burned his fingers. How stupid could he be! Mylo had said they should use oil or watercolor for this first task. He'd hardly drawn a line and had already embarrassed himself.

"That's right. You haven't worked with paints like these before," Mylo said softly, presumably because no one else was supposed to hear. Still, a mocking snort sounded from the next table, where Maximilian von Auerwald was busily applying oil paint to his canvas.

Alexander, reassured a little by Mylo's confidential tone, shook his head, ashamed.

"These paints are water soluble. You only need to dip the brush into the jar of water a little and then into the paint, like this," Mylo said, demonstrating. "Depending on how much or how little water you use . . ." The other two men on the committee looked on with consternation as Mylo showed Alexander how to handle the paints.

What a wonderful voice Mylo has, Alexander thought, fascinated. Melodic and deep—almost like Anton's. And he explained things so well, or at least it seemed to Alexander that he did.

"Now just paint whatever you already had in mind," Mylo said, bringing his explanation to an end.

Alexander murmured a thank-you. His hand shaking, he dipped a brush into the water jar and then onto the little crucible of ocher yellow. The colors were easy to work with, he discovered with joy after a few strokes of the brush.

While Mylo and the other two men stood by an open window and conferred in low voices, Alexander's ideas began to take shape on the paper in front of him.

After an hour, Alexander's hair was tousled from running his hand through it excitedly as he worked. His eyes hurt because he'd barely blinked, and his hand was cramped from holding the brush tightly for so long. But his watercolor painting was done.

The second task consisted of painting a rainbow with the watercolors, focusing on a gradual transition between the individual colors but also watching the shift in the colors from light to dark.

I can do that, Alexander thought, relieved.

"And now, gentlemen, we come to the third exercise," said Mylo, after the second hour of the exam had gone by and he had collected the two rainbows. "In the bowl in front of you, you will find a block of clay. We would like—"

"We're supposed to do pottery?" Maximilian von Auerwald interrupted him. "You don't expect me to model little dolls like a child, do you?"

"Why not?" Mylo replied with a smile. "The third dimension is a vital element in painting. It certainly cannot hurt to practice it, or to actually feel it, now and then. So take the clay in your hands and let it inspire you to a form. What you choose to model is entirely up to you. As you proceed, stay focused on good proportions and clean work, and keep your creation as close to real life as you can. We are eager to see what final form the material takes in your hands."

Again Alexander was taken with the way Mylo described things. He truly had never heard anyone speak so beautifully. There was nothing complicated about Mylo's words, but when he spoke, a task that might otherwise fill Alexander with anxiety transformed into one he could hardly wait to start. He reached eagerly for the clay. It was as big as a loaf of bread and felt moist, cold, and heavy. To get a feel for the unfamiliar material, Alexander began to knead it a little, and he found that as he did, the clay became warmer and more pliable. Smoother, too—as smooth and soft as his sisters' skin when they were born.

He didn't know why or how it came to him, but suddenly it was there: the inspiration. Throwing himself into the task, Alexander began to form an infant out of the clay, with tiny hands, tiny feet, and the face of an angel.

He was so engrossed in his work that he wasn't sure when it was that Mylo moved behind him.

"You're sculpting a newborn?" Mylo asked.

Alexander, who was working on the eyes, nodded. "My sister. She died in March, only a month after she was born." He hadn't even finished his sentence when he found himself regretting his words. What made him say that? It was nobody else's business.

But Mylo nodded, as if modeling a dead baby were the most normal thing in the world. "Make the forehead a little flatter. With newborns, the fontanels are not yet closed. The head only takes on its roundness later. And close the eyes, I would say, if the child is sleeping forever."

And then the exam was over. Alexander and Maximilian were led into another room where the secretary brought them hot chocolate and some big soft pretzels, still warm from the oven. Alexander ate and drank as if he hadn't had anything in his stomach for a week. How sweet the dark chocolate was, and how salty and crusty the pretzels. He couldn't remember the last time he'd eaten anything so delicious. Even if he failed the exam, the outing to Stuttgart would have been worth it just for these treats, he thought in a flash of dark humor.

"Aren't you hungry?" he asked when he saw that Maximilian was just sitting there with his arms crossed, staring into the distance.

"We're invited to a dinner later. I'm certainly not going to spoil my appetite now," he said with a sneer.

Spoil your appetite? With fresh pretzels? Alexander thought of the moldy bread they'd had the evening before at home. "Mold for beauty," his mother had said, as usual, and, also as usual, had done her best to scrape off the mold as completely as she could. He thought it over for a moment, then took a breath and asked, "Can I have your pretzels?"

Maximilian pushed the plate to him without a word.

CHAPTER 25

Hahnenkamm, Steinbeiss, and Mylo quickly agreed that the rainbows were well done by both candidates. The so-called "view from the window" exercise, however, was more difficult. Mylo had devised the exercise, which they had introduced to the exam this year.

Maximilian von Auerwald had chosen a view from the New Palace, with the musical pavilion clearly visible. "A pretty little painting, the kind that could hang in any drawing room," said Gottlob Steinbeiss.

Wilhelm Hahnenkamm nodded. "It looks as if the von Auerwalds are regular guests at the palace." There was a trace of admiration, perhaps even envy, in the director's voice.

"The painting is competent, I admit, but I'm missing the originality," said Mylo with a shrug. He held Alexander's watercolor up to the light. "Here, the long row of house fronts, the exceptionally subtle way the light finds its way between the individual buildings, the dark windows behind which one immediately suspects something shameful . . . *that* is original!"

"It's gloomy is what it is, my dear colleague." Gottlob Steinbeiss made a small noise expressing something between amusement and disdain. "Did you see how the boy held the brush? It might as well have been a pitchfork!"

"He's certainly wearing the right shoes," said the director with a smile. "Didn't they stop making straw shoes in the Middle Ages?"

Steinbeiss didn't respond but instead picked up Maximilian von Auerwald's clay cat, as big as the palm of his hand and depicted lying on a pillow, and held it in both hands. "Considering that he had no real interest in the task, the figure itself is accomplished. He's even worked in the whiskers," he said, turning the piece to observe it from all sides. Then he handed it to the director.

Wilhelm Hahnenkamm indicated the tassels with which the pillow had been decorated at each corner. "He certainly has an eye for detail. Gentlemen, I see nothing standing in the way of young von Auerwald joining our class, do you?"

Both Steinbeiss and Mylo agreed. The talent was certainly there, and the family could easily afford the fees—the school needed students like him.

Hahnenkamm checked a box on a form with a flourish. "Then we come to our potential scholarship recipient . . ." He looked at the other two men with a dubious expression.

"A deceased child? Heaven help us! What made him even think of something like that?" Gottlob Steinbeiss shook his head. "Just looking at this sculpture troubles me."

"Far more troubling is the fact that even today, where Alexander Schubert comes from, many infants still perish soon after birth," Mylo said fervently. His eyes sparkled like cold crystals as he looked from one man to the other. "I find it exceptionally courageous of the young man to represent this horrible situation artistically."

"Is that how he thought of it? Or does he just have a rather . . . morbid disposition?" Director Hahnenkamm shook his head disapprovingly. "There is no question that the execution is good, but who would want to show off a dead child in a display cabinet? God knows, a sculpture like this is certainly not something one could sell. And shouldn't we bear in mind that with everything we teach, we want our students to one day be able to make a living from their art? As one of the most successful architects of our time, Mylo, I am sure I don't have to remind you of that, do I? *Tout le monde* wants you to design their next villa!"

Mylo shrugged. "That may be, but I have never sought fame or fortune with my work. Substance has always mattered more. But to come back to Alexander Schubert, something tells me he is a diamond in the rough. I would be very interested to see what corners and facets come to light with the right support."

"I don't doubt he has potential," Steinbeiss said. "But shouldn't we also keep a few other aspects in mind? Does Alexander Schubert *fit* here, at our institute?" He looked from Mylo to the director. "I'm well aware that the scholarship is intended to give poor children an opportunity, but I wonder if the cleft between rich and poor, in this case, isn't perhaps too wide altogether?" He nodded in the direction of the adjoining room, where the two candidates waited. "The constellation we had just today was almost absurd: the son of a count, and the son of a . . ." He furrowed his brow. "I don't recall just now what's on the registration form. Where exactly is Alexander from?"

"Laichingen," said Mylo in a tone that sounded strangely emotional. "In all probability, he is the son of a weaver."

The other two men looked at him in surprise. The architect was well known for his at times mercurial style and occasionally unconventional declarations—which only made high society love him even more.

Director Hahnenkamm nodded. "That explains quite a lot. Gerhart Hauptmann dealt with the poverty of weavers in his most important work to date."

"That's my point," Steinbeiss added. "I can already see Alexander's fellow students humiliating him at the mere sight of his straw shoes. Do we really want to put him through that? Or would it be better not to bestow a scholarship at all this year? The candidates we had at the main examination were less than convincing, after all."

There was silence for a moment as all three men considered this question.

Hahnenkamm frowned. "It is not as if I couldn't be persuaded by the young man's talent . . . ," he said slowly. "And there's another aspect we can't afford to forget: if we don't make use of the scholarship money this year, who's to say whether it will even be available to us next year?"

Mylo nodded. "I think we should give young Schubert a chance. The Laichingen weavers may be dirt poor, but they're as tough as the flax from which they spin their cloth. Alexander Schubert will not have it easy here, but he's never had it easy in his life, I guarantee you. We won't be inflicting anything on him he doesn't know already."

"Did you see how the chimney sweep practically danced across the roof? And how he blackened that lady's nose? She didn't see that coming!" Christel's laugh rang brightly.

Anton blinked, then held one hand protectively in front of his face. After the dark theater, his eyes had to adjust to the glare outside. Christel, however, didn't seem bothered by the contrast. "And then how the cat ran across the street and the chimney sweep went flying with his ladder and . . ."

Anton grinned. He'd never seen Christel so lively. He listened happily as she recounted every scene, interpreting and reliving them in her mind.

He himself had taken in practically none of the film at all—he had far too much going on in his head. But now he had his thoughts in order and was ready to share them with Christel.

"I'll treat you to a lemonade. Come on, let's go in here," he said, pointing to a small pub a few doors ahead.

Christel, her mind still caught up with the theater, followed him as if in a trance.

They had not even settled into their seats when a waiter hurried over and asked Christel what he could get her.

Unbelievable, Anton thought. Christel commanded attention just by walking into a room! He wasn't a bad-looking fellow himself—at least, by his own estimation—but he still had to come out with one or two charming or brazen remarks or perhaps a compliment before anyone took any notice of him. All Christel had to do was breathe and people practically melted at her feet.

She was a rare gem. The thought came to him without warning, and he understood it literally. His fortune, his future. He'd always known she was something very special, he thought as Christel ordered two lemonades as casually as if she did so every day.

"How do you like our trip to the city?" he asked when the waiter left.

"How do I like it?" Christel said. "It's fantastic here!" She spread her arms wide as if she wanted to include all of Stuttgart. "All the elegant people on the street, the theater, it's so different from what we're used to. And it's not fair that other people have so much more!" Her brow creased grimly at her last words, but her face lit up again just a moment later when the waiter brought their drinks. "I think I could get used to all this very quickly," she said with a flirtatious flutter of her eyelids. She sipped the sweet lemonade.

Anton took her hands in his. "Then you finally understand it, too! Christel, you and me, we can do better. It's time we get away from Laichingen and make ourselves rich and famous."

"But how are we going to do it?" She put her glass down.

Did she really ask that? Anton thought in disbelief. *No protest? No "But the dear Lord gave me* this *life to live"? No "I can't just abandon my family"?*

"I've got it all worked out," he said. "Mimi Reventlow knows a businesswoman at Lake Constance who makes beauty products for women. I already told you about her. Clara Berg is her name. I'm sure she counts all kinds of important people among her customers. Nobility, the rich, and no doubt a few from the theater and film world. They need powder and makeup every day, after all. With her connections, this Clara Berg will be able to help us."

Christel was hanging on his every word. "You think we should go to Lake Constance?"

He nodded. He and Christel on the lakeshore. She with a lace-trimmed parasol and he with a walking stick, like a real gentleman. Passersby would look at them with at least as much admiration as they did here in Stuttgart. "The most important thing is to make our first contacts. Mimi Reventlow's friend there could be the lever we need to make you famous, at least as famous as the actress in that film just now."

Christel nodded as if they were talking about the most natural things in the world. "Where are we going to find the money to get there?"

"I'll take care of that," he said, and squared his shoulders. He'd do it, too, even if he had to build ten hunting blinds for his father.

Christel was so excited she bounced in her chair. "You should talk to Miss Reventlow on the train home."

Anton thought for a moment. The train trip was long. He would certainly have enough time to talk to her. But what if Mimi Reventlow had misgivings about their plans? Christel was easily influenced, and now that he had finally opened her eyes, he didn't want to risk anyone closing them again.

"Alexander doesn't have to hear everything. It's better if I talk it over with her privately," he said. "Besides, Alexander's exam is all we're going to talk about on the way back as it is. I just know he'll have been accepted. We won't get a word in edgewise. Trust me!"

Christel looked at him skeptically.

CHAPTER 26

In the evening, the group gathered at the station as they had agreed. Their train was due to depart in a few minutes, but instead of boarding immediately, all eyes were on Alexander.

"Well?" Anton said.

Alexander rubbed his chin. "I passed," he said quietly, as if he couldn't quite believe it himself. "And they offered me the scholarship."

After that, there was no holding back. Anton embraced his friend, secretly wiping away a tear. Mimi also threw her arms around Alexander and congratulated him. Even Christel shook Alexander's hand and told him he'd done himself proud.

"All aboard!" called the conductor, interrupting the excited chatter. Despite his achievement, Alexander was clearly exhausted, so Mimi took his crutches and Anton put his arm around his friend's waist and—bearing most of his weight—all but carried him up the two steps to the train.

They settled into their seats, then picked up where they had left off before boarding. All of them, after all, wanted to know what he'd had to do in the exam.

"It was fantastic. It's still like a dream," said Alexander. His voice broke with emotion and his eyes gleamed. "The paints! I couldn't believe you could get such brilliant colors out of a little box of watercolors. It was like magic. And the paper I painted on was so heavy! At the start, I hardly dared to touch it with the brush. My hands were shaking so much. And yet I don't think I've ever experienced anything as wonderful, ever."

"What were the other students like?" Anton asked.

"Well, because it's summer and the real exam was last month, there was only one other boy there. His name was Maximilian. He passed the test, too, but his parents are rich, so he doesn't need a scholarship."

"It's all so exciting!" Mimi could hardly sit still and would have loved to throw her arms around Alexander again. She was so proud of him it was as if he were her own son.

Alexander held out his hand to her. "I'd like to say thank you, Miss Reventlow. Without your help, I would never have had this chance."

"It was my pleasure," Mimi replied warmly as she grasped his hand.

"Now at least I know what I'm capable of—even if I have to turn down the scholarship." Alexander shrugged. "I didn't find the courage to tell the gentlemen there face to face. They would have been angry, I think, after giving me the chance and then letting me take the test later. But sometime in the next few days, I'll have to write them a letter." He laughed bitterly. "Gehringer's mill is waiting for me, after all."

An uncomfortable silence followed, until Mimi said, "Let's not get ahead of ourselves. Right now, we're just happy about your success, right?" She looked at Anton and Christel for support.

"Exactly," Anton said. "Who knows? Something might change . . ."

The conversation waned, and Alexander fell into gloomy contemplation. Anton and Christel whispered to one another.

The rumbling of the train made Mimi tired, and more than once her eyelids closed. But each time, when she snapped awake again, her eyes fell on a woman who had taken a seat two rows in front of them. She looked vaguely familiar.

They had nodded a brief greeting when boarding, and since then the woman had sat and gazed out the train window as if she did not want to talk to anyone. From where she sat, Mimi could only see the woman's profile. She was traveling alone, and Mimi guessed she was similar in age to herself, in her early thirties. She had thick, straw-blond hair showing the first strands of gray, and she had woven it into braids that circled her head like a crown. Where had she seen a coiffure like that before? Mimi wondered. The stranger's face had been browned and toughened by the weather, and she kept her lips pressed together so tightly that she looked as if she were holding in a scream. As powerful as the woman's face was in profile, Mimi could not decipher her expression.

After hesitating a few minutes, Mimi's curiosity got the better of her, and she got up and went over to the woman. She touched her shoulder gently, not wanting to startle her. "Excuse me for disturbing you, but do I know you from somewhere?"

The stranger looked up. Mimi could sense a slight annoyance at the intrusion, but the next moment, her expression transformed into puzzlement. She turned toward Mimi to see her more clearly. "I don't believe it," she murmured. "It was back in Esslingen. You . . . aren't you the photographer Mimi Reventlow?"

"I am. And you're the bride who had just picked up your wedding dress!" Mimi exclaimed, happy and stunned. Was it really possible? After all these years? "And I remember your name now, too—Bernadette, isn't it? The shepherdess from Münsingen." Mimi sat in the free seat beside the woman. "And here we meet, on a train of all places." She took Bernadette's hands in her own and said, "I hope you're not getting off at the next station? I'd love to find out how things went for you. And how the wedding was, especially—you must have been the most beautiful bride."

She would never forget how in love the woman had been back then, at their seemingly fateful encounter in Esslingen. She had gone on and on about her future husband and how she could hardly wait to be his wife. Her blue eyes had been as radiant as the sky on a gorgeous summer's day. And Mimi had realized back then that, while she liked him very much, she did not love Heinrich with all her heart. As a result, her decision to turn down Heinrich's marriage proposal and try her luck as a traveling photographer was closely tied to the stranger beside her. And now they'd met again, after so long . . . Mimi could not get over her astonishment, and it took her a moment to realize that Bernadette's expression had darkened as if a thunderstorm were moving in.

"The wedding . . . well, nothing came of it."

"But how? You were so happy," Mimi said in disbelief.

Bernadette sniffed. "Happiness is an illusion, nothing more. And love is a devious creature. I'm glad to have all that sentimentality behind me. You need a certain level of hardness to get through life undamaged." The radiant blue eyes were now as cold as a wintry lake.

Mimi was so shocked at Bernadette's words that she didn't know what to say.

"Don't look so surprised. Things often turn out differently than you expect in life. You must have seen that for yourself, haven't you?" said Bernadette, as if she wanted to console Mimi. "Tell me how things have been for you."

Mimi accepted the offer. She told Bernadette about her years as a traveling photographer and about how she'd been looking after her uncle in Laichingen since April.

"You ended up in *Laichingen*?" Bernadette laughed. "Then you're probably in the same boat as me. I'll bet that, as a woman, you have to be as tough as a man among the weavers for them to take you seriously."

Mimi shrugged. "It's more my sensitivity as a woman that inspires me. It's my signature as a photographer, and my customers appreciate it."

A slight frown played around Bernadette's mouth. "It's easy to see you haven't been in Laichingen long. Sensitive inspiration won't get you very far in the Swabian Jura. Wait and see. If you're successful, you'll find people just waiting for a chance to trip you up. Envy and resentment rule the world. You have to sense the knife they plan to stab in your back before they've even drawn it." She nodded as if to confirm the truth of her words for herself.

Mimi shook her head uncertainly. "The way you talk almost frightens me, Bernadette. People should have a little trust in God, shouldn't they?"

"Trust in God! Oh, Mimi, if that was all it took . . ." Bernadette sighed. She took a small notebook out of the large bag on the bench between them, tore out a page, scribbled something on it, and handed it to Mimi. "Here. My address in Münsingen. Come and visit sometime, and I'll tell you how life in the Jura really is."

End of conversation, thought Mimi. They parted with vague promises to meet again, and Mimi returned to her seat beside her companions.

"Who was that?" Anton asked, nosy as ever.

"An old acquaintance. She lives in Münsingen. Her family runs a sheep business."

Anton's interest faded instantly. Mimi was happy about that—she had far too much going through her mind to want to talk to him about Bernadette.

What had happened to the carefree young woman she'd once been? Why did Bernadette seem so bitter?

Depressed, Mimi put the piece of paper in her purse. A life without love, without trust in God—was that even possible?

Throughout the day, Eveline's thoughts kept drifting off to Alexander in Stuttgart, and she was consequently nervous and fidgety. She had forgotten the fifth petal of a flower in her embroidery, she had burned the *Schwarzer Brei*, and when she had collected the eggs from the chicken pen, she'd stumbled and almost fell with the valuable cargo. As she got ready for a long afternoon's work with the girls in the field, she hoped she wouldn't injure herself, as scatterbrained as she was.

How is Alexander? she wondered as she bent over and carefully loosened the soil around her potato plants. She must have asked herself that question a dozen times already. Had he held up bravely or lost heart? He'd never been away from Laichingen in his life, and he'd probably found the big city terribly daunting, especially on crutches. Why hadn't she gone along with him?

Her son would have the exam behind him now and would know the result. Eve didn't know what to wish for—that he'd passed or failed.

She straightened up and stretched. She didn't feel good about herself at all today. It had less to do with the sweat running in streams down her back or even worrying about Alexander and far more to do with her fight with Mimi Reventlow.

It had been more than a week since the incident in Helene's store, and she was still wondering what had gotten into her to make her lose her head as she had. Johann had told her openly that he'd invited the photographer to the festival. And, she reminded herself, he'd almost forgotten to pick Mimi up. Edelgard had jumped into the fray of gossiping women in defense of Johann and testified that he'd slept at home, and still she, Eve, had attacked Mimi.

As if that embarrassing incident weren't enough, two days later Johann had spoken to her about it and, with a laugh, had asked why she had acted like such a shrew. As calmly as she could, she explained the incident away as a minor exchange of words. Luckily, Johann had let the matter rest, but she had sensed clearly enough that he could not abide that kind of jealous behavior.

The longer she thought about everything, the more she was sorry it had happened. It was really not like her at all. As soon as she possibly could, she would apologize to Mimi, she decided, and clear the air between them once and for all.

The sun was setting slowly when Eveline and the girls set off for the village. When they reached the square, they were tired and hungry, and her daughters should really have been in bed already. But Eveline told them Alexander, Anton, and Christel would be back soon and that they'd wait for him. She pointed to the bench under the big chestnut tree as her gaze swept the square in front of her. Eveline also harbored a little hope that she might see Johann—the mill would have closed for the day, after all—but in vain.

Half an hour later, Alexander and the others came into sight.

"Alexander!" Marianne and Erika jumped up before Eveline could say anything.

Eveline gathered up the field tools, then she, too, walked toward the arriving group. From the middle of the square, she could already see the radiant smile on Alexander's face. He'd passed! Her heart bubbled over with pride and love when she saw how Alexander gave a pretzel each to Marianne and Erika. Even on his big day, he thought of his family.

Then she saw Mimi Reventlow. She hadn't known that the photographer had gone with Alexander, Anton, and Christel. When she saw Eveline, Mimi quickly looked away.

Eveline frowned. Hadn't she very clearly told the photographer to stay out of her life? Tight lipped, she went straight to Alexander.

"And? How was it?" she asked stiffly.

"I passed. They accepted me and offered me the scholarship," he croaked from a dry throat. "But if the others hadn't bucked me up like they did, I think I would have died of nervousness before I even walked into the school."

Eveline forced herself to smile.

"Time to celebrate!" Anton cried. "To The Oxen. A glass of cider for everyone to end this exciting day, my treat!" He was already waving Christel, Alexander, and Alexander's sisters up the steps of the inn.

From the corner of her eye, Eveline saw Mimi's hesitation, and she gave herself a push and walked up to Mimi.

"I'd like to apologize," Eveline said quietly. "I really don't know what came over me. I guess I just took out all my anger about our situation on you. I would dearly love to make it possible for Alexander to attend that school, but aside from a miracle . . . In any case, I'm sorry." She shook her head sadly, then held out her hand formally to Mimi. "Can we be friends again?" she said timidly.

Mimi hesitated for the blink of an eye, no more. "Of course," she said.

Mimi's handshake was not especially strong, but Eveline still let out a cry of pain. Mimi instantly released her hand. "My goodness, you've been bleeding!" Horrified, the photographer pointed to Eveline's hands, which were covered with scrapes and grazes.

"The work in the field, all the embroidery. Yesterday was washday, too. It all leaves traces," Eveline said, hiding them behind her back, ashamed.

"I have a good cream at home. If you like, I'll give you a little," said Mimi, clearly shaken.

Eveline nodded, then they followed the others inside.

The other guests at The Oxen quickly heard, of course, that Alexander had managed something great in Stuttgart. The weavers who had previously been so critical of his "harebrained idea" and who had mocked him, now came and clapped him on the shoulder and offered their congratulations. Many clinked glasses with him, or wanted to know what it was like in Stuttgart, or asked him about the school. It seemed to Eveline that people were suddenly proud of Alexander—he was, after all, "one of them." She was amazed at how well her normally so shy son handled all the attention.

Once Anton had set up glasses of cider for everyone, his mother, Karolina, came from the kitchen with a plate of bread and drippings and a bowl of sour gherkins. "Help yourselves! We've got plenty of cider, and you're our guests tonight," she said. To her son's surprise, she and her husband even joined them at the table.

Eveline felt a lump in her throat. As long as she'd lived in Laichingen, she could not remember the other residents of the village ever taking such an interest in her family. Edelgard and one or another of her neighbors helped her when they could, just as she did in return. But the solidarity and the warmth she felt now were new to her.

What a diverse group, she thought, her eyes moving from one face to the next around the table. Beside Alexander sat Anton with his broad shoulders, no longer a boy, but a man. He had proven to be a true friend to Alexander and had done so much for him. Beside Anton sat the beautiful Christel, and next to Christel was Mimi, the well-traveled photographer. On the other side of the table were Anton's parents, who had as little to say to each other as she and Klaus once had. What would Klaus think if he could see her here and now? Probably that the devil was dancing in the house, she thought bitterly, but she banished the thought as quickly as it came. If Klaus were still alive, Alexander would not have been able to enjoy this wonderful moment at all.

Suddenly, from across the table, she felt Mimi's eyes on her. She smiled bravely and raised her glass to the photographer.

CHAPTER 27

The next morning, the weather was as lovely as it had been for days. *All that nonsense about "half the year it's winter and the other half it's cold"!* Mimi thought as she carried plates, cups, and cutlery out to the garden. The coffeepot, the bread basket, butter, and marmalade followed. Then, she helped Uncle Josef outside with his walker—breakfast out in the fresh air would surely do him good.

And what would do her good would be to take each day as it came. She would not allow any more gloom or negative thoughts to find their way through. There was no need for her to have Bernadette's strange transformation on her mind or to constantly wonder why Eveline had been so unkind or why she was suddenly her friend again. Nor was there any need to pick apart everything Johann said for fear of missing out on some deeper significance. When it came to love, she was a fledgling at best—on what basis had she ever assumed that her relationship with Johann should take a certain course?

It also made no sense for her to always be thinking about how to boost her business when there *was* no business to be had. She was already doing what she could, and everything beyond that she would have to leave to the good Lord—just as the birds that sat on the studio roof, twittering happily, did.

What a tonic for her the day in Stuttgart had been, she thought later as she cleared away the remains of breakfast. As soon as she was finished, she threw a thin cape over her shoulders and marched off. She'd been planning to visit Sonja Merkle, and today she was making good on her resolution.

She wasn't even halfway across the square when she stopped short. Not ten yards away stood a man with hiking boots and a rucksack and . . . a small handheld camera. He was engrossed in photographing the *Hüle*.

An amateur!

"What are you doing?" Mimi shouted, unable to mask the irritation in her voice. Laichingen was her territory!

The man jumped but quickly gathered himself. "I'm taking a photograph," he replied proudly. He held up his small camera with just as much pride. "Are you interested in the craft, young lady? It's a marvelous pastime. Believe me, far more people will be enjoying it soon. There won't be any need for studios then, not with everyone taking their own photographs." He looked at her as if he expected her to applaud his insight.

"I wouldn't be so sure about that. You can hardly compare amateur photography to the art of a true expert," Mimi replied curtly, and felt her good mood vanish in an instant. If taking snapshots really did become fashionable, her entire guild might as well start packing its bags. Before the man could respond, Mimi set off again for Sonja's house.

After Mimi knocked, the door opened just a crack.

"Yes?"

"Luise! How lovely to see you here," Mimi said. "I came to visit Sonja and the baby."

"My daughter's resting." Luise opened the door wider, but instead of asking Mimi in, Luise stood in the threshold and looked at her doubtfully.

Mimi suddenly got the feeling it was strange to just drop in. "I brought a present for the baby. From Stuttgart." Hesitantly, she held up the silver rattle she'd bought on her way to the station the day before. It was a bit of an extravagance given her finances, but she was the baby's godmother after all. "If it's a bad time, I understand." Despite the amateur photographer and Luise's aloofness, she was still doing her best to maintain her newfound optimism.

Finally, Luise opened the door fully, but she still did not let Mimi inside. Instead, she beckoned Mimi closer and whispered in her ear: "Don't be frightened, but Sonja's suffering from the baby melancholy. All she does is lie in bed brooding and crying. She hardly has any interest in the child, and she doesn't want to eat anything. She's like this after every birth." Luise shook her head, worried. "The doctor says her depression will pass. But it's never lasted as long as it has this time, and we're starting to worry."

Christel wasn't exaggerating at all, Mimi thought. She raised her eyebrows with concern. "Should I leave?"

Luise shrugged, then said, "No. Maybe you'll be able to cheer her up a bit."

When Sonja saw the silver rattle, she only cried more. "It's so lovely. It's far too nice for us."

"Not at all!" Mimi said. "Just look at your delightful daughter. She's like a little princess." The baby girl lay in a cradle beside her mother's bed. She had the same gold-blond hair as her mother and Christel. "She's smacking her lips," Mimi said with a smile. "Is it true that means they're hungry?"

Instead of answering, Sonja began to bawl in earnest. "I've got another mouth to feed! And if the Lord above didn't show a bit of compassion once in a while, there'd be another one every single year. When is it finally going to stop? Life is getting to be too much."

"Don't say things like that. Children are a gift from God," Luise admonished.

Sonja glared venomously at her mother. Then she leaned over, picked up the baby, and placed her, without affection, at her breast.

For a while, the only sound was the infant's greedy sucking.

Mimi looked around furtively. Sonja and Paul Merkle's bedroom was tiny! It was smaller than her own room at Uncle Josef's house, and so full that it was hard to move around. Other than their bed, there was a second bed on which boys' pajamas lay. Did the boys sleep in one room with their parents? The entire house was small, and there wasn't even a proper kitchen. As at Luise's, there was only an oven in the hallway, Mimi had noted with astonishment when she'd entered. From what Mimi had seen so far, there was no sign of Christel's things—was it possible only she had a room of her own?

The lace curtains were the only decoration in the room—no pictures on the wall, no carpet on the floor, not even a mirror. Josef's house was a palace by comparison. And yet Paul Merkle must have earned relatively good money at Gehringer's.

To her relief, Mimi saw Sonja's face brighten as she fed her baby. But when she lay her daughter over her shoulder to burp her, Sonja began to sob again.

"I can't even give my child her mother's milk for long. When I start embroidering again in a few days, I won't have time for feeding. Mr. Gehringer would just love to see his pretty pillows covered in dribble."

"Then leave the work for now," said Mimi gently. "As Gehringer's assistant, your husband must earn enough for you to do without your income for a while, doesn't he?"

Sonja looked at her from red, weepy eyes. "He does, yes. But I hardly ever see my husband. Gehringer's got Paul tied up with a hundred preparations for the company anniversary jubilee next year, and there's so much to do, he spends hours on top of his actual workday.

Christel is starting as a model at the mill soon, too. I can't be the one to sit at home and twiddle my thumbs—what would people say if I suddenly started acting the fine lady?"

"Everyone has their lot in life," said her mother, nodding in agreement.

Mimi's eyes roamed the grim room again. How would she feel if she were surrounded by the same four walls day in, day out? "Maybe you just need a break for a day," she said. "See something different and have other people around you. If I think about how good the excursion to Stuttgart was for me—this morning I felt completely rejuvenated."

Mother and daughter both raised their brows as if to say, *Nice for those who can afford it . . .*

"It was very nice of your husband to let Christel make the trip to Stuttgart," said Mimi, who had seen their skeptical looks clearly enough. She decided not to say a word about how Anton had asked her to write to Clara Berg in Meersburg on Christel's behalf. Sonja would certainly not be thrilled about her daughter's daring to want to change anything about her *"lot in life." And nothing might come of it, anyway,* Mimi thought, feeling guilty.

Sonja sighed. "Since Christel got back last night, all she's done is go on and on about the movie and the theater. She's driving us all crazy with it! Now she has dreams of being an actress, if you can believe it. As if we don't already have enough theatrics here." Sonja burst into tears again.

Mimi and Luise exchanged a helpless glance.

"Did you hear that Alexander Schubert passed the admissions exam?" Mimi asked with deliberate cheerfulness.

"Christel told me," Sonja said as she laid the baby, who had fallen asleep on her shoulder, in her cradle. "I would never have believed we had such a gifted artist here in Laichingen. And young Schubert, of all people."

"There was a fellow here, a long time ago, who auditioned for the Ulm choir. But they didn't accept him," Luise said.

"It probably won't work out for Alexander, either," said Mimi with a sigh.

"But why not?" Sonja cried. "The possibility of Alexander going to that school is so important to Eveline. They say that's what she and her husband were always fighting about."

Mimi held back a smirk—apparently Sonja's depression had no effect on her ability to gossip. But maybe it would do Sonja good to turn her mind to the problems of others? Maybe it would even drag her out of her gloom? It was worth a try, Mimi decided. She sat down on the edge of the bed.

"Eveline simply can't afford to let Alexander go. The school itself isn't a problem, because he's been offered a scholarship. And knowing my mother, with all her contacts, she'll be able to come up with a charitable family who can offer Alexander room and board in exchange for a bit of help in the house. But as an art student, he wouldn't be earning any money, and the family can't live on what Eve brings in with her embroidery. I've been racking my brain for some way to help her, but I just can't think of anything." Mimi threw her hands in the air in frustration. "Do you have any ideas?"

The two women looked at each other.

"What if I gave up my field after all?" Sonja said after a pause, and so softly that, for a moment, Mimi thought she might have misheard.

Luise drew a shocked breath.

"Didn't you say just a little while ago that you might want to plant something there yourself next year?" Mimi asked, frowning.

Sonja waved it off. "The thought of dragging the baby off to the field with me is already too much. Paul won't be thrilled when he hears about it, but for once I don't care. If Eve doesn't have to walk so long just to get to her field, she'll save two or three hours every day. If she uses that time to embroider, that will also bring in some money."

"I . . . well, I don't know what to say. You're a treasure!" Mimi said, and she threw her arms around Sonja.

Sonja's pale cheeks reddened a little. "But just so we understand each other: Eveline gets my field only for the next three years," she said, and her mother nodded vigorously. "She will probably have a new husband by then and be provided for."

Mimi let out a laugh. Sonja seemed unable to entertain the idea that, as a woman, she could take care of her own livelihood.

"Mr. Gehringer won't be happy about not getting Alexander for his mill," said Luise.

"We all have to find our place, the Schubert family just like us or Mr. Gehringer," said Sonja with a hardness that took Mimi by surprise. As carefree as Sonja usually presented herself—her current melancholy notwithstanding—she apparently knew perfectly well what she wanted, and she had the will to see it through.

"You're right about that," said Luise.

For a moment, all three women fell silent, then Luise spoke up again. "Letting Eveline use your field is a start. But if we really want Alexander to go to art school, a lot of other people are going to have to pitch in. I could offer Eveline five eggs a week. Our hens are younger and lay more than Eveline's do. And you, young lady"—she pointed at Mimi—"could cook for the family once a week. I've already shown you how to make my soup."

"I'd be glad to," said Mimi, who could not get over her surprise. "But I fear a few eggs and a pot of soup aren't going to be enough."

Luise and Sonja exchanged a look.

"Edelgard is already helping with the children," Luise said. "If we ask Helene, I'm sure she'll help, too. And if Helene's in, then she'll bring Karolina Schaufler with her." She paused and took a deep breath. "Miss Reventlow, I believe it's time we pay a visit to a few people."

"Because we Laichingers are all so proud that one of our own can attend such a prestigious art school, we naturally want to support the family however we can. If we don't help, Alexander won't be able to go at all. Money, fruit or vegetables, chopping wood, helping in the field—anything and everything that might be of assistance. For example, I'm going to give them eggs every week and . . ."

Mimi listened in silent admiration as Luise got their various neighbors to pledge assistance, and they were not turned away from a single door they knocked on, regardless of how poor it looked. Two pints of goat's milk each week. A basket of firewood every month. Three jars of elderberry marmalade in autumn. For each person they visited, it was a matter of honor to do their little bit, and Mimi was deeply moved.

Last of all, they went to see Edelgard, who lived on the same street as Eveline. Mimi's heart was suddenly beating as if she'd just finished a footrace. Maybe, just by chance, Johann would be there? *Stop dreaming!* she reprimanded herself immediately. It was the middle of the day, and Johann was at the mill.

"Of course we'll do more for Eveline," said Edelgard when Luise had finished her speech. "Johann's going to start chopping wood for winter on the weekends soon. He can do enough for Eveline while he's at it."

And that means he'll have even less time for me, thought Mimi, disappointed. But aloud, she said, "An excellent idea."

Their mouths parched from all the talk, Mimi and Luise finally returned to Sonja's house. In the meantime, she had gotten out of bed and made a pot of tea. Honored and amazed, all three pored over the lengthy list of offers to help.

"We Laichingers are something of a special breed, aren't we?" said Sonja with pride.

"And you started it," Mimi replied, giving Sonja's hand a squeeze.

"That's all well and good," said Luise, tapping the list. "But the next question is, Who's going to tell Eveline about it? She's a proud woman. What if she's too proud to take our help?"

Mimi frowned. "Do you really think she might refuse?"

"Mother's right. Accepting charity would be very hard for me, too," said Sonja.

"But, Luise, you said we all need to pitch in. When we talk to Eveline, shouldn't we focus on that aspect in particular? We don't need to use the word 'charity' at all." Mimi thought of Eveline's damaged hands. Of Sonja's depression. Of the many other women who did so much and had so little of anything nice for themselves. And suddenly she had an idea.

She looked intently at Sonja. "Do you think you could manage to come visit me in the garden on Saturday afternoon? And you, Luise? For two or three hours? Bring Berta along, too. I'll get Eve, Karolina, and Edelgard to come."

"On a Saturday?" Luise grimaced.

Mimi laughed. "I know there are usually a thousand other things to do. But just this once?"

"Then I'd really have a chance to get out of here. But what in the world are you planning?" Sonja asked.

Mimi smiled. "Wait and see!"

CHAPTER 28

Josef Stöckle sat on his garden bench on Saturday morning and watched all of Mimi's activity with amusement.

Anton had helped her carry the kitchen table and chairs outside. After he left, Mimi began to set the table, and she brought out Traudel's best coffee cups and saucers—with Josef's permission, of course.

Now, just before one, Mimi stood back and cast a critical eye over her handiwork. In the middle of the table, she had placed a bouquet of sweet-scented wild roses and, alongside it, a marble cake she'd baked herself, working on it for most of Friday evening. Although it had cracked down the middle, Mimi had sprinkled it with sugar to hide the gap. The coffee grinder, filled to the brim with coffee beans, was also on the table, and a pot of water simmered in the kitchen—as soon as the women arrived, Mimi would put the coffee on. She'd also boiled a fruit tea the evening before and let it cool before pouring it into Traudel's best clay pitcher.

"What do you think?" she asked Josef.

"Child, I don't think the high-society ladies have ever seen a nicer coffee circle than this," the old man said. He stood up with a groan and reached for his walker, which he was leaning on less all the time. "I'll leave you to it. I'm sure you don't need me around."

Mimi laughed. While she knew it was still hard for him to move around, she was so happy to see him in good spirits that she could have hugged the world, but she did need to be sure everything was just as she pictured for her guests. "For once, you're right! I'll bring you a piece of cake later," she said. From the corner of her eye, she saw the first guests arrive at the gate at the back of the garden—Luise and her two daughters, Berta and Sonja, Sonja carrying her baby in a basket. It wasn't a minute later when Karolina, Eveline, and Edelgard arrived.

"Come in, come in!" Mimi called out happily.

Somewhat hesitantly, the women stepped into the garden. Karolina handed Mimi a bowl of blackberries and a bottle of wine.

"Coffee?" Luise's eyes got bigger and bigger the moment she spotted the grinder.

"And flowers on the table . . . It's as lovely as a wedding reception," said Berta.

"Did you bake that just for us?" Sonja looked at the marble cake in disbelief. "I thought you weren't really much for cooking. At least, Mother said—"

Luise immediately dug an elbow into her daughter's ribs. The other women giggled.

Mimi grinned. "Welcome to our little coffee circle!"

Luise clapped her hands. "I can't believe I get to do this, here in this garden! Traudel and I used to treat ourselves to a cup of coffee right here. I had to grind the beans, though. She always said I could grind them finer than she could." She smiled nostalgically, then pointed to the coffee mill. "May I? Like in the old days?"

"Gladly," Mimi said. "The water is simmering inside."

While Luise went into the house, the others sat down around the table.

"A coffee circle . . . I can't remember the last time I went to one of these," said Eveline, her voice filled with emotion.

"And I can't remember the last time I ate cake . . ." Sonja paused for a moment, then said, "Although now that I think about it, it was at Justus's confirmation in spring. It does look wonderful. When the baby is christened, I'll bake one myself. Would you give me the recipe?"

"Of course!" Mimi beamed.

"Coffee's done!" Luise called as she walked back to the garden, and when she'd poured a cup for each of them and taken a sip herself, she declared, "Just like it used to taste when Traudel was still alive; those were good times. We used to meet once a week in winter to do our embroidery and handicrafts together, just like our mothers and grandmothers did in their spinning rooms. We spent some very nice times together. But these days, people hole up alone in their own little houses."

"What's stopping you from resuming that tradition?" Mimi asked.

"Since we've gotten out of the habit, each of us has her own daily rhythm," said Edelgard vaguely.

"I can't get away from The Oxen," said Karolina.

"Someone has to look after the family," said Sonja.

Luise looked from one woman to the next over the rim of her coffee cup. "If that's all that's stopping us from a handicrafts evening, then come winter maybe we really should bring back the old tradition."

The others murmured words of assent.

The cake was good, the coffee, too, and the women laughed and enjoyed themselves immensely. At some point, Mimi gave Luise a small nod.

Luise cleared her throat. "Eveline, there's a matter we'd like to raise with you."

"I'm getting by, thank you," Eveline said, instantly on guard.

Mimi rolled her eyes—too much pride was really not a good thing at all. "Eveline, just wait and hear what it is."

"Exactly," said Luise sternly. "Because it's like this: Everyone in Laichingen is proud of your Alexander. We know you've been through a lot, so it should go without saying that everyone wants to help you and your family. Everything we can offer is listed here." She handed over a sheet of paper.

"You'll get my field, the one just behind the village," Sonja gushed. "You can get there in five minutes to do your fieldwork, and since you'll save at least two hours a day, you can get more embroidery done and benefit twice."

"My Johann is going to cut wood for you for the winter ahead," said Edelgard.

"And I'll come and cook for you once a week," said Mimi, and she sounded at least as proud as Sonja.

Eveline stared at the list and looked at each of the women around her. "You've all gone mad!" She shook her head. "You're teasing me, aren't you?"

The women shook their heads.

Eveline burst into tears. "I don't know what to say," she managed between sobs. "This . . . this is the nicest thing anyone's ever done for me. When I tell Alexander that he's going to art school . . ."

Mimi, who had a lump in her throat, saw Sonja covertly wipe a tear from her eye, while Luise focused intently on the cake crumbs on her plate. "Enough already," Mimi protested, half laughing, half crying. "I wanted this afternoon to make you happy, not sad."

Karolina Schaufler was the first to compose herself again. "I think we could all use something a little stronger than coffee and cake." She took a corkscrew from her skirt pocket and opened the bottle of wine she had brought.

The party was at its peak when an automobile pulled up to the gate.

"Are you expecting someone else?" said Eveline, frowning.

"That's Mr. Gehringer's car," said Sonja in a horrified tone.

"What does *he* want?" said Mimi, taken aback. But before she could do anything, the mill owner was standing in her garden.

He raised his top hat in greeting. "Ladies! Having a good time, I see. Cake and a glass of wine—I think I'd enjoy that myself," he said jovially.

The women exchanged abashed looks.

"How can I help you?" Mimi asked, an edge to her voice.

"Forgive me for bursting in on your little fete, but I've come on business."

Suppressing her anger at his interruption, Mimi quickly led him toward the studio. How annoying! What did the man want? And why *now*?

His assistant, Paul Merkle, had been right: Mimi Reventlow was leading the entire village down the road to decadence! *It's time to take her out of circulation,* Herrmann Gehringer thought as he followed her to the studio. Muffled giggling came from the garden. Were the women poking fun at *him*? Didn't they have work to do? And had he been mistaken, or was Paul's wife, Sonja, also there? Things were worse than he'd feared.

Mimi Reventlow stood beside her camera and tripod, her arms crossed, and in a cool voice said, "What is so important that it can't wait until later? You can see I have guests."

Wasn't she going to offer him a chair? He cleared his throat. "I'd like to make you an offer," he said. "As you know, my mill will be celebrating its thirtieth anniversary next year. I'm expecting important customers and high-ranking guests."

"And you'd like me to photograph your guests?"

He hadn't even thought of that. "Why not let me finish speaking first?" he said. "To mark the occasion, I'd like to publish a commemorative book in which I document the founding and growth of our weaving mill from its modest beginnings to the present day, in words and pictures. I would like to send this to all our customers and, of course, give a copy to each of my guests on the big day. Your task would be to take group photos of my weavers, the seamstresses, the embroiderers, and also some striking pictures of the mill itself and the grounds. And, of course, a portrait of me. I would gladly have given this work to your uncle, but I fear his health no longer allows. It is therefore my pleasure to do business with you instead," he said. His jaw hurt from forcing his smile so much.

"That would be rather a substantial job . . . and you want to hire me for it?"

Miss Reventlow's hostile disposition had vanished, but he still heard a trace of suspicion in her voice.

I'll have you in just a minute, Gehringer thought.

"The commemorative book itself is the smallest part of the job," he said airily. "I would also like you to take pictures of all our sample products. Until now, our wholesale catalog has used only illustrations, but I'm sure you would agree when I say that photographs are far more compelling."

The photographer, now utterly speechless, gawked at him and nodded.

"I also may be publishing a mail-order catalog in the near future. One has to move with the times as a businessman, after all, and selling directly to the customer promises to be quite profitable. Furthermore, I would also like a photograph of every item in our archive, to document the development of our products past to present."

"A job like that will involve a tremendous amount of work. What you want will take months," Mimi said, then added, as if to herself, "I'd have no time at all for the studio."

And that's the whole point, Gehringer thought.

"How you administer your other affairs is your business. If you accept the job, I want to see one hundred percent from you, not one percent less," he said flatly. "I have no doubt you'll be able to find someone to help you look after your uncle. I expect to see you in my office with an answer before Berta and Richard's wedding. The commission will begin immediately after the wedding. That's three weeks from now, but we have a good deal to prepare at the mill before you can start. We'll create a studio space where you can work, organize the sample garments for the catalogs, and pull from storage all the products from the archive for those photographs. Regardless, the pictures need to be finished by the end of October." He tipped his hat, about to take his leave. "You're correct about your time—you certainly won't have much left for coffee klatches," he said, and turned to go.

He was already at the studio door when Mimi called after him: "What payment terms are you proposing?"

Herrmann Gehringer flinched. In his entire career, he'd never met a woman so quick to talk about money.

"I beg your pardon," the photographer said, sounding as if she couldn't care less about his pardon. "But my decision is largely dependent on the pay."

As if she could even consider turning down a commission like this! thought Gehringer. Everyone in the village knew that she and her uncle had been just getting by for weeks. But the woman was pigheaded, he knew, and here it was again. He turned and looked directly at her.

"You know the prices for group and portrait photographs and for the factory pictures better than I do," he said. "As far as the pictures for the archive and for my catalogs are concerned, I will assume the material and overhead costs. For each picture you take of my garments . . ." He watched the photographer furrow her brow while he named his price.

"Forgive me, but that is very low. Whether I'm photographing a linen blouse or a building, in terms of lighting, processing, and any necessary retouching, the amount of work is always the same."

"Young lady, sometimes one has to keep in mind the motto 'It's the quantity that makes the difference.' By my estimation, we're talking about more than seven hundred pictures."

"Seven—"

Gehringer was satisfied to see the words stick in Mimi Reventlow's throat. Wonderful! His plan seemed to be working.

When Mimi returned to the garden, Eveline, Sonja, and Luise were getting ready to leave. Gehringer had soured the happy mood in an instant. In silence, the women gathered up the dishes, cutlery, and chairs and carried everything into the house. When Sonja asked Mimi what Gehringer had wanted, Mimi told them about the commission. The women nodded—the anniversary of Gehringer's mill certainly would gain a lot of attention. With assertions about how lovely the afternoon had been, the women went home. Disappointed by the abrupt end to the gathering, Mimi looked at the open bottle of wine. They hadn't even had the chance to drink that in peace.

A while later, after she'd washed the dishes, Mimi told her uncle about Gehringer's offer.

"Child, this is simply splendid," said Josef. "I always dreamed about such a job. Let's have a drink to that."

Mimi fetched the schnapps bottle from the sideboard and poured two small glasses. Before they drank, though, she said, "I still don't know exactly what to make of it. A project like this is certainly a challenge, and you know how much I love a new challenge. As for the money—which isn't much, by the way—it will go to good use, of course. But I don't like the man, and I am quite certain the feeling is mutual. So why me? Why would he give such a big order to me, even at the paltry rate he's offered?"

"Why not you?" Josef said. "You're a good photographer, and everybody around here knows it. Here's to your success!"

Mimi, with a strained smile, raised her glass to her uncle. But somehow, she could not shake off the feeling that Gehringer's offer had a catch.

Josef put his glass down, leaned toward her, and looked her directly in the eyes as if he seemed to sense her insecurity and wanted to support her. "I guess we humans will never get used to the way times change, will we?"

"What do you mean?"

Josef shrugged. "If I remember right, you just told me—and with a good dose of indignation—that you bumped into one of those hobbyist photographers here in the village and that he predicted the decline of studio photography?"

She nodded reluctantly.

"I'm not one to prophesy doom, but that man was probably right about what he said. In the next few years, there really will be more and more amateur photographers. When I flip through my photography magazines, I'm amazed by the low prices for good, compact cameras. If people start taking their own christening, confirmation, and wedding photographs, then professionals like us are going to have to fight even harder for every single customer. And whether it's even going to be possible to work as a traveling photographer . . . that's another story."

"You're really boosting my spirits, thank you very much," said Mimi ironically. It wasn't as if she hadn't had the same thoughts, but so far, she'd been able to push them away far enough to keep from drowning in worry.

Josef patted her hand. "I don't mean to make you nervous, child. I just want you to see that you're going to have to take more jobs that don't exactly inspire you. If you want to live well from your profession in the years ahead, Mimi, you'll have to be flexible."

"So you think I should start being flexible by accepting Gehringer's job?" She let out an exaggerated sigh as she realized she probably wouldn't have a choice anyway.

Josef Stöckle smiled. "Yes, child, I do."

CHAPTER 29

It was two weeks later when Mimi and Johann finally saw each other again. Saturday evenings were among the few times he neither had to work nor be at his mother's beck and call. Sometimes, Johann spent Saturday evenings with some of his fellow weavers at The Oxen, but this evening, he and Mimi went for a walk outside the village.

"Now, whenever I walk this way, I think of the *Heumondfest*. What a wonderful time . . . ," Mimi said, pointing toward the big meadow with a sigh. It wasn't hard to relive that night in her mind: the sparks flying from the fires and into the darkness like fireflies, the stirring music, Johann dancing with her, the night spent together . . . She sighed again and cuddled against him as they walked, but he quickly pulled away from her.

"Sorry, but it's really too hot," he said brusquely.

Mimi inwardly rolled her eyes: Johann really wasn't the romantic type sometimes. Instead—and from a virtuous distance—she told him how Gehringer had shown up in the middle of her party and about the photography job he'd offered her.

"No respect for the leisure time of others, that's just like him." Johann shook his head. "I'm guessing he almost had a fit when he saw you all drinking coffee, didn't he?" he added with a grin.

Mimi laughed and nodded.

"And he's planning a commemorative book? All about his own personal destiny, I'll bet. Have you thought about how you're going to photograph Gehringer's slaves, meaning us? I'm sure you have ideas about that." As ironic as he sounded, Mimi also heard a certain aggressive tone in his words.

"You're the one who called the weavers slaves, not me! Don't worry. If I take the job, I'll make sure you all look your dignified best," she said coldly.

"If you have any say in the matter. You know, Gehringer will be your boss, too."

Mimi grimaced. That was the last thing she needed to hear. "I know, but I'll only be taking the job for the money. You have to be flexible as a photographer these days," she said, unintentionally repeating her uncle's words. "I'm happy for any money I can earn. If Josef needs more care in the months ahead, I don't know if I'll be able to work at all. It would be good to have some money put aside. Besides, who let himself get employed by Gehringer the minute he came back to town?" Now she was the one with the belligerent tone.

"OK, OK!" He raised his hands defensively. "But you know perfectly well why I took the job with Gehringer."

Mimi's annoyance did not completely evaporate. Johann's intentions were oh-so-noble, and yet he implied that her own were not!

"He wants me to come and see him soon to talk everything through," she said, keeping her calm.

"Does the man think you've got nothing else to do?" Johann asked.

Despite herself, Mimi had to smile. His protective instinct toward her felt good.

"Probably. Unfortunately, he's right," she said, her smile transforming to a frown. "It's not as if people are lined up waiting to get into the studio, which means I'll probably take the job. Still, I can't say I'm happy about it. I simply don't like the man."

Johann looked at her thoughtfully. "Money aside, some other aspects of the job might be useful. In Gehringer's office, you're bound to pick up bits and pieces about what he and my dear brother are planning. You could give me information. I'd know what was going on before—"

"You want me to be your spy?" Mimi frowned.

"Who said anything about spies? You just need to keep your eyes and ears open, that's all."

"We'll see," said Mimi, and they walked on hand in hand. "Are you going to Berta and Richard's wedding next week?" Although Berta was Sonja's sister, and Sonja was married to Johann's brother, Paul, the animosity between the brothers justified Mimi's question.

"No. I have no interest in spending any more time with my brother than absolutely necessary, and besides, I've promised my mother I'll chop wood for winter. I've already bought a few felled trees. Winters in the Jura often come with no warning. We could be a foot deep in snow by November, so I have to get started with the wood now, especially since I'll be chopping for Eveline, too."

"But does that have to happen *next* Saturday? Wouldn't you prefer to spend a nice day with me at the reception?" Mimi felt disappointment wash over her.

Johann grinned. "Don't be upset—remember, you're the one leading the charge to help Eveline's family."

A week later, on August 19, the wedding couple, serious but also excited, stood on the platform in the studio and waited for Mimi's instructions. As Mimi had recommended, Berta and her fiancé had come in before the wedding ceremony. Once the photographs were taken care of, they could enjoy the ceremony and reception that evening without distraction.

While Mimi arranged a stack of glass plates, she thought about how best to frame the couple. Richard Hausmann was not only considerably older and far less talkative than Berta, but also a head shorter. Could she stand him inconspicuously on a stool? If she did, she would cover their feet with a length of fabric, or otherwise retouch the photograph to make the stool disappear. *Not a good idea,* Mimi thought. Maybe she shouldn't let the height difference bother her at all—clearly Berta didn't mind. And yet, visually speaking, she was not happy.

"Your white dress is beautiful," she said to Berta. "It's not common for a bride to wear white. Most brides I've photographed have just worn their black Sunday dress and added a white veil."

"Well, we may not have much money, but we've got plenty of white fabric," Berta replied proudly. "The dress is an heirloom. My mother and Sonja both wore it."

"It's a lovely tradition," Mimi said admiringly. She fanned her face a little—it had been oppressively hot the entire week, and everyone was longing for a little cooler weather and some rain, although Mimi hoped that a thunderstorm wouldn't ruin the wedding.

"Right, let's get started. Berta, can you stand to the right of your fiancé? And, Mr. Hausmann, if you could shift your left foot forward a little? Crook your arm a little more, your elbow behind your fiancée's . . . yes, like that . . ." Mimi peered through the viewfinder while the bridegroom did his best to follow Mimi's instructions.

Traditional wedding photos didn't allow much artistic flexibility. Usually, the couple stood beside a small table, with the man just behind the woman in a protective pose. The woman would hold a small wedding bouquet in front of her body. That was the only staging required, though typically, various accoutrements, including the bridal crown and the groom's top hat, were visible on the table beside them.

But weren't rules meant to be broken? Mimi wondered.

"Mr. Hausmann, would you mind putting the top hat on? And Berta, if you could hold the bouquet only in your right hand," she said, so as not to put all the responsibility for following instructions on the groom.

With the top hat in place, bride and groom were now the same height.

"Very nice, thank you. You make an exceptional couple!" Mimi said, satisfied. "Smile!"

An hour later, Mimi found herself in front of her armoire looking for something to wear. It was too hot to wear her travel outfit. Her purple silk dress seemed far too elegant, but the flowery blouse and skirt she wore most days were not formal enough for a wedding.

"Do you mind if I go through Traudel's clothing again?" she called down the steps to her uncle. When she and Johann had gone for a walk in Laichingen the first time, he had admired her in the blouse she had borrowed from Traudel's collection.

"Take anything you need. Traudel would be happy to know that a beautiful young woman like you was wearing her clothes," her uncle answered.

Mimi had her doubts about whether she would find anything suitable for the wedding, but Josef's deceased wife had owned lovely hand-stitched garments. A finely embroidered blouse. Skirts with eyelet embroidery around the hem. Linen collars of every kind, closed with the finest mother-of-pearl buttons. *Traudel certainly had good taste in clothes,* Mimi thought, more undecided than ever about what to wear.

"Richard Hausmann told me this is his first marriage. That surprises me a little. I mean, he's not the youngest," said Mimi, wearing a tea-colored linen dress and sitting at lunch with Josef. She had prepared a slice of bread and honey for each of them. The wedding reception was going to take place at The Oxen, and she planned to ask Karolina to make a plate of food for Josef.

Her uncle laughed, which triggered a short attack of coughing. "Well, not everyone makes it to the altar young, certainly not loners like Richard," he said when he'd recovered. "I was sixty myself before I married, you know."

"Luise mentioned that people in Laichingen tend to marry late since marriage means needing some space you can call your own. She explained that with the lack of space here in the village, that's almost impossible."

"Yes, that's it exactly. And usually that means a grandparent dying first, or a room or two being vacated for some other reason, before a couple gets to say 'I do.'"

"Why don't people build a new house?" Mimi found the idea of living in her parents' house as a married woman, with only one or two rooms to call her own, very strange.

"Child, haven't you realized it yet? The people here are poor." Her uncle looked at her as if she were a little dim witted. "Another thing: when you go to The Oxen after the church ceremony, be prepared for the meal to be a little less grand than you might expect."

Mimi laughed. "Are you afraid I'm going to get myself in hot water with extravagant requests? Don't worry, I won't embarrass myself. I'm not even going to dance." Without Johann there, she had no interest in dancing anyway, she thought.

"Dance? I'd be very surprised if there were a band at Berta's wedding."

Was he joking? "But a wedding is meant to be a celebration!"

As a traveling photographer, Mimi had been invited to weddings in the Black Forest, in Hegau, and various other places. While the couples enjoyed including Mimi for her unusual travel stories, they inevitably hoped they might get a few extra photographs for free. And Mimi was always glad to grant their wish.

"I probably won't stay very late," she continued when her uncle said nothing about a celebration. "Once I've taken a few nice pictures of the party, I'll bring you dinner."

CHAPTER 30

The church ceremony, like the confirmation in the spring, was an almost grim affair. While the priest sermonized at length about the hard times a married couple had to get through with each other, Mimi could only think about the modern, optimistic sermons delivered by her own father. *Father, Mother, I miss you so much.* If Josef hadn't been so ill, and if he hadn't suffered a broken leg, she might even have considered making a short visit to Esslingen. But as things were, she needed to be with him, so travel was out of the question.

The wedding guests, twenty in all, formed a kind of guard of honor on either side of the church door at the end of the service. Mimi raised her eyebrows when she saw that Herrmann Gehringer had pulled up at the front of the church in his automobile. Like a chauffeur, he held the door open for the bride and groom to climb inside. Berta Hausmann's cheeks were flushed, and in her excitement, she caught her right shoe in the hem of her dress and would have fallen if Richard hadn't caught her arm in time. Mimi found the simple gesture touching. With the other guests, she walked behind the automobile as it rolled across the square to The Oxen. To catch each other should you fall—Mimi would like to have that with Johann.

Anton didn't like wedding parties. Usually, the couple getting married had little money to spare because they had to set up a home. This meant that only the simplest meals and drinks found their way onto the tables, and tips were proportionately meager. And yet the guests expected the best service and a round of schnapps on the house—a wedding was a joyful occasion, after all.

His mood only worsened when he saw that Christel was wedged between her father and Herrmann Gehringer. And as if that wasn't enough, Gehringer now waved the photographer over to join him at the main table, as if *he* were the father of the bride and not Georg Neumann. Still, Anton thought, Mimi did not seem particularly enthusiastic about *everyone* she had to sit with—she took a seat at the far end of the table, as far from Gehringer as possible.

"It was very nice of you to invite me," Anton heard Mimi say to Berta Hausmann when he brought a tureen of chicken soup, the entrée, to the table.

"It's our pleasure," the bride replied in a low voice. "We don't have many friends. With all the work, it's difficult to keep up with people as one should. An afternoon like the one we women spent with you recently, just to sit and talk and have a bit of fun, well, we're just not used to that kind of thing. All we do is work, work, work . . ." She cast a careful glance around the table to make sure Gehringer wasn't listening, but he seemed to be deep in conversation with Paul Merkle.

"All that hard work means we deserve a good time occasionally, right? I'd be very happy to arrange another gathering in my garden," Mimi said with a smile.

While Luise, as mother of the bride, served the soup, Anton used the opportunity to catch Christel's attention. Aggravated as he was, he couldn't help but appreciate how golden her hair was in the sunlight streaming through the windows.

Christel, who seemed to have caught his look, put her napkin aside, whispered something to her mother across the table, then stood and went in the direction of the restroom, without a glance at Anton.

A few seconds later, he followed her as inconspicuously as he could. He locked the restroom door behind him.

"Did you hear? I'm a model for Mr. Gehringer now, at the mill! I've already modeled aprons, skirts, and blouses twice—just this week," she said before he could say a word. She looked at him intently, practically daring him to protest.

"No doubt the buyers bought twice as much as usual," Anton said, forcing a grin while trying to keep from grinding his teeth. The thought of Christel showing herself off to random old men was almost more than he could bear.

Christel was taken aback for a moment, then laughed brightly. "You're right, as it happens. Gehringer says I'm the best advertising he could get for his linen. And it gets better . . ." She leaned toward him. "Mr. Gehringer's arranged for someone to make an advertising film about the mill! It's for the big anniversary. Maybe I'll get a chance to act in it." She sounded breathless—as if the very thought might overwhelm her.

"A film about weaving linen. How incredibly exciting that's going to be. Where would you come into it?" Anton asked mockingly. He didn't like how Christel was immersing herself in her work for Gehringer. "Sounds to me like Gehringer's slowly losing his mind."

"As long as you don't lose yours and you're still working on our plan to leave here, everything will be fine," Christel replied archly. "What about Mimi Reventlow's contact in Meersburg? Clara Berg, isn't it? Has she been in touch?"

He shook his head.

"Have you at least managed to get some money together? We're not going to get out of here without money, and you know that perfectly well."

Anton frowned. What kind of tone was that? Not so long ago, she practically jumped down his throat if he even dared to raise the subject of leaving Laichingen. And now he couldn't make it happen quickly enough?

"I'm taking care of everything, like I promised," he said, irritated. "But you're earning more from Gehringer than before. You could put that money aside."

"My father takes my wages," Christel said sourly. "He says because I live with him for free."

Anton could do nothing but scowl. The smell of the freshly cooked fritters, the next course, filled the air.

"Anton? Anton!" he heard his mother call the next moment. He took Christel's hand in his, pulled her closer, and peered into her eyes. "I promise you this: we'll soon be able to turn our backs on Gehringer, your father, and all of this. A life of wealth, fame, and glamour is waiting for us. When we get married, it's going to be quite different from what your aunt's getting here. The finest food, a band playing dance music. And we'll drink champagne from crystal glasses. Trust me!"

She nodded half-heartedly, then returned to the main room. Anton trotted into the kitchen, where the fritters were waiting.

With two fully laden plates, Anton returned to the wedding table.

"Tell me, what are your plans for after the wedding?" Mimi was just asking Berta.

"Plans?" The bride shrugged. "What sort of plans do you mean?"

Anton sighed. Couldn't the photographer see that topics like that were a waste of time in Laichingen? The only plan anyone there should be making was for how to escape!

"Well, you know, what you want to do next," Mimi replied a little helplessly. "Some people plan a honeymoon trip. Others might open a business together. Most look forward to children."

"Children, yes, that would be nice. A whole house full!" The bride's face flushed red. She glanced uncertainly at her husband.

Anton grinned to himself. Christel's aunt could count her blessings if she got even one child out of old Richard.

"But now that you ask," Berta went on, "there's one thing I'd like to try. I'm already a seamstress, but I'd love to learn how to sew a traditional outfit. You know, one with an underdress, a skirt, an apron, a complicated blouse, and everything that goes with it." Berta's eyes sparkled almost more than they had earlier at the altar when she'd said "I do."

"So what's stopping you? You can learn anything," Mimi encouraged her.

Anton was refilling cider glasses when Gehringer leaned across the table toward the two women.

"Did I hear right?" he said to Berta with feigned horror. "Are you planning to quit your job?"

Anton poured the cider as slowly as he could, not wanting to miss a word.

Berta instantly turned chalk white and turned to her groom for support. "Good heavens no! Why would you think that?"

Instead of answering Berta, the businessman addressed Christel in a loud voice. "Miss Merkle, have you ever modeled a traditional outfit for me?"

Christel shook her head.

"Then what *do* you model when our esteemed customers come, Miss Merkle?"

"Your anniversary garments, your—" Christel began.

How proud she sounds, Anton thought. As if it were an honor to be allowed to even touch one of Gehringer's damned garments.

"And can you tell me, my dear Miss Merkle," Gehringer said, cutting her off, "how many of these anniversary designs we are making?"

Anton saw with satisfaction how Christel suddenly looked as unsure of herself as the new bride. It made no difference to Gehringer who he put on the spot, Anton thought bitterly. The main thing for the businessman was to have his big moment.

"Where the numbers are concerned, I'll be glad to help," said Gehringer to Christel and Berta, his smile as saccharine as if he were handing out candy to children. "The anniversary designs are to be produced in a run of thirty thousand. For that, I need hardworking people on the looms *and* the sewing machines." His smile froze in place. He looked directly at Berta. "So I would be very grateful to you if you would concentrate on your work, just like the rest of us do. Maybe the day will come when traditional outfits are produced in quantity here in Laichingen, but until that day, we must devote ourselves to what we are able to do, and what the good Lord expects of us here on earth. And to the best of my knowledge, that is still the production and finishing of linen." Gehringer dabbed at his lips with his napkin, pushed his plate away, and stood up. "My ladies, gentlemen, bride and groom—I'm afraid I must leave you. Work awaits. My responsibility is to ensure that, in the future as today, enough food finds its way onto every plate in Laichingen."

Then he straightened his arm and pointed his index finger at Mimi Reventlow.

"And you, young lady, I expect to see you in my office early on Monday morning to discuss my commission. You were supposed to have given me an answer before now. If you are not interested, please tell me—a replacement is easily found."

CHAPTER 31

Mimi, perplexed, could only stare in the direction of the departing businessman. What was that performance all about? An awkward and embarrassed silence hung over the table like a cloud.

"Everybody ready for dessert?" said Anton loudly to change the mood.

Luise nodded to him gratefully. Then, in a reprimanding voice, she said to Berta, "Did you have to do that? You know Gehringer doesn't like immodest talk."

Berta, already berated enough for one day, let alone her wedding day, only sank lower on her seat.

"The company anniversary next year is going to take dedication from all of us. No one will have time for hobbies," Paul Merkle chimed in. "Some people in the industry fear that many linen weavers won't survive the price war with the low-cost cotton producers. We can count ourselves lucky that Gehringer is ahead of the pack in every respect. It isn't too much for him to demand our best efforts, is it?"

"Pardon me for saying so, dear brother-in-law, but this is still our wedding day," said Richard Hausmann, so sharply that Mimi actually flinched. "My wife can think and say whatever she likes. She can also talk to whomever she wants." Stroking his gray beard, the groom turned benevolently to face Mimi. "If my wife wants to learn how to sew a traditional outfit, then she will. We work for Gehringer, it's true, but what we do in our own time is no business of his. If it had been up to me, I wouldn't even have invited the man to our wedding." He looked reproachfully in his mother-in-law's direction.

Everyone stared at the groom. No one seemed to have expected a speech like that from him. Paul Merkle clenched his jaw, as if fighting back the urge to pick a fight with his new brother-in-law.

"Anton, where's the dessert?" Richard called out. "You marry only once in life, so let's make a celebration of it!"

He wrapped one arm protectively around Berta, and she sighed deeply. She straightened her shoulders, smiled, and with newfound confidence, said, "Eat! Drink! We have enough of everything."

After Gehringer's departure and the groom's firmly spoken words, the atmosphere kept improving. Richard told funny anecdotes, there was plenty of laughter and talk, and Anton decided to treat everybody to a second round of plum schnapps.

Only Mimi's mood was subdued. She still could not fit Gehringer's performance into her scheme of things. If Johann had been here, he would surely have said that the weaver baron had been reminding people of their "place." But to Mimi, when Gehringer turned on her, it had seemed more like a power struggle between him and herself. But if that was the case, then why? Because he found her too forward? Too modern? And it made no difference anyway, she thought—one way or another, everything inside her rebelled against doing business with the man.

"Gehringer isn't a bad man, believe me," Luise whispered to her as if she could read Mimi's mind. "He never really got over the way his son disappeared so soon after his wife passed on." She shook her head sadly. "It's been fifteen years . . ."

Mimi looked at her neighbor. "What happened?"

"That's just the problem: no one knows if Michael's dead or missing or something else. He went on a trip to Italy and never came back." Luise seemed to drift off into her thoughts for a moment before she said, "It's funny, but I've found myself wondering about Michael Gehringer recently. He was such an artistic young man, just like the young Schubert. Alexander reminds me of him, in a way." She shrugged.

Mimi said nothing. What was she supposed to say?

"But what about you?" Luise asked, putting on a smile and changing the subject. "What do you think of our wedding here?"

"It's been a wonderful time. As mother of the bride, you must be very happy." Mimi, smiling herself, let her eyes move from one to another of the merry guests. "And your daughter looks very happy with her husband," she added. Johann would surely have stood up for her in such a situation, just as Richard had for Berta.

"In a village like ours, there aren't many unmarried men and women to choose from. Sometimes you have to take what you can get," said Luise pragmatically, but not without affection. "You have to figure out how to make a marriage work. In good times and in bad . . . they don't say that for nothing, not here."

Mimi raised her eyebrows. "I believe Berta and Richard Hausmann are very attached to one another, from their hearts."

Luise reached over and squeezed Mimi's hand. "As a traveling photographer, I'm sure you haven't had an easy time finding a husband. But it will happen. You'll meet a good man somewhere along the road. You'll marry, settle down, and have your own happy life. Then you'll have a livelihood, too."

Mimi, chagrined, extricated her hand from Luise's. Even if her neighbor's words were well intentioned, they still hurt. Yes, she knew that society regarded her as an old maid. But so far, her work had always been closest to her heart. And so far, too, it had given her a decent livelihood without the need for anyone else to provide for her. Now, though, she could imagine getting married, but if she walked to the altar, then it would be because she unreservedly loved the man at her side. Because she admired him, and enjoyed being with him. Because she would like it if they challenged each other occasionally. Because they thought in similar ways. And because their hearts beat with the same rhythm.

Like with Johann. Johann and her.

"Can you make sure your sisters get to bed soon? I have to go out again," Eveline said to Alexander as she combed her hair in front of the mirror.

"Yes. Is there anything else I should do?" Alexander said. He was sitting at the table, embroidering a cushion.

"Now that you ask, there is. The stove needs to be swept out."

Alexander nodded. "I'll take care of that!"

Eveline smiled to herself. Ever since they had known for certain that Alexander would start at the art school at the beginning of September, her son had been a different person. No more inward suffering, no more brooding. Instead, he helped her around the house as much as his leg would allow. And he had taken up embroidery!

It had been his idea, not hers. "I can't help you in the field with my leg like this, but if you show me how to use a needle and thread, I'll help with the embroidery. No one needs to know," he'd said just a few days before.

She had thought it over. Why not, in fact? And so she had shown him how she first "drew" each pattern with little pinpricks, and then completed the embroidery itself with satin, stem, and feather stitches. With his very first practice piece, Eveline could see that her son was more adept at the art than some who did it professionally, and perhaps nearly as good as she herself.

One last pin, and her hair was finished. *Almost as nice as Mimi manages,* Eveline thought, satisfied. It felt good to pay attention to her appearance. And was she mistaken, or did she look less haggard than she had since Klaus's death? *Being in love will do that to you.*

She smiled as she picked up the food basket she'd prepared earlier in the evening. Gone were the days when they had nothing but moldy bread to eat. Thanks to the help they got from the neighbors, she'd been able to put more and better food on the table for the past few weeks, and she'd been able to add a few tasty morsels to her basket.

"Where are you going?" Alexander asked.

"To visit your father's grave," Eveline replied.

"With food?" Alexander raised his eyebrows doubtfully.

"Maybe the prayers will make me hungry," said Eveline, then she closed the door behind her. Since when did she have to justify herself to her son?

It was as if, deep down, everything was fitting together like the pieces in a great mosaic, Eveline thought as she passed the field that Sonja Merkle had decided to let her use for the next three years. It was little more than a stone's throw from her house, but she doubted that she would use it for as long as even two years. Her period of mourning would end the following year, in June 1912, and if all went well, she would marry Johann in the autumn. Then he would provide for her.

Johann . . . the very thought of seeing him soon made her heart race. No one would disturb them today. Johann's brother, Paul, and their mother, Edelgard, were at Berta's wedding. Eve was planning to make good use of the time she and Johann would have alone.

A few days earlier, Eveline had asked Edelgard where the Merkle family felled their firewood. "If Johann is chopping wood for me, then the least I can do is take him a decent meal and a jug of cider," she'd said to Edelgard. The elderly seamstress had nodded her appreciation.

Or had there been more in Edelgard's look? Eveline wondered as she drew closer to the patch of forest where Johann had purchased the felled trees. Affection. Goodwill. The way Johann's mother looked after the girls, or sometimes simply embraced her or silently consoled her, was so loving . . . as if Edelgard could already see in Eve her future daughter-in-law. Edelgard liked her—Eve could sense it. But there was probably more to it than that. If Johann married someone from the village, he wouldn't soon pack up and leave again. *Never fear, dear Edelgard,* Eve thought, *I'll make sure Johann stays.*

The forest where Johann worked was steep and hard to access. High ferns, grasses, and thistles grew alongside the narrow path that Eveline followed, and she had to stop often to disentangle her skirt. Carrying her basket carefully so she wouldn't spill anything, she picked her way up the hillside. But when she finally saw Johann, his torso bare and sweat on his brow, running the saw powerfully back and forth through a log, all the strain and struggle were forgotten.

"Johann . . ." It was no more than a whisper, but he looked up instantly.

"Eveline!"

How he smiled! As if the sun rose just at the sight of her, she thought blissfully. She lifted the basket. "I've brought you something to eat." She was looking around for a place for them to sit when Johann took the basket from her hand.

"I could use a break. But not here. Come on, I know a better spot," he said, and reached out his free hand for hers.

Holding his hand tightly, they clambered farther up the steep slope. *He smells so good,* she thought, breathing in the scent of fresh sweat, wood, and fir tree sap. Her heart beat harder, but it had little to do with the physical exertion of the climb.

After a few minutes, they reached a small raised clearing. Johann set down the picnic basket and spread his shirt, which he'd tied loosely around his waist, on the ground. "If I may, my lady?" With an elaborate flourish, he invited her to sit.

The ground was soft—*Soft as a love nest,* Eveline thought, and she had to resist the urge to snuggle against him.

"This is one of my favorite places," Johann said when he was sitting beside her. He smiled and went on, "When I lived in America, I often dreamed of coming up here one day with you. I thought about you far more than was good for me."

Eveline felt her face flush with joy. With trembling hands, she opened the picnic basket and took out what she'd prepared. Bread and drippings, and a portion of the sweet dessert—*Ofenschlupfer,* a Swabian dish made from leftover bread and apple slices—that she and the children had had at lunch earlier.

But instead of taking the bread and drippings, as Eveline had assumed he would, he pulled the dish of *Ofenschlupfer* closer. "How did you know this was my favorite dish?" With a fork, he dug hungrily into the apple-bread mixture, which she'd sprinkled with extra sugar.

Eveline looked at him affectionately as he ate. "It just occurred to me that you wouldn't have had anything like this in America."

He nodded. "As uncertain as I was at the start, now I know I was right to come back. I'm in the right place at the right time, I could even say." He laughed. "And you?"

"What do you mean, me?"

"Laichingen isn't your home. Why didn't you go back to your parents after Klaus died? They would take you back, surely. You'd be rich. You wouldn't have to worry about money or anything else."

"Then I'd have to leave you," Eveline said, half joking, but she immediately grew serious again. "There were moments I considered it. Other than his farewell letter, Klaus left us nothing. He didn't give a thought to how we were supposed to get by without him. I have to watch every pfennig, and the children and I still go to bed hungry sometimes. If it wasn't for my neighbors' help, and if I didn't have you to chop wood for me, well . . . I don't know how I would get by. It's true that all these cares would disappear if I went back to my parents' house, but I would have to prostrate myself before my father. 'It was all a terrible mistake. Please forgive me and take me, poor sinner, back into your house!'" she said melodramatically.

Johann, scraping the last crumbs from the plate, laughed softly.

Gazing out over the valley, Eveline continued, "But you know what the hard years at Klaus's side taught me? That there's something at least as important as a full belly, and that's freedom—on the inside. That's what killed Klaus: he had no inner freedom. He choked to death on all the conventions and unwritten rules that go with living here." She frowned as she pointed down toward the village. "Everything we did had one aim: to lead a life pleasing to God and to Gehringer, and it was Gehringer calling the shots. No one bothered to ask how we felt about it. I never wanted to bow to him, but . . ."

Johann put the plate aside and took her hand in his. *Why am I telling him all this?* Eve wondered, realizing at the same time that these were thoughts she'd never before dared to speak aloud. Inner freedom . . . was that what had separated Klaus and her? And was that the bond that tied her to Johann?

"If I went back to my parents, I would only be trading one despot for another. Father would want Alexander to work in his factory, no doubt, and my mother would turn Marianne and Erika into little ladies and drag them around to high teas and receptions and such, whether or not they wanted to go. I wouldn't have any say at all," she said bitterly.

Eve paused and glanced at Johann, whose expression seemed sympathetic. Still, she shook her head and continued. "No, I didn't make it through all those years at Klaus's side for that. His death had to be good for something. I want my children to grow up free! Alexander must go to art school, though it practically kills me to accept alms from half the village so he can. My daughters, too, when the time comes, should be able to choose for themselves how they want to live. If they really want to be embroiderers or seamstresses like the other young women here, I won't stand in their way. But I would much rather that they go out into the world and use all their wonderful talents to lead good and beautiful lives. The times of the great Gehringer and Karl-Otto Hoffmeister will one day pass—you can't tell people how to lead their lives forever. People like us have rights, too. I don't care if it costs me everything, I'll fight for this freedom."

Suddenly, tears sprang to her eyes. *Oh God, why am I so worked up?* She had wanted Johann to see her as attractive and seductive, and yet she could do nothing to stop the flood of tears—tears of fury, tears of despair, tears of sadness, and tears for all the years she had lost.

"Eveline, Eve . . ." Johann wrapped his arms around her. "You have no idea what your words mean to me. I knew before I left all those years ago that you were different from the other women here. In America, I felt that kind of freedom on the inside, but since I've been back in Laichingen, I'm as much at the mercy of the old conventions as ever. It's almost as if I never left, and all my experience out in the world feels wasted. I'm angry at myself for letting people drag me this way and that. Damn it, how can I stay master of myself? It's what I'm encouraging others to be, after all. Masters of their own lives—at least in regard to work, and that will give them mastery over all the rest of their lives."

Eveline was taken aback. Such doubts were the last thing she'd expected from Johann. And who was dragging him around? His mother? Gehringer? Or was he somehow alluding to the expectation that they would not meet like this during her year of mourning?

"Sometimes, one has to betray conventions to stay true to oneself," she said, her voice raw with emotion. "Not everyone needs to understand that or welcome it, but for the sake of your own freedom, you can't feel tied to every rule. Each of us has the right to decide for ourselves when the old rules no longer apply. Life means change, even when it's usually easier to cling to tradition."

Johann looked at Eve, and she thought she saw admiration in his eyes.

"Betraying convention to stay true to yourself . . . is that perhaps the secret behind everything?"

"Perhaps," she said airily. "Just do what your heart tells you is right. Like me . . ." *Enough theory,* she thought, and kissed him.

"This feels damned right to me," he whispered between kisses, and pulled Eve closer.

A warm thrill ran through her as she felt his arousal.

Then it all happened so quickly that, later, when she replayed the scene over again in her mind, Eveline had trouble recalling the exact sequence. His resin-sticky hands unbuttoning her blouse. Her skirt torn from her body. His trousers torn from his. Quickly! They had already lost so much time. Her groans of pleasure as he pressed her into the soft floor of the forest. Her outspread legs, her body, greedy, taking him in.

"Eveline!" Her name on his lips. A cry of triumph at the climax of his lust.

"Johann . . ." His name, no more than a whisper on her lips, washed away with the torrent of her emotions.

CHAPTER 32

The hot summer weather had held through the wedding ceremony and reception, but the next day, the relief from the heat everyone had been longing for finally came. When the thunderstorms passed, they left behind rainy and cool weather.

When Mimi stepped outside on Monday morning, the day after the storm, it seemed to her that for mid-August, autumn was getting a little ahead of itself. She became a little anxious, too: Didn't they say that autumn was when people passed away?

She'd gone back inside the house to put on a cardigan before walking to Gehringer's mill for their meeting when she heard a horse whinny loudly on the square in front of the shop. A reason not to have to see the man, perhaps? She looked out the window and saw a wagon similar to the one her uncle had once used for his traveling business. Josef's Sun Coach had been painted black with elegant gold lettering, but this wagon was a garish red. In the muted light of the rainy day, it looked like something descended from another planet. Large letters inscribed on the side of the wagon announced, "Photographic Accessories of Every Kind—Max Mutter."

"What does *he* want?" Mimi murmured to herself. She had met the shifty salesman two or three years earlier in Pforzheim. Mimi turned to her uncle, who was sitting at the table reading a newspaper, and said,

"A salesman just pulled up. Max Mutter. Have you done business with him?"

Josef frowned. "With that crook? Never! Everything is twice as expensive as it should be and half as good." His frown turned to a smile, which gave way to a coughing fit.

Mimi took a step back. It was important not to get too close to Josef when he coughed, the doctor had told her many times. A good constitution can certainly prevent an infection, but a little caution was always better than regret. For several days, Josef had been suffering sweaty fevers, and cool compresses hadn't seemed to help. His chest hurt from all the coughing, and he hadn't touched the chicken soup from Berta's wedding.

"That was my impression of him, too, when I met him a couple of years ago. I'll send Mr. Crook on his way," she said with feigned gaiety. She shouldn't let her concern for Josef show, Dr. Ludwig had told her recently, and he advised her of the importance of being optimistic around her uncle.

"Optimistic"! Mimi thought bitterly as she stepped out and walked around the side of the house to the shop. Every day, she watched her uncle being eaten away by tuberculosis, and there was nothing she could do. How was she supposed to stay optimistic?

"You?" The traveling salesman looked as if he'd seen a ghost. "You're Mimi Reventlow, the traveling photographer!"

"We meet again," said Mimi flatly. *What a strange man,* she thought as the man looked her up and down. Max Mutter's crow-black hair was slick with pomade, and his suit—from too much wear and too little washing—looked as greasy as his hair. The skin beneath his right eye had a light bluish-purple tinge to it, the color of a wilting violet. Rarely had she met anyone who seemed more obviously untrustworthy than the photographic accessory salesman. When she'd met him in Pforzheim, he had palmed off a poorly painted and very overpriced backdrop of Neuschwanstein Castle to the photographer with whom Mimi had been working at the time. When she returned from an errand, she walked into the studio just as a princely sum from the cash register was placed in Max Mutter's hands.

Horrified by the kitschy backdrop, Mimi had asked cautiously whether it really fit with the style of the studio. Mutter, who had already shoved the money in his pocket, had glared at her venomously and left quickly. It wasn't long before the studio owner was tearing his hair out about his misguided purchase. "How could I?" he said, pointing to the pink fairy-tale castle. Mimi hadn't known whether to be amused or sympathetic. In the end, she and the photographer had gone after Max Mutter, but every attempt to persuade him to make good failed—the peddler would not cancel the transaction, which earned him quite a few choice words from Mimi.

"I heard that Josef Stöckle's business was in new hands," he said. "If I'd known it was you—" His eyes sparked with hatred.

"Well, it looks like you've driven all the way out to the Swabian Jura for nothing." Mimi turned to go back to the house, but the salesman caught her sleeve.

"Who knows? A new broom sweeps clean, as they say. And in that respect, my new selection of backdrops might be just the ticket. Why not take a look?" He put his hand on Mimi's back, and though she tried to shake him off, he pushed her in the direction of his wagon, opening the doors zealously. "Here: a stage set from Franz Lehár's *The Merry Widow*. And here: a view of the Lorelei and the river Rhine. And one that's been selling very well: a biplane! Your male customers will love to see themselves as princes of the air!"

Against her will, Mimi was impressed: each canvas was more horrifying than the one before.

"Thank you very much, but my uncle's studio is already outfitted perfectly well for my purposes."

Instead of giving up, Max Mutter pulled a basket from the interior of the wagon. It was filled with silk flowers and colorful fans. "Why bore your esteemed customers with your uncle's old props? Here, for your female clientele. You have to keep up with fashion, young lady!"

"I don't *have* to do anything." Crossing her arms over her chest, Mimi narrowed her eyes at the salesman.

"You don't think you're going to get rid of me so easily, do you? I came all this way, after all. That means you should buy something from me, or else . . ." The man took a threatening step toward Mimi.

"Could you go to the bank in Amstetten for me today?" His mother's voice was so weary that Anton had trouble understanding her.

"Mother, what's the matter?" he asked uneasily across the breakfast table. She'd been getting tired a lot lately, which was not like her at all.

But Karolina Schaufler waved away his concern. "Nothing to do with you," she said gruffly. She took the old money pouch, soft from years of service, from her skirt pocket and put it on the table, then removed the banknotes and slid them into an envelope, which she handed to Anton. "This is our take from the last two weeks and the wedding on Saturday. I don't like to have so much money lying around. Your father's off hunting again, so it would be good if you could take it to the bank."

Anton nodded and smiled. Amstetten wasn't Stuttgart, but going anywhere was always better than peeling potatoes.

Fifteen minutes later, he left the inn, whistling as he stepped out into the square. A whole day to himself—he could hardly believe his luck. Should he ask Alexander to come along? No, Alexander would be heading off to Stuttgart in a couple of weeks, and no doubt still had a lot to prepare, and he had been busy taking care of what he could to help his mother.

Christel, though—she'd love to go. Maybe there was a movie theater in Amstetten? But then he remembered that Christel would be modeling for Gehringer today. Blast it! He kicked a stone across the square. It bounced straight toward a horse and wagon in front of Josef Stöckle's shop. Anton had never seen the wagon before. A visitor? Maybe a doctor from another town? But the wagon didn't look respectable enough for that.

Anton looked at the time. It would still be a while before the train left. He'd go and see what was going on at the Stöckle place. Maybe Miss Reventlow would like to go to Amstetten with him?

A peddler, Anton realized when he drew close enough to see the inscription on the wagon. Then he heard Mimi say, "I don't *have* to do anything." She sounded combative.

Anton frowned. Was the man harassing her? His suspicion was confirmed when the salesman said, "You don't think you're going to get rid of me so easily, do you? I came all this way, after all. That means you should buy something from me, or else . . ." Then he stepped toward her aggressively.

Anton raced around the wagon and planted himself between the stranger and the photographer. "Get the hell out of here!" he snarled at the man. Then he put one arm around Mimi's shoulders and led her back to the house.

"Thank you," she said, her voice trembling slightly. "What a horrible man. I'm glad you came along when you did."

Anton nodded grimly. "That guy really looked like he could be dangerous," he said. Then an idea came to him—he ran through the necessary steps in his mind and decided it might just work. But he had to act quickly . . .

"You're all right?"

Mimi nodded.

"OK, I have to go. I've got a train to catch. My mother's sent me off to the bank in Amstetten. I've never thought about getting robbed before, but after what just happened with that man, having all this money on me is suddenly worrying . . ." He put on a fearful grimace. *Don't overdo it, you idiot,* he warned himself.

"Then watch out for yourself," Mimi called after him as he hurried away.

"You go in there and look for Christel Merkle. She's probably in the glass pavilion. Got it? Tell her I have to talk to her urgently and that she should come out," said Anton to a boy around eight years old. Anton had stopped him on the way to the station and asked if he wanted to earn ten pfennigs. It was still summer vacation, and lots of children earned a bit of pocket money running errands and doing other little jobs in the weaving mills. One boy more or less wouldn't be noticed.

Anton held the ten pfennig coin up in the air. "For you, but only if you get Christel out here fast. Now go, hurry!"

Christel was there within a few minutes, dressed in a black skirt and a fine white lacy blouse and looking every bit like Gehringer's personal secretary. The boy with her held out his hand to Anton, demanding his pay, and Anton gave him the coin. With a broad grin, the boy ran off.

"Are you crazy? What's gotten into you, interrupting me at work like this?" Christel snapped at him, looking nervously back toward the mill. "If Gehringer or my father catches me standing out here with you . . ."

It was certainly true that he didn't want anyone to see them, Anton thought. "If it wasn't so important, I wouldn't have bothered you, I promise. Give me five minutes, all right?" As he spoke, he grabbed Christel's hand and pulled her with him. Along the side of Gehringer's mill ran a small path, to the left and right of which grew hedges of prickly hawthorn bushes and wild roses.

"Ow! This is dangerous—I'm ruining my blouse!" Christel protested when Anton pulled her up the path.

He looked around frantically. He'd come up with his plan in seconds, and now he had to put it into action just as fast. But for that he needed a suitable tool. He found it a few yards farther along. He pushed his way through the spiky hawthorn, ignoring the prickles, and picked up a branch as thick as his arm.

"Right, now you have to bash me over the head with this." He held out the branch to Christel invitingly.

"What? I'm supposed to hit you? You have lost your mind!" She turned to go, but Anton held her firmly by the wrist.

"I know it isn't easy for you, but it has to be this way. This is about no less than our future." He frantically sketched out his plan for Christel.

She listened closely, then looked at him with something like a mixture of repulsion and fascination. "You'd do this? For us?"

Anton straightened his shoulders. "This and a lot more, if I have to." He took the envelope of cash out of his trouser pocket. "Here's the money. Look after it. If my mother found it, well . . ."

Without hesitation, Christel lifted her skirt and tucked the envelope between her underwear and girdle. "No one's going to look for any money here," she said, grinning. "And I've already got a good hiding place in mind at home."

Anton, already weak at the knees from the sight of Christel's bare thigh, held out the branch to her again. "Now do it! Hard!"

Before he knew what happened, an intense pain suddenly filled his right ear and he felt so nauseated that he almost vomited. Blood ran into one eye, and he staggered away, trying to find something to hold on to, but there was nothing but the thorny hedge.

"Are you all right? Oh God, was that too hard?" he heard Christel's voice as if through a heavy fog. "Can I leave you alone? I have to go . . . Anton, say something!"

"I'm OK," he groaned. Then he collapsed, and everything around him turned black.

CHAPTER 33

The aggressive salesman had just pulled away in his wagon when the mailman arrived with a letter for Mimi from Esslingen. Still standing in the doorway, Mimi tore open the envelope. The question of where Alexander would live during his studies had been settled, her mother wrote. Friends of friends would take him in. They lived in Bad Cannstatt, a beautiful suburb of Stuttgart. The man was French and worked for the city; his wife was originally from Remstal and worked as a nurse at the Olga Hospital. Her mother had included the address on a separate note and said that the hosts were looking forward to welcoming Alexander as their guest on the fourth of September. The family wanted no money, but expected the student to help them with the housework.

Thank God, Mimi thought. The letter came just in time since Alexander was due to arrive in Stuttgart in two weeks. She had to give Alexander and Eveline the good news right away.

It was afternoon when Mimi finally set off for Gehringer's mill. She didn't care that it was long past the morning meeting he'd commanded. The detour to the Schubert family had been worth it. Eveline had been so radiant, and Alexander had nearly knocked her over with his embrace! Mimi had never seen either of them so happy.

On an impulse, before going to the mill, she went back to the studio and took her camera, tripod, and a stack of packed glass plates along with her. After the rain that morning, a diffuse light now filled the day, painting the square and the surrounding buildings almost golden. Maybe she would be able to take a good picture of the mill grounds.

On her way to Gehringer's factory, she noticed the ever-present clacking of the looms from the mills in the village grow louder and louder. Mimi smiled. It was the same sound she had heard on her arrival in Laichingen, back when she had first walked along the main road leading into the village, her suitcase in her hand. That had been in April—not even half a year ago, but for Mimi it felt like half a lifetime.

Arriving at the front gate, Mimi introduced herself and then asked the way to Herrmann Gehringer's office. The gatekeeper explained that the office was in the left wing of the building, but that Mr. Gehringer was doing his final daily inspection of the weaving shed. He pointed to the large, elongated wooden building to the right of the entrance.

Mimi thanked the man. On her way, she passed the glass pavilion. When she'd first visited the mill, with Eveline, shortly before Klaus's death, the glass pavilion had not yet been built. She was certain she could take a striking picture of it.

On that visit, it had been deathly quiet, and Gehringer had been in the middle of a speech to the weavers. Today, when she opened the door of the weaving shed, she was greeted by a deafening roar. A din of motors and gears, hissing, the clacking looms . . .

My God, is it always this loud? she wondered as her eyes slowly adjusted to the twilight inside. There were certainly enough windows, but they were so dusty that daylight hardly seemed to penetrate at all. The air also was filled with dust, and it was terribly hot and stuffy. Mimi wiped the beading sweat from her brow. No doubt it was correspondingly cold in winter. Would she be able to take photographs in that soupy gloom at all? She'd do well to try a test image right away, she thought, gazing at the many looms lined up on the long sides of the rectangular building—before coming here with Eveline, she had never realized just how immense the looms were.

Somehow, the word "loom" conjured an image of a simple handicraft one could manage sitting down. But there was something monstrous about the machines. And no one sat around comfortably. No, the men were constantly on the move, left and right, adjusting a lever here, checking thread tension there. No one seemed to have noticed her presence yet, or if they had, none of the weavers looked up from his work. Their eyes were on their looms, where everything seemed to be in motion—warps, drive belts, shuttles, spindles—and the hissing and clacking continued unabated. *How could anyone work here day after day without going mad?* Mimi wondered, then she quickly positioned her tripod, attached the camera, and disappeared beneath her black cloth for a first look. Through the camera's viewfinder, the looms, if anything, appeared even more threatening, and the weavers themselves skinnier, more weary, more exhausted.

Gehringer was nowhere in sight, but she saw Johann at the far end of the building. He gave her a quick nod, but did not come over to her. Looking closely, she saw that, in this section of the weaving shed, Johann and his colleagues looked after not just one loom but two at once.

"Piecework." Johann had talked to her several times about the agonies bound up with the word, but this was the first time she was seeing with her own eyes the incredible workload it involved. *Oh, Johann,* she thought, her heart aching. Now she understood why he was often too tired in the evening even to go for a walk, and why he seemed to prefer moistening his parched throat with a glass of cider in The Oxen to spending time with her.

Mimi's thoughts were interrupted when a boy with an oilcan in one hand almost ran into her. What were children doing here? Mimi wondered. Young boys scurried between the looms, bringing the weavers water. A boy to Mimi's left was working hard to retie a broken thread on a loom, and another swept the floor, which only kicked more dust into the air. Like the grown men, the boys also looked pale and tired, and most of them were skinnier than Alexander! Horrified by this alien world opening up before her, Mimi took several photographs. She had never thought it would be so loud, hectic, and dusty. No doubt these were not the pictures Gehringer expected from her, she thought cynically. But now that she was here . . .

If she positioned herself at the end of the aisle that ran between the machines, she would have the looms on both sides of the image. A fascinating symmetry, she thought, and felt her skin tingle with excitement. She quickly disappeared beneath her black cloth and swapped the exposed glass plate for another.

The cloud of dust hovered in a yellowish shimmer over each of the looms. The children in their rags, so small and fragile against the enormous looms. The glassy eyes of the weavers, trapped in the rhythm of the wooden shuttles shooting the linen wefts in a relentless tempo left to right to left . . . Before she knew it, Mimi had exposed a dozen glass plates. One more picture, she thought, a photograph of Johann working two machines at once. But just then she heard a cry beside her unlike anything she'd heard before.

"My eye!" screamed one of the weavers, holding both hands over his face. It was an elderly man, and he began to stagger, then fell to the floor beside his loom. Johann shut down his looms and came running almost instantly.

"Record this," Johann shouted as he passed. "*This* is the reality, not the picture-book idyll the damned owner has in mind."

Helpless, Mimi could only watch as Johann kneeled beside the injured weaver. "Gustav, what's happened?"

The man only whimpered. Tears—or some other eye fluid?—ran down his cheek beneath his hands.

"The shuttle flew out of the box and hit him in the head," called the man from the loom behind.

"Shit," Johann muttered, and he bit down on his lip so hard it turned white. "Come on, Gustav, I'll get you to the doctor."

He tried to help the injured man up, but Gustav couldn't move from the floor and curled there in his misery. "I can't get up. My feet . . . after so many hours . . . I'm so weak!"

Johann's stifled fury, the helplessness of the other weavers, who couldn't even step away from their monstrous machines, Gustav's whimpering—suddenly, it was too much for Mimi. *How do the men put up with it?* she asked herself, on the verge of tears. All but hidden behind her camera, she framed the entire scene in her viewfinder.

"What's going on here?" she heard a voice behind her.

Mimi turned and saw Gehringer stalking down the aisle, Paul Merkle at his heels. She quickly stepped in front of her camera and tripod, hoping that she'd be able to conceal the setup behind her back.

"An accident, boss," said one of the weavers.

"Gustav! Not watching out again? You and your clumsiness. How many times have I told you all to be careful!" Gehringer waved his assistant over. "Johann, Paul, get the man on his feet. Paul, drive him to the doctor." Then he turned to Mimi. "What are you doing here?" he snapped. "Not taking pictures, I hope."

"The gatekeeper said I'd find you here. Because I was already inside, I just tested the light conditions for a moment, that's all."

"Can't you read? On the door outside, very clearly, it says 'No Unauthorized Entry Permitted.' What if you'd gotten caught in a running loom?"

"And what if one of the children here gets caught in one?" Mimi countered. "What are they even doing here? Child labor is against the law, unless I'm mistaken."

"Excuse me?" Gehringer said.

Can't you learn to hold your tongue? Mimi thought, angry at herself.

"The boys you see are ten, eleven, maybe twelve. They *don't* work here but will probably start as apprentices as soon as they finish school.

Right now, they are merely visiting their mothers and fathers here in the weaving shed and the sewing room during their summer vacation. Am I supposed to forbid them that? I'm not a monster."

Mimi stared at the floor.

Gehringer clapped his hands loudly. "Enough standing around gaping. Back to work! Johann, what do you think you're doing, shutting down your looms? Get them going again, and you'll make up the short pick count this evening, is that clear?" He turned to Mimi again. "As for you, young lady, to my office!"

CHAPTER 34

"I apologize. I really didn't see the sign on the door," Mimi said when they were in Gehringer's office.

"Sit down," Gehringer growled, then he took his own seat behind his large desk.

"It's so quiet in here compared to the weaving shed," Mimi said. "I don't know how the men can put up with all the noise."

"They stuff something in their ears," Gehringer said with a dismissive wave. "Besides, weavers are used to noise. They're cut from tough cloth here in Laichingen."

"So I've noticed," Mimi murmured.

Gehringer looked at her from across his desk. "I don't believe an outsider can ever really understand our little world. The looms keep moving here regardless of what happens anywhere else. It's been that way for hundreds of years, and nothing and no one is going to change it. Now, to your commission," Gehringer said. "I assume the fact that you're here, albeit very late, means that you've decided to accept the job?"

"I have," Mimi said, returning his gaze.

"Good. No doubt you've seen the glass pavilion, you've been inside the weaving shed, and tomorrow morning I'll show you the warehouse, the sewing room, and our archive room, where we keep a sample of every model we've ever produced. We've created some space there for you, and that's where you'll be working. I assume you will bring your camera, glass plates, and any other equipment you'll need. If you have any special wishes, out with it!"

Putting on her most charming smile, Mimi rattled off a list of what she needed for her pictures: lamps, stands, pins, backdrops, supports . . . She was already planning to bring some of that with her, but Gehringer ought to know how much equipment the art of photography entailed. Finally, she added that she would need an advance each week to cover the cost of her materials.

The businessman just nodded. "No problem at all. When you arrive tomorrow, we'll have everything ready. In return, I expect pictures of the very highest quality. My commemorative book has to be perfect. It would be best that you start tomorrow. Everything needs to be finished by the end of October." He held a piece of paper out to Mimi. "Your contract. All I need is your signature."

While Mimi read through the document, she could not shake off the feeling that she was signing over more than just her photographic skills to Herrmann Gehringer.

The photographer had just left when Paul Merkle returned. "Dr. Ludwig says the impact of the wooden shuttle on Gustav's eye injured it so badly there's no saving it," he said, not bothering to soften the news.

Gehringer, assessing the extent to which he, as the employer, could be held responsible for the accident—and by whom!—said nothing. When it came down to it, no one but the weaver himself was responsible, he concluded. There were enough signs on the walls telling the workers to pay attention to their looms at all times.

"Excuse me for asking . . . ," Paul Merkle said when he got no response from Gehringer.

"Yes?"

Merkle pointed toward the exit. "The photographer—may I ask why you contracted Mimi Reventlow to take pictures? Hasn't the woman caused enough trouble already? Didn't you want to send the catalog samples to a photographer down in Stuttgart?"

Gehringer smiled. As smart as his assistant might be, Merkle still couldn't match his own intelligence.

"I studied the bid from the Stuttgart photographer very closely. Having the pictures done here will be considerably cheaper. Besides, I like the thought of having Mimi Reventlow under my control for the next few months. In our little 'studio,' she is well provided for and can work undisturbed. Even better is that while she's here, she can't stir up trouble anywhere else."

"So that's why I've been setting up the old archive room as a studio. I couldn't figure out why you chose that cold, remote room with its tiny windows facing the rear yard as a workplace for Miss Reventlow. The linenwares could just as easily have been photographed in one of the storerooms or offices. But you're absolutely right, of course—nobody ever goes all the way back there, so Miss Reventlow can work without interruption." Paul Merkle chuckled.

Gehringer, satisfied with himself and his plan, nodded. "When the woman emerges in the evening, dog tired and half-frozen, she's not going to launch into any big speeches, that much is certain."

"Brilliant! One has to think around several corners to come up with a plan like that. Well done, Mr. Gehringer!" Merkle said.

Gehringer, who'd steeped long enough in his assistant's admiration, waved it off and changed the subject. "Has the Schubert boy finally signed? The new apprentices are starting next week, and the only contract missing is Alexander's."

Merkle's face turned grim. "As far as Alexander is concerned, you're too late, I'm afraid. He's going to go to that art school, and there's no way to stop him. Worse, though, is that half the village is helping him get there. People are practically breaking down Eveline's door with offers of help. My own wife—"

"What about your wife?" Gehringer snapped, eyeing him sharply.

"Nothing," Merkle said. "I just wanted to say that my wife, Christel, and myself, of course, cannot approve of this turn of events."

When Anton came to, it took him a few moments to realize where he was. His right ear was buzzing, and his head hurt as if he'd drunk too much homemade liquor. He tried to blink to clear his vision, but his eyelids were glued together. He wiped his face with his hand and recoiled at the sticky blood on his fingers.

He was still lying in the narrow, overgrown path beside Gehringer's mill, but how long had he been there? From the position of the sun, hours must have passed.

He'd been unconscious for hours? What if he'd never woken up at all? His heart pounded when he realized the risk he'd taken. Christel really hadn't needed to hit him as hard as she had, he thought as he slowly pulled himself together and got to his feet. It took him a moment to steady himself. The fall into the thorny hedge had torn his shirt, his trousers were dirty, and one shoelace had come loose. Together with his bloodied and beaten face, it was more than enough for what he had in mind.

When he reached the inn, he saw that the first guests were already there, so he went to the back door and stumbled into the kitchen, where his mother was washing dishes. At the sight of him, Karolina was so shocked that a cup slipped from her hand and smashed on the floor.

"My boy! Oh my goodness, what's happened?" She crossed herself, her eyes wide.

For a moment, Anton felt sorry for all the playacting.

"I . . . I don't know." He cleared his throat. His voice sounded as rough as a worn-out saw blade. With one hand pressed to his painful ear, he slumped into a chair. He didn't need to fake the poor condition he was in. His mother ran to the sink and returned with a cool, wet cloth. Anton wiped it over his face and shook his head, but the pain remained. "I went over to the photographer's place. I wanted to ask her if I could bring her anything from Amstetten, but when I got there, a pushy salesman was harassing her. I got in between them and told the man to take off, and then headed for the train station just after that. I had to relieve myself, so I turned off onto a little path. A wagon pulled up on the road at the end of the path. I didn't even have my trousers buttoned when someone came up on me from behind."

"The salesman? The one who was pestering Miss Reventlow?" Karolina asked.

Anton shrugged. "I don't know. It all happened so fast. Before I could turn around, someone whacked me on the head, then everything went black."

"My Lord above," his mother whispered. "He could have killed you! The way you look, it's a miracle you're still alive."

"Mother, it gets worse. He robbed me. All the money is gone."

CHAPTER 35

"Have a good trip. And look after yourself."

"You'll be rich and famous one day."

"Keep your eye on your bags!"

"Always be polite, and always say please and thank you, like I taught you," said his mother, holding on to him so tightly it was as if she didn't ever want to let him go. Alexander stroked her cheek awkwardly. "Everything will work out, Mother."

Eveline nodded bravely. "I'm so proud of you," she whispered.

It was the fourth of September, and many had gathered at the train station to see Alexander off. Aside from his mother, his sisters had come, along with Mimi and Edelgard. Anton was also there, as were Sonja Merkle and Christel. Again and again, along with all the good wishes, Alexander heard the advice to look after himself. After Anton had been so violently robbed, people were scared, especially because the crime had not been solved.

As much as Alexander had been longing for this day to come, now that it was here, he was more than uneasy. He shook hands and smiled—all while hoping he wouldn't faint from fear. While they all waited for the train, Alexander looked at each person in the crowd. It wasn't just him going off to Stuttgart, he thought. Rather it was the people of Laichingen, too, through the things they had given him. Alexander didn't know whether to find the thought consoling or frightening. The suitcase at his feet had belonged to Josef Stöckle. Mimi had given it to him, along with a suit and a few of Josef's shirts. Edelgard had altered the suit and shirts to fit Alexander. From Anton, he'd received five marks. Alexander hadn't wanted to accept so much money, but Anton insisted. "Just to get you started," he'd said, grinning.

These helping hands, and others—those who gave his mother food and firewood and more, so she and his sisters would be taken care of—touched Alexander deeply, and he was extremely grateful. At the same time, however, an even heavier burden weighed on him. What if he let all these people down? Then the suitcase and clothes for him, the eggs and flour for his family—all of it would have been for nothing.

"Don't forget your suitcase on the train," Anton now reminded him for the third time. His friend was just as excited as he was, Alexander realized. Ever since he'd been a toddler, they had seen each other almost every single day, had shared joy and sorrow. Their three-year age difference had never mattered. There was no one he was closer to than Anton. Now everything would change, and it wouldn't just be a train trip that separated them, but a whole new life.

"We'll write, OK? And maybe you'll come visit?" Alexander said, his voice heavy as he fought back tears.

Anton nodded, then turned away.

The train journey itself was uneventful, and Alexander disembarked in Bad Cannstatt. His host family didn't live in the middle of Stuttgart, but out in this picturesque suburb. He carried the note with the address in one hand and Josef Stöckle's suitcase in the other and marched off. At least he didn't need his crutches anymore, he thought as he made his way along the uneven pavement. His gait wasn't back to normal yet, and, especially when he was tired, he still limped on his injured leg. But he could put his full weight on it again, and that was something.

The Leucate family's house was situated on the edge of the suburb, Mimi Reventlow's mother had written, halfway up a hill, out where the vineyards started.

It amazed him that complete strangers would let him live with them, just like that. He was sure the Leucate family must be very rich, or they wouldn't be able to afford an extra mouth to feed.

His thoughts were interrupted when he arrived at a large plaza crossed by several streetcar lines. Alexander saw cars, too, some even bigger than Herrmann Gehringer's. Looking carefully left and right, he hurried across the plaza. What would it be like to travel in a streetcar? he wondered, then decided he would probably never find out. He had no plans to waste Anton's five marks on such extravagances.

His route led him past a church that reminded him of the church in Laichingen, but that was the only similarity he could see. The pretty half-timbered houses of Bad Cannstatt were much bigger than the weavers' houses, and there were all kinds of shops and businesses. Alexander passed a soap shop, a tobacconist, and a newspaper kiosk—all close together. A street sign revealed that, if he went right, he would find the Terrot textile machine factory. An advertising column announced that a circus was in town, performing on the shore of the Neckar River, and that the Stuttgart maternity home was running a donation drive.

Between the sidewalk and the street grew magnificent trees, and everything was laid out much more generously than in the narrow alleys at home, where the sun was hardly able to find its way between the closely packed houses. Women carrying elegant handbags strolled along the sidewalk, studying the displays in the windows of the stylish boutiques, while men smoking fine cigars walked their dogs on leashes. From an inn, the odor of gravy wafted out to the street, and Alexander felt an immediate pang of homesickness. Anton would love the spirited atmosphere here in the city on this mild September day, he knew. He would write all about it to his friend.

The house in which he was supposed to live for the next three years looked like all the others on the street—not particularly large, but also not particularly small. *A family could live well in there,* Alexander thought. He knocked tentatively.

A moment later, a tall, slender woman with dark-brown hair and sparkling eyes opened the door.

"Hello. I'm Alexander Schubert, from Laichingen," he croaked. Before he knew what was happening, the woman threw her arms around him in an effusive hug.

"Welcome! I'm Anna Leucate, but you can just call me Anna. We like to keep things *très léger,*" she said, and she led him by the hand through to the garden, where several people sat around a table beneath a huge cherry tree.

"Allow me to introduce our new house guest, Alexander. He's from Laichingen, and starting tomorrow, he'll be going to the Stuttgart Art School." She presented him as a conjurer might pull a rabbit out of a hat. Then she introduced the people at the table. "This is Yvette, Karl, Gretchen, Frank, and my husband, Pierre. You'll get to know your roommate, Otto, a little later. He's at school right now."

Alexander nodded to the people shyly, thinking as he did so that they were dressed rather strangely. The women wore colorful skirts and blouses, with only Yvette wearing the black that predominated in Laichingen. The men wore loose trousers and linen shirts, and had colorful kerchiefs tied around their necks, which reminded him of Mylo. Who were they? Didn't they have any work? Were they poor, like him? Or perhaps even travelers, like the musicians who played at the *Heumondfest*? And if that were the case, how could they afford a party like this? The table in front of them was covered with bottles; a board with sausage, cheese, and bread; and a plum cake on which the wasps were having a party of their own.

"Excuse me, I . . . I didn't mean to disturb your family gathering," he stammered, shifting his weight nervously from foot to foot. "Maybe you can show me where my room is . . ." He thought of his suitcase, standing unwatched in the hallway. And he had to go to the toilet, too, but didn't dare ask about that right now.

"Family gathering?" The people at the table laughed, but not in an unfriendly way.

"We like to gather after work at someone's house. It's what we do here," Anna Leucate explained. "Come, sit down. You must be hungry and thirsty after your long trip."

A chair was pulled up for him, and he sat down at the table. Someone offered him a cigarette, which he declined politely, inwardly shocked. The woman named Gretchen poured him a glass of a dark-red beverage that looked like cherry juice, and Anna's husband cut him a slice of bread and added a chunk of cheese.

"So you're going to the art school," said one of the men, who Alexander thought was Karl.

Alexander nodded. He reached thirstily for the glass. A mouthful of cherry juice would be just the thing, he thought. His throat was bone dry after his long journey. But he almost spat the liquid out again: it tasted like the wine in church, from which they all got to sip during their confirmation. Was it really wine? In the middle of the afternoon? That would explain the relaxed atmosphere, he thought, in a daze.

"From what I've heard, the Stuttgart Art School and the National Academy of Art currently represent two very different schools of thought. The art school, apparently, has dedicated itself more to the modern and the new. Was it difficult for you to decide between the different styles of study they offer?"

Alexander could only shrug.

"Alexander has been awarded a scholarship for the art school," said Anna, and she sounded almost as proud as his own mother. "Your roommate, Otto, by the way, is also on a scholarship. He attends the Royal Conservatory of Music."

Who was this roommate, Otto? Were they hosting another boy? How could they afford that? And why would they? Alexander wanted to ask, but he was unable to give voice to his questions.

"Speaking of music," said Karl. He picked up a guitar that had been leaning against the table and began to play. Yvette, who had long black hair to match her dress, began to sing a song in French, while a young man—Alexander guessed he was about the same age as himself—patted out a rhythm on the top of the table with the palms of his hands . . . This was Frank, Alexander recalled.

Where had he landed? he wondered, dumbfounded, and drank another mouthful of the wine while the others joined Yvette in her song.

An hour later, he sat on the bed in his room and wondered whether he should even bother unpacking his suitcase.

He was in a madhouse, a lunatic asylum, he thought, while the sounds of laughter, the clinking of glasses, and the smoke from many cigarettes found their way from the garden up to the second floor. The group around the table had grown in the meantime. People wandered in through the garden gate, greeted those already there, and pulled up a chair. Yvette and Karl left—Anna had said that they were both actors in the newly founded playhouse and they had to prepare for the evening performance. She had also told Alexander that he must pay a visit to the playhouse at some point, that it was in the middle of the city, on a street named Kleine Königstrasse, and offered an extremely varied program.

Alexander, already somewhat dizzy from the wine, had only nodded. Actors. Of course.

Was this the broad way his father had always warned them about? If Klaus knew what his son had gotten himself into, he'd turn over in his grave.

The thought made him smile, and for the first time in hours, he relaxed a little. Still smiling, he let his eyes roam around the room. Here and there were some personal items—a comb and a sweater—that must have belonged to Otto. Anna had finally explained that Otto was indeed another boy whom she and her husband were hosting, and she hoped that sharing the room was not a problem for Alexander. Of course not, Alexander had wanted to say, but he had only shaken his head.

He tested the bed, bouncing up and down on it a little. The thickly upholstered mattress sank and rebounded agreeably. He turned back the blanket carefully and lifted the linen sheet underneath. The mattress showed no signs of straw, and neither did the pillow or blanket. Perhaps they were filled with feathers? How elegantly some people got to sleep, Alexander thought with reverence. But the idea that he himself would be sleeping on a down pillow from now on was too much for him to imagine.

The next moment, the door opened and a boy more plump than any Alexander had ever seen came in.

"Oh, you're the new roommate. Welcome to Little Paris! I'm Otto Angerbauer," he said, reaching out his hand to Alexander. Then he went over to the little table that stood by the window and sat on one of the chairs.

"Alexander Schubert," Alexander murmured. His head was still spinning, and he knew he shouldn't have drunk the wine.

Otto nodded toward the window. "I guess you've met our host parents and their friends?"

"Hmm," Alexander said, noncommittal.

"And?" Otto asked, amused.

"They seem very nice, but a bit . . . different. Don't they?" Alexander said cautiously.

Otto Angerbauer laughed so hard that his stomach actually bounced. "'Different' is about right! Quite a few things are different in Little Paris."

"Little Paris?"

Otto leaned toward him confidentially. "That's what people call this quarter of the city, because like Pierre, lots of French people have settled here."

So was that a good thing, or bad? Alexander couldn't tell. Little Paris . . . he liked the sound of it.

"I know everything is new and strange for you. But don't worry. If you study hard, you'll do fine in the Leucate house. Just don't start slacking off, or Anna will teach you a thing or two!"

Anna Leucate could be strict? He found the thought somehow comforting. Alexander pointed to the thick pile of sheet music that Otto had just pulled out of his case and put on the table.

"You're a musician?"

"I actually study singing. I'd like to be a famous tenor one day," Otto said, and his already red cheeks reddened a little more. "I hope it doesn't bother you too much if I do my voice exercises."

Alexander grinned. "As long as I don't have to sing along. In the confirmation lessons, the priest always said my singing would scare the church mice," he said, and both boys laughed.

He'd get along fine with Otto, Alexander thought with relief. Then he lay back on the bed to sleep off the wine. Tomorrow was his first day at school, and he had to be at his best!

CHAPTER 36

The next morning, Alexander was relieved to find that the daily routine was not so much different to what he was used to from Laichingen. Everyone wanted to use the toilet, everyone wanted to get to the washbasin, and everyone was in a hurry. His roommate seemed to be grumpy in the morning. At least, Otto didn't say a word to him. Alexander didn't care—there was so much going on in his head that he doubted he could have put together a single coherent sentence in a conversation anyway.

In the kitchen, there was a pot of oatmeal. Pierre was already finished with breakfast and was rinsing his bowl at the sink, and he said Alexander should help himself.

Alexander approached the stove uncertainly. At home, his mother had always dished out the food. He was not used to taking anything for himself. So much oatmeal for four people? And there was honey to go with it. Amazed, but also hungry, Alexander filled a bowl to the brim and added a spoonful of honey. The oatmeal itself tasted almost as bland as his mother's *Schwarzer Brei*, he thought, and had to grin.

Anna Leucate, rushing around as she tried to get out of the house on time for work, handed him an apple, a sausage sandwich, and a ticket for the train to Stuttgart—train travel was included in the scholarship. She stopped in the doorway and turned around. "In case you're home first, there's a key to the front door in the first flower box on the left, in an old jam jar. Oncc you've unlocked the door, please put the key back." She wished him a good day and left, her skirt billowing behind her.

Now it gets serious, Alexander thought as he pulled on Josef Stöckle's altered suit jacket. Not only did he have to get on the correct train, but when he reached the station at the other end, he had to find his way to the school. He didn't even want to think about what was waiting for him once he got there. It felt little short of a miracle that he was able to stand up to all the excitement and didn't drop dead on the spot, he thought, and again he had to grin.

"Welcome to the Stuttgart Art School! My name is Gottlob Steinbeiss, and I am the senior art teacher here. It is my honor to introduce you to the conventions of our institution and to give you your class schedule and, I hope, some other useful pieces of information." Stroking his handlebar mustache smooth, the teacher looked from one student to the next.

Alexander, sitting by himself in the front row, stared straight ahead.

Only when his classmates had already entered the classroom had Alexander dared to step inside, discovering, to his horror, that the only free desks were in the front row. So he had awkwardly taken a seat at the front. He had given a general greeting to the others, but no one took any notice of him. Everyone else was too busy sizing up whoever was sitting next to them.

"This year's incoming class has sixteen students," the senior art teacher continued. "Before I come to organizational matters, we'll do some introductions." He nodded as if to lend weight to his words. "Let's start in the first row. Name, where you come from, and anything else you'd like to tell us."

Alexander felt himself blush. *Oh God, it had to be me to go first.*

"My name is Alexander Schubert," he said. "I come from Laichingen, in the Swabian Jura."

"From *de Jura-raaa*, you could say," said a classmate in an exaggerated Swabian dialect, drawing laughter from the other boys.

Alexander wished he could vanish under his desk.

Gottlob Steinbeiss glared sternly at the boys in the back rows, then turned to Alexander.

"Thank you, Mr. Schubert," Steinbeiss said. "Next!"

"My name is Erich Liebermann. I live in the Killesberg district of Stuttgart and went to Karl High School. My parents own the Liebermann department store at the end of Kronprinzstrasse."

No one laughed. Instead, a respectful hum circulated through the room.

"My name is Franz Macke. I'm from Dinkelsbühl, where my parents own a brewery. I finished high school at a boarding school in Munich."

"My name is Maximilian von Auerwald. My father is Count Karl-Albrecht von Auerwald."

Alexander looked around covertly. He almost wished he and Maximilian had become friendly when they'd taken the entrance exam. At least then he might not feel quite so out of place.

"Yes?" said Gottlob Steinbeiss, who, like everyone else, was waiting for Maximilian von Auerwald to add a sentence or two to his introduction. But the young count merely shrugged, as if to say, *Everyone knows who we are.*

"Next, please."

"I come from Ulm," Alexander heard a melodic, almost girlish voice say, and he pricked up his ears. "My name is Bernhard von Hoffheim, fourth duke of Hoffheim. My family owns the Hoffheim private bank."

Alexander's shoulders slumped. What was he doing here with all these stuck-up, privileged jerks?

When the rest of the students had introduced themselves, Gottlob Steinbeiss said, "Thank you very much. I'm sure that you will get to know each other very quickly. Our students, faculty, and staff maintain friendly, collegial associations with one another, and we expect the same from you as the incoming class. Anyone unable to adhere to that will have to accept the consequences."

"And those would be?" came a brusque voice from behind Alexander. He thought he recognized the voice of Franz Macke, the brewery owner's son. A question like that in a village school would have earned a rap on the knuckles, at the very least.

Gottlob Steinbeiss raised his eyebrows in surprise, and perhaps also annoyance. "Anyone not abiding by our code of conduct, depending on the severity of the transgression, will receive a letter of reprimand, a temporary suspension, or will be expelled from the school entirely," he said matter-of-factly. "But I am certain that the class before me consists only of decidedly friendly, eager-to-learn, and artistically gifted young men, and that our catalog of punishments is therefore of little interest to you. Please correct me if I'm wrong."

Was he mistaken, or did the teacher sound at least a little ironic? Alexander was puzzled, but Steinbeiss was already moving on.

"You will meet your various teachers throughout the week. The faculty are presently all in class, so, unfortunately, we can't complete our introductions here and now. It's time that I hand out your class schedules." Steinbeiss waved Alexander to the front. "Mr. Schubert!"

For heaven's sake, what did the teacher want, and why did he want it from *him*? Hesitantly, Alexander stood up and took the few steps to the front of the classroom. He did his best to not let his limp show.

"If you would please pass these out," Steinbeiss said, handing him a stack of papers.

Alexander went through the rows with the pages. Here and there, he got a nod of thanks, but others snatched the schedule from his hand without so much as looking at him, as if he were a servant and not a classmate. *They're all wearing such beautiful suits,* Alexander thought. Hair neatly cut and parted, shoes of the finest leather, cheeks red, bodies well fed. None wore trousers that were too short, none had bony shoulders visible beneath thin shirts, as had been the case for him and his classmates at his old school. None were bleary eyed for lack of sleep, no one coughed, no one's stomach cramped with hunger. They pored over their schedules and didn't have a care in the world.

Not for the first time since his arrival in Stuttgart, Alexander had the feeling that he was not only in another town but in a whole other world. Suddenly, he thought of Anton and his mocking smile, in which lay both a deep love of life and so much suppressed anger. What would his friend think of these "gifted young men"? Would he try to make friends? Would he poke fun at them because they all looked so similar with their ironed shirts, ties, and breast-pocket handkerchiefs?

How he would love to have Anton sitting at the next desk right now, Alexander thought as he took his seat again. Then, like all the rest, he looked over the schedule.

Sketching and drawing with pencil, charcoal, ink and chalk, From sketch to finished work, Oil painting—structure, classical techniques, and their application.

Alexander forgot all the differences between him and the others. Forgotten also was his doubt. With the name of every class, his excitement grew. He wanted to pinch himself, so sure that he was dreaming now, as he had so often in the past, about being an artist. And now . . . could it really be true that he was an artist, or at least soon would be? Greedily, like a man dying of thirst and finding water, he read on: *The portrait in all its aspects, Drawing the nude*. Drawing the nude? Alexander's eyes widened. But the shock had no time to settle in, for Gottlob Steinbeiss was talking again.

"Gentlemen, as you can see, you have, from now on, a very full schedule. In addition to the hours spent in class, you will need to find time for homework. He who seriously wants to achieve anything here will do so only through discipline and dedication."

Alexander nodded fervently. He was ready for anything!

"Please get something to write with, and I will read a list of materials you will need to procure by the end of the week, if you don't already have them."

At five in the afternoon, Alexander arrived back in Bad Cannstatt. As if he'd called the place home for years, he fished the key out of the jar in the flower box, but when he found the door already unlocked, he returned the key to its hiding place. Neither Pierre nor Anna Leucate were inside, and the garden was empty, but he heard Otto doing his voice exercises from the floor above.

Alexander carefully climbed the stairs—his leg was throbbing badly. He had walked farther in this one day in Stuttgart—and without crutches—than he had since he'd been injured. His leg didn't like it, he realized, worried. But it wasn't just his tired leg that was bothering him.

He knocked once before entering the room.

Otto stood by the open window. He had one hand on his chest, the other on his stomach, and ran his voice up and down a scale.

"Lalalalala . . . Lalala . . . Lalalaaaaa . . . Well? How was your first day?"

Exhausted, Alexander flopped onto the bed. "Don't ask. I'm trying to decide whether I should pack up and go home now or tomorrow morning."

"Why would you do that?" Otto asked, and he circled his tongue in his mouth.

Alexander rummaged in his bag. "Here, my shopping list. All the materials we're supposed to have by the end of the week. India ink, brushes, compasses and rulers, paints, and lots of other stuff." Alexander looked up from the list. "I thought I had a scholarship! And now I discover I have to buy all this myself."

Otto circled his tongue one last time, then said, "It was the same for me last year. I didn't need paints or brushes, of course, but I had to buy sheet music, songbooks, and scores." He shook his head. "I had no idea how much a single score could cost."

Alexander frowned. "How did you pay for it? Your parents aren't rich, too, are they?"

"Good God no, they're dirt poor," Otto said, and laughed loudly. "Poorer than the church mice you'd scare off with your singing."

His roommate's humor and openness did him good. "So what did you do?"

Otto shrugged. "The first week I was here, I went looking for work. Since then, I've been working two nights a week in a small restaurant down by the river, and I also run errands. The money covers everything I need."

Alexander looked at his throbbing, painful leg. Working in a restaurant? Running errands? He was happy that his leg had simply survived a normal day.

"It doesn't have to be in a restaurant," Otto said as if he could read Alexander's mind. "What else can you do?" He picked up an apple from their table, cut it in half, and handed one half to Alexander.

"Thanks," Alexander said, taking a big bite. "I don't think I can do anything," he said as the delicious juice filled his mouth. He'd never had an apple that sweet in the Jura.

"Everyone can do something," Otto contradicted him. "You wouldn't be here otherwise."

"That's true . . ." Alexander took another bite of his apple. "I'm good at drawing, but how am I supposed to earn money from that? If I'm lucky, I'll be able to live off my artwork later on, but that's why I need the training."

Otto nodded. "And if you talk to your teacher and tell him how things stand financially?"

Alexander shook his head. "I'm already the poor little dope stuck in with all the sons of department store owners, bankers, and nobles. For them, the shopping list is nothing. They'll probably get a servant to go buy it all for them. No, I'm not going to make more of a fool of myself than I already have."

While Otto returned to his voice exercises at the window, Alexander thought hard about what he really could do. The money from Anton popped into his mind. But he didn't want to spend that right away and leave himself with nothing. Damn it, there had to be some way for him to earn money.

He heard the front door open, and Anna Leucate called out, "I'm home!"

Maybe there was something he could do in the hospital where she worked? But even if there was, considering the full schedule and the homework they'd already been warned about, he would need to be careful about taking on anything too time consuming. He already had to do some chores around the house in return for his board and lodging.

Then he had an idea.

"I think I know what I can do," he murmured to himself.

Ignoring his sore leg, he got to his feet and hobbled down the stairs.

Anna Leucate was in the kitchen, cutting slices of bread and putting them in a basket.

"Can I help?" Alexander asked, looking around.

Anna nodded toward the table, where fresh vegetables lay. "You can wash the radishes and carrots. We're having salad and bread for dinner."

Glad to have something to do, Alexander moved the radishes into the sink. It felt almost like being at home with his mother, he thought, while Anna and he worked side by side.

"So how was your first day?"

Alexander told her about his rich classmates, about how happy he was that the classes would really get going in the next few days, and about the supply list.

Anna shook her head, clearly annoyed. "When are the people who run these schools going to get it into their heads that a scholarship should cover everything, including the items you need to study there?" She looked at him. "Do you have an idea of how you can earn some money?"

Alexander chewed on his lip. It was a little embarrassing to him, but he said, "I can do embroidery. Rose petals, vines, leaves, eyelets . . . if you know anyone who'd like to have a blouse or a cushion cover embroidered?"

Anna, who was opening a block of cheese, looked at him with fascination. "A young man who can do embroidery. How unconventional! I have to tell my friends about this. I'm sure they'll be thrilled, and of course you can also embroider one or two of my blouses, but . . ." She looked at Alexander and frowned. "I don't suppose you can also do darning?"

"Of course," he said boldly. At least, he'd watched his mother do it often enough. First she secured the edge of the hole with small stitches so it didn't get any bigger. After that, his mother put horizontal stitches in place and finished with the vertical weave, all very fine and strong.

"Excellent!" Anna wiped her hands on a kitchen towel and hurried out of the room. When she returned, she had a basketful of socks and other garments that needed to be darned.

"I hate darning," she said passionately. "If you can take this off my hands, I'd be eternally grateful. And I'd pay you for it, of course. Does two marks sound right?"

For a moment, Alexander was speechless: he already had his first job! "I think I could buy the brushes I need with that. But . . . isn't two marks too much?" He held his breath.

Anna sighed. "I was planning to use the money to buy some pork for the weekend meal, but it's more important for you to have what you need for school. Who needs meat? We'll make do with an onion cake instead, all right?"

"I don't know what to say," Alexander stammered. "This is really a great help. Thank you very much."

Anna waved it off. "I'm just happy I can buy my way out of darning. Later, when our friends come by, I'll tell them about your embroidery. I'm sure you'll have a lot more to do very soon."

Alexander felt a great weight lift from his shoulders. "That's wonderful!" he said, thrilled.

Two hours later—Otto had just left for the restaurant—Alexander sat by the open window, needle and thread in his hand, and he darned socks. *Just like Mother back home,* he thought, not sure whether to laugh or cry.

CHAPTER 37

At the beginning of September, Herrmann Gehringer had announced that the two extra hours of work at the mill each day would continue. The anniversary garments were more of a hit with their customers than anyone had imagined, and they were being produced and sold in large numbers. The looms were running at full capacity, and the factory workday only came to an end at eight in the evening.

It was left mainly to the women, now that the grain had been harvested, to plow the fields. Those who could afford it paid a local farmer to turn their fields with his plow and a team of horses. Those who had no money had no choice: they worked the soil themselves, with shovel and rake.

After months at this pace, men and women alike collapsed on their beds in the evening, exhausted and with aching limbs. Some just managed to wash off the day's sweat and grime; others were so worn out they didn't even want to eat.

Mimi, too, was kept busy. By the end of September, she'd been working for Gehringer for almost six weeks—and she had hated every single day of it.

On her first day, Paul Merkle had led her to what he called her "studio in our venerable old archive." *"Venerable old archive"* . . . that didn't sound so bad, Mimi had thought as she followed him along a dusty footpath around the side of the mill. In the back corner of the factory grounds, Merkle stopped in front of a small wooden shack. With a grand sweep of his arm, as if ushering her into a fairy-tale castle, Merkle opened the door. "Your studio!"

"I'm supposed to work here?" she'd asked, horrified.

"Here you will have the peace and quiet you need for your creative work," Merkle had replied, unperturbed. "As you can see, we've prepared everything you said you'll need. Lamps, stands, backdrops . . ."

Mimi had scanned the dilapidated room.

"Perhaps it's best if I bring the garments to my uncle's studio and take the photographs there?" She thought that would be ideal.

Paul Merkle shook his head and remarked that Herrmann Gehringer insisted that the photographs be completed on the factory grounds. "You can process the plates and take care of any necessary retouching at your studio and shop, but the garment samples are archival and they must stay here."

It had been clear to Mimi that she had no choice.

Since then, day after day, she'd been taking photographs of linenware of every kind. Lace-collared and plain nightshirts. Decorative cushions with seemingly countless variations of embroidered blooms. Aprons with eyelet borders. Aprons with an upper section and no decorative border at all. Underskirts. Underwear. Tablecloths with lace borders and without.

Mimi quickly discovered how hard it was to set up the white linenware in the brilliant light from the lamps in such a way that the entire photograph was not overexposed. It was also important to photograph the lace and embroidery so that it could be clearly differentiated in the catalog later. She spent many hours with various dark and light cardboard panels, lighting, shading, framing until she achieved the perfect illumination. After three days of rejects—and who was going to pay for those? she wondered—she finally had what she considered an ideal setup for the job, and it allowed her to place one garment after another in the same framework without starting all over again.

Position a lace blouse, straighten, rearrange, focus, click. Put the glass plate away in its paper sleeve. Write the coordinating information on the sleeve according to the small label attached to the item—each step took time. On average, she needed thirty minutes for one perfect picture. For seven hundred pictures, she would need three hundred and fifty hours. And that didn't even include the time for the group photographs of the weavers and seamstresses.

One day at a time—only with that motto in the back of her mind was Mimi able to save herself from dying of boredom and fatigue.

By evening, her shoulders and head hurt. Often, she was so tired that she nodded off at the kitchen table when she finally got home. She would have been only too happy to meet Sonja or Eveline or Berta, but she could hardly find the time even for a chat with Luise. Luckily, her neighbor had been willing to start looking after Uncle Josef again during the day. Otherwise Mimi would not have had a quiet minute at all. The feverish spells that had plagued him just a few weeks earlier had disappeared. Mimi didn't know if she should be happy about that, because when she helped him wash or stroked his skin for comfort, he felt unnaturally cool, almost chilled. *Like a dead man,* she thought sometimes, scaring herself.

The only thing that made the monotony of her days and her concern for her uncle bearable were the hours here and there spent with Johann. After his long day at the mill, there was always some task to do for his mother. Then there was the work he did for Eveline's family. It took up so much of his time that Mimi sometimes regretted ever asking him to help her. But she didn't complain, because she was so busy with her own work and looking after Josef.

All their obligations only served to make the brief hours they had together more valuable. On the few warmer evenings they still had in late September, they had managed to meet for a stroll just outside the village. When it was cooler, Johann visited Mimi at Josef's studio—and only when it was dark, of course, so nobody would see him come or go. To Mimi's disappointment, however, their meetings were never particularly intimate. Both of them had too much on their minds.

"Why did I ever accept this job? Sometimes I think I'm going to be violently ill if I see one more piece of linen." Mimi, sitting at the table in the studio and looking at the abundance of photographs on the table in front of her, shook her head in exaggerated revulsion. "I did nothing last week but take pictures of cushions. I would much rather have spent that time with my uncle. Or with you."

Johann, sitting on the edge of the platform with a bottle of beer, laughed. "Don't complain! Twelve hours at the loom is no walk in the park. And when it comes to monotony, I think we weavers can hold our own with anybody. And our work's more strenuous and dangerous, too."

Mimi sighed. They all worked so hard.

As she always did when Johann visited, Mimi had pulled the curtains closed and lit a few candles. She had also bought him a few bottles of beer at Helene's store.

How romantic the candlelight looks, Mimi thought, and wondered why she felt anything but romantic. She hid a yawn behind her hand.

"Did you ever develop the photographs you took on your first day in the weaving shed? The ones that showed Gustav's accident?"

Mimi frowned. "Now that you mention it, I'd completely forgotten about them. They're probably no good at all, as gloomy as it was in there."

"But it's the real-life photographs that are so important. Those are the ones to show to Gehringer, and everybody else," Johann said. "You've got more than enough of the pretty photos you earn your money with."

"And I have neither the time nor the opportunity to spend any of that money!" she said, suddenly angry. "If I don't get out of that shack for a day very soon, I think I'm going to go insane." She went over and sat down beside him, wrapping her arms around him. "Johann, please—let's take the train to Ulm next weekend. I feel like I haven't been out of here for an eternity. If I ask Luise, she would certainly keep an eye on my uncle for one night. We could go back to the little wine bar where we first got to know each other." A glass of red wine, candlelight, and a pretty little guesthouse after that . . . Mimi sighed rapturously. Just to get away from all the prying eyes. And Johann would also be more relaxed, she was sure.

"You get some ideas. As if I could find the time to flit off to the city now, when there's so much to prepare and think about." Johann gave her a light tap on the nose. "On the other hand, if I don't come up with something about which to confront Gehringer soon, then I'll have to do some traveling anyway. But then I'll be heading for Augsburg. I know the head of the Textile Workers Association for South Swabia there. He's a smart man, very experienced. Maybe with him I'll find a solution to the dreadful state of things here."

Augsburg? Mimi looked at Johann with interest. That would be even better than Ulm. "I know a lovely little restaurant in Augsburg," she said. "And believe it or not, it's right in the middle of the textile district. When do we leave?"

"Mimi, hold on. I'm not even sure I'll be going yet. Even if I do, I have to put my personal pleasure aside. I've been marking time here for months. Gehringer knows labor laws back to front, and so far I haven't found anything I can use against him." He took out the worn copy of the Labor Protection Act of June 1, 1891, that he always carried in his pocket and held it out to Mimi. "As helpful as this law has been in numerous other strikes, it's no use to me here in Laichingen. According to this, children under thirteen are not allowed to work in factories. Youths under the age of sixteen can't work for more than ten hours a day, and women a maximum of eleven hours. Night work for women and children under sixteen is also prohibited. But none of that applies to Gehringer's mill. The fact that it's unacceptable for the men here to slave away at a loom until they can hardly stand—frankly, the law has nothing against that. As long as an employer pays the stipulated overtime, there's nothing we can do."

"Why don't you simply speak to him?" Mimi said. Sometimes she got so sick of all this talk. "Maybe he has no idea about the level of dissatisfaction at the mill." A simple conversation instead of relying on some "workers' revolution"—wouldn't that be a start?

"Labor disputes don't work like that," said Johann sharply. "I have to find some way to get to Gehringer . . . failing to meet safety guidelines, not sticking to break times . . ."

And talking about it all the time isn't going to improve the situation, either, Mimi thought. Sometimes she truly felt as if Johann were chasing his tail . . . but she would never actually tell him that, of course.

"And if it really goes to a labor dispute, then . . ."

Mimi felt her eyelids drooping. She took a fan—one of the props—from a basket beside her on the platform, and waved a little air over her face. *Don't drift off now,* she warned herself—the little time she had with Johann was far too valuable for that.

"I understand that it's important for you to stick up for the weavers of Laichingen," she said, her voice strained. "But isn't it also important to enjoy life a little? You can find new energy and inspiration. You won't be talking day and night with your union friends in Augsburg, will you?"

Johann shook his head in annoyance, as if a fly were bothering him. Ignoring her question, he went on: "And then there's the matter of what kind of strike we should even be aiming for. That's something else I have to start thinking about. Do we just stop work? Or maybe a work slowdown would function better? Or maybe we should be looking at collectively staying home sick? The question is really . . ." And Johann was off again.

"Mimi? Mimi!"

Someone was shaking her shoulder. Mimi woke with a start. "What . . . what is it?"

"You fell asleep," Johann said accusingly. "If that's how you show interest, then I know where I stand with you. I thought you could stand by me and help me in my struggle. My God, it's not as if I'm drowning in supporters here, after all." He set his beer bottle down loudly and rose to his feet.

"I'm sorry. I just nodded off. It has been a long day . . ." She blinked, dazed.

"We all have long days. I plan to deliver my first speech soon, and I wanted to talk to you about my plans for what would come next. But the way things look, I can't rely on your support at all, now that you're in cahoots with Gehringer," said Johann angrily.

"'In cahoots' . . . that's nonsense! Johann, stay, please!"

Distraught, Mimi could only watch him go.

CHAPTER 38

On her way to Mimi's house, Eveline dropped off Erika and Marianne with Johann's mother. The girls, who had come to regard Edelgard as if she were their own grandmother, were excited to help her make caramels.

Eve knew she should really be getting home and using the time she had for work. The evening before, Paul Merkle had brought a basket filled with linen to the house and asked her to have the embroidery done by Tuesday, and she would have to work hard to manage that. But it could wait half an hour—after all, she didn't have such good news to report every day.

The chestnut trees had changed color beautifully, she noted as she arrived at the square. "I'd give anything to be able to paint all those colors one day," Alexander had said to her the previous autumn. And now he was at the art school and could paint to his heart's content, whatever he wanted. She was so happy that wish had come true for him.

She wondered if the trees in Stuttgart were as colorful as they were in Laichingen. *They must be,* she decided, and pulled her shawl closer around her.

It was the start of October, and there was already a chill in the air. When Eveline had left the children with Edelgard, the old woman had remarked that the first frosty nights were not far off. Eveline had only smiled. She didn't care if the frost lay inches thick across the land! With the warmth she felt inside, she was well equipped for the coming winter. Too, thanks to Johann, she had a huge pile of firewood stored in her shed. And with his help, she'd already brought in the entire potato harvest and stored it away—not a single potato would freeze on them this year!

The last few evenings, they'd been at the field until well after sunset, their hands and feet chilled. When they arrived at Eve's house under the cloak of darkness, the wagon piled high with potatoes, he had lit a fire in the stove and warmed water for a footbath.

Eveline had been so moved and so grateful to him that she had been unable to hold back her tears. In all their years together, Klaus had never once done anything as loving as that for her.

But Johann had a sense for these things. He always knew how she felt. And when she lay in his arms, all the toil and tribulations fell away, and she was the happiest woman in the world.

Still smiling, she knocked on Mimi's door. A few moments later, it swung open and Mimi was standing there, her hair down and several hairpins in her hand. She seemed momentarily taken aback, as if unsure whether Eveline's visit was a good one or not.

No wonder, Eveline thought, considering how she had acted toward Mimi after *Heumondfest*. And while they had reestablished their friendship since the incident in Helene's store, both of them were still a bit reserved.

"Eveline! What a nice surprise. Come in, I'm just doing my hair," Mimi said after a brief hesitation.

It struck Eveline that the photographer was a very beautiful woman. Her glossy dark-brown hair fell almost to her hips, and Eve thought it a shame that she kept it so elaborately pinned up all the time. She reflexively lifted her hand to her own hair, which she had woven into two simple braids. The braids made her look like a young girl, Johann had said to her only recently, and she'd responded by laughing and asking him if he couldn't see the silver strands she'd already had for a year or two. Still, the compliment had made her happy.

"I don't want to disturb you if you're busy . . ."

"I have to go and see the man Josef always buys his firewood from. Our woodshed is empty. But it can wait. It's Saturday after all, and in any case, I always have time for a cup of tea with you." She waved Eve into the kitchen. "Come, sit, I'll be with you in just a minute. Uncle Josef is still asleep. He rarely gets out of bed before ten these days."

While Mimi turned on the water for tea and put her hair up in front of the mirror in the hallway, Eve looked around the roomy kitchen. So much space for two people! The big table, the nice white cupboards. And then the colorful souvenirs from Josef's travels on the shelf and the small paintings adorning the walls. Her own house would never look as cozy as this. But on the other hand, she *did* already have her winter wood supply sorted out. And there had been a few other changes, too. Before the potato harvest, Johann had gone down into the old *Dunk* and built her a shelf with different sized bins—something she'd wanted for years—in which she now had the entire potato and turnip harvest stored. But for Klaus, the *Dunk* had always been such a sacred place . . . As if there was anything sacred about an old, dark basement.

Johann and me. Eve smiled absently. Somehow, she could not believe that her dreams had come true. And, as she waited for Mimi to return, she could not help but think about Johann's visit a few nights earlier.

They had been lying in Eveline's bed at the time, sweat soaked and exhausted from their lovemaking. "You were right, you know. When you said I should just do what my heart tells me is right," Johann had said. "We'd be missing out on so much if we followed the unwritten rules of the mourning year. Everyone has their own way to mourn, don't they?"

That was true, absolutely, she'd assured him. Their love did not make her a bad widow. She still visited Klaus's grave regularly and prayed for his soul. Then she had summoned up all her courage and asked Johann the question she couldn't let go of.

"Does your heart also tell you that you should keep meeting Mimi Reventlow?" She had held her breath in anticipation of his answer.

To her dismay, Johann had nodded. "I last saw her a few days ago. I wanted to talk to her about my plans at the mill, but she was too tired. She's a special woman, and for a while I thought that she and I . . ." He had waved the thought away.

A black knot of disappointment, jealousy, and anger had formed instantly in Eveline's gut. Her reaction was not lost on Johann, who said, "Don't look as if you'd like to throttle her. There's no reason to. She's smart, and I like smart women, it's true. But you cast a spell on me the first day I met you. My heart beats only for you."

His words had been spoken plainly and honestly, and had put her mind at ease. "What does Mimi Reventlow know about the hard life of a weaver? Why not talk to me in the future about your plans?" she'd offered, and added, "Besides, when it comes to a fight with Gehringer, I'll be on your side, unwavering, I promise."

He nodded vigorously several times. "I know it. And you give me so much more, Eveline. You've shown me a way to find my inner freedom again, despite all the worn-out old conventions here in Laichingen. Since we've been together, I can actually imagine living here again."

Did that mean he'd been thinking about leaving? she'd wondered, but quickly banished the thought. He wanted to stay, for her. That was all that mattered.

But were Johann's meetings with Mimi really just about the poor working conditions the weavers faced? Eveline wondered now, when the photographer joined her at the table with two cups of tea.

"How are you? What does Alexander write? Tell me! And if I may say so, you look wonderful, so happy and carefree," Mimi chattered. "I admire so much how you stay on top of everything. Looking after the children, keeping up the house, all the work for Gehringer and out in the field."

Eveline felt herself flushing red. "It's not as hard as you make it sound," she said. "I have a lot of support now, after all, thanks to you organizing everyone."

Mimi nodded. "Yes, it's really fantastic how the whole village is pitching in so that Alexander can go to art school. Still, you must miss him terribly."

Yes and no, Eveline thought. If she were honest with herself, she was glad that her son wasn't at home. Of course she was thrilled that he was now able to live his dream. And with him away, she, too, could live at least part of her own dream. While Eve could hide from her daughters the fact that Johann sometimes spent the night, she would not have been able to keep it from Alexander. She could picture vividly his accusatory stare.

"Everything is good the way it is," Eve said with resolve. "It's important to be happy about the small things. I think about that all the time. It helps me get through the jobs I *have* to do, and to do them with pleasure."

"You're very brave, you know? You have a wonderful approach to life," said Mimi, her voice full of respect. "If I could borrow just a bit of that for myself, but the thought of going back to Gehringer's shack on Monday to take pictures of linen garments makes me feel ill."

"Oh, I believe you," said Eveline, smiling. "But perhaps I can cheer you up a little?" She handed Mimi an envelope.

"From Alexander?" Mimi's face brightened instantly. Rapidly, she scanned the few lines he'd written. "He's already made a lot of friends. I'm glad about that! And the classes are better and more exciting than he ever thought they would be. Oh, Eveline . . ." Mimi gazed at her with shining eyes. "Isn't it wonderful how everything has turned out?"

Eveline nodded. It certainly was.

"The October sun is shining a particularly lovely shade of gold today—what do you say, gentlemen? Shall we pack our watercolors and move our painting class to Wilhelma Botanical Garden? Does everyone have thirty pfennigs on them for the entry?" Their teacher, Mylo, looked around the classroom inquiringly, and murmurs of assent came from every side.

"Then we can go straight to the beer garden afterward," Franz Macke said from the back row.

Alexander's shoulders slumped. While everyone else packed their things, he didn't make a move.

"Alexander?" Mylo looked at him, frowning. "What are you waiting for?"

"Sorry, I . . . I forgot my wallet," Alexander whispered so quietly that he thought only Mylo could hear him. Apparently he wasn't quiet enough, however, because a groan came from behind him.

"Sure he did," he heard Maximilian von Auerwald mutter to the young man next to him. "The pauper can't pay the entrance fee."

"Much more of this and our bank will have to give him a loan," Bernhard von Hoffheim replied, and both of them laughed maliciously.

Alexander only slumped more.

Mylo glared at the young nobles, infuriated. "You're in a particularly hilarious mood today, gentlemen. But humor at the expense of others is not something I appreciate, as you should know by now. In the light of your oh-so-fraternal comments, consider my suggestion null and void. The class will take place here." Mylo began unpacking his bag.

"Oh no . . ."

"Blast it, I was looking forward to being outside!"

"Seriously?"

If looks could kill, I'd be dead, Alexander thought. He could practically feel the glares of the boys behind him.

"Just a moment. If it's all right, I'll pay for Schubert's entry," Franz Macke said loudly.

Mylo looked up. "Mr. Schubert? Would that be all right with you?"

Alexander shrugged uncertainly. In the month or so he'd been here, none of his classmates had done him any favors. They barely said a word to him, in fact.

"I'll pay it back tomorrow," he murmured, hoping that Anna had a few more socks to be darned.

"Thanks for putting up the money for my ticket. It's very nice of you," said Alexander to Franz Macke as they departed the classroom.

The son of the brewery owner snorted disparagingly. "Nothing to do with nice. I just don't want to spend a great afternoon like this sitting in that musty box because of you. As for paying it back—don't forget the interest!" He grinned spitefully. "Mylo will probably have us all drawing dragonflies or butterflies again. You're good at that, so a small watercolor for me by way of interest shouldn't be too difficult, should it? I'll sign it myself and call it a 'genuine' Macke." He laughed as if he'd made the joke of the century.

Alexander gritted his teeth.

CHAPTER 39

Mimi had thought that the sight of her pantry filled with the cabbages, carrots, and potatoes from their small vegetable garden would make her happy, but the opposite was true. It had been days since Uncle Josef had had any solid food. Only when Mimi cooked a strong vegetable broth did he manage to swallow a few spoonfuls. Now, with the start of the colder months, the last of his vigor had run its course.

"They're already advertising Christmas pyramids from the Erzgebirge." Mimi held the Ulm paper in front of her, from which she'd been reading to Josef for half an hour. She tapped the advertisement, which showed one of the traditional pyramid-shaped Christmas decorations with its carousel, nativity scene, angels, and more. "But Christmas is still more than two months away."

"Do you remember how you always looked forward to the Christmas holidays?" Josef said so softly that Mimi could barely hear him. "Your mother always made twenty-four chalk marks on the door to your room at the start of Advent. Every day, you were allowed to wipe one of them off. She called it 'Mimi's own Advent calendar.'" This was more than he had said for days, and his voice was raspy.

Mimi nodded nostalgically. "Advent is a very special time. When I was a young girl, I could hardly wait for the Baby Jesus to arrive, and for the gifts he brought with him, too." She laughed and eyed her uncle. It was rare for him to comment on anything she read to him. Most of the time, he only listened, or not even that. But Mimi made sure she read to him every day. There was so little she could do for him otherwise.

"I won't see the Baby Jesus arrive this year. But I'll make up for it—God will take me in his arms instead. At least, I hope he will."

Mimi, close to tears, said nothing.

"Life is change, my child, and my life was richer than most, you know. Or at least it seems that way to me, so there's no need for tears. I have no fear of death. I'm ready to go. And you should be, too."

Mimi started. "What do you mean?"

Josef smiled, and for a moment she saw in his eyes the mischievous charm with which he'd won people over all his life. "Well, you have to go to Gehringer's. You're already very late. I don't want you to lose your job on my account."

"In the box on the left are the pictures for your anniversary book. The prints on top are the ones you haven't seen yet. The box on the right has the first batch of product photos for your wholesale catalog," Mimi Reventlow said.

Herrmann Gehringer took the photographs one by one and examined them closely. He knew that she normally spent Saturdays processing glass plates and making prints in her darkroom at home, so he had gotten into the habit of checking her progress every Friday. It was as cold in the old archive now as it had been hot and stifling at the start of September. He resisted the urge to rub his hands together to warm them, but he did not have to be there very long, he reminded himself.

The woman knew her craft, that was clear, he admitted silently as he inspected the perfectly lit photographs. Although he knew every item his weaving mill had ever produced, he was nevertheless impressed to see the products in all their abundance in front of him. The recipients of his anniversary book would no doubt be just as amazed.

He placed two photographs side by side to compare them. "It's hard to see the difference between the lace trim on blouses F22 and F28 in these pictures."

Mimi Reventlow leaned across the table, so close that he could smell her perfume. Perfume! Here in the village!

"That's because those two blouses are practically identical," she said with a slight smile.

"Then you should pay even more attention to highlighting the differences in your photographs. How else are our future customers supposed to choose?" He was pleased to see the photographer's jaw tense, as if she were swallowing a retort. It must certainly be a new experience for her not to have her way, he thought mockingly.

"I'd like you to retake those photographs. Is that understood?"

"Perfectly," she replied.

Satisfied, Herrmann Gehringer took out his wallet, counted out several banknotes, and put them on the desk in front of the photographer. "Your advance for the week."

"Thank you."

Was that it? Was that all that occurred to her to say? She should keep in mind that one certainly didn't earn that kind of money every day as a traveling photographer, he thought angrily.

Mimi Reventlow cleared her throat. "Autumn is showing it's prettiest side, and the sun is shining particularly beautifully at the moment. If it's all right with you, I'd like to find the time for the group photographs of your various staff. I think I'll need about half a day for them."

Gehringer thought it over. Earlier, making his way around the outside of the mill, the facades of volcanic tuff from Gönningen had indeed glowed as if dipped in gold. Still, he dismissed her suggestion. "The men will be tied up with a major order until the end of October. I can't sacrifice a half day's production now. And in the first week of November, the film company is coming to shoot an advertisement for our mill."

"Film people? Here?" Mimi Reventlow was taken aback.

"Why should it only be the champagne makers who advertise their products with a film?" he said casually. And didn't that take Miss High and Mighty by surprise! She should have figured out by now that anyone trying to keep up with him didn't have a chance. "The group photographs will just have to wait until November."

"But you said you wanted everything done by the end of October. And besides, by November the trees will have lost all their leaves!" she said, horrified. "And if it's foggy . . ."

He looked sternly at her. "Young lady, as a good businessman, I have to know how to set my priorities. And as a good photographer, *you* should know how to get the best out of any situation. If all else fails, then you can always do a bit of retouching. If the sun isn't shining, then you'll just have to add the light to the picture. You can do that, can't you?"

"Of course. But—"

"No buts!" he interrupted her. "I already have the impression that your mind isn't entirely on your work. Look here . . . ," he said, and tapped a finger on one of the photographs, which showed a decorative pillow. "Couldn't you have straightened that before you took the picture?"

"Excuse me? That pillow is as straight as anyone can make it," the photographer replied in a curt tone.

"I see it differently, and I insist that you redo this picture, too. Or is it asking too much for me to expect perfection?" he said without flinching.

"But the photograph *is* perfect! Forgive me for saying this so openly, but this is nothing short of harassment."

"Harassment?" He gave her an exaggerated look of puzzlement, as if he didn't understand the word. "Who is it who only arrived here at midday today?"

"I wanted to spend a little time with my uncle," Mimi Reventlow defended herself.

"And what about Wednesday?" Paul Merkle said you left at three in the afternoon."

"No doubt he also told you that one of the lamps was broken. No light, no photographs," she countered.

How he hated women who always had to have the last word. "Then what about Monday? What happened then? You left without a word in the middle of the afternoon."

"You know how sick my uncle is. Dr. Ludwig had scheduled a visit to my uncle at home, and I needed to be there," she said, her head bowed.

Gehringer, happy to see at least a touch of regret, said, "It's all well and good that you look after your uncle as you do, but this is a major commission, the kind of thing a photographer gets perhaps once in a lifetime. I had believed that you were aware of the great honor accorded to you. It would appear, however, that I was mistaken. Taking pictures of the good citizens of Laichingen in absurd poses in your studio seems to interest you more than focused work of the highest level." He rapped his walking stick on the floor imperiously. "By next Friday, I expect to see a considerable improvement in your performance. Otherwise, you and I will have a serious problem." He gave her a final intimidating glare before leaving. *So much for who has the last word around here,* he thought.

"And it's really all right if the girls spend the night with you again?" Eveline asked with feigned concern, while Erika and Marianne ran past her into Edelgard's house without so much as a goodbye.

Edelgard patted her arm. "You know I'm happy to have them here. Go and spend a nice Saturday evening with Johann. But you watch out—people here don't need to know my boy stops by as much as he does."

"Thank you," said Eveline, touched. "There's not many who could"—she waved her right hand as if she could snatch the word she wanted out of the air—"manage this situation as well as you."

"We all need to get by, one way or another," Edelgard said. "Now go."

Eveline smiled with gratitude and left. All she and Johann had done in the last few weeks was work, work, work. Today, she wanted to remind him that there was more to her than just work.

The wood stove was doing its job well, she thought as she unlocked the door of her house and was met by a cozy warmth. At the end of October, the house with its old stone walls was already chilly, but whenever she'd dared to heat it decently in the past, Klaus had reproached her for being wasteful. Now, thanks to Johann, her woodshed was filled to the roof, and she could allow herself this small luxury, at least now and then. And for what she had in mind, it had to be warm.

From the stove, Eveline took one of the large pots of water she'd set there two hours earlier, then she poured the contents into the large metal tub she and her children bathed in. She immediately put another pot of water on to heat so she could keep adding more hot water.

How lovely it would be to have some bath salts, the kind that she and her mother had used in Chemnitz. With the scent of lavender or roses . . . She thought for a moment, then she went down to her new pantry, from the ceiling of which she had hung various bundles of herbs to dry. The verbena leaves smelled so fresh—she would throw a handful of those into the bathwater.

Satisfied with herself and her idea, Eveline climbed the stairs again. Now all she needed was to light a few candles, draw the curtains, and . . . Ten minutes later, she sat on the edge of the tub, wearing nothing but a linen sheet draped around her shoulders. She had let down her hair, and after a hundred strokes with her brush, it shone like a young girl's. She looked down at herself. Her breasts were not as full as they once had been, and the births and the years of hunger had left their marks on her body. And yet she felt more beautiful and more feminine than she had for a very long time.

She glanced at the old clock. It was just after seven, and soon her lover would arrive. Eveline let out a small moan of pleasure as she let one hand glide over her breast. *"You cast a spell on me,"* she suddenly heard Johann's words in her mind. Her eyes darkened with passion. A bath together, and a night of lovemaking to follow. Tonight, Johann would learn that she had only just begun to deploy the weapons in her woman's arsenal.

It was early on Saturday evening when Anton took Christel by the hand and led her down the stairs to the cellar where the beer was stored. They didn't have much time. The Oxen would open in half an hour, and then he wouldn't have a minute for the rest of the evening.

"Not so fast," Christel hissed. "The steps are slippery. You'll make me fall if you're not careful."

How he hated having to resort to such furtive moments together. If they only had some place nearby where they could meet without the risk of being disturbed, Anton thought, not for the first time. But regardless of how much he thought about it, he could come up with nothing better than the beer cellar. Just a few days earlier, he'd taken a closer look at his father's hunting blinds out in the woods, but had been disappointed to see that they would not work as a place to meet Christel. High in one of those flimsy constructions, they would be practically on display for the world.

When they reached the bottom of the stairs, he took Christel in his arms and kissed her. "I've missed you so much," he murmured. She felt so good, so womanly. He pressed closer against her, but she pulled away.

Her eyes sparkled with excitement as she said, "Next week the film people are finally going to be here! And there's an opera singer coming, too. She's supposed to be super famous, and she's going to be the main character in Gehringer's advertisement—a diva visits the mill, that's the story. I get to play a seamstress! Isn't that great?"

Christel looked at Anton expectantly, and he nodded obediently. Gehringer and his stupid film—every time he saw her, it was all she talked about. He was slowly running out of patience.

"I've got some good news, too," he said. "Mimi's friend Clara Berg finally got in touch. She said she hadn't had any jobs open in her factory during the summer, but now she's looking for a new cosmetics apprentice for her beauty salon in Baden-Baden. Mimi Reventlow thinks you should definitely apply. With your looks and personality, you've got a good chance." He'd asked Mimi about Baden-Baden, and learned it was a city where the rich and beautiful from all over the world came and went, and there was also a casino.

"You want me to wash strangers' faces? Put cream on their feet and lotion on their cheeks?" Christel cried, clearly disgusted by the thought. "If that's the best you can come up with for our future, then we don't have one!" She looked at him with disdain.

"OK, OK, it was just an idea," Anton said, although he still thought it was a good idea. "Then let's just strike out on our own. We've got enough money." When Anton thought about how he'd gotten his hands on that money, however, and how he'd lied to his mother, his conscience still stung.

"We'll see," Christel said grumpily. She licked her index finger and pressed back into place a few strands of hair that had come loose when he'd kissed her. *Always making sure she looks her best,* Anton thought admiringly.

"If it were up to me, we would leave tomorrow," he said. "Pack up whatever we have, and whatever else we need we'll just buy. The best silk clothes, clips and pins for your hair, elegant hats, gloves—I'll dress you like a queen," he said. In the heat of the moment, he reached forward and let his hands glide lightly over her breasts, and to his amazement, she did not shy away, but instead she pressed his hands to her so tightly that he turned dizzy with desire.

"If we go, we go *after* the filming. I am not going to miss out on that. Now I have to get back. Gehringer said I could choose anything I wanted from all his clothes to wear in the film. I'll see you again, soon." She turned and began to climb the steps, holding her head high.

"Stay! Let's make plans . . ." *And maybe work in a caress or two,* he felt like adding, but she was already gone.

"Who gets women?" he murmured to himself. There he was, laying the world at her feet, and all Christel could think about was Gehringer's linens.

If only Alexander were here, he thought as he trudged upstairs. With his best friend, at least, he could let off some steam about Christel and all her airs and graces. Alexander had always been there to talk to, and damn it, he felt his absence now: their conversations, the trust they shared.

But his friend would not really have been able to give him any advice about how to handle Christel. Unlike Anton, Alexander had never had a girlfriend, and had so far shown little interest at all in the opposite sex. *He'll probably make up for that in Stuttgart,* Anton thought, grinning to himself.

At the top of the stairs, he paused and listened in the direction of the kitchen window. His mother seemed to be busy with preparations for the evening meal, and it was still dark in the bar area, which meant no guests, at least not yet.

Anton decided to take advantage of the situation and look in quickly on Eveline Schubert. Alexander's letters to him so far had been hurried and infrequent, but maybe his friend had written more to his mother, he thought as he quickly made his way through the alleys to Eveline's house. And maybe she could already tell him if Alexander would perhaps be home for Christmas.

He saw a low light beneath the door of the Schubert house, so Eveline was at home, and he was about to knock when he saw a shadow crossing the curtain. He heard low laughter and a man's voice, and he paused with his hand in midknock. Did Mrs. Schubert have a visitor? Would he be interrupting?

Maybe he ought to make sure first, he thought. The curtains were closed, certainly, but on the right side of one window, a small gap remained uncovered. *Just a quick look,* he told himself as he rose onto his tiptoes.

He blinked once. He blinked twice. But the image he saw through the narrow opening didn't change. Johann Merkle sat in a bathtub as naked as the day God made him, with Alexander's mother, just as naked, straddling him.

CHAPTER 40

For the first time perhaps in her entire life, Mimi did not attend the service in the church on Reformation Day. Luther's theses could wait. She wanted to spend every free minute she had with Josef.

That morning, her uncle had expressed a wish for chicken soup. "You're in luck," Mimi had told him as she stroked his cheek. "Helene mentioned just yesterday that she was going to kill a few chickens. I'll go to her store, then I'll cook you the best chicken soup ever."

Josef had smiled his gratitude.

After she had washed him and combed his hair, Mimi made her way to the store. Although it was already after ten, the sky was dark and leaden. Mimi's gaze turned wistfully across the market square, empty except for a few leaves driven by the wind.

The stately chestnut trees in front of the church were bare, their sap drawn down into the earth. It seemed to Mimi that the people of the village were copying nature, and tending likewise toward the earth. Luise and her husband, Helene, the priest, even Herrmann Gehringer—all looked somehow more stooped than they had just a few weeks ago. One complained of a pain in the back, another of sore knees, and yet another of aching shoulders. In autumn, the sad grew sadder, and even those lighter of heart laughed less than they did in summer. The winter would be long. Quiet, lost in their own thoughts, Laichingen's residents prepared for the cold season.

In her years as a traveling photographer, Mimi had made it her habit to travel to warmer climes no later than November. To Baden-Baden in the Rhine valley, where the frost came only now and then. Or to Lake Constance. She had once spent the winter in the Palatinate, and recalled Landau as a particularly pretty little town.

Where would she spend this winter? she wondered as she pushed open the door to Helene's shop and stepped inside. Josef would die soon, she knew. What then?

As on any other morning, a group of women had gathered at the store. And just as on any other morning, they chatted among themselves while they waited their turn at the counter. Mimi said a general greeting, and the women replied with friendly nods and took up their conversation again.

"My Beppo hardly slept a wink last night. He said his eye was twitching so badly he couldn't even close it," reported a woman with a careworn expression. Mimi knew her face, but not her name.

"My husband was almost sliding off his chair at dinner, he was so tired," said Fritz Braun's mother.

"Is it any wonder? The men have been at it twelve hours a day for the last four months. So much for a 'temporary production increase'!" mocked another.

"All because of those stupid anniversary designs," Franka Klein practically spat. "I'm telling you, it won't be long before we're burying the next one after Klaus."

The women looked at her, shocked, and crossed themselves.

"Maybe it's really time someone did something about the conditions here," said Mimi quietly. "If everyone stood up and said, 'We've had enough of all the overtime! We're not doing it anymore!' then Gehringer would have no choice but to reduce the number of hours to a reasonable level, wouldn't he?"

The women looked at her but said nothing.

So much for my future as a unionist, Mimi thought. She was slowly beginning to understand how hard it was for Johann to turn the men toward a strike.

"In the past, our men were starting work as autumn weavers at this time of year," said Helene nostalgically.

"Autumn weaver? I've heard the expression, but what exactly does it mean?" Mimi asked.

"Before the factories came, the farmers worked the fields in summer, and in winter, went down to the *Dunk* to weave. Everything had its place back then. People worked hard, but nobody worked themselves to death," Franka Klein explained.

"Speaking of working oneself to death," said the woman with the careworn face, looking around the group expectantly, "Johann was over at the widow Schubert's house *again* last night! He took her a rabbit and who knows what else."

"Ah-ha! So the prodigal son turns out to be a consoler of widows," said Franka Klein, and the women around her laughed.

Mimi's expression darkened. "Personally, I find it admirable that Johann Merkle is doing his part to help the Schubert family," she said calmly.

"But is it just a bit of help that Johann has in mind?" Franka Klein raised her eyebrows meaningfully. "Eveline Schubert is still a very pretty woman."

"Eveline also happens to be in her mourning year, and she knows well enough what's decent, so stop talking nonsense," said Helene from behind her counter. "Now who's next?"

"A mourning year also passes," Franka Klein murmured to Mimi, who was standing behind her. "If you ask me, they make a good couple."

Mimi opened her mouth for a sharp retort, then changed her mind. Johann had nothing but good intentions in helping Eve and her family, and suddenly people were pinning all kinds of misbehavior on him!

She was starting to see that his concern for her reputation was not misplaced.

Or was there perhaps something to all the talk? No smoke without fire, they said.

"Miss Reventlow? What can I get you?"

Mimi was so caught up in her gloomy thoughts that she hadn't realized it was her turn at the counter.

While the chicken and vegetable soup simmered on the stove, Mimi went up to check on Josef in his bedroom. She found him staring at the ceiling with a strangely rigid gaze. Mimi's hands flew to her throat. Was he dead?

"Mimi, child . . . ," she heard him say in his frail voice, and she breathed again.

"Doesn't the whole house smell good? It's the chicken soup. It will be done soon," she said with forced cheer.

He nodded vaguely. "My last meal. It's almost time."

Mimi shivered.

"It was a rich life, and I drank deeply from it. But the moon no longer lights for me. Only the dark night is waiting."

Mimi sought frantically for something to say, but Josef took her hand. "My child, I have to talk to you. I had my last will and testament written up a long time ago. The house, the studio, the shop . . . when I'm gone, it will all belong to you."

"I don't want to inherit anything!" Mimi cried in despair. "I want you to keep on living."

"My time has come, and both of us have to come to terms with that." His eyes glistened, but no tears came. "When I put you in my will as my sole heir, I thought that, one day, you would sell everything. And you can still do that, of course. All you have left to finish of Gehringer's commission are the group photographs, and after that you're as free as a bird. But I want to be honest with you, child. Now that my end is near, the thought that the studio will go unused makes me sad. So I want to ask you directly, dear Mimi: Would you like to stay on and take up my legacy?"

Confused and terribly upset, Mimi found herself standing at the stove in the kitchen a few minutes later, picking the chicken meat from the bones. She cut it into small pieces and put it back into the broth. The long talk had made Josef tired, and he had fallen asleep before Mimi could answer his question. She was glad about that, at least. What was she supposed to say?

Would she stay in Laichingen forever? Since Johann had come home, it was a question constantly on her mind. But now that Josef wanted an answer from her, she found it hard to say, *Yes, I'll stay.*

It was already afternoon when Josef woke again. Mimi, who had kept the soup warm for hours, took him a small bowl and began to feed him, but after a few spoonfuls, he'd had enough.

"My last meal in this world. It was wonderful," he whispered. "Thank you for your company. And thank you for everything else."

With trembling hands, Mimi put the soup bowl aside. Suddenly, she could no longer stand the smell of fat and chicken meat. Never again would she eat chicken soup without thinking of this moment, she thought, and the tears she had tried so hard all day to hold back trickled from her eyes.

"Don't be sad, my child. I'm not. Finally, I will get to see my Traudel once more." Josef patted her hand consolingly, then fell asleep once more.

Hour after hour, Mimi sat by his bed. She read a little, but most of the time she sat and stared at nothing, her head filled with thoughts, her heart heavy. She had planned to use the day to sort the most recent batch of Gehringer's product photos. But she did not want Josef to be alone when he died.

For Josef, phases of wakefulness alternated with spells of fitful sleep. He said nothing more, now, but she felt his eyes on her, questioning, waiting. She wished she could easily tell him, *I will keep your studio going just as you want.* But something stopped her from making that promise, though it would have pleased him and perhaps even eased his last moments. What was she waiting for? Laichingen was beautiful, and the studio with its glass wall was a wonderful construction. Johann was here, she had neighbors ready to help whenever necessary, and she had even made a few friends. Too, her encounter with the amateur photographer not long ago had shown her that it would get harder and harder to make her living as a traveling photographer. Josef had never—not once in her entire life—demanded anything of her. How could she even think about turning down his request?

It was just after six in the evening, the sun long since set, when Mimi left the room briefly to use the toilet. When she returned, she knew in an instant that he was gone. Josef's mouth was slightly open, and his eyes, too. Still, she checked his pulse and laid one ear to his chest to listen for his heartbeat. But there was nothing.

He had chosen to die in the five minutes she was not in the room.

CHAPTER 41

Ruthilde Rudy, the famed soprano and a familiar figure on all the great stages of Europe, was used to traveling with a large entourage. Whether to the National Theatre in Munich, the Bolshoi Theatre in Moscow, the Vienna State Opera, or Laichingen, it made no difference to her. With her came her hairdresser, maid, personal chef, and personal assistant—a short, weedy man who disappeared behind Ruthilde Rudy's prodigious back—and Oleg, a muscular Russian who was Ruthilde's personal masseur. And with Ruthilde Rudy and her entourage came the film crew from Munich: six men and twice that number of crates of equipment arrived the morning of November 1.

When Herrmann Gehringer, who had been so excited the previous night that he'd been unable to fall asleep, saw the new arrivals for the first time, he almost lost his nerve. Simply putting them all up in a hotel in Blaubeuren for the next three days would cost him a fortune. A few advertisements in the Stuttgart paper would have been far less trouble . . . But then he got a grip on himself. Great men were men of vision, after all. He could already picture himself at his anniversary celebration next year, presenting the film they were shooting today—his customers and competitors alike would be left openmouthed at such a bold move! Perhaps he could persuade Ruthilde Rudy to appear on the day. And since the film could have no sound, maybe she would even sing in person? In case she could find the time between Verona and Vienna . . . If not, never mind, he was already counting on a large contingent of journalists, and even the king of Württemberg was likely to be in attendance, so no expense could be spared. It was high time for the world to learn of the monumental importance of the linen industry for the entire empire! And his colleague Morlock, so proud of his pretty showroom in Ulm, might as well pack his bags.

Herrmann Gehringer took a deep breath and was ready for whatever had to be done.

While everyone except Ruthilde Rudy—who was given a seat in Gehringer's heated office—stood around in the entrance area of the mill and waited for instructions, Gehringer took Max Mühlzahn, the director, aside and explained to him how he envisioned the film: He saw Ruthilde making her way majestically through the mill, admiring this and that, exchanging a few gracious words with one of the weavers before moving on to the sewing room, where she would delight in the fine embroidery of one of the seamstresses, played by Christel Merkle. The final sequence of the film was to show Ruthilde Rudy smiling as she stepped out through the company gates, laden with Gehringer linenwares.

The director listened attentively to Gehringer's vision, then said, "Splendid, splendid. To be sure, though, every advertising film needs a certain amount of drama, if you take my meaning. What do you think of having Ruthilde Rudy sitting elegantly atop one of the looms, legs crossed, belting out a song? When we show the film at your gala, we could, for example, play a recording of Mrs. Rudy singing an aria from *La Traviata*. Of course, we'll need some dramatic lighting. Perhaps we could set up a couple of flaming torches somewhere? Then we'll get a few of the weavers to carry Ruthilde through the mill on a chaise longue—an operatic diva only ever walks by herself if absolutely necessary, and we'd able to show off your strong weavers to best advantage."

Gehringer frowned. Flaming torches? Was the man out of his mind? Was he supposed to stand and watch everything burn while Ruthilde Rudy warbled out an aria? And what strong weavers? His weavers were certainly a tough breed, but he couldn't picture them doing what Mühlzahn was proposing.

"Then we cut away—making any film dramatically interesting means finding the ideal way to cut the individual scenes together—and we see Ruthilde sitting in a circle of beautiful seamstresses. She is also sewing something and still singing away."

Gehringer felt an uncomfortable churning in his belly. Was it fear? Panic, even?

He coughed a little, and almost choked on his own spit in the process. "I can see I'm talking to a true master," he said, with a pat of recognition on Max Mühlzahn's shoulder. A little praise at the right moment never hurt. "But I should point out that a film shot in a weaving mill has to take certain . . . restrictions into account. The aisle between the looms is unquestionably too narrow to accommodate a chaise longue and bearers. If it is in any way possible, then, and not asking too much, it would be far better if our dear Mrs. Rudy walked by herself."

The director thought this over for a moment, then threw his head back so vigorously that his slicked-down hair flew backward. "Done!" he announced loudly. "She shall walk."

Gehringer exhaled with relief. The director would find out for himself soon enough that Mrs. Rudy's trilling would be inaudible anyway over the racket made by the looms. And Mühlzahn would also have to forget the flaming torches—the fire risk was simply too great. With a bit of luck, he'd be able to deflect the rest of Mühlzahn's grandiose ideas.

Lamps were unpacked and film cameras set up on large stands. The film people were an arrogant bunch and ordered Paul Merkle and the weavers around as if they owned the place. To Gehringer's annoyance, the looms had to be shut down—they were simply too loud. But what did the loss of three days' production count compared with a filmic work of art directed by Max Mühlzahn?

Then Ruthilde Rudy refused to appear in the mill for a rehearsal. The dusty air would not do her vocal cords any good at all. Could they wipe the place down with wet cloths before her performance? They could. Paul Merkle quickly reassigned two of the seamstresses to cleaning duty.

While the two seamstresses went to work with buckets and rags, Christel stood in the farthest corner of the mill and watched the proceedings with wide eyes. After an enormous amount of pleading, both Gehringer and her father had given her permission not just to be there for her own small part but to watch the rest of the filming, too. Now, like a sponge, she soaked up every nuance.

"What's a pretty girl like you doing among all these men?" she suddenly heard a male voice say beside her. She couldn't quite place his accent.

She looked around and saw an attractive middle-aged man with coal-black hair and a rakish mustache. He had come in with the director, but Christel did not know what his position was. Like her, he was just standing around.

"I don't work in the weaving shed. I model Mr. Gehringer's clothes when customers come. I'm supposed to play one of the seamstresses," she said proudly. "My name's Christel."

"Crystal—that's a fine name." The man raised his neat dark eyebrows. "I'm Freddy Forsythe, a friend of the director, at your service. Pretty as you are, this can't be the first time someone's asked you to be in a film, can it?"

Christel reddened. "It really is my first time. But our local photographer is going to take my picture next week, Mr. Gehringer said. He wants to have me on the cover of his new mail-order catalog."

The man snorted with laughter. "Forgive me for saying so, young lady, but that is a monumental waste!" He looked around as if to make sure nobody could hear their conversation. Leaning close to Christel, Forsythe said in a confidential tone, "Someone with your beauty and grace does not belong on the cover of a mail-order catalog, but on the big screen."

"Really?" said Christel, excitedly twirling a lock of her golden hair.

Forsythe nodded vigorously. "I know what I'm talking about. I emigrated to America many years ago, and I'm only back here in the homeland for a short visit. When my old friend Max told me about his job here in the Jura, I decided on the spur of the moment to join him. Little productions like this can be quite a lot of fun sometimes. But I normally work in America."

"So you're not one of the film people at all?" Her words carried a touch of *So why am I even talking to you?* Why, when there was so much excitement going on?

But her interest was piqued again when Forsythe said, "Not one of *these* film people, exactly. I work as a cameraman and director in Hollywood. You know, where they make the really big films, like *The Great Train Robbery* and *Frankenstein*. My friend Carl Laemmle—another German emigrant, by the way—has a film company called Independent Moving Pictures Company, and tens of thousands of Americans come to see the films his company makes. We like everything big, you know?"

Christel's eyes grew wider, and she nodded, impressed. "I think I could get to like 'big,' too," she said slowly.

Freddy Forsythe grinned. "Young lady, you have the very best prerequisites for making it big. Take my word for it. You don't just have beauty—you have a radiance and a way of moving that will entrance audiences. Even here in this dark and dusty hole, you have a luminosity I have rarely seen. Once we get you into a film studio . . ."

Christel gulped. She had known today would be very special, but she had never dared to dream about something like this.

"You really think I'd have a chance all the way out there? In Hollywood?"

"If you meet the right people at the right time—without a doubt." Freddy Forsythe glanced out into the mill—still no one was paying them any attention. He took Christel's hand in his and said solemnly, "Crystal, I believe today is your lucky day. I can make you bigger than you would believe! If you're serious about this, then listen to me very carefully . . ."

CHAPTER 42

Slowly, the horse and wagon carrying Josef Stöckle's coffin rolled from the church to the graveyard. A long row of people clad in black walked behind, stony faced. Heavy fog swirled around the mourners. The day seemed to suit a burial—certainly more so than in late June, when Klaus Schubert had been carried to his grave. Back then, everything had been green and growing—which had only served to make Klaus's death appear more senseless.

But now everything felt transitional. Everything had its time. The light and the darkness. The joy, the suffering. Life and death.

At Mimi's request, Anton had pushed all the tables at The Oxen into a U shape for the reception after Josef's funeral. Mimi sat in the center of the base of the U. On her left were her neighbors, Luise and Georg Neumann, and on her right her mother, who had come from Esslingen. Her father had not come—a heavy cold had prevented him from traveling.

Mimi thought she could probably count on one hand the days on which her mother had been there for her. As a priest's wife, Amelie Reventlow was simply too busy all the time, and Mimi had feared that she would be left by herself this time, too. She had been relieved when her mother arrived, although it had taken Josef's death to get her to come. But despite Amelie's presence, Mimi felt more alone than ever—it was the first time she had ever lost someone so close to her. And it was as if her grief, like a wild animal, would tear her apart.

Of course she had known that her uncle would die. But can one really prepare for a person's death? Mimi, at least, had been unable to. Her eyes stung from all the tears she had spilled in the last few days.

In her years of wandering and, really, long before, as a young girl, Mimi had been aware of her beloved uncle's role in her life. Without Josef, she never would have found the courage to go traveling at all. He had never said a harsh word to her, never criticized her, not even when, some years earlier, she had rather unceremoniously turned down his offer to take over his Sun Coach. And in recent months, when they lived under the same roof, his presence and importance to her had become more and more clear. He had always believed in her. That much was clear, too, with his request that she take over his studio . . . But in the end, she had been unable to give him an answer.

Nor had Josef ever resorted to the stale old "you'll never make it as a woman, anyway." On the contrary, he had always encouraged her to try new things. *"Life is change, my child"*—how many times, with his characteristic smile, had he told her that?

Oh, Josef, I feel so lost, Mimi thought as she saw Berta approaching. Smiling bravely, Mimi grasped Berta's hand.

"My condolences," Berta said. "I'm sure you must miss your uncle. And my condolences to you as well," Berta said to Mimi's mother. "Your brother was a much-loved man here in the village."

Tears immediately welled in Amelie Reventlow's eyes, and she took out a handkerchief and dabbed them away.

Berta looked away for a moment and then back at Mimi. "I know this isn't a good time, but when you were at our wedding, you asked about my plans for the future, and I had mentioned wanting to learn how to sew a traditional outfit . . ."

"Yes?" Mimi said from her daze. She wanted to sound encouraging but didn't think she'd managed it.

"Well, I've actually started to work on my first one. And Richard is carving the buttons for it from horn. And the—"

"Berta, I would so enjoy talking with you about this and seeing your work. Might we do just that in a few days? It will give me something to look forward to."

"Of course, yes. Again, my condolences," she said, then turned and left.

Mimi's mother sat next to her, twisting her handkerchief in her fingers as she sat in silence.

Eveline approached the table next. "I'm sorry about your uncle, Mimi. He was a good man and will be remembered for a long time. Alexander wanted me to be sure to tell you that he would have liked to come to the funeral, but, well, it is hard for him to leave school." She turned to Amelie. "And I am sorry for the loss of your brother. I know if Alexander were here he would want to say the same and to thank you for your generous help with the art school. Art means everything to Alexander—it's all he's ever wanted." With a kind smile to both Mimi and her mother, she walked away.

"That's the mother of the boy you helped get into art school?" Amelie whispered in Mimi's ear.

Mimi nodded. She noticed Johann across the tables, looking in her direction. At the church, he had sat beside her, and on the way to the cemetery, he had even offered her his arm to lean on. Having him so close was good, Mimi thought, picking her slice of *Hefezopf* apart without eating any of it.

"What a fine-looking man," her mother whispered. "Could *he* be the reason you stayed in Laichingen?"

"I stayed because of Uncle Josef," Mimi replied, stung by a moment of regret that her mother had come at all—Johann would be where her mother was sitting now, instead of next to Eveline. And he would not leave her alone later, when this day was finally over, but would stay to console her, and be her shoulder to cry on.

"Should I bring out more coffee?" Anton said, coming up beside her and dragging her out of her thoughts.

"Yes. One or two more pots, please," she said. She looked up at him and frowned. "What's the matter with you?" she asked, speaking softly. "You look more down in the dumps than I. It can't just be because of Josef, can it?"

Anton's shoulders collapsed so abruptly that Mimi pictured someone releasing the strings of a marionette. "It's Christel," he whispered. "She's being so strange. Ever since the film people were here, she's been acting like she's better than the rest of us, and as if I'm just some kind of man Friday she can push around any way she feels like."

Mimi sighed. She could imagine too well how the film experience had gone to Christel's head. "It will be all right," she said sympathetically.

"I'm not so sure." Anton glared toward one end of the table, where Christel was sitting with her family and Mr. Gehringer. "Gehringer has managed to drive a wedge between Christel and me after all." His brow creased in anger, and he stalked off.

"It's amazing, isn't it, the absoluteness with which young people express themselves." Amelie Reventlow shook her head with a smile. "I'll tell you this, dear, I'm impressed with the trust the people here seem to have in you. It appears you've become an important person for the citizens of Laichingen. Who would have thought that you would one day follow in my footsteps?" she said, moved.

Mimi, despite her grief, had to smile. She hoped she was still a long way from following in her mother's footsteps!

She rose to her feet. "I'll be back in a minute," Mimi said, and she made her way to where Gehringer sat.

"Thank you for coming today," she said.

The businessman nodded. "I wouldn't have missed it. I held your uncle in high esteem."

And yet you always used to order your photos from Ulm, Mimi thought. "I'll finish the last of the group photos in the next few days. My uncle's passing shouldn't cause any delay."

Gehringer dabbed at his lips with his napkin. "I should hope not. Now that the film people are gone, a little peace has returned to the mill, and it's time to take those pictures. Oh, by the way, I have another photograph in mind that I'd like you to do."

"Yes?"

"Paul Merkle's daughter Christel," said Gehringer. "I want a picture of her in our prettiest linen blouse, one to grace the cover of our new catalog. And then you're done. I'm sure you can hardly wait to get out on the road again, can you?" he remarked, a smirk playing on his lips. "When the time comes, just say the word and I'll have Paul drive you to the train station in Ulm."

Apparently, Gehringer couldn't get rid of her fast enough.

"I'm not going anywhere soon," she said flatly. "There is still a great deal to sort out. I'll go to Blaubeuren next week to meet with a notary about my uncle's will. After that, there are several decisions to be made. But thank you for the offer," she said, doing her best to be polite.

"Maybe I can help you with those decisions?" Gehringer said. "We can sit down together soon, and I'll make you an offer. I'm still interested in your uncle's shop."

Could he get to the point any faster? Mimi thought, annoyed and hurt. There was nothing more she could say in that moment, nor could she stop herself from giving Gehringer a scathing look before returning to her seat.

"I'm going to miss your uncle," said Luise with a sigh when Mimi sat down. "Thank God I have you as my neighbor. And now that you're one of us, the people will be more willing to visit your studio."

"One of us"? Mimi thought, saddened by all the decisions she needed to make. *If only it were that simple. I still don't know if I'm even going to stay.*

"Have you thought about what you're going to do with Josef's clothes?" Amelie was sorting through a thick file that contained her brother's personal papers. "If you like, we can clear out his wardrobe together."

"I don't know," Mimi said. Clear out Josef's wardrobe? She dreaded the very thought.

"It's all here—title deed, registry notice. My brother was very organized," her mother murmured, and a nostalgic smile appeared briefly on her face. But a moment later, she said, "And what about all the bits and pieces in his wife's wardrobe? Who do you want to give all that to? If you want help before I leave again the day after tomorrow, we'd better get started."

Mimi nodded unhappily and sat down opposite her mother at the kitchen table. "There are two or three blouses I'd like to keep, but the rest I'll give away. Luise will be happy to have a few things to remember her best friend by, I'm sure. And Alexander's mother will be able to use some of it."

"That's a start," said Amelie. Her eyes turned toward the window, and Mimi saw her shudder slightly.

"What a grim village," she said. "How on earth did Josef put up with it? More importantly, how have *you* put up with it for so long? With all due respect to Josef's final wish, I hope you're not planning to stay." Amelie looked intently at her daughter over the rim of her reading glasses.

Mimi took a deep breath. "I've been thinking about nothing else for days, but I just don't know. Josef's final will . . . It's so hard to choose. It fills me with pride and joy that he's entrusted his studio to me. But then, I love my life on the road." She leaned across the table for an envelope. "It's been a long time coming, but I've just recently had a new inquiry. A town down in the Black Forest wants to know if I can come and take pictures of their new ski lift, together with the skiers. They're publishing an advertising brochure. If I wanted to, I could leave within a few days. It's tempting."

The letter had arrived the day after Josef's death, and she had only glanced at it. Despite her long break from traveling, people still wanted her services, she had realized with some relief. Being on the road again, meeting interesting people, getting to know new places, and recording all these impressions with her camera—after the hundreds of garments she'd recently photographed, the life of a traveling photographer seemed more diverse and vibrant than ever. But would she be able to just pick up and leave so easily? The thought of leaving Johann, and Laichingen and its people, too, was hard for her to accept.

She let her hands fall helplessly into her lap. "Somehow, I have the feeling that I'm not finished with things here, and not just because I still have to take the group photos for Gehringer." She looked at her mother, who had so far only listened in silence. "Even though I've known things would change after Josef died, when I was working in Gehringer's makeshift studio, it was easier to push aside all thoughts of the future. I only had to look as far ahead as the next garment. But now I have to make a decision."

"And not only you, but a certain gentleman does, too, right?" said her mother gently. "That attractive man who stood beside you at the graveside is surely one reason for how torn you feel."

Mimi nodded, and stared at her hands in her lap. "I don't know where I stand with him." In a few words, she told her mother how she had met Hannes in Ulm and then become reacquainted with him here in Laichingen, as Johann. "Leading the weavers of Laichingen into a labor dispute clearly means more to him than anything else," she finished sadly. But as she told her mother the story, she felt a spark of hope flare inside her. Would Johann declare his feelings for her more easily now that Josef had passed? Perhaps he would even propose to her, now that she owned Josef's house? To live in peace with her, would he give up on his long-sought strike?

Amelie Reventlow laid a hand on Mimi's arm. "Have a little trust in God, dear child. The Lord will show you the road ahead, as he has always done. But if you want to hear my honest opinion, then I can hardly imagine that your future lies in this remote place. The world is big and exciting and wonderful!"

Mimi let out a faint laugh, but it was tinged with her despair. "Laichingen is also wonderful, though it may not look like it on a gray November day. Besides, as you've seen, I've taken the people here into my heart, and they me. Poverty is everywhere, and the mill owners exploit the workers. Like Johann, I would like to help them. Can you understand that?" *Of course she can understand that. If not Amelie Reventlow, then who?* Mimi thought, before she'd finished speaking.

But to Mimi's surprise, Amelie said, "Your unionist Johann can do whatever he likes. But if you want my advice, child, then don't fall into the same trap I did. All my life, I've wanted to help anyone I could. It made no difference if it was an alcoholic I tried to wean off schnapps, or a poor fishing family on the Neckar with no money to fix their boat, or some other emergency—I was always there when I had to be. Sometimes, what I did actually helped, but often it didn't. How many times have I put our family—you, your father, Josef—in second place just to help strangers?" Her mother shook her head.

Mimi, listening speechlessly, could hardly believe it.

"It's not as if I regret all of it, good gracious no," said Amelie quickly, as if she'd seen Mimi's surprise. Her mother's expression was stern as she went on, "Today, though, when I hear about the latest crisis, I stop and think first what kind of help is needed, or if my help is really needed at all. Each of us is the architect of our own fortune, and maybe there's more truth in that saying than I used to think. Each of us has the freedom to decide what we really want in life."

"But what if the people are not able to help themselves? What if they rely on the aid of others?" Mimi was starting to feel completely lost. Would Fritz Braun have gotten his apprenticeship with Mr. Meindl if she hadn't spoken up for him? Would Eveline have been able to send Alexander to art school without help from the other villagers? Would Alexander even have had the opportunity without help from Amelie and Mimi herself? She doubted it. And what about the weavers for whom Johann wanted to stand up? Without his leadership, would they ever dare to rebel against Gehringer and the other mill owners? "Sometimes people need someone to walk ahead of them, to give them courage, to show them the road to follow," Mimi said softly.

"That's true. And that's why there are people like your Johann. As much as you stand up for others, Mimi—and it is good that you do—one part of you will always be a photographer. It is your calling to give people the gift of beauty. Don't underestimate how important that is," said her mother. "Quite apart from that: one can't force people to be happy. Somewhere along the way, I came to realize that. Change has to take place in people's heads and hearts. And the courage to change doesn't grow any faster just because you hold up someone's failings in front of them, or count off all the things they could do better. Besides, what gives us the right to say we know what's good for someone else?"

Mimi could only sit there, stunned.

Amelie took her daughter's hand. "I would love to spend a few extra days with you, but your father needs me. When he's suffering from a cold, it's like he's at death's door."

Amelie smiled, and Mimi saw in her eyes the love that still held sway after all the years her parents had been together. "Come and stay with us at Christmas. Papa would be overjoyed to see you. We'll have a lovely time, and you can find some peace and quiet to think about what you want to do next. And who knows?" Her mother smiled mischievously. "Maybe Esslingen's charms will tempt you to settle there with us, instead."

Mimi laughed. "With a photo studio of my own, right? I'm sure old Mr. Semmer would be thrilled."

Amelie joined in her laughter. "I've heard Felix Semmer will be retiring soon. Should I bring up your name as a possible successor to his business?"

"Thank you, no!" Mimi said, raising her hands defensively.

Before Mimi knew it, Amelie had wrapped her arms around her and rocked her side to side like a child. "Things will work out—love-things and work-things, it doesn't matter. You will do what's right, Mimi, as you've done all your life. I don't have the slightest doubt about it."

CHAPTER 43

"Hello. My name is Anton Schaufler. This is my wife, Christel. She's looking for work in film, so—" Anton, cleaning windows in The Oxen, abruptly stopped talking to himself. Didn't his name sound a little plain? Maybe if he made it sound a touch more foreign? Anthony or Antoine? He dunked the towel into the bucket of ice-cold water and wrung it out.

He usually hated cleaning the windows in winter. On days like this, the water froze on the windowpanes faster than he could wipe it dry. His hands were raw and chapped, and he already knew that Christel would complain later if he tried to stroke her cheek or hold her hand. If it were up to him, they'd simply ignore the damned windows in the cold. But today, even this hated chore could not sour his mood.

"Good afternoon, my name is Anthony Schaufler. My wife, Christel . . ."

"My wife"—those two words sounded marvelous to him, and a warm thrill ran down his spine as he scrubbed the windows. He could hardly wait to make Christel his wife. They would stay true to each other and hide nothing.

His discovery that Johann Merkle was spending nights with Alexander's mother had certainly been a shock. The man had been kissing and cuddling Mimi Reventlow not so long ago. How could anyone be so two faced? Johann was just one more example of what the ever-so-virtuous Laichingers were capable of, and it made Anton more determined than ever to escape the place.

"Let's get through New Year's first," Christel had said to him a few days before when he'd asked her impatiently what they were still waiting for. "The new year is a good time for a fresh start."

He'd had nothing to counter that argument. Maybe it was good to spend Christmas in the circle of their families—he didn't want Christel suddenly homesick and miserable when they were already many miles away.

In the meantime, he hadn't been merely biding his time. On the contrary! When the film people had come to The Oxen one midday the week before last, he'd peppered them with questions—albeit as subtly as he possibly could. He'd discovered that there were film studios in Berlin and Denmark, and that the film industry was burgeoning. Berlin would be their first stop! And if they didn't have luck there, then they would travel on to Copenhagen. In his mind's eye, he could already see himself standing at train stations, smoking cigars, waving for a porter to stow his and Christel's baggage in one of the compartments on board. On top of the considerable sum he'd passed on to Christel through his sham robbery, he'd put some additional coins aside: tips and the money his father had given him for helping build another blind in the woods. One thing was certain: they would start their new life with more than enough for a while.

Anton scrubbed pigeon shit vigorously from a pane of glass.

He was just pouring the dirty water down the gutter when he saw Paul Merkle running across the square. *Is he late for work, maybe?* Anton thought, grinning. But his grin froze when he realized that Christel's father, his face twisted in anger, was headed straight for him. Before he knew it, Merkle had him by the throat. The wash bucket clattered onto the cobblestones as Anton struggled just to breathe.

"Where is she? What have you done with her?"

"Who? What? What are you talking about?" Anton choked out, and every word hung like a little cloud in the cold air.

"You know perfectly well what I'm talking about!" Merkle shouted. Then, with a growl that came from deep in his throat, he finally released Anton. "Where is my daughter? Speak, before I really lose control!"

"What about her? What do you mean?" The thought that something might have happened to Christel made Anton's heart hammer faster. His pupils widened, and now he was close to grabbing Merkle by the collar. "Speak, man! What's going on?"

Paul Merkle's glare bored into Anton, as if he were sizing him up and expecting him to betray himself in some way. But Anton felt just as it seemed Christel's father did—fearful, uncomprehending, desperate.

"Christel is gone," said Merkle, and suddenly all his strength seemed to drain out of his body. "When she didn't stoke the fire this morning and put water on to heat like she usually does, we thought she'd overslept. My wife was furious, but when she went to wake her, all she found was an empty bed. She hadn't slept in it."

"I don't believe it," Anton said, his voice flat. Suddenly, he felt as if he might faint, and he looked around for something to hold on to.

Merkle, more distressed than furious now, said, "We've looked everywhere for her. We've asked the neighbors. She's disappeared."

"It's not possible. Christel can't be gone," Anton said despairingly. Not without him. "She must have stayed at a friend's place, and everything's just a misunderstanding."

"You really don't know where she could be?"

Anton shook his head. *It's not possible,* he kept telling himself, over and over. They had planned to leave together, just after New Year's!

Paul Merkle turned in circles while pulling at his hair. For a moment, he looked as if he were about to burst into tears, but he quickly caught himself.

"We have to keep looking. All of us! Can you get a search party together?"

Herrmann Gehringer had asked Mimi to put the photographs in order by the years in which the items had been produced—the earliest at the bottom and on up to this year's designs.

Now, as Mimi inspected the many pictures stacked on Uncle Josef's kitchen table, she couldn't help but be impressed. The work, indeed, had been monotonous, but that only added to her sense of accomplishment in maintaining the quality of her pictures from the first image to the last.

Also in accordance with Gehringer's wishes, she began to sort each year's pictures into its own box. Those intended for the catalog went into one box, the group pictures of the weavers and seamstresses into another, along with the exterior photographs of the mill and grounds.

The work was a welcome distraction from the loneliness she had felt since Uncle Josef's death and her mother's departure: in the mornings, when she was by herself with a cup of tea and a slice of bread for breakfast; during the day, when she sat in the studio and waited for her few-and-far-between customers; and in the evenings, when she waited in vain for Johann to come, or after he stopped by for a few minutes before leaving again. The work also distracted her from making the decisions she would have to make sooner or later.

At some point, most of the pictures were organized, but at the corner of the table, there was a small pile still unsorted. *Now what are those?* Mimi frowned, hoping she hadn't made a mistake somewhere along the way. She had no desire to go back through everything again. A little annoyed at herself, Mimi reached for the pile, and saw that they were the pictures she had taken the day before she started at the mill. She'd developed the plates and made some prints after Johann had asked her about them, then put them aside to focus on the photographs for the commission. Now she looked at the pictures again, with a mix of fascination and repulsion.

Here were the long rows of looms and the children running among them. Their skinny arms, their thin, gangly legs . . . And how fast could a child's hand find its way into one of the machines? According to Gehringer, the children were only there to visit their parents at work.

Weavers with pale faces, eyes on the flying shuttle. What did they think about when they stood at a loom for twelve hours a day? About the many thousands of picks that made up their daily quota? About green meadows and blue skies? About the work still to be done out in the fields?

Mimi's gaze stopped on the picture of the weaver who had had the accident in front of her and collapsed to the floor. His face covered in tears, his eye injured. Did he still work at the mill? She hadn't even asked about him afterward, she realized now, feeling guilty.

Never in her life had she photographed reality like this.

A knock on the door startled her. Johann? Mimi hurriedly put the pictures aside and ran to the door.

"Mr. Gehringer!" she said in surprise when she opened the door. "I've just finished sorting your photographs. I planned to bring them to you tomorrow, but if you like, you can have them now."

"I'm not here about the photographs. I came to see how you are getting on after your uncle's death," Gehringer said as he followed her into the kitchen. "You must feel very alone."

Mimi quickly gathered up the grim images and put them away in the kitchen table drawer—no need to upset the man with pictures like that.

"Sit down, please. Would you like a cup of coffee? My mother brought me fresh beans."

"Cider would be perfect, if you have some," Gehringer replied, then sat on the chair Mimi offered. "Here is the rest of your fee, by the way," he said as he placed a hefty envelope on the table.

It was a sizable sum, and Mimi thanked him. But how long would the money last? she wondered. Then she fetched the jug of cider and poured her visitor a generous glass.

"Your uncle collected many things in his lifetime of travels, didn't he?" Gehringer asked as he surveyed the exotic souvenirs that filled the shelf and decorated the walls.

Mimi smiled wistfully. "Josef was very attached to them. To be honest, I still don't know what to do with all of them. I can give my uncle's clothes to the needy, of course, but what do I do with a medieval sword? Who do I give the beer steins from the Hofbräuhaus in Munich to? Are you interested in them?" she asked jokingly. She had no idea why she was suddenly so relaxed with him.

Gehringer laughed with her. "Wouldn't you also like to sit?" he asked, gesturing invitingly, as if they were in his kitchen and not hers. "I'd like to propose an idea. If you like it, you won't have to give up either Josef's sword or his steins."

Mimi was taken aback. "What do you have in mind?"

"I'd like to buy the property from you, all of it—house, shop, and studio. It's true that I no longer need the shop as a showroom for my goods—the glass pavilion on the company grounds has proven to be quite an attraction for my customers, and when Christel models the garments, no one takes any notice of their surroundings in any case." He laughed as if he'd made an exceptionally funny joke.

"But I have big plans! Laichingen has always been good to me. The town and the mill have made me a wealthy man. It's time I came up with something special for the village in return." He leaned across the table toward Mimi, as if taking her into his confidence. Then he finally showed his hand: "I'd like to transform the entire property into a museum. A museum about the history of weaving, to which my mill has, of course, made a substantial contribution. The well-lit rooms would be ideal for all kinds of exhibits—historical looms, ancient specimens of the embroiderer's art, spinning wheels, a timeline showing the history of weaving. And who knows? Perhaps we could also show something of the history of your uncle's studio. What do you say?"

"A museum here?" Mimi said. Her voice sounded a little shrill. "This comes as quite a surprise. I don't even know yet whether I'm going to leave or stay in Laichingen." She knew that Gehringer was not a man reluctant to speak his mind, but couldn't he even wait until the reading of the will, scheduled for the next day? she thought, annoyed.

"You? Stay here? Young lady, with your talent, the world is at your feet. It is to your credit that you think about continuing your uncle's work with his studio, but believe me, within a few months, you'll be so bored you won't know what to do with yourself. Do you really think you'll be happy taking pictures of christenings, confirmations, and an occasional wedding forever?"

Mimi said nothing. One did not live for work alone, she thought. There was also love . . .

"Thank you. I'll think about your offer," she said politely.

"Don't think about it too long. Ideally, I'd like to have the museum ready to open during the anniversary celebrations in March."

CHAPTER 44

Mimi was rinsing out the cider glass when there was another knock at the door.

"Anton!" she exclaimed when she opened the door. It was good to see him. But her smile disappeared when she saw the desperation on his face.

"Miss Reventlow, we need your help. Christel has disappeared."

Everyone in the village was involved in the search. Every house and every cellar was scoured at least twice. Christel's old school friends were questioned, as were the neighbors, all the employees in Gehringer's mill, even Gehringer himself. Speculation was rife, and over the next two days, the theories as to her whereabouts grew more and more outlandish. Had she been kidnapped? Unlikely. Did the film people have something to do with her disappearance? That was also considered unlikely—they had left Laichingen ten days ago. Did the person who'd robbed Anton also have a hand in Christel's vanishing? Some certainly thought it possible.

Anton, who knew better, asked: "What if she just went for a walk and had an accident?" So people went out and searched every patch of forest, every meadow, every field for miles around. Small groups walked every path, used and unused. Paul Merkle and Anton hardly slept at all, and Johann was also out searching day and night—Gehringer had given both brothers the time off.

The police in nearby villages were notified; train station attendants and mailmen were told to be on the lookout.

The Oxen became the meeting point for the search parties. Karolina Schaufler had food and beverages available at all hours. At first the mood was optimistic, but after two days of fruitless searches, that confidence faded with each cup of tea and every spoonful of soup. Paul Merkle aged years, his usual self-importance gone. Slumped in a chair, staring at nothing, he paused his search only to warm himself up with tea or soup that he didn't actually taste. His cup or bowl was hardly empty before he was out the door again. Maybe they had overlooked a clue somewhere, somehow.

On the third day of the search, Mimi, the Merkle brothers, Anton, and a few others were taking a short break at The Oxen. Other than Mimi's trip to Blaubeuren for the reading of the will, she also had been searching around the clock.

"I was lost myself, once," said Mimi. All eyes instantly turned to the photographer. "I was a little girl," Mimi began, both hands wrapped tightly around her cup of hot tea. "I'd caught a fat caterpillar, and I hoped that it would turn into a beautiful butterfly. I wanted to build a cage for the caterpillar out of an old box, but my mother scolded me and said, 'There are no lovely cages. A caterpillar can only turn into a beautiful butterfly if it has room to move' . . ." Mimi, suddenly deep in her memories, trailed off. Her mother was a smart woman.

"What's that have to do with Christel?" Anton snapped at her.

Mimi jumped. She hadn't noticed that she had gone silent. "I went off into the woods. I wanted to collect some leaves for the caterpillar, but I fell into a poacher's pit. It was camouflaged so well that you couldn't see it at first glance. Later, my father said the search parties had passed by that exact spot several times. It was only when they brought in a tracking dog that I was found."

Paul Merkle looked dubiously at Mimi, then at Otto Schaufler, Anton's father. "We don't have pits like that around here, do we?"

Anton's father shrugged. "They're prohibited, of course. But that doesn't mean they don't exist."

"Christel's probably fallen into just such a pit!" Paul Merkle cried. Frightened and hopeful at the same time, Merkle looked at Anton, who had become a kind of ally to him.

Anton was already on his feet. "We need a dog!" he said to his father. "Which of your hunting friends has the best?"

Tracking dogs were brought in, and the search continued. The dogs' excited barking and yelping found its way through the windows into every house. But another day passed, and there was still no sign of Christel Merkle.

The search had been going on for five days, and with each passing day, the number of volunteers grew smaller. As much as people wanted to help, they had children to care for, they had work to do, and they needed to sleep. But the core group did not give up.

Christel's family sat at the table where the mill owners usually met. Sonja, her eyes red and swollen from crying, had the baby on her lap. Three of her sons; her mother, Luise; and her father, Georg, surrounded her. Only Christel's brother Justus wasn't there. Johann was also present, along with his mother, Eveline, and Mimi Reventlow. No one talked much. Each sat alone with their thoughts.

Anton looked down at himself. *This brown apron—how long have I been wearing it now?* He couldn't remember the last time he'd washed or changed clothes.

Christel was gone. With his money. Without him. She had left her clothes behind to make everything look innocent, but she had taken the envelope with his money. If it had still been there, Christel's parents—who had turned her room upside down several times, looking for some clue—would certainly have found it.

She'd run away.

With his money.

Without him.

Christel was free, while he was still stuck in Laichingen.

The same thoughts kept hammering away in his head, like a blacksmith beating relentlessly on an anvil. There were moments when he wanted to bawl out his pain, fury, and disillusionment, and other moments when he wanted nothing more than to smash everything around him to pieces. In between, he kept hoping it was all just a bad dream. But no. Christel had betrayed him in the worst possible way. Disgusted, he reached for the bottle of schnapps that, for days, had been standing on the bar of The Oxen for anyone who wanted it, and refilled his glass.

"Drinking too much won't make it better," said his mother, but he took no notice.

The next moment, the door jerked open and Christel's brother Justus came in. Bewildered, the boy—who, like the others, had slept far too little in recent days—came up to the table nearly breathless. "I went through Christel's room again, and I found this," he said, waving an envelope. "It was caught inside the fold of her pillowcase somehow."

Anton was instantly alert. Was that the envelope with his money? Had his suspicions about Christel been unwarranted?

A breathless silence prevailed while Justus opened the envelope and took out a sheet of paper. He unfolded it clumsily and began to read:

"'Don't look for me, because you will not find me. Dear parents, I did my best to be what you wanted me to be, but now I know that my happiness lies elsewhere.'"

Anton doubled over as if somebody had stabbed him in the belly.

He'd known it. Deep inside, in his gut, from the very first moment, when Paul Merkle came running to The Oxen with the news of Christel's disappearance. But knowing something and actually believing it were two different things.

The others seemed to feel the same. If anything, the silence only deepened as each of them tried to make sense of what they had just heard. Christel had actually *chosen* to leave?

"Mimi, your mother was right," Sonja's voice rang out, high and clear. "There are no lovely cages."

Anton spun around to face her. Had Christel's mother lost her mind? No, her expression was calm as she continued, "I'm sure Christel is well and where she wants to be. She always wanted more for herself. And now she will get more, God willing."

Drunk on schnapps and pain, Anton was suddenly overcome with anger. "So it's God's will that Christel's gone? What 'more' is she going to get now?" He looked around at the group, his eyes burning. "More freedom? More money? More love? Nobody loved her more than I did." He swallowed a sob. "But all of you, sitting here, you all missed something about her. Not one of you saw that Christel was something special. For you, she was the nanny, the household help. For free. Never a trip to the city, never allowed to meet me, never able to go to a movie. If you'd only left the cage door open, just a crack, she'd still be here."

"What nonsense is that?" Paul Merkle snarled at him. "Christel had it good with us! You were the one putting crazy ideas into her head."

Anton let out a hard laugh. "Your daughter didn't need to have crazy ideas put into her head. She had them all by herself." The way she acted sometimes, like a prima donna. And then she'd gone and made her own plans to escape. Without him, but with his money! The thought that she was sitting somewhere right now, laughing it up at his expense, while he spent night after night searching for her like an idiot . . . A sound escaped his throat, something between a cry and a lament.

"Anton," said Mimi in a soothing tone that enraged him even more. "For now, let's be happy that nothing bad has happened to her."

Suddenly, Anton could no longer stand the sight of those around him, but it was Mimi Reventlow who took the brunt of his wrath. "Nothing bad? How exactly do you know that? You think you're so clever, but you don't even see what's going on right under your nose," he shouted at the photographer. "You'd have done better to listen to your friend on the train when she said that love is a devious creature. She was right. I know that now. You need to give up dreaming about the love of your life. It's no more than an illusion."

"Anton, that's enough!" he heard his mother say sharply, but there was no stopping him now.

"For once, I'm the one to decide when it's enough," he said. He pointed to Johann and Eveline. "Those two have been carrying on a little affair of their own. I've seen it with my own eyes. If our prodigal son's been whispering sweet nothings in your ear, Miss Reventlow, then they've all been lies." His hand trembled as he lifted the schnapps glass to his mouth. "To hell with it—you're a pack of liars, all of you," he snarled, then he threw back the liquid. Almost simultaneously, his mother slapped him hard on the side of his face, and it burned like the schnapps in his throat, but he stood his ground and glared at the glass in his hand.

The photographer froze in her seat. "Say it isn't true," she whispered in Johann's direction after a long moment of silence.

"It's nonsense, drunk talk. Eveline Schubert is in her year of mourning," Johann said adamantly, but his guilty eyes gazed at the floor, telling a different story.

Mimi slowly turned to the right. "Eveline?"

Alexander's mother twisted her hands in her lap. "Anton's too drunk. He doesn't know what he's talking about. Besides, you know how quickly people here talk. Johann's just been very helpful, that's all," she said, her cheeks red with shame.

But everyone could see the glow of love in her eyes.

CHAPTER 45

Distraught, Mimi ran blindly across the market square. She did not feel the cold of the November night. She did not feel the rainwater in the puddles soak through her shoes. She did not feel the tears streaming down her cheeks.

Johann and Eveline? But Eve was her friend. At least, Mimi had believed she was. How could Eve deceive her like this? She ignored the notion that Eveline knew nothing about her relationship with Johann. And Johann . . . how could he have betrayed her this way?

"Mimi!" she heard him calling behind her. "Wait, please! Let me explain things, at least."

How could he possibly explain? She stopped at Josef's gate and turned around, panting as if she'd just finished a footrace. "How long has this been going on?" she spat.

He took a step back, shocked, suddenly silent.

"Cat got your tongue? You're normally so happy making speeches," she said with contempt as she wiped the tears from her face. How guilty he looked, standing there. She wanted to beat his chest with her frozen hands. She wanted to hurt him as badly as he had hurt her. But she kept her hands by her sides and instead balled them into fists.

"Mimi, please, can we talk about this inside?"

"So nobody hears anything? You seem to be very good at hiding things, I'll give you that," she said, pulling open the garden gate. "Then come inside," she added harshly.

"I didn't want this. You have to believe me," Johann said, the moment they were standing in the hallway of the house.

"Really? Did Eveline force you into it? Is she the guilty one? Wait, no, how could I forget?" She slapped the palm of her hand against her forehead. "Mr. Gehringer's to blame, isn't he? Just like he always is."

"No one's to blame, and you know that perfectly well," Johann replied quietly.

Mimi, who had expected more excuses, looked away. As quickly as her fury had flared, it now dissolved. Her shoulders slumped, she threw both hands over her face and sobbed, "No. You are to blame. *You* are. I thought you loved me! You came to Laichingen for me."

Johann let out a deep sigh, placed his hands on her shoulders, and guided her into the kitchen. Mimi allowed him to do this.

"I have no regrets about following you here," Johann said when they were sitting opposite one another at the kitchen table. "Without you, I probably never would have returned to Laichingen. I will always be grateful to you that I came back."

Oh, wonderful, Mimi thought. While she sat there in defiant silence, Johann continued. "You know how much I like and admire you. And yes, perhaps we could have been something together. But then . . ."

She frowned. What "then"? She was trying so hard to comprehend what was going on.

He looked at her pleadingly. "I don't know how to explain it. Eveline . . . I had strong feelings for her in the past, years ago. Too strong. Back then, I felt I could accept the limitations of Laichingen with her beside me." He gazed off, lost in older memories.

"'Accept the limitations'—that sounds so passive," Mimi said. "No one is stopping you from breaking free of those limitations again. How many times did I suggest going to the city for a weekend? But no, you didn't want that."

He nodded, then went on as if she hadn't raised an objection at all. "To be honest, Eveline was the main reason I left in the first place. She belonged to Klaus, and I knew I could never call her mine. But when Klaus died, and when you encouraged me to help her . . ." He shrugged helplessly. "Suddenly, everything looked different, and everything changed."

Mimi snorted. Now she was to blame?

He took her hands in his. "Mimi, I'm sorry. But if you look at the situation dispassionately, you know I never made you any promises. I think, deep inside, I probably realized very early on that we were not meant for each other."

"And what about all the evenings when you came to me to talk about your workers' revolt? You held me in your arms. You kissed me! I was good enough for you as a patient listener." She shook her head, still unable to comprehend.

"What's wrong with listening?" he retorted. "The Laichingers are close to your heart, or else you would not have stood up for Alexander, Eveline, and the others the way you have."

And unlike you, I've done more than just talk, Mimi almost said. "But none of that is any reason to lie to me. You must at least have suspected that I was dreaming of a future for us—you and me, together. Why didn't you simply come out and tell me that you and Eveline were a couple? Anton is apparently well aware of the fact."

Johann threw up his hands. "I have no idea how Anton even found out," he said. "Eveline is in her year of mourning. We were careful not to be seen together in public."

"Of course, how could I forget? You're always so mindful of the good reputation of women," she said, her voice heavy with irony. Every word was a knife in her heart. She wondered who she was hurting more with her harsh words—him, or herself?

She breathed in and out deeply, arming herself for what was coming. Her goodbye.

From the kitchen table drawer, she took out the small stack of photographs. She gave them to him with trembling hands.

"Here. The pictures from Gehringer's mill. They should be a good memory jog, just in case you're so in love that you lose sight of why people here are suffering. Use them. At least then our relationship will have been worth something. Now go."

As poised as Mimi had been with Johann, the moment he left, she once again broke down in tears. How *could* he? What had she done to be betrayed like this? Their meeting had seemed to her so fated—how dare he ruin it like this?

Half-blinded by tears and with a broken heart, she hunted through the kitchen cupboard for the bottle of schnapps that her uncle hadn't finished. She poured the last of it into a glass. Would it be enough to erase all her dreams? Or to make her forget what had happened?

She took her first mouthful.

There would be no wedding.

Another mouthful.

She had no future with Johann. And no future here in Laichingen, either.

A third mouthful, and this one burned with a special bitterness in her throat. Her friendship with Eveline was an illusion.

She drank the last drop. The glass was empty.

She was alone, just as she had always been.

A few days later, Mimi had more or less collected herself again. She knew with certainty that she did not want to stay. Whether she wanted to sell her property to Gehringer, however, she hadn't yet decided. He had been to see her twice since that first visit, adding pressure each time. Either he gave her time to think or he could forget all about it, she had told him in no uncertain terms the third time he came.

Running her fingers wistfully over the sideboard, the kitchen table, the shelf with Uncle Josef's souvenirs, she made her way through the house one last time. Everything was tidy and sparkling clean. The kitchen, the parlor—there wasn't a crack in the wall through which so much as a mouse could get inside. She hadn't forgotten any bread in the bread box, and she had cleared out the pantry completely, giving away the last of the food. The windows were latched.

Apart from a few mementos, she had given away all of Josef's and Traudel's clothes. He had wanted it that way. But she hadn't yet done anything with the furniture or souvenirs: for now, everything in the house stayed the way it had always been. She had returned the retouching desk to the studio and put away or covered the rest of the equipment and props.

The page-a-day calendar on the wall caught her eye. It was the twenty-fifth of November. As long as her uncle had been able, the first thing he did every day was to tear off the previous day's page and read the motto on the reverse. When he'd been confined to his bed, Mimi had taken over the task for him.

She took a deep breath, tore off a page of the calendar for the last time, and turned it over. *There'd better not be something like "Romance is the icing, but love is the cake,"* she thought grimly.

But the daily aphorism came from Alexander Pope's *The Dunciad*: *Quod petis in te est*—"What thou seek'st is in thee."

Was that really true? Well, with God's help, she would find out. With a lighter heart and grateful soul, she folded the torn-off page in two and put it in her handbag. In the hallway, she picked up her suitcase and slung her camera bag over her shoulder.

Outside, it was snowing lightly. Tiny, delicate snowflakes danced and sparkled around her—soon, they would cover the land. *The circle closes,* thought Mimi. In April, when she arrived in Laichingen, ice crystals had glittered in the air. She found the memory consoling, in a way. With a smile, she locked the house in which her uncle, in his old age, had found his greatest happiness. Since April, it had also been her home. And yes, she had been happy here. She had made up her mind to preserve in her heart everything she had experienced here. Her memories of her uncle. The friendships she had made. The trust the people of Laichingen had in her. There was only one thing she wanted to leave behind: the illusion that this might have been a home for her, forever.

"You really don't want to stay?" Her head tilted slightly to one side, Luise Neumann looked inquisitively at Mimi.

Standing in the doorway of her neighbor's house, Mimi shook her head. She had delayed stopping at Luise's until the last moment. The day before, she had said goodbye to Sonja and Berta and a number of others, but she had chosen not to visit either Eveline or Eve's future mother-in-law, Edelgard. At every stop, she had been met with sympathy and kindness, but no one openly asked after the reasons for her departure. Only Sonja had grasped her by the arm and whispered, "He isn't worth your tears, believe me." Then she had made Mimi promise to keep her eyes open for Christel.

"Oh, I've been happy to have you as a neighbor," said Luise. "I never would have imagined it when you first arrived, but you kept your head up so fearlessly."

Mimi laughed, genuinely moved. "That's true, actually. When I think that I didn't even know how to wash clothes when I got here! But thanks to you, I can now claim to be able to run a household."

"And you're a hardworking gardener. All the cabbages and turnips you gave us. It's a shame you won't be eating them yourself," Luise said, and she smiled wistfully.

Mimi's gaze turned back across the garden fence to Josef's garden. Who would have thought that she, the photographer, would have dug in the dirt with her own hands?

"I loved the garden work especially," Mimi said with a sigh. "I think I'm going to miss it terribly."

"Then you'll just have to come back! You always have a home here," Luise said resolutely. "Now that I mention it, what's to become of your uncle's house?"

"I don't know yet," said Mimi. Then it was she who looked inquisitively at her neighbor. "Can I leave the key with you so you can look in from time to time, just to check? I'll get in touch as soon as I've sorted a few things out." She held the house key out to her neighbor, along with an envelope containing some money.

Luise nodded warmly. "I'll poke my head in every day. There won't be any mice making a home there, that's a promise."

"Thank you," said Mimi, relieved. "If it's all right with you, I'll write once a month and tell you where I am. And in case you hear anything about Christel, would you let me know?"

Luise's eyes grew moist. She nodded. "I'll write back and tell you all the news, all right?" she whispered through her tears.

Then the two women embraced for the first and last time.

Mimi had just reached the train station when Anton came running.

"Miss Reventlow! Wait! Please!"

Mimi stopped and turned around. "Yes?" she said coldly.

Anton shifted his weight nervously from one foot to the other. In the distance, a low rumbling signaled the approach of the train. "My behavior a few days ago . . . I was such an idiot. All the worry about Christel, the whole situation—suddenly, I couldn't hold my anger inside anymore, and you're the one I took it out on. You, of all people, when you wished nothing but the best for all of us. I'm so terribly sorry."

Mimi looked at him and saw that he really meant it. “Maybe it was good that you opened my eyes for me,” she said.

“Really? You can forgive me?”

Mimi nodded. “And where is *your* journey taking you?” she asked, glancing toward the travel bag in his hand.

He shrugged. “No idea. Away from here. That’s a start, and after that, I’ll have to see. And you? Do you have a plan?”

“A hotel owner in the Black Forest has asked me to come and take pictures of his hotel, a newly opened ski lift, the skiers, and the village.” As she spoke, she felt the familiar thrill inside that she got when she was about to leave for a new place.

“The Black Forest, that’s as good a start as anywhere else.” Anton looked at Mimi, sizing up his chances. “May I come with you? For now?”

AFTERWORD

All characters and events in my novel are fictional. The arrangement of buildings in Laichingen, the train station, power station, etc. is not historically accurate, but the product of artistic license.

It is, however, true that for centuries, Laichingen was an important center for the weaving trade. Laichingen linenwares were quality products, like knives from Solingen or clocks from the Black Forest. Until the late twentieth century, linen from the region was an indispensable part of the trousseau of every Swabian girl.

According to a Laichingen historian, nothing is known about accidents at the Laichingen looms. My research in other linen-weaving centers, however, has shown that accidents—from minor to fairly serious—were commonplace. I've assumed, for the sake of my story, that industrial accidents also occurred in Laichingen.

The *Heumondfest* in Laichingen and the tradition of giving forget-me-nots in the morning are my own invention.

Whether Alexander, Anton, Mimi, and Christel could have made it from Laichingen to Stuttgart and back by train in one day in 1911 is doubtful, but because of the expense and for other reasons, I did not want to have them spend a night somewhere along the way.

At the time my story is set, the National Academy of Art (Staatliche Kunstakademie) already existed in Stuttgart. Alexander's invitation, however, comes from the Stuttgart Art School, an invention of my own.

At some point, I began collecting historical photographs myself, and you will see some included in each book of the series. My research materials are far too beautiful to keep to myself—I simply must share some with my readers.

I hope you have enjoyed Mimi Reventlow's journey so far, and I wish you many pleasant hours reading about her—not only photographic—adventures in the books to come!

Petra Durst-Benning

IMAGE GALLERY

Laichingen in the Swabian Jura. Photographers in the early 1900s earned at least part of their income with postcards like these.

Laichingen was a stronghold of the linen-weaving industry. In 1825, there were more than four hundred looms in the town. Practically every house had one, housed in what was known as the Dunk—a cold basement room. Weaving at home gradually gave way to small and then larger mills.

The span of a lifetime, captured in the photo studio. As a memento of the first phase of life, baby pictures and christening photographs brought in many customers.

The first day of school marked the transition from toddler to schoolchild. Behind the children is a backdrop showing a reproduction of Burg Teck, a ducal castle in Württemberg. These pictures were taken in Otto Hofmann's famous Kirchheim studio, and Hofmann painted the backdrop himself. The girl with the schoolbag in the second picture is Anna Hofmann, the photographer's daughter. Hofmann's studio still exists and can be visited at the open-air museum in Beuren, near Stuttgart, in Germany. His studio is the inspiration for Josef's.

Holy Communion or confirmation marked another important milestone in life, frequently recorded photographically.

Wedding photographs represent the start of another phase of life.

For many years, children were photographed very much like stern little adults, with no perceivable emotion on their faces.

Otto Hofmann
Kirchheim u/T.

Otto Hofmann
KIRCHHEIM U/T.

But times changed. Photographers like Mimi Reventlow fought for children to be able to smile for the camera, and for people to be able to show their emotions.

ABOUT THE AUTHOR

Petra Durst-Benning was born in Baden-Württemberg in 1965. For more than twenty years, she has been writing historical and contemporary novels. Almost all of her books have been Spiegel Publishing bestsellers and have been translated into several languages. Petra Durst-Benning's novels also have been celebrated in the United States. She lives with her husband and two dogs in the countryside south of Stuttgart.

ABOUT THE TRANSLATOR

Photo © 2016 Dagmar Jordan

Born in Australia, Edwin Miles has been working as a translator, primarily in film and television, for more than fifteen years. After undergraduate studies in his hometown of Perth, he received an MFA in fiction writing from the University of Oregon in 1995. While there, he spent a year working as fiction editor on the literary magazine *Northwest Review*. In 1996, he was short-listed for the prestigious Australian/Vogel's Literary Award for young writers for a collection of short stories. After many years living and working in Australia, Japan, and the United States, he currently resides in his "second home" in Cologne, Germany, with his wife, Dagmar, and two very clever children.